Death, Taxes, and a Skinny No-Whip Latte

DIANE KELLY

St. Martin's Paperbacks

DEATH, TAXES, AND A SKINNY NO-WHIP LATTE

Copyright © 2012 by by Diane Kelly.
Excerpt from *Death, Taxes, and Extra-Hold Hairspray* copyright © 2012 by Diane Kelly.

All rights reserved.

For information address St. Martin's Press, 175 Fifth Avenue, New York, NY 10010.

ISBN: 978-0-312-55127-8

Printed in the United States of America

St. Martin's Paperbacks edition / March 2012

St. Martin's Paperbacks are published by St. Martin's Press, 175 Fifth Avenue, New York, NY 10010.

10 9 8 7 6 5 4 3 2 1

To Mom, for kicking my butt when I needed it

$\mathscr{A}$cknowledgments

Many thanks to my smart and hardworking team at St. Martin's Paperbacks: To my insightful and intuitive editor, Holly Blanck. It's both a privilege and pleasure to work with you! Thanks for making my work shine! To Eileen Rothschild and Katie Dean. Thanks for spreading the word about my books! To Danielle Fiorella. Thanks for creating such fun and eye-catching covers! And to everyone else who had a hand in bringing my books to readers, thank you!

To Trinity Blake, Cclyn Bowers, Angela Cavener, Vannetta Chapman, Angela Hicks, and Kennedy Shaw. I appreciate your invaluable input, support, and friendship!

To *mi amiga* Gina Mendez Bushnell. *Muchas gracias* for your help with the *español!*

To Julia Hunter. Thanks for sharing your knowledge of firearms!

To the clever and creative Liz Bemis and Sienna Condy of Bemis Promotions. Thanks for all your hard work on my Web site and promotions!

To the IRS special agents who assisted in my research. I'm in awe of what you do! Thanks for sharing your intriguing world with me.

And lastly, to my readers. I hope this book brings you lots of LOL moments!

CHAPTER ONE

It's a Terrifying Job, but Somebody's Gotta Do It

"I'm scared shitless, Eddie."

I looked over at my partner as he pulled his maroon minivan into the parking lot of the downtown Dallas post office. Eddie Bardin was tall and lean, sporting a gray suit and starched white dress shirt with a mint-green silk tie. Though Eddie was African-American, he was more J. Crew than 2 Live Crew, like a dark-chocolate version of President Obama. Not that Eddie'd ever condescend to vote for a Democrat.

Despite the fact that my partner was a conservative married suburban dad and I was a free-thinking single city girl, the two of us got along great and made a kick-ass team. Problem was, the current ass we were aiming to kick was a very frightening one.

A row of cars stretched out in front of us, a solid red line of brake lights illuminating the early-evening drizzle. Apparently I wasn't the only slacker who waited until April fifteenth to file their tax return.

Eddie pulled to a stop behind one of those newer odd-looking rectangular cars. Cube, was it? Quad? Shoebox? He glanced my way. "Scared? You? C'mon, Holloway. You've been slashed with a box cutter and shot at and lived to brag about it." His scoffing tone might have been more believable if I hadn't noticed his grip tighten on the steering wheel. "We're invincible, you and me. Like Superman. Or toxic waste."

I scrunched my nose. "Ew. Couldn't you have come up with a better metaphor?"

"I'm exhausted, Tara. And besides, it was a simile." He muttered something under his breath about me being the child the education system left behind.

I might have been offended if I thought he truly meant it. You didn't become a member of the Treasury Department's Criminal Investigations team without a stellar academic record, impressive career credentials, and a razor-sharp intellect, not to mention a quick hand on both a calculator and a gun. Not that I'm bragging. But it's true.

I toyed with the edge of the manila envelope in my lap. "Battaglia and Gryder were chump change compared to Marcos Mendoza, and you know it."

Eddie and I had recently put two tax cheats—Jack Battaglia and Michael Gryder—behind bars, but not before Battaglia had sliced my forearm with a box cutter and Gryder had taken pot shots at me with a handgun and pierced Eddie's earlobe with a bullet. Not exactly polite behavior. What's more, neither of those men had a history of violence prior to attacking us. The focus of our current investigation, Marcos Mendoza, was an entirely different matter.

Due to a lack of evidence, Mendoza had never been officially accused of any crimes. Yet his business associates had a suspicious history of disappearing.

And resurfacing.

In Dumpsters.

In pieces.

They'd found parts of Andrew Sheffield, a former employee of Mendoza's and presumably his most recent victim, spread among garbage receptacles from Harlingen, to Houston, to San Antonio and beyond. The sanitation department of El Paso found Sheffield's right foot, still clad in a pricey Ferragamo loafer, in the trash bin behind the police headquarters. Andrew had yet to be fully accounted for.

Hence my scared-shitless state of mind.

We inched forward, the only sound the occasional swish of the intermittent wipers as they arced across the windshield.

I knew Eddie well enough to know his lack of response meant he agreed with me. But perhaps some things are better left unsaid.

Think happy thoughts, I told myself. *Fluffy kittens. Colorful rainbows. Big tax refunds.* Of course it would be easier to think happy thoughts if my right arm wasn't bearing a plaster cast. I'd fractured my wrist diving out a window to evade Gryder. The con artist was rotting in jail now.

Hey, now there's a happy thought.

Finally, we reached the bleary-eyed postal worker standing in the parking lot. She wore a dark blue rain slicker and held an umbrella in one hand, a white plastic box bearing the postal service eagle logo in the other.

I unrolled my window, letting in the dank air, and dropped my return into her nearly full bin. "Thanks. See you next April fifteenth."

A drop of rain rolled off the tip of her nose as she forced a feeble smile.

How much longer would I file single? I wasn't yet ready for diapers, playdates, and PTA meetings, but the thought of joint tax returns didn't frighten me as much as it used to. Maybe because of Brett Ellington, the sweet, brave, and incredibly sexy landscape architect I'd been dating the past few months.

I rolled up my window and checked my watch. "Six thirty-seven P.M. That's a personal best."

Eddie snorted. "I filed my return two months ago. Already got my refund."

I cut my eyes to him. "Oh yeah? And what did Sandra and the twins spend the money on?"

He turned away, letting me know my jab had hit home.

"Ha! You are whipped, dude."

"Better to be whipped than to be a procrastinator."

"Hey, I've been busy." Busy shopping and packing for my upcoming trip to Fort Lauderdale with Brett. I'd made no less than three trips to Victoria's Secret before deciding on the red satin teddy with black trim and those little clip thingies to hold up a pair of old-fashioned fishnet stockings. I couldn't wait for Brett to see me in it. He was a perfect gentleman in public, but in the bedroom, well, let's just say he left his decorum at the door.

A new red chiffon cocktail dress had made its way into my shopping bag, too. The spaghetti straps and handkerchief edge gave it a feminine and festive feel. It was the perfect outfit for the American Society of Landscape Architects' awards banquet, where the society would bestow its prestigious Landmark Award on Brett for his work at city hall. I'd scored the dress forty-percent off at an after-Easter sale. Christ may have risen, but Neiman's had lowered its prices. Hallelujah!

I stifled a yawn. Not surprising I was tired since we'd been on the job since nine o'clock that morning and at the office until midnight the last few nights reviewing paperwork. The Mendoza case was so highly sensitive we'd been forbidden to discuss it with anyone, even our coworkers. To maintain secrecy, we'd been forced to perform some of our work after hours.

Why the secrecy? Three years ago, a special agent named Nick Pratt had infiltrated Mendoza's operations and purportedly obtained evidence that Mendoza had earned enormous sums of illegal, unreported income. Though the details were sketchy, Mendoza allegedly got wind of the investigation, bought off the agent, and set up the traitor in a luxury beachside condominium in Cancún, Mexico.

Tough life, huh?

Lawyers at the U.S. Department of Justice fought to extradite Pratt back to the U.S. on charges of obstruction of justice and theft of government property, but the Mexican judge refused to cooperate, claiming all Pratt did was quit his job at the IRS, which wasn't illegal. He argued the theft charge wouldn't stick since Pratt's government-issued cell phone and laptop were mailed back to the department. Of course all of the data had been wiped clean, the hard drive erased. Presumably Mendoza had the judge in his pocket.

If only money were at stake, the government might have let the case go. But given the recent increase in body count, the case was reopened.

Come hell or high water, Mendoza had to be stopped.

And it was up to Eddie and me to stop him.

We'd been on the case only four days, since Eddie had returned from his medical leave, sans one bullet-damaged earlobe. We'd finally finished our review of the documentation. We'd painstakingly searched through Mendoza's tax filings and those of the businesses linked to him, document by document, page by page, entry by entry. But this guy knew how to cover his tracks.

We'd found no evidence. No leads. *Nada.*

Nada damn thing.

CHAPTER TWO

Caffeine Fiend

Eddie drove on, pausing at the exit to the parking lot. "Where to?"

I pulled the papers out of the manila envelope and riffled through them until I found the printout listing directions to Pokornys' Korner Kitchen, a small Czech bakery and café located in an older section of Garland, one of the many mid-sized cities making up the sprawling Dallas suburbs.

"Central north to Loop Twelve," I instructed.

Eddie gave me a salute. "Aye, aye, captain."

He took a right turn out of the parking lot and in minutes we were driving north on Interstate 75, known to locals as Central Expressway, one of a dozen freeways that crisscrossed the extensive Dallas metroplex area. We had a seven-thirty appointment scheduled with Darina and Jakub Pokorny, the owners of the bakery.

Early last week, the head of the Treasury's Criminal Investigations Department had flown in from Washington,

D.C., to meet with our boss, Lu Lobozinski, aka the Lobo. George Burton had asked Lu to put her top agents on the Mendoza case. She'd immediately assigned Eddie to the investigation. Eddie was one of the more senior special agents, experienced, clever, and intuitive, the crème de la crème of the Dallas team. As a rookie, I hardly qualified as crème of any sort yet. I should've been flattered to be put on the case. But I feared it was my skills with weaponry rather than my skills with a calculator that landed me the assignment. If ever there'd been a case that called for an agent adept with a gun, this case was it.

As far as career enhancement was concerned, this was definitely the job to be on. As for my boyfriend Brett, well, if he knew what I was up to he'd shit a brick. Maybe even a cinder block.

Before coming to work for the IRS, I'd spent several years in the tax department of Martin and McGee, a large regional accounting firm. I'd learned a lot at the CPA firm, earned a lot, too. But sitting in a cubicle day after day, week after week, year after year, sorting through paperwork and staring at a computer screen, had eaten away at me. I'd felt unsatisfied, caged, trapped. It was a good job, but it wasn't right for me.

Of course I still dealt with a fair share of paperwork and computer screens at the IRS, but I loved the action in Criminal Investigations, hunting down clues, the thrill of the chase, the sense of purpose and justice. My job called for financial savvy, investigation expertise, and weapons proficiency, a unique skill set possessed by very few. This job was made for me.

Still, Brett worried about the risks my job posed. Who could blame him? He'd recently witnessed me cowering in a hole amid a shower of bullets and risked his own life to rescue me from certain death. Of course I'd done my best to convince him that the attack was a fluke, that the vast majority of tax evaders surrendered peacefully, that most special agents went their entire careers without facing real danger.

But I wasn't most special agents. As Eddie'd once pointed out, something about me brought out the homicidal tendencies in people.

Forcing that ugly thought aside, I rubbed my eyes, which were beginning to feel heavy. "I sure could go for a latte."

"Not a bad idea."

Eddie took the next exit and pulled into the drive-thru of a twenty-four-hour coffeehouse. New York isn't the only city that never sleeps. Dallas doesn't doze, either. "The usual?"

"Yep."

The barista at the drive-thru opened the window, releasing the invigorating aroma of French roast. I closed my eyes and took a deep breath. "Mmm."

Eddie placed our order. "Small coffee. Black." Eddie was a purist. I was anything but. "And a large caramel latte. Extra whipped cream, heavy on the drizzle, sprinkle of cinnamon on top."

Just the way I liked it. Eddie knew me well. I handed Eddie a ten from my wallet. "My treat."

When we received our drinks, I removed a dark-skinned doll from one of the cup holders. "Nice job on Barbie's hair," I said, holding up the doll. One of Eddie's girls had pulled the doll's hair up into a ponytail on the top of her head and the black locks cascaded down on all sides of the doll's head, making her look like a palm tree.

"That's not Barbie," Eddie said. "That's Christie. Barbie's black BFF."

"Oh yeah?"

"Yeah. My girls set me straight on that right away."

I tossed the doll into the backseat. "Girls'll do that for ya'." I sipped my hot drink. Yum. I could live on these things.

Eddie stuck his cup in the holder, pulled out of the drive-thru, and headed back onto the freeway.

My thoughts returned to the case, to Mendoza and the earlier agent he'd bought off. What kind of guy would turn like that? Give up his job, his reputation, his life for money? Nick Pratt had to be one sorry-ass son of a bitch. "Hey, Ed. I was wondering. How well did you know Nick Pratt?"

Eddie hesitated a moment, seeming to consider his words. "Nick and I partnered on several big cases, had a beer together after work every now and then. He covered for me when the twins were born."

I snorted. "You make him sound like a nice guy." As if. Nice guys don't sell out.

"You would've liked him. He was a country boy, wore snakeskin cowboy boots with his business suits. Didn't take crap from anybody." Eddie cut his eyes my way. "He was a lot like you, only with—"

"Guy junk?"

"I was going to say more muscle and less mascara. He could handle a gun almost as good as you, too."

I offered a derisive snort. "Nobody handles a gun as good as me." They didn't call me the Annie Oakley of the IRS for nothing.

Eddie rolled his eyes. "I said 'almost.'" He stopped talking for a moment and looked solemnly out his window as if looking for answers to questions that had none. "When Pratt disappeared, Lu told the rest of us he'd turned in his resignation. Claimed the stress of the job got to him."

"Did that seem odd to you?"

"Odd? Yeah. He was smart as they come. Hardworking, too. But he could be a little intense at times, so we bought the story. Figured he'd burned himself out. It happens." Eddie's jaw flexed as he clenched angry teeth. "But I can't believe he turned on us."

"Guess you never can tell, huh?"

Eddie turned back to me then, our eyes locking. "People aren't always who they seem to be."

CHAPTER THREE

$\mathcal{N}$ice Buns

Twenty minutes later, our nerves buzzed with caffeine as Eddie and I pulled into the cracked asphalt parking lot next to the bakery. We climbed out of his minivan, lugging our briefcases with us.

Pokornys' Korner Kitchen was clearly a mom-and-pop—or should I say *matka*-and-*tata*?—operation. The redbrick storefront was narrow with plate-glass windows bearing white eyelet curtains. Their posted hours were from six A.M. to three A.M., their market primarily the breakfast and lunchtime crowd. A sign saying SORRY WE MISSED YOU! sat in the front window next to a cardboard clock with red plastic hands noting the bakery would reopen at six o'clock the following morning.

The front porch light flickered in the evening dusk as we approached the door. Although the seating area at the front of the café was dark, a light shone through an open doorway leading into the kitchen and storage areas at the rear. Moving shadows indicated people working in the back.

We stepped up to the door and Eddie rapped on the glass. A short, plump woman poked her head out of the backlit doorway inside. She gave us a wave, set aside her broom, and headed toward us. As she unbolted and opened the door, the warm, enticing scents of cinnamon and vanilla greeted us. Apparently the couple was getting a head start on the morning's baking.

Darina Pokorny was an attractive woman in her early fifties, with a round face and pink cheeks. Her blond hair bore undertones of white, her short curls springing from her head like a pack of frisky poodles. She wore white cotton pants and a long-sleeved white shirt covered by a red-and-white-checkered apron that, in turn, was covered by powdered sugar and smudges of what appeared to be lemon cream filling.

Mrs. Pokorny flipped on the lights and offered a pleasant but cautious smile. "Come in, please." Her Czech accent was still thick despite more than two decades in Texas.

I stepped through the door. Before me stood a lighted glass-front display case containing cookies and cakes, pastries and pies, tarts and tortes. Some were slathered in chocolate, others oozed vanilla cream. Sugar crystals sparkled, glazes glistened. It was all I could do not to rush to the case and press my face to the glass.

Should've had more than a latte for dinner.

"Down, girl," Eddie said from behind me. I swear the guy could read my mind.

Forcing my eyes from the display case, I stuck out my hand to Mrs. Pokorny. "Tara Holloway," I said by way of introduction.

"And Eddie Bardin," my partner said from behind me, likewise extending his hand.

After we shook hands, Mrs. Pokorny directed us to one of the red vinyl booths. "Make yourselves comfortable."

"Thanks." I slid into one side of the booth, Eddie slid in after me, and my gaze slid back to the refrigerated case. A pastry on the bottom shelf oozed thick purple goo. Grape jelly? Blueberry filling? Blackberry jam? Couldn't tell for sure. Regardless, the thing looked delicious.

"Jakub?" Mrs. Pokorny called back to her husband. Since she spoke in her native tongue, I wasn't sure what she said next. The only part I understood was "IRS."

A few seconds later, Jakub Porkorny emerged from the back room and joined us at the table. He, too, was dressed in white, including his apron. Like his wife, he bore a sturdy build, fair skin, and fair hair. Unlike his wife, he wore a burr haircut, a thick mustache, and a St. Christopher medallion around his neck. Some believed such medallions would keep the wearer safe. I wasn't usually superstitious but, under the circumstances, figured the medallion couldn't hurt.

Jakub nodded to me and Eddie as he took his seat.

I nodded back. "Good to meet you, Mr. Pokorny. You two have a nice place here."

The Pokornys smiled, obviously proud of their little bakery. And rightfully so. They'd built the business themselves from scratch. According to the information Burton had provided, the couple had left their homeland shortly before the Berlin Wall fell and the Velvet Revolution put an end to communism in Czechoslovakia. They'd been in the U.S. just long enough to settle in and squeeze out a couple of children. They chose to stay here to raise their family rather than tear up their newly formed roots and return to Europe.

On the wall above the booths hung framed recipes written in both Czech and English, including one for *palacinky*, which, according to the translation, was a type of Czech crepe. Large photographs of Prague landmarks, including two identified by hand-lettered tags as Prague Castle and Saint Vitus Cathedral, hung on the wall behind the display cases.

Another frame contained a dollar bill, the first the bakery had earned, alongside a photograph showing a smiling Darina and Jakub in their bakery garb with their arms around the shoulders of their now-grown son and daughter. Both of the children were fair skinned and fair haired like their parents. Their son sported a green-and-gold Dallas Stars jersey, their daughter an excess of eyeliner, skintight jeans, and a low-cut tee. All-American kids.

Mr. Pokorny's thick brows pulled together as he folded his hands on the tabletop. "Is there a problem? We thought everything was settled now."

"No. No problem," I reassured them. "We just had some questions about your loan." And about the fruit tart calling to me from the middle row of the glass case. "Is that lemon cream or custard filling in the tart with the kiwi on top?"

"Lemon cream," he said.

A soft sigh escaped me.

During a recent routine audit, the auditor had noticed the Pokornys' interest deductions seemed unusually high. When asked for documentation relating to the loan, the couple produced a faxed copy of a "Loan Contract." Although the contract identified Darina and Jakub Pokorny by name, the party making the loan was identified in the documentation only as "The Lender." The signature block contained lines for Darina and Jakub's signatures but none for the lender's representative. The contract required all payments be in the form of a money order made payable to bearer and be sent to a post office box in Dallas. The contract charged an interest rate of thirty percent, far above market rates and in excess of the legal rate for loans between private parties.

When the auditor traced the Pokornys' money orders, she discovered they had not been deposited in a bank account. Rather, they'd been cashed at various check-cashing businesses in the small agricultural towns of south Texas, otherwise known as "the Valley."

What caught the attention of higher-ups in the IRS was the fact that Mr. and Mrs. Porkorny had first approached their financial institution, North Dallas Credit Union, for a business loan. NDCU shared corporate DNA with other entities owned, at least in part, by Vicente Torres, who'd been the initial target of Nick Pratt's investigation years earlier.

All of NDCU's stock was owned by a parent company, AmeriMex Inc., which also held interests in horse-racing tracks throughout the U.S. and several *maquiladoras,* factories in Mexican border towns where labor could be obtained cheaply. Venture capitalists not involved in the day-to-day operations of AmeriMex owned a combined 49 percent interest in the company. The remaining 51 percent controlling interest was owned by Torres.

Torres was a Mexican national. American citizenship was not required to establish a business in Texas. Anyone willing to set up shop here in the Lone Star State and provide jobs and tax revenue was more than welcome. That's Southern hospitality, y'all.

Torres lived in Nuevo Laredo, Mexico, a city situated just across the border from Laredo, Texas, and just outside the jurisdiction of U.S. law enforcement, including the Treasury Department's Criminal Investigations Division.

Muy convenient.

But Marcos Mendoza lived and worked primarily in the U.S., within our jurisdiction. Mendoza was designated in paperwork as the assistant manager of AmeriMex, a position for which he was purportedly paid a salary in the mid six figures. His reported salary was high enough to support his lifestyle in the U.S. But it wasn't nearly enough to cover the cost of the enormous mansion he owned in Monterrey, Mexico, not to mention the extensive full-time staff who ran the place.

Things didn't add up.

I eyed a chocolate drip on Mr. Pokorny's sleeve, my stomach rumbling audibly now.

"You sound hungry." Mrs. Pokorny motioned to the case. "Can we get you something?"

I thought you'd never ask.

Two minutes later, we were again seated at the table, the gooey purple pastry and fruit tart in front of me. Of course I'd paid for the treats. Didn't want to be accused of abusing my authority. Now, which to try first? Eeny, meeny, meiny, mo . . .

Given that my mouth was stuffed with pastry—*blueberry, mmm*—Eddie began the questioning. "It's our understanding the two of you first approached your credit union for a loan. Is that correct?"

Jakub nodded. "Yes. We needed eighty thousand dollars.

But the credit union would not give a loan to us." He explained they'd needed the funds to replace their industrial ovens, refrigerators, and display cases, all of which were outdated and not heating or cooling properly.

The loan officer at the credit union denied the loan due to a lack of collateral or consistent income to cover the loan payments. The Pokornys' home and shop were mortgaged, their retirement and investment accounts held only nominal balances, and, thanks to the sluggish economy, their bakery business was barely hanging on. It was no wonder their loan application had been refused. No legitimate financial institution would take such a risk.

I swallowed. My God, the thing was delicious! These people should sell franchises. "After your credit union turned you down, did you apply for a loan at any other banks?"

Jakub shook his head. "We thought if the place where we kept our accounts would not lend to us, we would have even less hope elsewhere."

Eddie jumped back in now. "So how did you end up getting the loan?"

Jakub nervously twisted the end of his mustache. "Just a few days after the credit union turned us down, we received a call from a man who said he could help us."

"Did he tell you his name?" I asked.

"Yes," Jakub said. "His name was John Smith."

John Smith. Sheez. Why didn't crooks come up with more interesting aliases? Like maybe Isaiah Steele, I. Steele for short. Now there's a good alias for a crook. Or maybe Rip Yuoff. If these con artists were smart enough to set up complicated loan transactions, the least they could do is show a little imagination when it came to their imaginary identities.

Eddie and I exchanged glances. Presumably there was a connection between the loan application at the credit union and the subsequent phone call from the alleged "John Smith." How else would the caller have known the Pokornys needed some quick cash?

Darina leaned forward. "We were afraid we would have to close the bakery. When Mr. Smith said he could loan us the money, it was a godsend." She raised her hands and looked heavenward. "He saved our business."

Mrs. Pokorny's comment highlighted the problem with loan sharks. They never seemed like sharks at first, more like lifeguards tossing out a ring to save a drowning victim from going under the waves. It wasn't until the borrower got behind on payments that the shark's pointed teeth came out and began to tear bits of flesh from its victims.

"How is your business doing now?" Eddie asked.

"Not much profits," Jakub said, "but we are able to pay our bills." Shortly after obtaining the loan, he explained, they'd had the good fortune of landing a deal to supply kolaches to a local grocery store chain. They were managing to stay afloat. At least for now.

When we'd obtained as much information as we could from the couple, we thanked them for their time and stood to go.

"One last thing," Eddie said, meeting their eyes to ensure they were paying close attention. "It's very important you tell no one that we've been here. Understand?"

The couple nodded.

Eddie and I left with their promise to keep mum and a half-price day-old apple strudel.

CHAPTER FOUR

The Pressure Builds

I arrived at the office Friday morning with another extra-whip, heavy-drizzle caramel latte in my hand. As I stepped off the elevator, Lu's secretary, Viola, glanced up from her desk down the hall, her gray curls bobbing. She eyed me over her plastic-rimmed bifocals, keeping an eagle eye on the office activity, as always. I gave her a smile and a wave, and headed to my office.

Josh Schmidt, one of my fellow special agents, passed me on his way up the corridor. Josh wore his standard attire of khaki pants and blue button-down shirt. He stood just five foot five, with a deceptively cherubic face given he was such a huge pain in the ass. Yep, no amount of Preparation H could counter the effects of Little Lord Fauntle*roid*.

Though the computer geek could interface with technology like a pro, his people skills were sorely lacking. We other agents tolerated Josh only because he had the best cyber-sleuthing skills around. The guy could crack computer code in less time than the rest of us could crack our knuckles. But his condescending attitude, competitive nature, and sarcastic jabs made the rest of us want to crack his skull.

"'Morning, Josh," I managed. Just because I didn't like the guy didn't mean I wouldn't be cordial. I'd been raised in the South, after all, where we're taught to always be pleasant. Or were we taught to be hypocrites? Fine line there.

His eyes cut to my briefcase. No doubt he was trying to summon X-ray vision so that he could read the documents inside. *My case is bigger than your case,* I wanted to say. *Neener-neener, you little wiener.*

"Uh, yeah," he said, when he realized I was eyeing him. "'Morning."

I continued on to my office and slid into my wobbly desk chair, dropping my purse into the bottom desk drawer. The red voice-mail light on my phone blinked, alerting me to an awaiting message. I dialed into the system and listened.

The message was odd and cryptic. Loud techno dance music in the background and a deep male voice that muttered a single, frustrated word. "Fuck."

Strange. Must've been a wrong number.

I pulled out a pen and legal pad, ready to get to work. Unfortunately, when I went to write the date on the pad, the tip tore at the paper. Out of ink. Not a good start to the day.

I rummaged around in my pencil cup, then my desk, then my purse. Not a pen to be found. Dang.

The supply cabinet was way at the other end of the floor so, being the lazy ass that I was, I'd taken to pilfering supplies from the unoccupied office across the hall, an office that had once belonged to the infamous Nick Pratt. I headed across the corridor and pulled open the top drawer of the desk. Empty. Looked liked I'd already cleaned it out. The second drawer contained a squishy blue stress ball and a half-used stack of sticky notes, both of which could come in handy. I slipped them into my pocket. In the bottom drawer I hit the jackpot. An entire box of ballpoint pens.

Also in the drawer was a box of business cards. I opened the box and fished out a card.

Nicholas Pratt
Senior Special Agent

Humph. *Double Agent* was more like it.

I glanced around the room, wondering what else I might find. Surely the room had been thoroughly searched after his defection, so I didn't hold out much hope of finding anything important. Still, maybe something here would yield a clue about Nick, why he'd traded a good job and a good life for a dirty bribe, why no one had seen it coming.

The desk blotter calendar was three years out of date. I flipped through the oversized pages. While handwritten notes appeared on the top page, the following pages were pristine, unused.

His bookshelves held only the standard special agent manuals and a dusty Dirk Nowitzki bobble-head doll. Looked like Nick was a Mavericks fan. Were NBA games broadcast in Mexico? I hoped not. Would serve the guy right to miss out on them.

In the credenza I found an aluminum baseball bat and a blue nylon duffel bag. The duffel bag contained a pair of athletic shorts, a pair of tennis shoes, a T-shirt that read IRS-CRIMINAL INVESTIGATIONS, and a jock strap. Size extra large according to the tag. Not surprising. Accepting a bribe and fleeing the country knowing you'd become a federal fugitive would take some pretty big balls.

I returned the items to the bag, zipped it up, and closed the credenza.

Nothing I'd found had told me anything useful about Nick. But now I wondered something else. Nick had been gone for three years. Why hadn't Lu reassigned the office to another agent?

I spent the rest of the morning on the phone, speaking with the managers of the check-cashing businesses where the Pokornys' money orders had been cashed. The calls proved to be a total waste of my time. Given that money orders are prepaid and virtually risk free, the check-cashing businesses had been more than happy to cash them, for an exorbitant fee, of course. Moreover, because the money orders were payable to "bearer," meaning anyone possessing them had the legal right to cash them, the staff had taken only a cursory glance at the identification proffered by the customer. No permanent record had been kept.

A dead end.

Dang.

I met my best friend, Alicia, at a downtown sandwich shop for lunch. While I was a part-time, bargain-basement sophisticate, Alicia was überchic, a platinum blonde with a short, angular haircut and a cutting-edge sense of style. Today she wore a royal blue satin blouse with a dark gray pencil skirt, along with a pair of pointy-toed black stilettos. Her look was polished and professional, yet feminine. I looked professional in my gray suit, too, though far less feminine. Hard to look too girlie when your clothing has to accommodate a hip holster. And since I never knew when I might have to chase down a suspect, rubber-soled loafers were more my style.

I glanced up at the menu board and debated. Soup, sandwich, or salad?

Alicia stepped up to the counter in front of me. "Bottled water. Garden salad. Fat-free ranch dressing." Always watching her figure.

"I'll have the same," I said, "but not with that icky fat-free stuff. Give me regular dressing."

Alicia cut her eyes my way. "You'll regret that decision someday."

"Maybe," I said, "but it won't be today."

Alicia and I had met in college, in our first accounting class, and instantly hit it off. When we graduated, we'd both taken jobs at Martin and McGee. Though I'd felt stifled and had since moved on to my special agent position at the IRS, Alicia thrived at the CPA firm. She'd recently been promoted to a junior management position, a job which came with a cushy office and a twenty-percent pay increase.

We paid for our lunch, took our trays, and found seats at a table in a corner.

The skin under my cast itched like crazy. I grabbed the plastic fork that came with the salad and eased it under the plaster near my thumb, scratching at my skin. Relief. *Aaah.* Unfortunately, the fork became stuck inside my cast. After several attempts, I managed to fish it out, though two plastic tines broke off and eluded me. I retrieved another fork from the bin on the counter to eat my lunch.

When I sat down again, Alicia looked at me across the table and frowned. She plucked two slices of cucumber off her salad and held them out to me. "Here. Put these over your eyes. They'll help with those dark circles."

"That bad?"

She nodded.

I took the cucumbers from her, but dipped them in my ranch dressing and ate them instead.

She spread her napkin in her lap. "When was the last time you got a full night's sleep?"

The night before the Lobo and George Burton assigned me to the Mendoza case. "About a week ago."

Alicia didn't push me further. She knew I was working a highly sensitive case and couldn't share the details. "When this case is over," she said, "I'm taking you to the Four Seasons spa for a massage and facial. My treat."

"Wow, thanks."

"I'm a junior manager now. I can't be seen with you looking like death warmed over."

I shot her a look across the table. "Feeling a little less grateful now."

She smiled for a brief moment then her face scrunched in concern. "Be careful, okay? I don't want to have to find a new best friend."

I didn't want her to have to find a new best friend, either.

The scent of menthol cigarettes and industrial-strength hairspray registered with my nose a split second before my boss stepped into my office later that afternoon. Lu sported a strawberry-blond beehive, heavy on the strawberry, along with false eyelashes over blue-shaded lids and bright orange lipstick. Her outfit today was a sixties-style pantsuit with a Nehru jacket in size twenty-two Velveeta-colored velveteen.

Though Lu's fashion sense was questionable, her other mental faculties remained acute. She'd reached the minimum retirement age and had previously planned to retire once the department collected a hundred million under her watch. But when Eddie and I had recently helped her reach her goal, she'd changed her mind, decided she wasn't yet ready to throw in the towel.

Lu closed my office door behind her. "Tell me you've got some solid leads on Mendoza."

"Wish I could, Lu." I told her about our interview with the Pokornys, my futile calls to the check-cashing facilities.

She chewed her lip in an uncharacteristic act of anxiety. It wasn't like the Lobo to worry. But the Mendoza investigation wasn't the typical case, either. No doubt George Burton was breathing down her neck, wanting it resolved ASAP.

"They found more of Andrew Sheffield," she said, pulling a cigarette and lighter out of her pocket. "His left hand turned up in the weeds near a rest stop outside Abilene."

"Oh God." I put a hand over my mouth, hoping my salad would stay down. If not, well then it really didn't matter that I hadn't opted for the fat-free dressing, did it? "How'd they know it was him?"

"Wedding ring. His initials were engraved on the inside."

When Andrew Sheffield vowed to love his wife *till death do us part,* I'll bet he never realized just how short that time would be.

Lu stuck the cigarette between her lips and clamped down, speaking out of the side of her mouth. "I don't want any more dead bodies on my conscience."

"Sheffield's death isn't your fault, Lu."

"Oh yeah?" she spat. "Tell that to Sheffield's widow. Tell that to his little boy. If we'd taken Mendoza down three years ago, Sheffield would still be alive." Lu lit the cigarette, took a deep drag, then pointed it at me. "If you and Eddie don't nail that bastard soon, the next body's on your heads."

The stomach that had just threatened to spill its contents now shrank into a tight, painful ball. "Great motivational speech."

Lu ignored my sarcasm. "I'm counting on you, Holloway. Mendoza hasn't just cost the government a bunch of money, he cost me the best special agent I ever had."

"Gee, thanks," I replied dryly.

"Don't get your panties in a wad. You're better with a gun, but Pratt was a workhorse. Smart as a whip, too. Brought in more money for this agency than any other agent in history."

Ironic, then, that he'd been bought off. I wondered if Mendoza would try to buy off me and Eddie, too, if he got wind we were after him. No amount of money was worth sacrificing my personal integrity, of course. Still, I was curious what personal integrity was going for these days.

"How much do you think Mendoza paid Pratt?" I asked Lu. "Five million? Ten? More?"

She shrugged. "Don't have a clue."

"If Nick was willing to leave his entire life behind, it must've been a shitload." Hmm. What was the exchange rate between shit and U.S. dollars?

Lu looked down at the floor and took a slow, sad drag on her cigarette.

I eyed her. "Seems like you took his leaving personally."

Lu was quiet for a moment. When she spoke, her voice was unusually soft. "You have no idea just how personally, Tara."

Nick Pratt had been assigned to the earlier investigation after U.S. customs agents made an interesting discovery during a routine border stop in Laredo. The agents found a large stash of Mexican five-hundred peso bills concealed in a box among others filled with children's footie pajamas. The pj's had been produced at one of the *maquiladoras* that cropped up in Mexico's border towns after the enactment of the North American Free Trade Agreement in 1994. In the preceding presidential election debates, Texan candidate Ross Perot had warned voters that, if passed, the pending bill would result in a "giant sucking sound" of jobs heading south of the border. Bill Clinton was elected and had promptly signed the controversial bill. Then again, President Clinton was known for sucking sounds.

The *maquiladora* factories were supposed to be a win-win situation, bringing jobs and money into Mexico while eliminating tariffs and thus keeping prices down for products imported into the U.S. Instead, the end result had been the exploitation of Mexican workers paid so little they were forced to live in slums, with the bulk of the profits going into the pockets of the factory owners on both sides of the border. The rich get richer . . .

After the cash was found hidden among the pajamas, the customs agents did some research into the driver's purported destination only to discover an abandoned warehouse was located at the address. After further interrogation, the driver admitted he'd been provided the warehouse address as a decoy and had been told he'd receive a call on his cell phone later that afternoon with instructions on where to deliver the shipment.

When the call came in that afternoon, the agents intercepted it. Unfortunately, the call came from an untraceable prepaid cell phone. The caller asked the driver for his current location and, when the driver hesitated, the caller realized things were not right and terminated the call without giving a delivery address.

The lackey driving the truck claimed to have no knowledge he'd been transporting cash. After several hours of interrogation, the agents determined he was telling the truth. Officials did more digging and linked the pajama shipment to a Mexican textile company owned by Vicente Torres. A little more digging linked Torres to AmeriMex in Texas. Unfortunately, Torres was on the wrong side of the border and there wasn't enough evidence to arrest anyone in the U.S. The Mexican authorities were notified, though Torres asserted his innocence, claiming the driver must have been transporting the cash for someone else.

The pajamas and funds were seized. No one showed up

to claim them. The sleepers were sent to a local children's charity, while the funds went into the U.S. coffers. *Muchas gracias*. Customs tipped off the IRS about the questionable cash and Pratt had been discreetly dispatched to investigate whether AmeriMex was engaged in financial shenanigans.

Pratt discerned that, despite being listed only as an assistant manager for AmeriMex, Marcos Mendoza was really the head honcho of a vast financial enterprise. Unfortunately, that tidbit of information was all Pratt shared with the Lobo. He'd told Lu that he'd need to go undercover inside AmeriMex to obtain proof. He'd subsequently checked in a few times, indicated he was building a solid case, then *poof!* The traitorous asshole disappeared quicker than a man served with a paternity suit.

Weeks later Pratt mailed back his laptop and cell phone from Cancún. But without the cooperation of Mexican authorities, there wasn't much else the IRS could do at that point.

So here we were, trying to resurrect a case against Mendoza, to rise like a phoenix from the ashes of the previous investigation, to boldly go where one man had gone before. The only viable lead George Burton had been able to provide us was the Pokornys, and the only lead the Pokornys provided us was the post office box to which they'd sent their loan payments.

"Eddie's gone to the post office," I told Lu. "Maybe he'll come up with something."

"Keep me informed," Lu said. "I want daily reports. Got it?"

"Got it."

The Lobo turned to leave.

"Lu?"

She turned back.

"How about we go ahead with your party?" I said. "Even though you've decided not to retire, collecting a hundred million is still reason to celebrate. It's a huge achievement." Not to mention the fact that I'd called the country club and been told we'd forfeit our sizable deposit if we canceled.

"What the hell," Lu said. "Wouldn't be right to be the pooper of my own party, would it?"

I was glad she agreed to go ahead with the celebration. Something told me we'd need something fun to look forward to.

CHAPTER FIVE

$\mathscr{L}$ie with Me, Not to Me

Brett and I had standing dates each Friday night, though ironically, these standing dates usually ended with us lying down. We'd been dating for a few weeks and suffered a rough patch when I'd suspected he might be involved with a con artist. Thankfully, I'd been mistaken.

Brett wasn't perfect. He sometimes mumbled in his sleep and liked to watch golf on television. Somebody kill me, please! He also didn't understand my enthusiasm for bargain hunting and target practice. But we shared a fondness for furry four-footed creatures, ethnic foods, and offbeat British comedies, not to mention incredible chemistry. Not a bad start for a relationship, right?

Brett had suggested dinner and a movie out tonight, but I'd countered with pizza and a DVD in. After the long hours I'd put in all week, I wasn't sure I'd be able to stay awake for an entire movie, and if I were going to fall asleep I'd rather it be on Brett's couch than in a public theater where I might drool all over myself.

I drove to Brett's house and let myself in with the key he kept hidden under the decorative birdhouse on his front porch. Two wagging tails greeted me. One belonged to Napoleon, a small Scottie mix, the other to Reggie, a pit bull–Rottweiler cross Brett took in after I busted the dog's owners and got stuck with the enormous beast. Given his large size and muscular build, Reggie looked scary as hell, but Brett's doting care had transformed him from a wary and intimidating watchdog to a sweet, spoiled-rotten mutt.

I gave each of the dogs a quick scratch behind the ears and took them out to the backyard for a potty break. After changing into my comfy red nightie, I flopped onto Brett's overstuffed sofa, dug my cell phone out of my purse, and checked the screen. No messages. Eddie hadn't yet called to tell me how things had gone at the post office. Either it had been another dead end or he was still there.

As long as I had the phone out, I figured I might as well call my parents. It had been a few days since we'd last talked. I dialed my mom and dad's number in Nacogdoches, my hometown back in East Texas.

Mom answered, her voice coated with a sugary Southern accent. "Well, hi there, sweetie."

Given that I'd been a rough-and-tumble tomboy during my growing years and was now a gun-toting, ass-kicking federal agent, "sweet" wasn't a word most people associated with me. But my mother would forever view her only daughter through rose-colored glasses.

We chatted briefly. After she lamented the heat that had scorched her heirloom tomato plants, I told her about my upcoming trip with Brett to Florida, describing the beautiful chiffon dress I'd bought but neglecting to mention the sexy lingerie. No sense shattering those rose-colored glasses.

"Be careful if you go into the ocean," she warned. "Your father's been watching shark week on the Discovery Channel. Those creatures like to scare me to death."

I didn't fear the predatory fish nearly as much as the loan shark Eddie and I were after. But, again, no sense telling my mother—something that would just cause her to worry. "I'll be careful."

"I'd love to come out and see you," she said. "Maybe do a little shopping?"

Though Nacogdoches offered a relaxing pace and a small-town sense of community, it offered little in the way of retail. Mom routinely made the drive to Dallas, her frequent visits allowing us to bond while shopping for clothing, jewelry, and assorted housewares.

"I'll check my schedule and get back to you." I hated to put my mother off, but until Eddie and I figured out how we'd bring Mendoza down I had no idea when I'd have time for a visit.

Mom begged off then. She and Dad were off to a dance at the VFW hall, where they reigned as the king and queen of swing. Their jitterbug wasn't bad, either.

"Y'all have fun."

"Always do." Mom made a kissing sound in the phone. "You take care, hon."

As I ended the call, I noticed my cell phone battery was nearly dead. I also noticed the dogs looking up at me with hunger in their eyes.

"Who wants some dinner?"

Their wagging tails said what their mouths couldn't—*we do!*

I carried my phone into the kitchen and plugged the device into an outlet beside the microwave to charge. Then I opened a can of dog food and split it between Napoleon and Reggie.

A half hour later, the dogs and I were curled up together on the couch when Brett arrived with a warm, delicious-smelling pizza. With his sandy brown hair, sage-green eyes, and lean athletic build, Brett could certainly turn a woman's head. He'd turned mine. And it hadn't since turned elsewhere.

He shifted the pizza box in his hands and gave me that special smile, the one where he cocked his head, locked his gaze on mine, and just slightly raised one side of his mouth. "Hi, honey. I'm home."

"How was your day, dear?"

It was a silly, clichéd spiel, but what the heck. What we lacked in originality we made up for in sincerity.

Brett slid out of his suit jacket. "My day was long and hard."

"Long and hard, huh?" I pointed a finger at him. "That's just how I like you."

He gave a lustful groan.

"I'll give you two minutes to get out of that suit and into me." I lifted my nightgown and playfully flashed my lace panties.

He all but threw the pizza box on the coffee table and dashed to his bedroom to change out of his work clothes.

I wanted Brett, sure, but I wasn't quite the sex-crazed skank I may seem to be. The fact was, I was tired to the bone and if we didn't get the sex out of the way first I was afraid I'd be too tired later. Wouldn't be right to leave my man disappointed, would it? Besides, he might be offended if I fell asleep and started snoring in the middle of the act. This stretch was the longest we'd gone without making love since our first time a few weeks ago. I hoped Eddie and I would bust Mendoza soon. The case was costing me too much sleep and seriously impeding my orgasm quota.

While Brett changed out of his suit, I grabbed a couple of plates and napkins from the kitchen, as well two stem glasses and a bottle of our favorite wine from the stash he kept in his pantry. I'd learned to manage pretty well despite the darn cast on my wrist. Nothing was going to slow Tara Holloway down.

Napoleon and Reggie had followed me back into the kitchen, and now sat side by side on the tile floor, patiently watching me with their big, brown eyes, their expressions hopeful. *Arf?* asked Napoleon. Reggie followed up with a husky, *Woof?*

"You got it, boys." I retrieved two crunchy dog biscuits from the cookie jar on the counter and tossed them to the dogs.

Reggie wolfed his down, while Napoleon caught the biscuit in midair, wagged his tail in thanks, and carried his treat into the living room to eat it on the rug. I followed the dogs, my arms full, and arranged everything on the coffee table.

Brett returned from the bedroom, now wearing only a pair of soft cotton lounge pants, black with bright-red chili peppers printed on them. Yep, I'd bought the tacky things. Hot pants for my hot boyfriend. He took the glass of wine I offered him, his eyes darting from me to the pizza. "Hmm. Not sure which one I want to devour first."

What a tease. I gave an indignant grunt. I could give as well as I could take. I sat down on the couch, leaned back against the cushions, and ran a lazy finger up and down my thigh. "Does this help you make your decision?"

Brett moaned with desire. "I'll take you hot and the pizza cold."

Take that vegetarian supreme.

Brett pounced on me and we rolled around on the couch for a moment, him chuckling, me giggling. He shifted so that he lay to my side and I turned toward him, all silliness gone now. I slid one foot up along the back of his leg until my thigh draped over his.

Brett brushed my hair back from my face, his rough fingertips leaving warm, sensitive trails on my cheek. He leaned in to kiss me, softly, sweetly, a gentle warm-up promising much more. Seconds later, the kiss deepened, growing hotter, more demanding.

I was fully prepared to meet his demands. And I had some of my own, as well.

I ran my fingers up his chest, running my red-tipped nails over his pecs, through his coarse chest hair. Maybe it's just me, but I have no idea why men shave or wax their chests. I like my man to look and feel like a man. And Brett definitely felt like a man, from his downy chest to the rock-hard, ready arousal pushed against my inner thigh.

My fingers continued up over his bare chest, over his shoulder, around the back of his neck, and up into his hair. He shifted, positioning himself on top of me now, my left leg crooked around his waist. His mouth left mine, traveling down my neck, his breath hot against my skin. His hand ran down my side, his thumb grazing my alert nipple through the fabric of my nightshirt, his palm coming to rest, cupped around my hip bone. He ran his thumb lightly back and forth over my bare abdomen, tracing a line just above the waist-band of my panties. *Mmm.* He knew exactly what to do to get me going.

He nuzzled under my chin now, forcing my head back, my chest arching upward. Only a thin layer of fabric separated us, but it was too much to bear. He grabbed the hem of my now-rumpled nightshirt and eased it upward. Straddling my hips, he sat back and pulled my upper body forward, releasing me from my clothing in one swift, expert maneuver. There's a lot to be said for an easy-on, easy-off style.

Brett tossed the shirt over his shoulder. Napoleon dashed over to pounce on it when it hit the floor. The mutt was just as playful as his master.

Brett looked down at my bare torso, his eyes roaming over my features with appreciation. Though my breasts were small, they were proportional to my petite frame and rested above flat abs toned from hours of hard work at the Y. But as good as Brett's admiration felt, I craved his contact more. I reached my hands up, hooked them behind his neck, and pulled him down again until we were chest to chest, skin on skin. He felt so warm, so good, all conscious thought left my brain.

Mendoza who?

We kissed some more, touched some more, and when I could wait no longer, I used the leverage of my hip to push Brett to his side. His lounge pants and boxer briefs hit the floor next to my nightshirt, my lace panties coming to rest beside the latest edition of *Architectural Digest* on the end table.

Taking charge, I took him in, all of him, in one swift, slick motion, gasping with pleasure as he filled me. He countered with a moan of utter bliss and the two of us began the rhythmic dance that ended in absolute, mind-blowing bliss.

* * *

An hour later, minds blown and lusts quenched, we were back in our nightclothes, our hair mussed, satiated smiles on our faces. We nuked the pizza in the microwave and ate it while watching the previews at the beginning of the DVD, a romantic comedy, of course. It had been my turn to pick. Last time, Brett had selected an art film that had won all kinds of awards at the Sundance film festival. We were nothing if not versatile. We couldn't quite figure out the plot of the four-hour flick, though. Something about two pickle farmers in search of their true destinies. It seemed their destiny was to bore us to death as they made vat after vat of dills. Brett had ended up slipping me his pickle while we watched.

Tonight's movie, on the other hand, was fun, cute, and romantic. Still, I soon found myself yawning, my lids growing heavy. With both my physical and sexual hungers sated, I fought to stay awake.

Apparently I'd lost the fight. I awoke in Brett's bed the following morning with no recollection of how the movie ended. He must've carried me to the bedroom.

I sat up and rubbed my eyes. Striped light filtered through the slats of the wooden blinds, much brighter than I would have expected for early morning. Reggie lay sprawled belly up on Brett's side of the bed, dozing peacefully on his back, what remained of his boy parts shamelessly exposed. The bedroom door was cracked open a couple of inches and I could hear a soft voice from Brett's home office across the hall, Brett chastising an impatient, growling Napoleon. "Hush, boy. Tara needs her sleep. How 'bout a tummy rub?"

I could go for a tummy rub, too. But first I needed to check my phone to see if Eddie had called. Unfortunately, when I stood, nature placed an even more urgent call.

After freshening up in the bathroom, I stepped into the hall. Brett sat at his drafting table, Napoleon lying on his side at Brett's feet. Brett looked intently over a set of blueprints, rubbing the dog's stomach with his bare foot while marking the plans here and there with a colored pencil.

Brett's reputation as the must-have landscape architect of Dallas continued to grow by leaps and bounds. Not only did he understand the different types of local soil and the plants that would flourish in each, but he had an artist's eye for color and design. He picked up a scarlet pencil and dabbed at the blueprint, his pencil giving off a soft squeak against the shiny paper. When he was finished, he leaned back in his chair with a smile on his face. Obviously, he loved his job.

Just like I loved mine.

The floorboard creaked as I tried to tiptoe past the door.

Brett lifted his head. "Hey."

Busted. My cell phone would have to wait a little longer. "'Mornin'," I managed, my voice gravelly from sleep.

"About time you woke up," he said.

"What time is it?"

Brett held out his arm and tapped his watch.

I stepped toward him and checked his wrist. "Noon? Gosh, I slept for—" I tried to mentally calculate but my mind wasn't awake enough yet for mathematics.

"Thirteen hours," Brett said, beating me to the punch. "Give or take."

"Haven't done that since college." When I'd been hungover after a kegger at the Beta house. This Mendoza case was going to kill me.

"I drove to the coffeehouse at ten and got you a latte," he said. "I was sure you'd be up by the time I got back." He watched me for a moment longer, his expression concerned. "You've been working extra hard lately. How much longer is this going to keep up?"

Until we either bust Mendoza or die trying?

That wasn't the answer Brett wanted to hear and, besides, with Burton swearing me and Eddie to secrecy, I couldn't reveal any specifics about the case anyway. "I'm not sure." It was as honest as I could be.

"What kind of case are you working on?"

"I could tell you," I said, stepping up behind him and nuzzling the back of his neck. "But then I'd have to kill you."

How was that for evasive? And now, an attempt to change the subject. "What are *you* working on?"

I stepped into place beside him and looked down at the blueprint. Unlike most of Brett's projects, which tended toward high-end residential and large-scale commercial projects, the structure pictured in the blueprint appeared to be a basic, modestly sized house.

He slid the pencil into a cup on his drafting table. "It's a Habitat for Humanity project. I volunteered to do the landscaping at a house they're building in Oak Cliff."

"That's wonderful!"

Brett reached out and took my arm, pulling me toward him until I was sitting on his lap. He nuzzled my neck. "I hope you wrap up your case soon. I miss spending time with you."

"Me, too." I tilted my head to give him better access to the sweet spot where neck meets shoulder. "But don't worry. I'll make it up to you in Fort Lauderdale."

He found the spot—*mmm*—then left a trail of soft, warm kisses as he moved up to nibble my earlobe. "I'm going to hold you to that."

I reluctantly left him and walked to the kitchen to heat the now-cold latte in the microwave. I would have a hard time getting it down. My stomach had clenched back into that tight knot. After I'd withheld information from Brett on my last case, including the fact that I stupidly suspected he might be involved in a fraudulent scheme, I'd promised Brett there'd be no more secrets between us. But here I was, keeping things from Brett again.

It didn't feel right.

In fact, it felt pretty damn wrong.

CHAPTER SIX

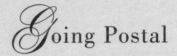

Going Postal

My latte now warmed, I checked my freshly charged cell phone. Three voice mails awaited me.

Uh-oh.

All of the messages were from Eddie, each one progressively less cordial.

Message number one, left at eight o'clock yesterday evening: *Tara, it's Eddie. I've got some important news about the P.O. box. Call me as soon as you get this.*

Oops. The dang phone was set to vibrate, the ringer turned off. No wonder I hadn't heard Eddie's calls.

Message number two, left just after midnight : *What part of "call me as soon as you get this" did you not understand?*

Message number three left at nine this morning: *Get your skinny white ass out of bed and over here to the post office or, so help me God, I will feed you headfirst through the shredder!*

Yikes. With the volume of confidential information we handled at the IRS, our shredder was an industrial-sized unit with blades the size of chain saws. The device could make short work of a school bus. I called Eddie back immediately. "I'm on my way."

His only response was to hang up on me.

I threw on the same clothes I'd worn yesterday, bade a cursory good-bye to Brett and the dogs, and hopped into my car.

Twenty minutes later, I pulled into the post office parking lot, taking the spot next to Eddie's minivan. I climbed out of my car and into his vehicle. Despite the fact that he'd parked in the shade of a tree, the heat inside was sweltering. That's Texas for ya.

Like me, Eddie was still wearing yesterday's clothes, though he'd stripped down to his undershirt, his white button-down in a ball on the backseat. He cut angry, bloodshot eyes my way.

I cringed. "Were you here all night?"

"Gee, Tara. What was your first clue?"

"I'm sorry. Really."

"You better be." His eyes narrowed at me. "You look well rested."

True, I'd gotten lots of sleep last night. Lots of sex, too. My orgasm quota was back on track. Heck, I'd even accumulated a surplus. "What did you find out?"

"I spoke to the manager on duty. He gave me a copy of the rental application." Eddie reached into the pocket of his pants, retrieved a folded piece of paper, and handed it to me.

I unfolded it and looked it over. The application indicated the P.O. box had been rented in the name of ARS Financial Corporation.

My heart tripped over itself. "ARS? As in Andrew Richard Sheffield?" As in the one-time member of NDCU's staff who was later *dis*membered?

Eddie nodded. "One and the same."

When Sheffield's appendages had surfaced, the local police departments in each city had opened separate murder investigations. After one of the detectives pieced Sheffield's pieces together and realized that a single victim had been sprinkled across several cities, the local police turned the matter over to the Texas Rangers, who had statewide jurisdiction. When the Texas Rangers had been unable to solve the case, they referred it to the FBI.

Per the FBI files, Andrew Sheffield had left NDCU a couple of years ago to form his own one-man financial services company. Although the banking records for ARS Financial indicated a number of suspicious transactions, including a significant number of cash deposits and withdrawals, no direct evidence could be found to link the transactions to Mendoza.

As primitive as cash transactions were in this day and age, they were the best way to move money without leaving a trail. The FBI report made note of other deaths surrounding Mendoza, including an AmeriMex employee who'd been the victim of an unsolved carjacking and another who'd perished in a suspicious house fire.

Interestingly, there'd been no reference to the P.O. box in the FBI's investigative reports on Sheffield's murder. "I'm surprised the FBI didn't find out about the box."

Eddie shrugged. "You know how these things go, Tara. There's a lot of luck involved."

True. Investigating a crime wasn't nearly as easy, or as quick, as they made it look on television shows. Clues didn't exactly jump out at you and holler "Here I am!" You had to hunt them down.

Eddie leaned toward me then, speaking in a low voice. "Of course it's also possible that the FBI's investigators didn't *want* to find the post office box." He raised a suspicious brow.

My throat constricted, my voice coming out tight and squeaky, like one of Alvin and the Chipmunks'. "Does the manager at the post office know about Sheffield? That he's . . ." I couldn't bring myself to say it out loud.

"Dead?"

A nod was all I could manage.

"No," Eddie said. "I didn't tell him. Didn't want him closing the account. He told me the box rental had been renewed a month ago. Prepaid in full for an entire year."

Given that Sheffield was killed more than a month ago, he couldn't have been the one who'd renewed the box. "Who paid the fee?"

"Good question. The manager said the payment was made by mail. In cash."

Again, untraceable.

My mind whirled. Could this box be the missing link? The one that would tie Mendoza to Sheffield's murder?

Maybe.

Maybe not.

But hopefully it would be. I wanted this case closed. Quick. I wasn't sure my nerves could take a lengthy investigation. I didn't like keeping things from Brett. And I sure as hell didn't want a dead body on my conscience.

Eddie took the rental application from me and slid it into his briefcase on the backseat. "With Sheffield gone, somebody else must be picking up the loan payments from the box. Maybe the same person who paid the renewal. We have to find out who that person is."

Which meant we'd have to continue a round-the-clock watch on the box. Good thing I had those surplus orgasms to keep me going.

CHAPTER SEVEN

$\mathscr{F}$rugal Fashionista

Stakeouts required stealth, special equipment, and, of course, a carefully planned wardrobe. If I were going to spy on the post office for several days, I had to vary my look or risk being noticed. Problem was, the tightwads in the IRS accounting department weren't exactly generous when it came to reimbursing agents for business-related expenses. I'd learned that lesson the hard way. Good thing I was resourceful.

I phoned Alicia from the post office parking lot on Monday afternoon. "Meet me after work at the downtown thrift store."

"Making a donation?"

"No," I said. "Buying some new clothes."

"They don't sell new clothes at the thrift store."

Duh. "Not *new* new. New to me."

"You're going to wear some stranger's used clothes?" Her tone was incredulous with a hint of revulsion. "Seriously?"

"Yes, seriously." I rolled my eyes, grateful she couldn't see through the phone. I adored Alicia, but she could be tad particular at times, perhaps even snobby. She took that whole *dress for success* and *clothes make the woman stuff* to heart. "People wear secondhand stuff all the time. Haven't you heard of *The Sisterhood of the Traveling Pants*?"

"Of course," she said. "It's a horror movie. Four girls sharing used jeans they don't even wash? That's disgusting. They could get an STD."

Sheez. "Get over it."

She reluctantly agreed to accompany me, but it wouldn't have surprised me if she showed up in a hazmat suit.

When Eddie arrived at five o'clock to relieve me, I drove to the secondhand shop downtown. Alicia sat out front in her sleek black Audi, an expression of distaste on her face. She climbed out of her car and we met at the front door.

"Ready?" I asked.

"Ready." She took a deep breath and held it.

I eyed her. "Are you going to hold your breath the entire time we're inside?"

She nodded frantically, her face already turning red.

"You're nuts." I yanked the door open and we stepped inside.

The place wasn't fancy but it was clean, smelling faintly of pine-scented disinfectant. Decorative items and small household appliances were situated near the front of the store, followed by racks of clothing, with a display of shoes and accessories along the back wall. Signs hanging from the ceiling indicated the men's, women's, and children's sections.

I pulled a shopping cart from the corral and aimed for the women's department. Alicia followed, gasping for air behind me as her lungs gave way.

I stopped at a rack of blouses and began to sort through them. A T-shirt that read FOXY GRANDMA. No, thanks. Ditto on the bright green polyester blouse with the enormous, eighties-style shoulder pads. Next was a black leather vest trimmed with silver studs, only three of which were missing. Now that had possibilities, both for the stakeout and, come October, a biker chick Halloween costume. Into the cart it went.

Beside me, Alicia squealed and yanked a champagne-colored blouse off the rack. "Ohmigod!" She checked the label and looked at me, her eyes wide and gleaming with excitement. "This is Versace!"

"*Secondhand* Versace." I couldn't help myself. What are friends for if not to razz each other? "You might get an STD, remember?"

She checked the price tag. "For four bucks I'll risk it." Alicia stepped to my other side, quickly moving hangers aside. "Ohmigod! Ohmigod! Ohmigod!" *Squeal! Squeal! Squeal!*

"You sound like a piglet."

Her only response was to squeal again.

I suppose it shouldn't have been surprising the downtown thrift store would have some designer pieces. More than likely they had been donated by wealthy female executives who worked in the city's nearby financial district.

I continued sorting through the tops, adding a colorful striped tunic, a lace-trimmed peasant blouse, and a teeny half-shirt with HOOTERS printed across the front.

I moved on to the dresses and coordinates next. A pastel blue and white polka-dot set caught my eye and I pulled it from the rack. Though the label indicated the top was a size small, it seemed oddly spacious. Then I noticed the matching pants contained a solid white stretchy panel across the front. A maternity set. What the hell. The outfit was the perfect disguise. No one would suspect a pregnant woman of being an undercover agent, right?

I added the set to the stack accumulating in my cart. I also selected a pair of blue scrubs with BAYLOR MEDICAL CENTER stamped on the chest and a muted floral dress with long sleeves, a long skirt, and a collar that buttoned all the way up. I'd look like a Sunday school teacher in that one, or maybe a cast member from *Little House on the Prairie*.

Next came pants. I passed on a pair of stretchy stirrup pants, as well as an outdated pair of high-waist black dress pants. A pair of leather-trimmed jeans made their way into the cart, though, as did a pair of white cotton Capris with red roses embroidered on the pockets and hem.

I looked up to see a salesclerk unburdening Alicia of the enormous load in her arms. We headed to the shoes and accessories next. A pink pillbox hat complete with a gaudy silk flower and netting sat on a shelf, along with a matching pair of gloves.

I slid into the gloves, then slapped the hat onto my head at a jaunty angle, pursed my lips, and did my best Queen Elizabeth impression. "Charles dear, you simply must stop boffing Camilla on the dining room table, especially during breakfast. You're causing my poached eggs to jiggle in an uncomely fashion."

Alicia giggled and grabbed the hat off me, placing it on her head now. "Camilla, you detestable, boorish whore. How dare you soak your soiled naughties in the kitchen sink!"

We shared another laugh and Alicia put the hat back on the shelf. I returned the gloves, too. That set was a little too much. I was trying to avoid attention, not attract it.

I found a pair of black leather ankle boots with silver chains in my size, as well as a studded leather belt. I also found a blue-and-yellow-print Vera Bradley purse that would go well with the maternity outfit.

A few feet away, Alicia checked the tags on a colorful silk scarf. "Hermès for six bucks? Unbelievable! This place is a gold mine."

We left the store a half hour later, loaded down with bags. Alicia had twice as many as me, as well as a zippered garment bag that contained a gorgeous Monique Lhuillier wedding gown she'd scored for the ridiculous sum of seventy-five dollars, a mere fraction of its original price.

"You better hide that dress from Daniel," I warned as we headed to our cars. "If he finds out you've bought a wedding dress he's going to freak."

Alicia was determined to one day marry her boyfriend, Daniel Blowitz, even if she had to drag him down the aisle kicking and screaming. Though Daniel was nuts about Alicia, he suffered from a chronic case of commitment phobia, no doubt brought on by interactions with the divorce attorneys at the law firm where he worked as a litigator. Of course we all assumed he'd come around eventually, probably when his hair began to thin and his middle began to thicken. Maybe then he'd realize he wasn't a kid anymore and it was time to man up.

"You're right," Alicia said. "If Daniel saw the dress, he'd think I was trying to send him a message. It's going home with you, then. You'll keep your cats off it, won't you?"

"Sure." We'd been friends for years. The least I could do was sacrifice some closet space for her.

She followed me to my car and laid the dress across the backseat. I stowed my bags in the trunk and slammed it closed.

Alicia headed to her car with her remaining bags, looking back over her shoulder to toss me a cheeky "Ta-ta!"

CHAPTER EIGHT

$\mathscr{B}$ig Whoop

Eddie and I spent the next week doing twelve-hour tag-team shifts watching the post office box. I took the noon-to-midnight shift so that Eddie could spend the evenings with his wife and daughters, while he took the midnight-to-noon shift.

The post office where the Pokornys' payments had been sent was a neighborhood branch in the northwest Dallas suburbs. The building was located on a corner across from a strip mall containing a convenience store and a Laundromat. An elementary school sat next door, the sounds of children at recess drifting over from the playground. *Ready or not, here I come!*

In movies, stakeouts are portrayed as exciting events, a team of agents set up in a tricked-out van or vacant building using the latest hi-tech gear to spy on the bad guys, tap into telephone conversations, collect evidence.

This stakeout was nothing like that.

I performed my surveillance from a musty, nondescript

white rental car. The tightasses in the IRS accounting department would only spring for a subcompact, so there was no room to stretch my legs. The best I could do was lean the seat back in an attempt to create more space. What's more, the entire car seemed to be made of plastic. I suspected the word "Mattel" was engraved on the car's undercarriage.

I sat in the car for hours at a time with a pair of my dad's oversized field glasses, staring through the plate-glass window of the post office, waiting, hoping to see someone stick a key in box 1216.

I went on high alert early one evening when a large, middle-aged man in a trench coat and fedora-type hat entered the post office. Nobody dressed like that in North Texas, especially when it wasn't raining. He headed for the section containing box 1216.

I leaped from my car and hurried inside, the floral church-lady dress swishing around my legs. So as not to rouse suspicion, I had a stack of mail under my arm, letters I'd written while sitting in the car. My aunt Darlene would be thrilled to finally get a thank-you note for the check she sent me years ago for college graduation. It's not that I'm ungrateful. It's just that correspondence is at the bottom of my to-do list and I never get to the bottom of my to-do list.

I approached the man slowly, pretending to be sorting through my letters when in reality I was looking at him from under my bangs. The guy was Caucasian, with a thick salt-and-pepper beard concealing the bottom half of his face. Turned out the man was only buying stamps from the automated machine situated nearby.

Damn. So close yet so far.

I went ahead and mailed my letter to my aunt. Also one to my congressman proposing a tax exemption for pets. Heck, I spent as much money on my spoiled cats as most people did on their children.

After slipping my letters through the mail slot, I headed back to the door. The guy held it open for me.

"Thanks."

He noted my prim, prissy dress and offered a toothy smile. "My pleasure."

I returned to my car, the only one in the lot now. I'd just settled in the seat, locked my door, and cracked the window a couple of inches for ventilation, when a tap sounded at the glass. I turned to find myself face-to-face with the man in the raincoat. Well, not face-to-face exactly. More like face to exposed genitalia.

The trench coat suddenly made sense.

Now you might think I'd scream or gasp, but this wasn't the first penis I'd encountered on the job. Just last month I'd cuffed a guy around the ankles with his pants down. After a while, you grow immune. Besides, if this guy tried anything, he'd be sorry. My Glock was in my purse on the passenger seat, within easy reach.

Ignoring the man, I picked up the mystery novel I'd been reading earlier.

The guy bent down and spoke through the window opening. "Hey, lady. I think you missed something."

I flipped through the book, looking for the dog-eared page that marked my spot. "Nope. Don't believe I missed a thing."

He emitted a frustrated huff. "Come on. Look!"

"At your wiener? Urk. No, thanks." There we go. Page eighty-seven.

He knocked again. This guy did not take rejection well.

I contemplated calling the cops, but didn't want to bring any unnecessary attention to myself. Besides, I had bigger fish to fry than this neighborhood exhibitionist. "Go away," I said. "I'm busy." I turned my back to him.

"Just a quick peek?" he begged. This pervert was persistent.

"If I take a quick peek, will you go away?"

"Yeah. Sure."

I turned to the window and looked. Mostly all I could see was his round, hairy belly. The guy had obviously indulged in a little too much beer and barbecue. I motioned at his stomach. "You're going to have to lift your belly."

He put a hand under his gelatinous abs and lifted. There it was. His junk. Big whoop. Actually, average-sized whoop at best.

"Okay, I looked." I waved him away with my hand. "Now shoo."

His shoulders slumped. "But you didn't scream or anything."

"Screaming wasn't part of the deal. If you wanted a scream, you should've negotiated for it."

He curled his fingers over the top edge of the window now and peered in at me. "Please? Just once?"

This guy was really starting to annoy me. What did he think it was, be-kind-to-perverts day? Still, it was clear he and his middle-aged man parts weren't going anywhere until I showed the proper amount of alarm and dismay.

I put a hand on either side of my face and emitted a high-pitched scream like Macaulay Culkin's famous scream in *Home Alone*. There. Shock and ew.

The guy leered at me now.

"I screamed," I said. "Now go. That was the deal."

Unfortunately, the perv breached our agreement. He didn't go. Instead, he pressed his junk firmly against the glass. Guess I should've gotten the terms in writing.

Now the only thing more disgusting than a saggy scrotum is a saggy scrotum smashed flat against glass only inches from your face.

"That's it." I jabbed the button to roll up the window, trapping him by his fingers.

"Hey!" he hollered.

I pulled out my cell phone and dialed 911, giving the dispatcher my location.

The guy tried to pull his hands out of the window, but couldn't. "I can't feel my fingers!"

I looked at his fingers. Even in the dim light of the parking lot, it was clear they were beginning to turn purple. Still, I didn't want to risk him running off and I sure didn't want to engage in a physical confrontation with him unless absolutely necessary. This stupid dress would impede my movement.

I jabbed the cigarette lighter. When it ejected seconds later, I held the orange glowing surface a few inches from his fingertips. Not close enough to burn him, but close enough to determine whether his fingers really had grown numb.

"Shit!" he shrieked. "That's hot!"

I shoved the lighter back into its slot. "Your fingers are fine."

Grunting now, the guy tried to force the window downward. Given that the car was a cheap P.O.S., he'd likely be successful.

"Stop that," I ordered. "You'll break the window."

He didn't stop. The window gave a squeak, about to give way.

Out of options, I took a deep breath, unlocked the door, and shoved it open with all my might. The outside door handle hit the guy square in the nards. Howling in pain, he hunched over and instinctively tried to step backward, but couldn't with his fingers still trapped in the window. He collapsed against the door, slamming it shut again.

I locked it.

"My balls!" he screamed. "I'll sue!"

Fortunately, a squad car pulled up then. A butch-looking female officer climbed out. Despite his pain, the man turned to the cop and kicked his leg out, opening his coat and exposing himself to her, too. She rolled her eyes. Clearly not her first on-the-job encounter with a penis, either.

I unrolled the window to release the guy's fingers. He turned to run, but the officer was ready for him, sticking her foot into his path. He tripped, falling to his hands and knees on the pavement, his coat riding up on his back, exposing his bare buttocks. She put a foot on his ass and shoved. The naked man sprawled forward. Before he could gather his wits, the officer had his hands jerked up behind him and cuffed.

I climbed out of the car in case she needed assistance, but this officer was self-sufficient. She shoved the perv into the back of the squad car, took a quick report from me, and left.

I turned back to the rental car, noting a scrotum-shaped smudge on the glass. Ick. I wasn't sure if the rental company would charge extra to clean the glass, but I sure as hell wasn't touching it myself.

Alone again, I resumed my surveillance.

CHAPTER NINE

$\mathscr{A}$ Stakeout's More Fun with a Friend

Watch duty was nothing short of miserable. Besides the cramped car and the itchy cast on my wrist, I had to deal with the discomfort of infrequent potty breaks. I suppose I could've worn an adult diaper like that crazed female astronaut who'd driven nonstop from Houston to Florida after learning her boyfriend was cheating on her, but I just didn't have it in me. Then again, she'd been trained to pee in zero gravity so she had an advantage.

I wondered how long we'd have to watch the box before someone would come to pick up the contents. We assumed that payments for loans other than the Pokornys' were being sent to the box, too, but we couldn't be certain. For all we knew Mendoza could have multiple boxes at multiple post offices, maybe even a single box for each loan. After all, renting a box was cheap, less than a hundred bucks for an entire year. Compared to the huge profits the loans generated, the box rental fees were chump change. The Pokornys had made a payment only a few days earlier. It could be weeks before the box was checked again.

Every day it was harder to stay awake, despite the caramel lattes. I'd pick up two extra-large cups on my way to the post office each day, drinking one right away, pouring the other into a thermos to drink later when my concentration began to wane.

I'd checked in with my parents by phone several times, for once not minding when my mother rambled on with the small-town gossip from my hometown. She'd continued to press me for a good date to come visit, growing suspicious when I kept putting her off, her maternal instincts telling her that her daughter was working a big and dangerous case despite my insincere assertions to the contrary.

I'd searched party supply Web sites and ordered decorations for Lu's upcoming party. I'd watched a dozen DVDs on my laptop, finished nearly as many mystery novels, and given myself a mani/pedi, twice, all the while keeping one eye on the post office. I'd read each day's newspaper, cover to cover. I'd never been more informed. Or more bored. Or more lonely.

I missed Brett and Alicia. I missed my cats. I missed my normal life.

It chapped my ass that Marcos Mendoza was free to go about his business while here I sat, growing stiff and uncomfortable. What's more, due to our tag-team schedule, Eddie and I weren't able to perform our usual afternoon workouts at the Y. I could feel my butt growing wider, the blood congealing in my veins, my muscles beginning to atrophy. How long would it be before I developed hemorrhoids? To make matters worse, the Lobo demanded daily updates on my progress. She wasn't happy to hear there'd been none.

"You and Eddie need to step it up," she barked. "Mendoza's probably planning to kill another one of his associates as we speak."

"Don't remind me." Really, please! I didn't need any more pressure.

* * *

On Thursday I dressed in the blue hospital scrubs. At least I'd be comfortable today. The things felt like pajamas.

The post office had no benches outside or inside, probably to discourage the homeless from loitering. But it was simply too damn hot to sit in the car all day.

I went inside and stood at one of the workstations where patrons could assemble their packages for mailing. I'd bought a few things to send to my mother, big-city luxuries not available back home. A bottle of her favorite gardenia-scented hand lotion. An organic plant fertilizer made from bat guano. A patented, secret-formula antiwrinkle cream, which I also suspected was made from bat guano. These gifts were the least I could do for her. After all, she'd recently sent me a tin of her homemade pecan pralines.

Working slowly, and clandestinely keeping an eye on the nearby P.O. box, I wrapped each of the items in newspaper and placed them carefully in a red, white, and blue flat-rate box. As I wadded more newspaper to further cushion the gifts, an auburn-haired woman in a clingy, low-cut purple dress walked up to me.

"Are you a nurse?" she asked.

"Nurse?"

Her eyes flickered to the Baylor Medical Center logo on my scrubs. The soft cotton set was so comfortable I'd forgotten I was wearing the things.

"Uh . . . yeah," I said. "I'm a nurse."

"Does this look infected to you?" She turned her back to me, hiked her dress up over her hip, and pulled down one side of her panties, exposing a pasty, tattooed butt cheek. The tattoo was a red heart with the name Ricky in the center. If an ass tattoo with your lover's name on it didn't spell true devotion, I didn't know what did.

The skin around the tattoo was swollen and pink and—ew!—was it oozing? The latte and pralines in my tummy threatened to make a reappearance. "You should definitely get that looked at."

She pulled up her panties and dropped her skirt. "Thanks."

I received more health care questions as I finished assembling the package. An older man asked me to look in his ear, tell him whether the wax buildup he'd accumulated was normal. Urk. A young woman with an infant wanted to know if the baby should be producing three bowel movements a day. Double urk. A middle-aged woman asked my opinion on vaginal rejuvenation.

My opinion on *WHAT?!?*

I made up vague answers, hoping I wouldn't be arrested for practicing medicine without a license.

Another man tried to stop me on my way out the door, but I held up a hand. "Running late! No time for questions!"

The free medical clinic was now closed.

Early Thursday evening, I phoned Christina Marquez, a rookie DEA agent with whom I'd recently worked on an undercover case against a drug-dealing ice cream man. Nothing bonds two women like bringing down a sleazebag together.

"Hey, Tara." She sounded like her always bubbly self. "What's up?"

"I'm on a stakeout," I told her. "Come hang with me?"

"Where are you?"

"Spying on a post office."

"Oh God."

"It's even more boring than it sounds."

"Good thing you didn't go into sales as a profession," Christina said. "You'd have starved to death."

"Come on," I begged, scratching an itch on the back of my neck. "If I have to sit here by myself for another minute I'm going to self-combust."

She sighed. "All right. Nothing good on TV tonight anyway."

"Thanks. And speaking of starving to death, could you pick me up some dinner on the way?"

Christina showed up half an hour later, pulling up next to me in her sporty Volvo and giving me a friendly wave through the windshield.

Although the two of us were tough, capable, and clever, our similarities ended there. I was petite with a lean figure while she was tall and voluptuous. My chestnut brown hair was cut in a conservative shoulder-length style, while Christina sported long black tresses. My facial features were delicate, whereas hers were dramatic. She was the yin to my yang.

Christina wore a teeny pair of denim shorts, a sleeveless yellow top, and beaded flip-flops, looking nothing like the hard-hitting DEA agent she was. She unrolled her window, her gaze roving over my tiny compact car. "I can't believe they expect you to run surveillance from this piece of *caca*." She eyed the driver's window. "Weird. That smudge on the glass is shaped like a penis."

"That's because it was a penis."

"Oh." She, too, was unfazed. Nothing surprises a federal agent.

Christina kept an eye on the post office box while I drove to a residential area a few blocks away and parked the rental car. If whoever picked up the mail realized the post office was being watched, he might not go through with the pickup. Best to shuffle the vehicles around a bit.

I walked back to the post office lot, enjoying the brief exercise. Christina pushed her passenger door open from inside and I climbed into her car, thankful to be able to stretch out my legs. She'd brought me a sub sandwich and yet another caramel latte, extra whipped cream, heavy on the drizzle, sprinkle of cinnamon. Yum. I was addicted to the things.

I took a sip of my coffee. She took a sip of her antioxidant vitamin-infused karma-enhancing herbal tea. Like I said, yin and yang.

"So," she asked, "who we stalking here?"

"Don't have a clue. Just know which box to watch."

We sat in silence for a few moments, watching the box, sipping our drinks.

Christina finished her tea and slid the empty cup into a holder. "You and me on a stakeout. Reminds me of old times."

"Old times?" I repeated, glancing her way. "You mean last

month in the roach motel?" We'd recently spent a few weeks
on a stakeout in a former crack house, waiting to bust the
aforementioned drug-dealing, tax-cheating ice cream man.

"Last month is old times to rookies like us."

"True." I unwrapped my sub, releasing the scents of onion,
mustard, and banana peppers. I took a huge, ravenous bite.

Christina crinkled her nose and fanned the air with her
hand. "I should've told them to hold the onions."

I held my field glasses to my eyes each time I saw movement inside the post office. No luck. Nobody stopped at box
1216.

An elderly man supported by a four-pronged metal cane
stopped at a box a few rows over and removed several magazines in brown wrap. Girlie mags, no doubt, delivered to the
post office so the missus wouldn't know her husband was yet
another disgusting perv, getting his jollies ogling nude, big-
busted girls young enough to be his granddaughters.

When he emerged from the building, I couldn't help myself. I stuck my head out the window. "Those girlie mags,
Grandpa?"

The man looked at me, his eyes wide and wild. He clutched
his mail to his chest and shuffled to his car as fast as his
skinny, arthritic legs and cane would take him.

Christina snorted. "You're going to give that old fart a
heart attack."

"Would serve the skeeve right." Then again, in these hospital scrubs, I might be expected to perform CPR on the
guy. I was in no mood for mouth-to-mouth, especially when
it would likely be mouth-to-dentures. I could go without the
taste of Polident, thank you very much.

The last of the post office employees left soon thereafter,
the parking lot emptying, making our presence more con-
spicuous. We decided to drive next door to park at the elementary school.

The marquee in front advertised SPRING SHOW TONIGHT.
Cars streamed into the lot, which was nearly full. We found
a spot in the shade of the building and pulled in. We sat quietly for a few more moments, the faint, off-key sound of

children singing audible when a late-arriving parent opened the front door of the school.

"What do you do to entertain yourself when you're alone on a stakeout?" I asked Christina. Maybe she'd thought of something I hadn't.

She shrugged. "Sometimes I do crossword puzzles."

"I don't like crosswords." Mostly because I could never fully complete one and hated the sense of failure. I mean, really. Who knew the Russian city of Volgograd used to be called Stalingrad? Come on!

"There's always sudoku," Christina suggested.

"Do math for *fun*? Are you nuts?"

"If we were men we'd have more choices."

"What do you mean?"

"We could pick our noses or scratch ourselves or . . . you know." She made a fist and pumped it in a jerking motion.

"Ew." Thoughts of the flasher from the other day and the dirty old man with the magazines had my hands fluttering involuntarily. "Ick. Yuck."

"It's what guys do." She shrugged. "I'm just sayin'."

"Well, stop sayin'! And speaking of guys, how's Ajay?"

Due to a series of unfortunate mishaps on earlier cases, I'd come to know the doctor at the minor emergency clinic on a first-name basis. When Christina accompanied me on a visit a while back, the doctor had fallen hard for her. The two had been going strong for several weeks now.

"Ajay's great," she said.

"Tell him his favorite patient says 'hey.'"

We listened to the cricket song, the leaves rustling in nearby trees, the rumble of an occasional car engine. Try as I might, I couldn't stop thinking about the case, about Mendoza, about the people whose lives he'd ended, whether more lives would end before Eddie and I could nail the guy.

Christina must've sensed my tension. "This is a dangerous case, isn't it?"

I nodded, feeling my throat and chest tighten even further. Screw confidentiality. I needed a confidante. Christina would keep her mouth shut. I told her all about Mendoza.

"Wow," she said when I finished. "He sounds like a real asshole."

That was putting it mildly.

I looked over at her. "Do you ever wonder what makes people turn bad?" I wasn't thinking solely about Mendoza anymore. I was thinking about Nick Pratt, too.

She exhaled slowly. "Greed. Power. Thrills. Stupidity. Take your pick."

As far as Marcos Mendoza went, my money was on greed. Maybe power, too. He didn't seem to take many chances, so I didn't think he was in this game for the thrills. And the guy was anything but stupid. He'd earned an MBA from the University of Texas Business School, had even been named a distinguished alumnus. I wondered if they'd repo his trophy after we busted him.

But what made Nick Pratt turn from the office superstar into Benedict Arnold?

Christina hung out with me for a couple more hours, during which we huddled together, watching episodes of sitcoms she'd downloaded to her cell phone. Before it grew too late, I had her watch the box again while I took a quick potty break in the restroom at the convenience store and retrieved the rental car. I parked it in the lot of the Laundromat. When I was in place, I called her from my cell. "Thanks a bunch, Christina."

"Any time." She clicked off the call and flashed her lights by way of good-bye.

Then it was just me again. Me and my boredom and my imagination, which wandered into terrifying places, wondered how many pieces Mendoza might chop me into if he found out I was after him.

Five?

Ten?

An even dozen?

CHAPTER TEN

$\mathcal{S}$hifts and Shifty People

Over the weekend, my partner and I switched to six-hour shifts to enable each of us to have some semblance of a regular life. Eddie attended his twin daughters' soccer game in the early afternoon, while I enjoyed a date with Brett on Saturday evening, touring the new spring displays at the Dallas Arboretum, the place where we'd first met. Brett and his crew had installed a water garden area, complete with a pair of turtles paddling happily among the water lilies.

Brett was disappointed when I declined his invitation to spend the night at his place. He wouldn't like it if he knew I'd be spending the remainder of the night on a stakeout, so I fibbed and said I had some important work I needed to wrap up in the morning. It wasn't precisely the truth, but it wasn't a big lie, either. Just an itty-bitty, teensy-weensy white lie. Hardly more than a fib. Those don't really count.

How's that for rationalizing?

Sunday afternoon, I sat in the rental car, sweating in the late spring heat, smelling like I'd run a marathon. When I'd eyed myself in the mirror that morning, I thought I looked tough and sexy in the biker chick gear. In retrospect, the leather vest and ankle boots hadn't been the wisest choice. Leather doesn't exactly breathe.

When I stepped out of the car to stretch my legs, a skinny biker dude with a dark braid hanging halfway down his back offered me a pleasure ride on his hog. I assumed he was talking about his motorcycle, but he may have meant something else entirely. Either way, I declined.

To make things worse, that annoying itch at the hairline on the back of my neck had returned. Maybe I should buy some dry scalp shampoo.

I called Brett on my cell phone. It was a poor substitute for seeing him in person, especially since we couldn't snog and snuggle while watching BBC America.

I contemplated the pros and cons of offering him phone sex. Pros: no risk of pregnancy, no chafing, no vying for position, wrangling to see who gets to be on top. Cons: I wasn't exactly sure what phone sex entailed. Was it just talking dirty to each other? Or was there more to it? I could toss out a few *oohs* and *aahs,* but no way could I do something that was, essentially, um . . . er . . . *masturbation.* Sheez, I could hardly even say the word! Besides, I didn't find myself sexually attractive. I had the wrong parts. *It's not you,* I told myself, *it's me. I hope we can still be friends.*

My cell phone bleeped, indicating an incoming call.

"Do you need to take that?" Brett asked.

I pulled the phone from my ear and checked the readout. The call came from the 401 area code. The number didn't ring any bells. Probably my credit card company calling to pester me about buying credit insurance. How many times did I have to tell them no? I put the phone back to my ear. "It can go to voice mail."

The two of us discussed our upcoming trip to Florida.

"I reserved the hotel room," Brett said. "Got us one with an ocean view and a balcony."

How utterly romantic! "That sounds wonderful."

"You're bringing your new bikini, right?"

"Yep." And the beautiful chiffon dress and the sexy lingerie with the clip thingies. But no sense telling him and spoiling the surprise, right?

"Can't wait."

"Me, neither." Beautiful beaches, yummy seafood, the company of a sweet, sexy man. What more could a girl ask for?

Then it hit me. If Eddie and I didn't bust Mendoza in the next few days, there would be no trip to Fort Lauderdale with Brett. Dammit! My heart drooped in my chest. The Society of Landscape Architects was to present Brett with a major award at the banquet. This trip represented a significant event in his life. I needed to be there with him, to cheer him on, to show my support. To be ravished in my flirty new lingerie.

No. No way. I sat up straight, fortified with fresh resolve. I'd be damned if I'd let some tax-cheating loan shark keep me from fresh shrimp scampi and hot lovin' in a beachfront hotel. No matter what, we'd bust Mendoza before the trip to Florida. Yessiree, Bob!

When Brett and I ended our call, I dialed into my voice mail. It was another odd message. Blaring mariachi music in the background and a deep male voice that sounded much like the one who'd left the "fuck" message at my office number. "Jesus Christ, don't you ever answer your damn phones?"

At first I thought it was another wrong number. But how would the same caller have misdialed both my office number and my cell number? It didn't make sense. And the irritation in the caller's voice was strange. If the caller and I didn't know each other, what reason did he have to be angry with me? I suppose it could have been one of the taxpayers I'd investigated, or maybe one of their attorneys, but if so, wouldn't the caller have identified himself?

Curious, I dialed the number from which the call had been placed. Unfortunately, all I got was a computer-generated voice inviting me to leave a message. Looked like my mystery caller and I were going to engage in a game of phone tag.

"This is Tara Holloway returning your call," I said after

the beep. "Call me back. If I don't answer, leave your name and a good time to reach you."

The caller, whoever he was, was now "it."

On Sunday night, I changed into a thrift shop T-shirt and set up shop inside the Laundromat where I could stretch my legs and get a change of scenery. I was tired of staring over a plastic dashboard. So as not to raise suspicions, I'd brought along some dirty laundry to wash. I stepped inside and looked around. Only a couple of people were in the place, a large black man asleep in a chair and a cute Asian girl, probably a college student, engrossed in sending text messages from her cell phone, giggling at the apparently witty textual repartee.

Oh, to be so carefree.

A fluorescent light flickered behind a cracked plastic fixture overhead, a valiant bulb not yet willing to give up the fight. The place smelled simultaneously and somewhat ironically of both dirty socks and soap. Washers churned noisily, creating humidity in the warm air generated by the spinning dryers. Before long my hair would frizz. On the upside, maybe the steam would clear my pores.

I opened the lid of a washer at the end of the row closest to the front windows, set my wicker laundry basket on top of the adjacent machine, and began sorting through it, tossing in my whites. I had more than usual given I hadn't seen much of Brett lately and had therefore opted to wear my comfy cotton granny panties rather than the red lace models. I stuck eight quarters in the slots, slid the mechanism forward, and the machine kicked in, the tinny sound of water filling the basin adding to the white noise created by the other washers and dryers.

Taking a seat in a hard plastic chair in the corner, I stared out the window, waiting and watching. The glass reflected the word on my thrift shop T-shirt, the image backward, spelling SRETOOH.

When a car drove into the post office parking lot, I slipped outside to get a better view. I'd concerned myself unnecessarily. The driver came nowhere near box 1216. Back inside I went.

I retook my seat, fighting feelings of frustration and failure. When Nick Pratt had been on the case, he'd gotten the goods on Mendoza. But Eddie and I were spinning our wheels. Was Nick a better agent than us?

Nah. I refused to believe that. When Nick first started his investigation, Mendoza'd had no idea the Treasury was on his trail and had probably been less careful. Things had been different then, easier. That was my story and I was sticking to it.

And speaking of Nick . . .

I'd brought my laptop along and booted up the machine, logging in to the Treasury Department network. I ran a search for his name. Several documents popped up.

The first was a memo drafted by Lu and circulated to the staff, commending Nick for taking down a tax evader who'd embezzled four hundred thousand dollars from the car dealership where he worked as an accountant.

A second memo congratulated Nick for leading the Treasury Department's softball team to a win in the championship game of the interagency softball tournament. Thanks to Nick's three home runs, Treasury's team had beaten the pants off the dweebs from the Bureau of Labor Statistics.

I-R-S! We're the best!

When our opponents tried *Two bits, four bits, six bits, a dollar,* we jeered them with *Your little team ain't nothin' but a joke! We'll tax that dollar and leave you broke!*

The Treasury team hadn't won a game since Nick left.

The Lobo had issued a final memo, dated shortly after Nick's aborted investigation at AmeriMex. The memo informed the staff that Nick had resigned and that his large caseload would be reassigned. *Prepare to work your asses off,* Lu noted.

As long as I was in the system, I figured I might as well take a look at Nick's tax returns. I logged in to the taxpayer filings next. I didn't know Nick's Social Security number, so I had to search by name. I skipped over returns for several Nicholas Pratts, including a Nicholas A. Pratt who was a self-employed plumber in Boise and a Nicholas J. Pratt who drove a school bus in Walla Walla. After some searching, I found the Nick Pratt I was looking for.

My eyes skimmed over his return information for the year he'd disappeared. Whoa. In addition to his wages from the IRS—which far exceeded my salary, by the way—he'd reported some dividends, a few hundred in interest income, and a three-million-dollar "buyout."

That entry must be Mendoza's bribe.

The records indicated that Nick had mailed in a check for the full amount of the taxes owed. In the subsequent years, he'd reported sizable amounts of interest income paid to him by a Mexican bank, no doubt the place where he'd deposited his bribe money. The records showed he'd paid all taxes due on the interest, also.

Why would a double-crossing traitor report a bribe and pay taxes on it? Especially when he was out of the country and beyond the reach of American law enforcement?

Once again, things didn't add up.

I logged off the system, returned my laptop to its bag, and resumed my surveillance of the post office. The Asian girl finished her laundry and left, texting single-handed as she made her way to her silver Honda, her pink plastic basket perched on her slim hip. Other than the sleeping man I was all alone now, staring out into the growing darkness, watching the post office and trying to make sense of things that made no sense.

Sometime later, out of my peripheral vision, I noticed a young Caucasian man enter the place. He didn't have any laundry with him. An eerie tingle crept up my spine. Instinct kicking in and kicking hard.

Never, ever ignore instinct.

I watched his reflection in the glass. He wore baggy jeans, the crotch nearly reaching his knees and his plaid boxers sticking up above the waistband, along with a KORN T-shirt, complete with the band's trademark backward *R*. The guy's right arm bore a colorful sleeve tattoo. A dragon or a lizard. Hard to tell for sure from this angle.

He walked slowly past the sleeping man, his head angling first left, then right as he appeared to weigh whether he could shake down a man that size. He must have decided that, even with the advantage of surprise on the dozing man, it wasn't worth the risk. His head lifted and turned my way.

A conversation balloon reading "Bingo!" might as well have appeared above his head.

He'd chosen his victim.

And it was me.

Female, petite, cast on my arm, looking in the other direction, I probably seemed like an easy target. But looks can be deceiving, can't they?

As he circled behind the row of washers, trying to creep up slowly so as not to alert me, I, too, played nonchalant, easing my hand into my purse. My fingers crept over my Glock. Nah. When the cops arrived, they'd recognize the gun for what it was, federal agent standard issue. I didn't want to explain who I was or why I was here, what with this case being hush-hush and all.

After my earlier run-in with the pervert, I'd decided it couldn't hurt to have a personal weapon at my disposal, too. Good thing I had a concealed-handgun license and could carry a backup weapon from my personal collection. Some women accessorize with twenty-four-carat gold. Today I'd accessorized with a thirty-eight-caliber pearl-handled revolver. The perfect accompaniment to a Hooters T-shirt, don't ya think?

Moisture seeped from my pores onto my forehead and upper lip as I sat, muscles tensed, ready to spring into action. The guy crept around the corner, tiptoed up to me, and tapped me on the shoulder.

I turned and looked up at him. "Yes?"

He stuck out his hand and waggled his fingers. "Give me your wallet," he demanded, keeping his voice low lest he wake the sleeping man and roust a potential rescuer. "Now."

"My wallet?" I slowly rose from my seat, clutching my purse in front of me. "Now?"

"That's what I fucking said!" he spat in a whisper, glancing down at my purse. "Do it."

I narrowed my eyes at him. "Are you trying to rob me?" I made no attempt to keep my voice low.

"Fuck, lady!" He flapped his arms, looking like a frustrated ostrich. "Do I have to spell it out for you? Give me your wallet or I'll just take it from you."

"Yeaaah-no." I cocked my head. "That's not going to happen."

A flicker of confusion crossed his face. Obviously, he hadn't anticipated resistance.

I yanked my gun from my purse and shoved it up under his chin, forcing him backward until he was pinned against a whirling machine.

"I'll spell it out for you, doofus. You're going to sit down on this floor like a good little boy or I'm going to bust a cap in you." I'd always wanted to say that. "Got it?"

The sleeping man woke with a start, looked our way, and shrieked. He bolted from his chair, tripping over his own feet, and stumbled out the door.

With a look of disgust, my captive slumped to the floor and crossed his arms over his chest. "Shit. If I'd known he was such a pussy I would've robbed him instead of you."

Neener-neener. "Perhaps next time you'll choose your victim more wisely."

Headlights flashed across the street, a rusty pickup truck pulling into the post office. "Don't move," I admonished the twerp.

I stepped to the glass doors of the Laundromat and pushed one open, propping it ajar with my foot. With one hand, I held my gun aimed at the would-be robber. With the other I wrestled my binoculars from my purse and held them to my eyes. A man in a cowboy hat climbed from the truck and went inside. He stopped at box 1322, removing this month's copies of *Field & Stream* and *Guns & Ammo*. Also what appeared to be a past-due notice from a collection agency.

From his place on the floor, the thief snorted. "Spying on your boyfriend? What'd he do, cheat on you?"

I gave him a shut-the-fuck-up look. But he didn't shut the fuck up.

"It's no wonder he's cheating." He spewed a nasty chuckle, as he eyed my chest. "Hooters, my ass. You got no tits."

"Keep this talk up and *you'll* have no *balls*." I shoved the binoculars back in my purse. "And by the way, Korn sucks. They don't sing. They scream. And they stole the idea for the backwards *R* from Toys 'R' Us." Okay, so maybe insulting his taste in music was making this too personal. But he'd started it by insulting my breasts. They might be small, but they get the job done.

Pulling my cell phone from the pocket of my shorts, I dialed 911 and requested an officer. Déjà vu. At least this criminal had kept his pants on. Well, halfway on anyway.

Minutes later, a cruiser pulled up. The cop who climbed out was a young, nicely built Latino. He came inside and read the word on my T-shirt, eyeing my 32As in puzzlement before looking up at my face. "What's going on here?"

I explained what happened.

Still sitting on the floor, my robber shook his head, "She's crazy!" he shouted. "All I did was ask if she had change for the machine and she freaked out."

"Change, huh?" The cop hooked his thumbs in his belt and looked at me, raising one dark brow.

"He's full of crap." I rolled my eyes. "He doesn't have any laundry."

The cop looked back to the guy. "Where's your laundry?"

The guy gestured to the machine I was using. "In there."

"That's *my* laundry," I told the cop.

The officer stepped over to the machine. He raised the lid, peeked inside, and fished out a soggy pair of white nylon undies. His eyes went from the panties to my face. "Not getting any, huh?"

I sighed. "Not lately."

He held the dripping panties in front of the tattooed guy's face. "Still want to claim these as yours?"

The guy didn't respond, just glared at me.

I shook my head. "Didn't really think this through, did ya?"

The guy turned to the cop, jabbing an angry finger in my direction. "That bitch pulled a gun on me. Isn't that against the law?"

"That depends." The cop cut his eyes back to me. "You licensed to carry?"

I nodded and pulled both my license and my thirty-eight from my purse.

The cop took a quick look at my permit, then admired my gun, taking it from me and turning it back and forth in his hand. "Nice piece."

"Thanks."

"So, what?" the kid yelled from the floor. "It's legal to threaten someone with a gun now?"

"No," the cop said as he jerked the guy to his feet. "But it's legal to defend yourself."

Especially in the Lone Star State.

God bless Texas.

CHAPTER ELEVEN

Where Do We Go from Here?

The next week passed without incident. I suppose I should've been grateful, but at least the pervert and the mugger had added some excitement to my watch duty. Now two full weeks into this stakeout with no luck, my patience had run out. For all we knew, Mendoza was plotting to kill another of his minions right now. What's more, the date of my trip to Florida was growing near.

We needed to get this show on the road.

When I showed up at the post office for my noontime shift on Monday, I phoned Eddie from my cell. "This is getting us nowhere." The drizzle was back, the mist accumulating into droplets of water that slid down the windshield of my plastic-mobile.

Sitting in his own cheap rental car across the parking lot, Eddie scrubbed a frustrated hand over his head. "Let's talk to the manager again. Maybe we missed something."

We met on the sidewalk and went inside together, approaching the manager of the post office again. This time, the manager pulled all of the original records on the box and took us back to his stuffy, windowless office. He plunked himself down in his chair, stroking his finger and thumb over his chin as he looked through the paperwork. "Here's your problem." He handed us a piece of paper.

The paper was a completed forwarding request form, dated the day before Andrew Sheffield's disappearance. The order directed that all mail sent to box 1216 be forwarded on to another post office box, also rented in the name of ARS Financial Corporation, but located several hundred miles south in the border town of Laredo, Texas.

Shit.

Shit. Shit! SHIT!

Eddie and I exchanged exasperated glances. We'd sat there for two weeks, testing the limits of our determination and bladder control, for nothing. Nothing! To make matters worse, I'd gained six pounds sitting on my ass, drinking all those extra-large, extra-whip caramel lattes. I'd been unable to button my pants that morning, even when I sucked in my gut and held my breath. Thank goodness for the stretchy maternity pants I'd picked up at the thrift shop.

It would have to be skinny lattes only from now on.

No drizzle.

No whip.

I sighed. Was there any reason to continue living?

The manager made us a copy of the forwarding order. The two of us thanked him and stepped back outside.

Eddie let out a long, loud breath as we walked to our cars. He flicked the paper with his index finger. "This explains why the Pokornys' money orders were cashed in South Texas."

We'd assumed, wrongly, that the payments were being picked up here by someone who then transported them and cashed them in south Texas.

"The Lobo won't be a happy camper when she realizes we've wasted all this time." She wanted Mendoza nailed. Yesterday. Whoever broke the news to her was in for a thorough ass-chewing. I looked up at my partner. "How 'bout you tell her, big guy?"

"No way," Eddie said. "For better or worse, you and I are in this together."

Desperate now, Eddie and I returned to the office. Viola looked up as we approached her desk, which sat crossways a few feet in front of the Lobo's door, enabling Vi to serve as Lu's secretary, gatekeeper, and unofficial guard dog.

"Hi, Viola," I said. "Is Lu available?"

She punched the intercom button on her phone. "You up for visitors, boss? Got Agents Bardin and Holloway out here."

"Send 'em in," Lu's voice barked through the speaker.

Viola waved us through.

"Thanks, Vi."

Eddie closed the door behind us as we entered Lu's office. Today, a thick green scarf cut a path across Lu's pinkish-orange beehive, the loose ends tied behind her neck. She sported a tight polyester dress with a wide collar and belt, the bright gold on green checkerboard pattern playing tricks on our eyes, the fabric seeming to quiver on her body

We took seats in her wing chairs. Lu took one look at our faces and reached for the pack of cigarettes she always kept handy. After shaking one loose, she lit up. She took a deep drag, held it for a moment, then shot a stream of smoke out the side of her mouth, defying both the federal building's no-smoking policy and the rules of workplace decorum. "I take it you don't have good news."

Her gaze was on Eddie but, when the rat bastard hiked his thumb at me, she turned her focus my way.

"Hate to disappoint you, Lu," I said, giving Eddie a side-ways kick in the ankle. "But we've got squat." I explained how the post office box had been a dead end, how any checks addressed to the box had been forwarded to the post office down south.

She raised a brightly colored brow and looked back and forth between Eddie and me. "You mean to tell me you sat on your damn asses in front of that damn post office for two damn weeks for nothing?"

She took another drag so deep her right and left cheeks nearly met in the middle. It was a wonder her head didn't implode. She flicked the ashes into a plastic ashtray on her desk and propelled the smoke out her nose. "This is one case where time is not on our side. We need to keep this investigation moving."

"We understand that, Lu," Eddie said. "Problem is, we're not sure where to go from here."

The only idea we'd come up with on the drive over was to have someone from the Laredo office monitor the post office box where the mail had been forwarded.

Lu chewed the inside of her cheek. Clearly, she didn't like the idea. The fewer people involved in this investigation, the better. But without any more leads, what choice did we have?

Lu finally agreed on the condition the agent in Laredo be given no details on the case, as well as strict instructions not to confront the person picking up the mail. He was only to attempt to identify the person from a license plate or to discreetly follow the person and obtain an address. And the agent was not to be informed that Mendoza was the target of the investigation. The last thing any of us wanted was for Mendoza to be tipped off that we were on his trail again. If he knew, he'd keep even tighter controls on his organization, making it all that much harder for us to obtain information and bring him down.

Eddie and I slunk out of Lu's office with our tails between our legs.

As we made our way to my digs, we passed Josh standing at the copier. His eyes took in my loose polka-dotted outfit.

"Nice circus tent you're wearing," he said with a smirk.

Jerk. I didn't dignify his insult with a response. Well, not a visible response, anyway. I mentally willed his head to explode into a ball of confetti. No such luck.

When we reached my office, I plopped down in my seat and pulled Nick Pratt's stress ball out of my drawer, squeezing it over and over in a vain attempt to work off my frustration. "What now?"

Eddie perched on the edge of my desk. "Hell, I don't know."

The light on my phone flashed, indicating a voice mail message waiting for me. I picked up the phone, dialed into the system, and listened. There was one message. That same deep male voice. Despite my earlier instructions to leave his name if he called back, the mystery man once again failed to identify himself.

Once again, music played in the background. And, once again, his message was short. "Check last week's referrals from the Trade Commission."

Huh?

Whoever this guy was, he had to be an IRS insider, right? How else could he know both my office and cell numbers and have access to the Treasury's computer files?

But who the heck was it? And why did he suggest I look at the referrals?

I looked up at Eddie. "Have you received any unusual calls?"

"Unusual?" Eddie's brows drew together. "What do you mean?"

To tell or not to tell. Hmm. As Eddie had said, he and I were in this together. He was my partner, after all. Still, the caller had apparently chosen to call me and only me. Maybe there was a reason for that. Maybe I should keep the details to myself, at least for now.

I shrugged. "Cryptic messages. Loud music in the background."

"Didn't you call several deejays to get price quotes for Lu's party?" Eddie waved a hand dismissively. "It's probably one of them."

"You're right," I said, though I didn't buy that explanation for a second. "You think maybe we should check the files again? See if there's anything new?"

When Eddie and I had begun our investigation, we'd

painstakingly combed through every file that had even a remote connection to Mendoza and the companies with which he was involved. None of them had yielded a lead. But new information flowed into the department constantly. It was possible my mystery caller was on to something.

"It's doubtful," Eddie said, sliding into one of my wing chairs. "But it can't hurt to check again."

We unpacked our laptops and booted them up.

"I'll check the recent payroll tax filings," Eddie said. "Where do you want to start?"

"Hmm." I looked up, feigning a mental debate even though I knew exactly which files I'd search first. "How about the referrals?"

Occasionally, something that seemed like a tiny detail in one case would lead to a smoking gun in another. For instance, an odd deduction on one taxpayer's return could lead us to an abusive preparer who'd cranked out fraudulent returns on a wide-scale basis. We'd hoped the Pokornys' interest deduction would be just this type of clue, but until we learned more from the agent in Laredo, we had no idea if anything would pan out.

While Eddie typed away on his laptop, I turned my computer where he wouldn't be able to see my screen and logged on to the Internet. Although the office phone didn't have caller ID, I assumed today's call came from the same number as the call I'd received earlier on my cell. I checked the call history on my mobile phone and typed the number into the browser to see what might show up.

I pressed enter.

Bingo!

The number showed up on a roster for the Alpha Chi Omega sorority at Brown University in Providence, Rhode Island. According to the list, the phone number belonged to a sophomore art history major named Lindsay McFarland.

What the heck?

I was stumped. The person who called me was definitely not sorority girl Lindsay McFarland. Not unless Lindsay was a drag queen. Despite the advances in gay rights, I doubted the organization would allow a transvestite into its folds.

I sat back in my chair, trying to figure things out.

Eddie glanced over at me. "Got something?"

"Uh . . . no." I reached for my mouse and quickly exited the screen. "Nothing yet."

Later, when I was alone, I'd give Lindsay a call.

I punched some more keys and accessed the recent referrals from the Federal Trade Commission. Within minutes I hit potential pay dirt.

Florida, here I come!

"Check this out." I swiveled my laptop so Eddie could read the information.

In the Treasury files were three credit card fraud cases referred by the Federal Trade Commission. The FTC had sent the cases over only the preceding week, which explained why neither we nor George Burton had discovered them earlier.

Credit card fraud could be accomplished in various ways. In the simplest cases, the thief simply lifts a charge card from the victim's purse, wallet, or mailbox. In other cases, an identity thief applies for a new credit card account using the victim's name and Social Security number, but providing an alternate address to which the card is mailed. In the most sophisticated cases, the criminal actually manufactures a bogus duplicate card using the information from an existing charge card account. These three cases were all of the latter variety.

Credit card counterfeiting was a booming underground business. Counterfeiters could produce cards en masse for next to nothing and sell them for a pretty penny to unscrupulous thieves. Using a counterfeit card was safer than outright shoplifting since the party attempting to use the card could simply leave the store if the card were declined. The risk of being caught was small, nearly infinitesimally so.

As Eddie read the notes from the FTC files, a slow smile spread across his lips. "You may be on to something here, girl."

All three victims earned significantly above-average incomes. All three had perfect credit prior to the fraud. And all three held checking accounts with online bill pay at North Dallas Credit Union.

Coincidence?

We didn't think so.

More than likely, an NDCU insider had stolen the victims' credit card information from the financial institution's online bill pay database and supplied it to an outsider, who in turn manufactured and sold the bogus credit cards. But was that NDCU insider working on his own, or was he Marcos Mendoza's minion?

My money was on minion.

After the fraud had been reported to the FTC, the FTC in turn reported it to the IRS. The counterfeiting income and stolen property represented taxable income to the thieves and surely had gone unreported. If we could find the parties who'd used the counterfeited cards, perhaps, with a little persuasion, they would point us to the person responsible for manufacturing and selling the cards. And, perhaps, that person would then lead us on a trail to Marcos Mendoza's door.

I was thrilled to discover these new leads, yet I felt uneasy. The cryptic voice mail message had referenced the files from the trade commission. As much as I wanted to chalk this up to coincidence, doing so would defy logic. The caller apparently knew I was after Mendoza. George Burton, the Lobo, Eddie, and I were supposed to be the only ones privy to that fact.

Someone in the IRS had gotten wind of the investigation. Not good. At least the person seemed to be on our side.

Who was it who had called? And why had the person called from a coed's cell phone? Another mystery to solve.

But first things first. The first step was to find the identity thieves. And the first step to finding the identity thieves was milking the victims for information.

Eddie and I jumped on our phones and set appointments to interview the three victims. Fortunately, all three were eager to nail the assholes who'd screwed up their credit scores and got bill collectors calling them nonstop. Each of them agreed to meet with us that day.

We poked our heads in Lu's door and told her the news.

"Well, what are you waiting for?" She pointed out the door. "Get going!"

CHAPTER TWELVE

Charging Ahead

Our appointment with the first victim, an elderly widow named Ernestine Griggs, was scheduled for five o'clock that evening at Ernestine's home.

I changed out of the maternity clothes and into a peach-hued blazer, white silk camisole, and a faux-pearl necklace, along with a pair of slacks, top button undone to accommodate my newly acquired girth. Eddie wore a basic navy suit, crisp white shirt, and red tie, looking every bit the conservative Republican that he was, God save his soul. We appeared professional but not intimidating.

I sang along with the country music on my BMW's radio as we made our way to Ernestine's house. Eddie had the good sense not to comment on my choice of music or lack of vocal ability. He'd learned it only made me sing louder. After no less than three songs referencing tequila, pickup trucks, and blue jeans, we pulled up to the curb in front of Ernestine's house.

I switched off the engine and Eddie and I turned our

heads, taking in the fifties-era ranch-style gray brick home. Something didn't look quite right, but it took us both a few seconds to figure it out.

Eddie's mouth hung open. "You seein' what I'm seein'? Plastic daffodils?"

"Yep. And lots of 'em."

The front yard was AstroTurf, the flower beds filled with fake flowers and small white rocks instead of dirt. Not exactly yard-of-the-month material. Brett would cringe if he saw this place.

Eddie swung his door open. "What kind of person puts plastic flowers in their yard?"

"We're about to find out."

We climbed out of the car and made our way up the cracked concrete walkway to the front door. Mother Nature had turned her hairdryer on Dallas, and the warm winds had quickly dried up the morning's drizzle. The heat made my blazer feel too thick, too heavy. I lifted my shoulders to free my back from the cami that was now sticking to it. A skinny, solid orange cat emerged from the bushes next to the porch, made a chirping sound, and followed us to the door.

Mrs. Griggs jerked the door open as we came up the steps. The cat darted inside.

"You're six minutes late," she barked. She wore mismatched slippers over knee-hi panty hose and a blue housedress, her gray hair pulled up in a dozen pink sponge rollers. You'd never know from looking at the frump that she pulled in a cool sixty grand a year in dividends and interest.

"Sorry, ma'am," I said. "We ran into traffic. Hope we haven't interfered with your plans."

Eddie cast me a sidelong glance that said *What kind of plans could this woman have dressed like that?*

She impatiently waved us in. "*Judge Judy* starts in twenty-four minutes. We need to wrap this up by then."

We stepped into her house. The décor was baby blue and pink, as if the entire house were a toddler's nursery. The pink velour couch was so worn in places that the fabric sported a sheen. The blue carpet was threadbare in the high traffic areas. Wallpaper with alternating blue and pink stripes covered the walls, with dusty braided wreaths of twigs and paper roses hanging here and there.

The room was too warm, the ineffective ceiling fan overhead emitting an irritating *skree-skree* as it made its slow rotation. For God's sake, why didn't this woman have the air conditioner on? She was loaded. She could afford A/C. Then again, maybe years of penny-pinching is how she'd amassed her fortune.

Ernestine plopped down in a glider, propping her feet up on the matching ottoman. An oversized Siamese cat appeared out of nowhere, announcing his arrival with a quick meow before jumping into the woman's lap.

"This is Tom," she said, pulling the cat toward her. "Say 'hi,' Tom." She turned him around to face us, grabbed his paw and held it up, moving his furry little foot back and forth in a feline wave. The poor beast's expression was humiliated yet tolerant. He knew better than to bite the knobby old hand that fed him.

When she'd finished playing pussycat puppeteer, she gestured toward the couch, where a gray tabby lay, one leg kicked straight up in the air like a furry Rockette, happily licking his genitals. "Sit there."

Eddie and I took seats on the couch on either side of the tabby. I set my purse down on the coffee table next to a copy of *AARP Magazine* and pulled out my notepad and pen. Another cat wandered into the room then, this one a long-haired calico, primarily black, with white paws and an orange spot under her chin. The cat paused a moment, stretched out her front paws and fluffed her tail, then waltzed over to sniff my purse.

"Hello, kitty." I gave the cat a quick scratch under the chin and turned my attention to Mrs. Griggs, clicking my pen to take notes. "How did you find out you'd been a victim of fraud?"

She glided back in her chair. "Got a call from one of those smart-ass bill collectors. You know the kind. Threaten to toss you out of your house and take your retirement accounts if you don't pay up."

"When did this happen?"

"Let's see . . ." She looked down at the cat on her lap as if the answer were written on his back. She stroked the kitty a couple of times. "Last fall. October. I remember because he called right after I got back from visiting Martha Potter in the hospital. She fell and broke her hip. What a bitch."

I wasn't sure if the bitch was the broken hip or Martha herself, but since it wasn't relevant to the case I didn't ask for clarification. "What did you tell the bill collector?"

"That I hadn't used my Visa card in years and he could go fuck himself."

"And what did he say?"

"That I was the third person that day to suggest he fuck himself and if he could figure out a way to do it he would because women were too much trouble."

Eddie snickered. "Amen to that."

I elbowed him in the ribs. *Oomph*.

"What happened next?" I asked Ernestine as Eddie rubbed his side.

"The guy claimed I'd run up a bill of nearly ten thousand dollars. What a bunch of horse hockey. I called the lawyer who'd handled my husband's probate when he passed away—" She looked skyward and waved the cat's paw toward the heavens this time, a little "hello" to her hubby in the hereafter. "The lawyer sent a letter telling them to . . ." She squinched her eyes closed in thought and snapped her gnarled fingers as if the action would make the words she was searching for magically appear.

"Cease and desist?" Eddie filled in for her.

"That the legal term for 'eat shit and die'?"

"Pretty much," my partner said.

"That's it, then." The woman impatiently waved her own hand around now. "The lawyer got them to back off, got the delinquency removed from my credit bureaus. Which had been perfect by the way, never been late on anything in my life. The lawyer reported it to the Trade Commission, too. 'Course they didn't do nothing about it."

Unfortunately, with credit card fraud being the crime du jour, the FTC simply couldn't keep up. Instead, the staff at the commission had passed the information on to the Treasury. The other federal agencies treated the IRS staff like the cleanup crew at a rodeo, expecting us to take care of the shit they couldn't handle. Any crime resulting in financial gain to the perpetrator, most of which went unreported, was a potential tax case. So when federal agents couldn't nail someone for other violations of law, they counted on the Treasury to bring the bad guys in for tax evasion. Not necessarily a bad strategy. It had worked with Al Capone, after all.

"At the time this fraud occurred, where did you maintain financial accounts?"

"My retirement was with Charles Schwab," she said. "Had a checking account at North Dallas Credit Union. Certificate of deposit at Wells Fargo. Big 'un. Also a college fund for my grandson at Vanguard. Not that he'll ever use the money. The kid's dumber than mud. We'll be lucky if he graduates from high school."

She gestured to her gray brick fireplace. On the mantel sat a framed eight-by-ten photo of a skinny, shaggy-haired boy wearing a stained white T-shirt and a vacant expression.

"Maybe he'll surprise you," I said hopefully.

Ernestine snorted.

We continued our interrogation, asking how long she'd held each of her financial accounts, whether there had been any suspicious activity on any of them. Of course the only one we were really interested in was the NDCU account, but we didn't want to tell her that. Couldn't have her running down to the credit union and confronting the staff, blowing our case.

She picked up a piece of paper from her end table and jabbed it in my direction. "Here's the credit card bill you asked for."

Eddie moved the tabby cat and slid closer to me on the couch, reading over my shoulder as I reviewed the account statement. The bill revealed the standard MO. The thief had hit the card hard in a short period of time, running up charges at various gas stations, a grocery store, a pharmacy, and a half dozen shops in Collin Creek mall.

The grocery store and the mall were likely to be dead ends. Too many people coming and going and no way to identify them from a film clip. But the pharmacy posed possibilities and the gas station could have a security camera tape that would give us a license plate.

I stuck the bill in my briefcase for safekeeping.

When we were through asking questions, I jotted down the facts she'd given me on an affidavit form. We'd need her sworn statement to show Magistrate Judge Alice Trumbull when we went before her later to request a wiretap on NDCU's and AmeriMex's phone lines. I slid the affidavit and pen across the coffee table toward her. "Sign this at the bottom, please."

"If it'll put the bumfuckers who caused me this trouble behind bars, I'd be glad to." Ernestine plopped the cat down on the floor, where he stood angrily whisking his tail back and forth while she picked up the pen and signed the document.

"You'll need to keep our investigation confidential," I warned Ernestine as I took the signed document back from her. "If anyone gets wind of this, it could blow our case. Understand?"

She rolled her eyes. "I watch *Law & Order.* I get it." She made a motion as if zipping her lips then throwing away a key. She'd mixed her metaphors, but she'd made her point. She'd keep mum.

By that time, *Judge Judy* was coming on. Ernestine didn't bother seeing us to the door, just picked up her remote, pointed it at the television, and ignored us as we walked outside, yet another cat, this one a smushed-face gray Persian, trotting out the door with us.

That evening, we interviewed the other victims and obtained similar affidavits from them, as well as similar promises to keep quiet about our investigation. The other victims were a single hi-tech consultant in his early thirties and a married, middle-aged insurance salesman. Neither had a clue why their information might have been targeted or who the identity thief might be.

The fraudulent charges on their accounts were similar to those on Ernestine Griggs's billing statement. Grocery stores. Gas stations. Stores at local malls. Whoever had the insurance salesman's counterfeit card had spent a grand at one of the big box electronics stores.

Merchants had grown lax in asking for identification, making it easy for thieves to get away with credit card fraud. Then again, if the stores had asked for ID and rejected the counterfeit cards, Eddie and I wouldn't have some new leads to follow, would we?

When we'd finished for the day, I dropped Eddie at his minivan in the IRS employee lot. I glanced at my watch. It was 8:45. Just enough time to make a quick nooky run to Brett's. I dialed Brett on my mobile. "Get naked," I told him. "I'm on my way."

CHAPTER THIRTEEN

Making the Rounds

On my drive to Brett's, I placed a call to Lindsay McFarland's cell phone.

After three rings, she picked up. "Hello?"

There was no music in the background this time, only the sounds of girls shouting and laughing, a door slamming. Lindsay must live in the sorority house.

"Hello, Miss McFarland. My name is Tara Holloway. I received a call from your number a few days ago."

"Tara who?"

"Holloway," I repeated. "I work for the IRS."

"IRS?"

"Right."

"I never called the IRS." Her tone was confused.

"Actually it was a man who called from your phone. Someone with a deep voice."

There was a short pause as the young woman seemed to be thinking. "Oh yeah. It was probably the dude I met at Coco Bongo."

"What's Coco Bongo?"

"Only the best club ever! I went down there with my sorority sisters. We needed a weekend away, you know?"

If anyone knew about needing a weekend away, it was me. "When you say 'down there,' where do you mean?"

"Mexico."

Holy cucaracha. My heart rate doubled. "*Cancún,* Mexico?"

"Mm-hm. Coco Bongo has the best margaritas on the planet!" Assorted whoops sounded in the background. Sounded like the girls of Alpha Chi Omega were in agreement about the margaritas. But I was more interested in the guy who'd used her phone.

"So you let a man borrow your phone?" I asked, steering Lindsay's focus back to the caller.

"Right. He bought a round of drinks for me and my friends. It was the least I could do, you know?"

My mind whirled. Could it have been . . . ? Surely not. But what if . . . ? "Did he tell you his name?"

"He did." She hesitated a moment as if trying to recollect the information. "Gosh, I can't remember what it was, though."

Not surprising. Margaritas aren't exactly memory enhancers.

Lindsay polled her friends. "Anybody remember the name of the guy at Coco Bongo who bought us drinks?"

There were various voices in the background. None seemed to remember the man's name for certain, though they all remembered he was "totally hot" and at least two of the girls "would do him."

I changed lanes on the freeway to avoid an ancient Dodge sedan spewing a gray cloud of exhaust.

"Could his name have been Eddie?" I asked, tossing out the name only to have a control by which to judge the conviction of her responses.

"No," she said. "It wasn't Eddie."

"Josh?"

"No," she said again. "That doesn't sound right, either."

I tried to sound casual, though my heart was pounding. "Any chance his name was Nick?"

"That's it!" she said. "I remember now. When he bought us the drinks we teased him that he was like Santa Claus. We called him Saint Nick. My friend Kaitlyn tried to sit on his lap but she was so drunk she fell off."

Looked like Kaitlyn would be on Santa's naughty list this year.

That was all Lindsay could give me.

But it was enough to blow my mind.

I rolled off Brett, panting, and settled my head against the soft, plump pillow.

"I don't know what's gotten into you," Brett said, turning his head to me and giving me a sexy, satisfied grin. "But whatever it is, I like it."

Brett had been the unwitting beneficiary of my pent-up frustration and anxiety over the Mendoza case. All that energy had to go somewhere, didn't it? Lucky for Brett, I'd put it to positive use, treating him to, well, let's just say *enthusiastic* sex. He'd returned the favor, being up and ready for a second round in record time. We'd both be lucky if we could walk straight tomorrow. Maybe we could call in sick to work, claim to suffer a temporary bout of EBD—Excessive Boinking Disorder.

He glanced down at my chest then back at my face. "Is it just my imagination or have your breasts grown bigger?"

Not only were my breasts bigger, but so were my ass and my thighs thanks to all those extra-whip heavy-drizzle caramel lattes I drank while trying to stay awake at the post office. "I've gained a couple of pounds." Okay, so it was more than a couple. Sue me.

He was quiet for a moment, an odd look on his face as he seemed to be debating whether to follow up with something akin to "Big boobs! Woo-hoo! Gain away!" Or perhaps "Though these larger breasts are nice, I was perfectly happy with your A cups and you were never in any way inadequate as a woman." He chose, wisely, to say nothing. No way to win on that one.

As I lay there, snuggling up against him, my eyes began to drift closed. I blinked, forcing them back open, but an instant later the lids began to drift downward again. Ugh. I normally enjoyed the postcoital haze, the mindless bliss that followed the physical ecstasy, lying cuddled together as if nothing else in the world mattered and falling asleep in Brett's strong, warm arms.

But I couldn't stay here tonight. I had to be at work first thing in the morning to get a start on the new leads. Besides, I hadn't even been home yet to feed my cats their dinner. No doubt Henry, my arrogant Maine coon mix, was plotting revenge against me, doing his best to hack up a slimy hairball on my bed pillow or taking a dump in one of my houseplants. Anne, my skinny cream-colored kitty, would be worried, sitting on the windowsill, waiting and watching for my car to pull into the driveway.

I scratched at that darn itchy spot on the nape of my neck, then slid out of Brett's arms and out of his bed.

He groaned and propped himself up on one elbow. "Stay," he pleaded, patting the spot next to him.

"As much as I want to," I said, "I can't." I would've loved to stay. Brett was like a safe, calm refuge in my otherwise tumultuous, dangerous world. I leaned over and gave him a warm kiss, hoping it would soften the blow. "My cats need their dinner."

Brett grabbed me by the wrist and tugged me toward him. "They can survive for one evening on dry food."

True, I always left out a bowl of dry kitty kibble for the cats to snack on during the day, but they'd be expecting their usual Fancy Feast for supper. Still, the cats were only a convenient excuse, one that didn't require me to remind Brett that my current case was consuming my life.

He pulled me closer and began kissing my neck, working his way from the front to the side, where he began to suck gently on that tender spot where neck and shoulder meet. I felt my eyes drooping again, though this time it was with pleasure rather than drowsiness. If he didn't stop that right now, I'd never get out of there.

"No fair." I gently pushed him back.

He made a growling, grumbling sound. "When can I see you again?"

"Naked or dressed?"

"Either."

"Nice to know you appreciate me for more than my girl parts."

"So? When can I see you again?" Brett repeated, more than a hint of irritation in his voice.

I had no idea how the investigation would go over the next few days, but the Treasury Department couldn't fault me for taking a dinner break. A hungry agent would be an ineffective agent, right?

"How about dinner Wednesday? Maybe Chinese?"

"Great. Let's meet at Ning's."

First order of business Tuesday morning was a quick meeting with the other members of the Lobo's party planning committee. Despite the fact that sixty percent of the special agents in our office were male, all of the five volunteers were female. Typical.

After a brief debate over the country club's buffet options—barbecue, French, or seafood—we took a vote. In case my trip to Florida didn't pan out, I voted for seafood, which won by a three-to-two vote.

Lu stepped into my office a half hour later as Eddie and I were mapping out the gas stations, grocery stores, and malls we planned to visit. She closed the door quietly behind her. Today she wore a lemon-yellow Nehru-style jacket with a pair of white bell-bottom pants and cork platform heels. She clutched a rolled-up sheet of paper in her hands. She held the roll out to me.

"What's this?" I asked as I took it from her.

"Your vacation request," she said. "Denied."

"Damn," I muttered, though I was hardly surprised. Brett would go to Florida alone, and my beautiful red chiffon dress and sexy lingerie would go to waste.

I couldn't blame Lu for refusing me the time off. I could, however, blame Marcos Mendoza. One way or another, he would pay for making me miss this trip. I crumpled the paper into a tight ball and hurled it into my trash can. *Thunk*.

Lu let my little act of rebellion slide. "Andrew Sheffield's wallet turned up in the bushes outside the outlet mall in Hillsboro."

At least it wasn't a body part this time. "Any fingerprints on it?" I asked.

She shook her head. "Not a one."

I guess a break in the murder case was too much to hope for.

"How're things going?" The Lobo's brows rose in an expectant pinkish-orange arch as her eyes surveyed the maps on my desk. "Got some new leads?"

We gave her an update, told her of our plans.

The brows drooped. "Visiting a few stores? That's it?"

We knew the identity theft cases were a long shot, but they were all we had.

"We're doing the best we can, Lu." There was an edge in Eddie's voice. Apparently the stress of this case was getting to him, too. "There's not much to go on. Hell, the Texas Rangers and the FBI couldn't even get Mendoza."

Lu crossed her arms over her ample bosom and blinked her false eyelashes at us. "Perhaps I overestimated you two."

Ooh. Them's fighting words. The Lobo knew just how to push my buttons.

Maybe it was my naïveté, or maybe it was my need to prove to my boss that I could do this job. But whatever the reason, I rose to the bait. "You didn't overestimate us, Lu. Come hell or high water, we'll get this guy." Hell, while I was at it, why not promise to find a cure for cancer, achieve world peace, and stop global warming, too?

The Lobo jabbed a finger in my direction. "That's what I like to hear."

As soon as our boss left, Eddie glanced my way and frowned. "Girl, you shouldn't make promises you may not be able to keep."

"Shut up, Eddie."

He narrowed his eyes at me then. "*You* shut up."

"No, *you* shut up!"

Great. Now the stress had me and Eddie at each other's throats.

I walked past Josh's office on my way out, backtracking a few steps as an idea hit me.

He looked up as I entered his digs, his expression wary. Clearly the guy didn't get many social visits. "What do you want?"

There's the reason he didn't get many social visits. He really needed to work on his greeting.

"I've got a technical computer question I hope you can answer."

A smug smile spread across his face. "I can answer *any* computer question." Josh had often been accused of being a sniveling twerp and a whiner, but no one could accuse him of lacking confidence, at least when it came to his technical savvy. "What is it?"

"Is there a way to tell who has accessed a file in the Treasury's database?"

He cocked his head, his eyes narrowed. "Why do you ask?"

Yeah, Tara. Why? Think quick. "I had some files on the system. Stuff for Lu's party. The guest list seems longer than I remember, so I'm wondering if someone added to it." Flimsy. But the best I could come up with on short notice.

"Did the other members of the party committee know you were making a guest list?"

"Well, sure."

"Maybe one of them modified it."

Dammit, why wouldn't he just answer my question? "So is there a way for me to tell who it was?"

"Yeah." His voice was snide now. "Ask them."

"On the computer, Josh." My frustration was evident in

my voice. "Just answer the question, okay? Is there a way for me to run a history on the computer system to see who accessed the file?"

"No." He looked down, straightening a stack of files on his desk. "There are programs that can track that information but we don't have them on our system. No need. Everything is password protected. Only authorized staff can access the files."

My mind reeled. If only authorized staff could access the files, then how did Nick Pratt access them? Surely his username and password had been removed from the system when he'd left. Had someone here run the search for him? If so, that meant he'd stayed in contact with someone on the staff. Who would that person have been?

Could it have been Eddie? I doubted it. Nick and Eddie had partnered on earlier cases, so Nick would know that Eddie was a by-the-book kind of guy. Besides, Eddie had a family to support. He wouldn't do anything that would risk his job.

The faces of the other agents ran through my mind. Since I hadn't been with the IRS back when Nick had worked here, I didn't know who else he might have been close to.

Could it have been Lu? Every time she mentioned Nick's name, she seemed to become upset, as if she harbored regrets about how things had turned out in the earlier investigation.

I suppose it could've been Josh, but I had my doubts. He wasn't a likable guy.

What did all of this mean? Why would Nick Pratt feed me information that might help us nail Mendoza? Had things soured between the two of them, or was Nick simply toying with me, playing both sides again in some kind of sick game? And how did Nick know that I'd been assigned to investigate Mendoza?

I wished I could talk to the guy and get some answers. After I'd spoken to Lindsay McFarland I'd debated trying to contact Nick myself, but my instincts told me not to. Nick had taken pains to call me from public places using random phones that belonged to other people. Perhaps his phones were being monitored by Mendoza or Torres. I couldn't risk tipping them off that the investigation had been resumed. Of course that assumed Nick hadn't already spilled the beans. Still, something told me he hadn't. What would he have to gain at this point? I wished I knew exactly what he was up to.

Josh interrupted my scattered thoughts. "There's always the possibility that a hacker accessed the files. Some bored teenager from Hoboken might've thought it would be fun to see if he could hack into the IRS system. It's happened before."

A hacker, huh? Could Nick have hacked into the system? I had lots of questions. But I was short on answers.

The only one who had the answers was Nick Pratt.

"Thanks, Josh." I scurried back to my office and programmed my phone to forward all calls to my cell.

If Nick called again, I didn't want to miss it.

Eddie and I spent all day and evening Tuesday making our rounds of the gas stations, grocery stores, and malls at which the counterfeited cards had been used. Like Lu, we didn't hold out much hope we'd learn anything of importance. The cards had been used months ago and it was unlikely the stores would have retained any of the security videos or the employees would retain any recollection of the transactions.

All of these leads were dead ends. Rather than waste more time and gas traipsing all over town, on Wednesday morning I called ahead and spoke to the head of security at the electronics store, a woman named Courtney Schwartz. The electronics store had a better security system. Because employee theft was a big problem for the merchant, the management retained their footage for longer periods of time in case the video would be needed to nab and convict a thieving employee. Ms. Schwartz said the store had lost thousands of dollars last year in credit card chargebacks due to fraud and she'd be glad to help.

The store sat in the center of a strip mall. I went inside, checked in at the customer service desk, and waited for Ms.

Schwartz. In a few minutes, a woman with spiky dishwater-blond hair and minimal makeup met me at the desk. She wore the company's trademark neon orange knit shirt with navy pants and rubber-soled loafers, probably steel toed. She was lean and fit, like a female golfer. Her nametag read LOSS PREVENTION but her attitude read "Don't Fuck with Me."

"This way," she said, gesturing for me to follow her to the back of the store.

As we walked down the main aisle that bisected the store, separating the small electronics from the big-ticket items, a tall pale-faced boy with black-dyed flat-ironed hair came running toward us. The kid held a laptop computer tucked under his arm, no doubt the display model given the lack of packaging and the severed security cable trailing behind him. Following him was a male employee, a tiny wisp of a man who simply couldn't keep up with a teenager motivated by a free laptop if he could clear the front door and the possibility of jail time if he could not.

Before our minds registered what was happening, the thief ran past us, moving surprisingly fast in his skintight skinny jeans.

"Stop him!" the salesman squealed.

The security guard turned and ran after the shoplifter. On instinct, I turned and ran after her. In seconds, Courtney was on the kid's heels. The thief made his way outside and Courtney tackled him on the sidewalk. He grunted as he hit the pavement, the laptop crashing to the sidewalk next to him and exploding into a barrage of plastic and metal bits. A beat-up blue Hyundai that had been idling out front tore away from the curb, tires squealing. The getaway car no doubt.

The laptop lay in shattered pieces on the concrete, the keyboard's ESCAPE key lying, ironically, next to the thief. There'd be no escape for him.

Several employees, including the salesman, had gathered in the store's doorway. Courtney and the thief struggled on the sidewalk. The boy was on his back, doing his best to throw her.

I suppose I could've jumped into the melee, but I was

wearing my favorite red blazer today and didn't want to risk a tear. I yanked my Glock from my hip holster. "Freeze!" I hollered at the kid, adding "IRS!" out of habit.

The shoplifter looked up at me, his face contorted in confusion. He might not have understood why an IRS agent was brandishing a weapon at him, but he understood that running away from the scene was no longer an option. He stopped struggling. "Okay! I give up!"

Courtney glanced my way, too. "IRS agents carry guns?"

Always the same question. People generally thought of IRS agents as nerdy pencil pushers who merely performed audits. Society at large had no clue that the Treasury Department employed a team of crack agents whose job it was to pursue criminal tax evaders. And, yep, we carried guns. Pepper spray, too. I'd lobbied for nunchuks, brass knuckles, and Chinese throwing stars, but to no avail. Something about civil rights, abuse of power, yada yada yada.

I nodded and slid the gun back into my holster.

Once the police had been summoned and the would-be thief had become the responsibility of Dallas PD, Courtney and I headed to her office. She tucked her shirt back into her pants on the way, but otherwise seemed unruffled by the encounter.

"Nice job back there," I said.

She waved off the compliment. "Served two tours of duty in Afghanistan. That punk was nothing compared to a Taliban insurgent with an AK-47 and a rocket launcher."

"Boy howdy!"

Her office was a small room just inside the wide swinging door that led into the stockroom. A shadow box perched on top of a metal file cabinet displayed an assortment of military medals, including a striped white, red, green, and black ribbon denoting her service in Afghanistan.

She slid into the rolling chair behind her desk. Her tidy desktop supported a neat stack of manila files, a plain white coffee mug that served as a pencil cup, and a computer with an oversized flat-screen monitor. I took a seat on a folding chair in front of her desk.

I pulled the insurance agent's credit card bill from my purse and slid it across the desk, pointing to the entry for the electronics purchase. "I need to find out who made this charge."

"Okeydokey. Let's see what we can find." She positioned the paper next to her keyboard and angled the flat screen so that we both could see it. The monitor displayed a screen split twelve ways between the multiple security cameras positioned throughout the store and over the front and back doors. The image in the top left square showed an employee on the sidewalk in front of the store sweeping up the pieces of busted laptop.

Courtney maneuvered her mouse and minimized the video-feed screen, pulling up another screen containing blanks to be filled in. She typed the counterfeit credit card number into her system along with the sales date and pressed the ENTER key.

Her eyes squinted as she reviewed the information. "The charge was run through at 11:32 A.M. Register five."

Dang it, there was that annoying scalp itch again. It seemed to be growing worse. I clawed at the back of my head. Maybe I should make an appointment with a dermatologist.

Courtney clicked back on the video surveillance icon. The screen was again split twelve ways, but the notation at the bottom of the screen now showed the date for the day after Thanksgiving last year.

Black Friday. A smart time to use a counterfeit card. The stores would be swamped, the cashiers rushed and pressured to keep the lines of customers moving, hardly looking up as they rang up sales and processed payments.

Courtney dragged her computer mouse, forwarding the time to eleven-thirty and clicking on the feed that showed the cashier lanes. A single line of customers waited in a roped-off space, each proceeding to the next available checkstand when it was their turn. At the front stood a woman pushing a stroller, a thumb-sucking baby happily slapping at the spinning toy mounted on the seat in front of him. Couldn't be her. The card used here bore the name of the insurance agent, a man's name.

The first lane opened up and mother and baby headed to that register. The next person in line was a stocky white man, average height. The man wore a dark blue ball cap and windbreaker, both bearing the Dallas Cowboys star logo. The hat was pulled down tight on his head, the jacket pulled tight across his ample belly, the collar turned up to cover the lower part of his face.

The next lane to open was number five. The man in the cap moved to the register, growing larger on the screen as he advanced toward the camera. As he made his way closer, I could see he also wore blue jeans, tennis shoes, and dark sunglasses.

He'd taken care to make himself unidentifiable. The only thing I could tell for certain about the guy was that he hadn't hit the gym lately. Without more, I'd never be able to track him down. Heck, I probably wouldn't recognize him if he were standing right in front of me.

After the cashier had rung up his items, he pulled a credit card out of his wallet and ran it through the machine mounted on the counter. Plucking the stylus from its holder, he signed the screen. The checker bagged the iPod, video games, and Blu-ray player he'd purchased, then handed him the bag and receipt. She never asked for identification. The thief waltzed out the door, free as you please.

Courtney moved the mouse and clicked on the feed for the camera mounted over the exit door. We saw the thief walk into the parking lot. Problem was, he kept on walking, right out of camera range.

"Any help?" Courtney asked.

I didn't have the heart to tell her I'd just wasted her time. Mine, too. "We'll see." I thanked her and told her I'd let her know if I found anything out.

In the parking lot, I climbed into my car, rolled down the window to let out the heat, and called Eddie from my cell.

"Tell me you're having more luck than I am," Eddie said. "'Cause I got jack shit."

"I've learned that one of the men who used a counterfeit card is a white guy with a beer belly. Cowboys fan."

"Gee, Tara, that narrows it down to what? Half the men in north Texas?"

"True." I gripped my steering wheel and squeezed. Should've brought Nick's stress ball with me. "I'll run by the pharmacy on my way to dinner."

Maybe I'd have better luck there.

CHAPTER FOURTEEN

$\mathscr{R}$x for Love

I drove to the pharmacy, parked, and tried to tune out the sappy Muzak streaming through the store's speakers as I waited by the one-hour photo lab for the manager on duty. The way they'd cheesed up Avril Lavigne's hit song "Complicated" was nothing short of criminal.

A minute or so later, the manager arrived. Rectangular, plastic-rimmed reading glasses perched on the end of his pointy nose. His bald scalp was shiny, only a thin horseshoe of brown hair encircling his head.

I identified myself and showed him my badge.

He shook my hand. "Nice to meet you, Agent Holloway." He stepped behind the front counter and stuck a key into a cash register that stood idle. He turned the key, pushed his glasses back into place with his index finger, and punched a few buttons on the register, releasing a series of beeps. He looked up at me. "What's the credit card number?"

I rattled off the number on Ernestine Griggs's billing statement and he punched it in. He pressed a final key and *zzt-zzt,* the machine spat out a duplicate receipt. He handed it over and stared at me expectantly.

My eyes ran down the list. Some of the items I could identify. Chap Stick. Deodorant. Disposable razors. Others I couldn't. "What's LuvLub?" I pronounced the word with two soft *u*'s. *Love-lubb.*

The manager corrected me. "It's pronounced *love-lube.* And it's, uh . . . a sexual enhancement product." His bald spot turned crimson.

"Oh." I looked back down at the receipt. The final entry was "Rx" followed by an eight-digit number. I held up the receipt, pointing at the entry. "Is this a prescription?"

He nodded.

"Can you tell me who the prescription was for?"

"The pharmacist can look that information up for you."

My heart sped up. Finally, maybe, possibly, a viable lead. Hooray!

He gestured for me to follow him and I trailed his shiny pink dome to the pharmacy at the back of the store. He explained to the female pharmacist what I needed. She balked at providing the information to me, claiming she wasn't sure whether the Health Insurance Portability and Accountability Act's privacy rules allowed her to give me the information.

"I don't need to know what the medication was," I said. "I only need to know who the prescription was for and the person's contact information." I wasn't sure whether the HIPAA rules prohibited her from sharing that info.

She bit her lip. She didn't seem certain, either, but she eventually acquiesced. "I guess that would be okay." She pulled a pad of yellow sticky notes out of a drawer and read from her computer screen, jotting down the information. She handed me the note. I glanced at it. Although it was Ernestine Griggs's card that had been used here, the prescription was for a man named Zachary Merten. Apparently, the Ernestine Griggs imposter, whoever she was, had purchased the prescription for Merten. A pretty stupid move to buy something that could be traced but, unlike Marcos Mendoza, most criminals aren't all that smart.

I thanked the pharmacist and stuck the note in my purse. I thanked the manager, too. He returned to stocking laxatives in the Digestive Relief aisle. I snagged a bottle of dandruff shampoo, then went in search of a tube of LuvLub. Not that Brett and I needed anything to enhance our spectacular love life. But, then again, sex can never be *too* good, can it?

Brett and I finished our egg drop soup and lo mein, and cracked open our fortune cookies. I probably should've told him right off the bat that I wouldn't be able to go to Florida with him, but I knew how disappointed he'd be. I decided to break it to him as gently as I could.

I cracked open my fortune cookie and pulled out the white strip.

You will soon face grave danger.

My breath hitched. Weren't fortune cookies usually positive and optimistic? This wasn't as much a fortune as a cookie-coated threat. Sheez. This was the last time I'd eat at Ning's Noodle Palace.

"What's it say?" Brett asked, crunching down on his cookie and looking at me expectantly.

No way did I want to tell him what it said. It would only remind him of the dangers of my job. I'd rather endure a bikini wax than rehash this sensitive topic. "It says 'You will disappoint someone tonight.'"

His expression became puzzled.

I reached across the table to take his hand in mine. "I can't go to Florida, Brett. Lu denied my vacation request."

Puzzled became pissed. "She can't do that. You're entitled to two weeks off a year."

"She can," I said, "and she did. Eddie and I are working on a difficult case. She wants it resolved as soon as possible."

Brett sat back in his chair, putting a hand in his hair and pushing it up into angry spikes. "This is bullshit, Tara. We've been looking forward to this for weeks. This isn't something we can reschedule. I'm getting a big award, for Christ's sake. I want you there with me."

More guilt. Ugh. "I'm sorry, Brett. I'm not happy about it, either."

He looked away for a moment, his jaw flexing as he clenched his teeth. Finally he turned back. "Your job is taking over your life."

He had a point. But my job wasn't a typical job, either. Being a special agent wasn't just what I did for a living, it was a part of who I was as a person. It was as if the position had been made just for me, enabling me to combine my business smarts and marksman skills. The cases were interesting, challenging. We special agents ensured everyone paid their fair share to Uncle Sam, that honest taxpayers didn't bear an unfair burden. I was an instrument of justice. Still, as proud as I was of my work, it sucked when my job got in the way of my personal life.

"I'll make it up to you, Brett."

"How?"

I reached into my purse and pulled out the small bag from the pharmacy, tossing it to him across the table. He opened the bag and pulled out the tube of LuvLub. As he read the package, his expression changed from one hundred percent angry to equal parts angry and amused.

Two hours later, Brett and I lay in his bed, our bodies spent and our minds blown. The FDA may not have approved the product's claims, but they were true. And a round of mind-blowing sex was just what I needed to take my mind off Marcos Mendoza and the fact that I was letting Brett down in a major way.

Grave danger?

Not if I had anything to say about it.

CHAPTER FIFTEEN

*D*iseases and Immunity

I dragged my butt out of Brett's bed bright and early the next morning. I planned to stop by the address the pharmacist had jotted on the sticky note before Zachary Merten left for work.

I ran by my house to shower, using the new dandruff shampoo I'd bought at the pharmacy. I hoped it would relieve the itchiness. It was becoming damn near unbearable. I dressed, fed my poor neglected cats, and drove to the apartment complex in South Dallas.

I walked to the door of apartment 1D and, badge in hand, knocked on the door. There was no immediate response. I knocked again, louder, and heard a man's voice, muffled and irritated. "Jus' a minute. Fuck! Where's my underwear?"

Funny, I'd had to search for mine at Brett's earlier that morning, too. Turned out Napoleon had dragged them under the bed and chewed them to bits. I'd had to drive home commando style.

"You forget to pay the fucking rent again?" I heard the male voice ask someone else in the apartment.

A female voice responded. "I paid it, you dumbass. With no help from you. When you gonna get a fucking job?"

"When you gonna get off my fucking case about it?"

"When you get a fucking job. Duh!"

Looked like I'd worried myself unnecessarily about stopping by before working hours.

Eventually, the door was yanked open. "Yeah?"

In the doorway stood a man in his early thirties. He was, hands down, the hairiest person I'd ever seen. The hair on his head was shoulder-length and shaggy, and his face sported a scraggly beard. He appeared to be wearing a hair vest. His chest, shoulders, and what I could see of his back bore an apelike coating of dark fur. Urk. He looked like Chewbacca. He held a couch cushion in front of his crotch, his underwear apparently continuing to elude him, though he did sport one dingy sweat sock.

I fought a gag reflex. "Are you Mr. Merten?"

He looked me up and down, taking in my blue pin-striped suit, and closed the door slightly. "Who's askin'?"

"Tara Holloway. I'm a special agent for the IRS." I flashed my badge and eased my foot over the threshold in case he tried to shut the door.

"IRS?" He released his hold on the door and scratched at his ear. Fleas, perhaps? "What's the IRS want with me?"

"Actually, I was wondering if you could tell me who picked up a prescription for you last December at the pharmacy on Hatcher."

The guy visibly relaxed then, his shoulders slumping. He swung the door open and hiked a thumb behind him. "That would be her."

A big-boned thirtyish woman sat on a cockeyed recliner behind him, lighting a cigarette. She wore a stained pink T-shirt and a pair of black sweatpants cut off above the knee. Her hair was brown at the roots, the remainder blond, dry, and frizzy. She must have gotten her hair care tips from Dog the Bounty Hunter.

Merten turned and waltzed down the hall to the bathroom, tossing the couch cushion aside and giving me a view of his furry ass before he disappeared into the bath. I hoped the hair growth wasn't a side effect of the LuvLub. I might owe Brett an apology.

"You better not be getting a weapon, Mr. Merten," I called.

"I'm just taking a leak," he hollered back. "Chillax."

Chillax? Sounded like the ape had been watching a little too much *iCarly.*

The frizzy-haired woman took a long, slow drag on her cigarette and eyed me through narrowed lids. No attempt to get out of her chair. No greeting. Apparently her mother hadn't sent her to Miss Cecily's Charm School like my mother had.

I stepped further into the apartment, leaving the door open behind me in case I needed to make a quick exit. You never know. "Are you the one who bought the prescription for Mr. Merten?"

"Mr. Merten?" She chortled. "Never heard anyone call Zach 'mister' before. Sounds kinda funny."

"Please answer the question."

"Maybe I was, maybe I wasn't," she said. "I know my rights. I don't have to say nothin.'" She took another drag on the cigarette, narrowing her eyes further as she inhaled.

I gestured toward the bathroom, from which a loud flushing sound could be heard. "Mr. Merten just identified you as the one who purchased his prescription. It was paid for with a counterfeit credit card. That's enough for me to take you in."

She rolled her eyes.

This woman was really starting to piss me off.

"Where did you obtain the counterfeit credit card?" I scratched at the back of my neck again. That dandruff shampoo wasn't helping a bit.

The woman said nothing, just continued to stare at me, occasionally putting the cigarette to her lips.

I pulled my cuffs from my purse and stepped toward her. "You have the right to remain silent," I said. "You—"

She held up a hand and sat up in her chair now. "You're not after me," she said. "Not really."

She was smarter than she looked.

"You want to talk?" I asked.

"You want to deal?" She arched a brow in dire need of plucking.

"Sounds like you've been through this before."

She pinched a flake of tobacco from her tongue and smiled a knowing smile.

I hate it when they do that.

I spent the rest of the day in a small, stuffy conference room at the Justice Department with Ross O'Donnell, an attorney who regularly represented the IRS. I had the frizzy-haired woman, whose named turned out to be Lizzie Crandall, in tow.

Ross contacted a buddy at the Dallas County District Attorney's Office. Despite being a top-notch attorney, Ross initially had a hard time getting the DA's office on board. The assistant DA wanted to know more about my investigation, whom I was after, whether my target was a big enough fish to make it worth forgoing an open-and-shut credit card fraud case against Crandall. The DA's office liked easy cases. Good for their trial statistics. Besides, Lizzie Crandall already had a record for three misdemeanor thefts, one drunk and disorderly, and one possession of marijuana, each of which had been pleaded out and earned her only short periods of probation. The DA felt it was time to give Lizzie more than a slap on the wrist.

Ross finally convinced his buddy that we weren't pulling rank, that my investigation was highly sensitive because the target had not only done some evil stuff far worse than Lizzie's relatively minor infractions but had so far also managed to avoid arrest. Eventually, the lawyers worked out the details and the Justice Department and DA's office granted Frizzy Lizzie immunity from all charges relating to the credit card fraud on the condition she'd tell us all she knew.

I wrote down the date and Ms. Crandall's name on my legal pad. "How'd you get the counterfeit credit card?"

She leaned forward, elbows on the table. "I was sitting outside my apartment sometime last fall, smoking a cigarette, when some guy drives into the complex. He unrolls his window and asks if I'd like to buy a credit card. Said I could use it for days before anyone would find out."

"And what did you say?"

"I told him to prove it was good, take me to buy some beer and cigarettes."

"And did he?"

She nodded. "Bought me a six-pack of Bud and a carton of Camels at the convenience store on the corner."

I knew which store she was talking about. I'd spoken with the manager there on Tuesday. It had been one of my dead ends. Until now.

"What was the guy's name?"

She rolled her eyes again, as if I were an idiot. "Didn't need to know. Didn't ask."

"How much did you pay him for the card?"

"Two hundred," she said.

"Cash?"

"No." She chuckled a hoarse and sarcastic smoker's chuckle. "I used a credit card."

All right, I had to admit it was a stupid question. Still, scribbling the word "bitch" on my legal pad made me feel a little better. "So, cash then."

"Yeah."

Bitch paid cash, I jotted. *Bitch needs a trim and facial.*

"What did the guy look like?"

She looked up in thought. "Skinny little Asian guy."

Thin. Asian. Male.

"How old?"

"Twenty or so."

Twentyish.

"Any distinguishing characteristics?"

"Capped tooth in front." She tapped on her top right incisor. "Gold ring in one ear." Now a tug on her left lobe.

I made another quick note. "What was he wearing?"

She squinted, as if trying to conjure up a mental image of the guy. "Dark hoodie, black or navy. I forget. It's been a while, you know. Baggy jeans, maybe, or sweatpants. One of those goofy-looking knit caps. A red one, I think."

As I made a note of his clothing, I wriggled in my chair. Was it just my imagination or was my skin starting to burn *down there*? Sheez. As if my itchy scalp wasn't bad enough. "What kind of car was he driving?"

"One of them cheap little foreign pieces of shit."

P.O.S. Foreign.

"Color?" Wriggle-wriggle. Definitely starting to burn. Uh-oh.

"Silver," she said. "Or gray, maybe."

I scratched my head and wriggled again. "Texas plates?"

She lifted one shoulder, noncommittal. "Probably. Might've noticed if they weren't."

"Did he say anything that would give you an idea of who he was? Where he was from?"

She shook her head. "He gave me the card. I gave him two hundred bucks. He drove away."

"Have you seen him around again?"

She shook her head.

"Did anyone else at your complex buy a card from him?"

"Can't say for sure," she said. "Wasn't nobody outside but me when he pulled in. Wasn't nobody outside but me when he drove away."

"That all you got?"

"That's all I got."

Ross gave me a look then that said the immunity deal might not have been such a good one. But, hell, a girl's gotta do what a girl's gotta do, right? And I had to find a way to nab Marcos Mendoza. Besides, people like Lizzie Crandall didn't stay out of trouble for long. She'd rack up another offense soon and the DA could exact some real justice then.

I typed up an affidavit on my laptop, printed it out on Ross's printer, and had Lizzie sign it. She dropped the pen on the table and stood to go.

"One more question," I called as she walked to the door. "What was the prescription for?"

She turned in the doorway. "Jock itch."

I shuddered. Ick. Sorry I'd asked.

It was nearly six when I pulled into the lot of the minor-emergency clinic. Good thing the place was open twenty-four hours.

After a brief wait, a nurse led me to an examination room. Dr. Ajay Maju arrived shortly thereafter, pulling my chart from the plastic bin on the door and entering the room. Ajay might be short in stature, but he was big in personality. Today he sported torn jeans, bright green Converse high-tops, and a white lab coat that hung open to reveal a T-shirt with Oscar the Grouch on the front. "My favorite patient, back again."

Ajay might only work at a minor-emergency clinic, but he was nonetheless smart. Unfortunately, he was also a smart *ass*. He glanced down at the note the nurse had made on my chart then up at me, a grin tugging at his lips. "Your 'girlie stuff feels like it's on fire'?"

I rolled my eyes. I didn't think the nurse would write down what I told her verbatim. Still, it wouldn't have surprised me to see flames shooting out of my you-know-what. "I think I'm having a reaction to a product I used."

"A product?"

I nodded.

He waited a moment for me to clarify.

I didn't.

"Douche?" he asked.

"No."

"Yeast infection cream?"

"No."

"Feminine deodorant spray?"

"Ew." I crinkled my nose. "No."

"Vibrator? Dildo? Strap-on?"

"No, Ajay! Jeez!"

He cocked his head. "Should I keep guessing until we are both entirely disgusted or do you want to just tell me?"

I didn't want him to keep guessing. Given what he'd come up with so far, I could only imagine what remained on his list. "You have to promise not to laugh."

"No, I do not," he said. "I have to promise to do no harm and to keep your medical information confidential, but I am not legally required to refrain from laughing at my patients."

I looked down at my lap and wriggled on the crinkly paper as a fresh wave of prickly heat turned my nether regions into an inferno. "It was a sexual enhancement product."

He raised a brow. "Let me guess. The one from the television commercial where all the hot chicks are hanging on the nerdy guy?"

I shook my head. "No. I bought this one at a pharmacy."

"*You* bought it?" he said. "Not Brett?"

"Right."

A fresh grin tugged at his lips. "Is your man not satisfying you? Because I have several tricks I could teach him from the *Kama Sutra*."

I glared at Ajay. "Brett satisfies me just fine. I was just trying to spice things up."

"Next time try curry." He grabbed his prescription pad. "By any chance, was this product called LovLub?"

"You've heard of it?"

"You are my third female patient this month with the same problem. I should probably contact the FDA." He reached in a drawer, pulled out a tube of ointment, and handed it to me. "This cream will help."

"Thanks." While I was there, I figured I might as well ask Ajay about my itchy scalp. Maybe I had some kind of rash.

He donned a fresh pair of latex gloves, grabbed a tongue depressor, and began examining my scalp, using the wooden stick to separate locks of my hair. After a moment, he stepped back. "You have lice."

"What the hell!" Was my infestation some type of karmic payback for my insensitive thoughts about Zachary Merten's hairy body? "Where would I have gotten lice?"

Ajay shrugged. "You tell me. Have you been around any

young children? Maybe shared a hairbrush or comb with a homeless person?"

"No." But I had tried on the pink pillbox hat at the thrift store. So had Alicia. Oh, shit. She probably had lice now, too. She'd kill me. I may have given lice to Brett, too. Great.

Ajay shrugged. "Go to the pharmacy. You can buy medicated shampoo over the counter. Wash your hair with it today, then again in two weeks. Wash all of your bedding, too. Throw out all of your brushes and combs and buy new ones. That should take care of the bugs."

I closed my eyes. How humiliating.

The only positive thing about my visit to the clinic was that Ajay removed the pesky cast from my arm. Once the cast was gone, he plucked the broken plastic fork tines from my skin. "There. You are good to go."

Having full use of my arm again felt great, even if the skin was a bit pasty and clammy. After one last scratch and wriggle, I hopped down from the table. "Thanks, Ajay."

"Any time." He left the room whistling Elvis's "Burning Love."

Like I said. Smart ass.

CHAPTER SIXTEEN

$\mathscr{B}$edside Manners

As I left the medical clinic, I pulled my cell phone out of my purse. Then I did what I always did when I had a boo-boo and needed someone to make me feel better. I called my mommy. "Guess what, Mom? I've got lice."

She gasped, apparently disgusted by her own daughter. "Goodness, hon. How in the world did you get those nasty bugs?"

I told her about the thrift shop hat. "The doc says a medicated shampoo will get rid of them."

"There's no need to make a special trip to the store," Mom said. "Mayonnaise will do the trick. Just load it on real good. It'll smother those critters."

Ew. The thought of a mayonnaise massacre taking place on my head had my stomach rolling. Still, it would save time. When Mom and I finished, I phoned Brett and gave him the news.

"Lice I can handle," he said. "It would be a different story if you'd given me crabs."

I was fortunate to have such a forgiving boyfriend. However, I doubted my best friend would react the same way.

I dialed Alicia's number, closing my eyes to fortify myself for the hissy fit she'd surely throw once I gave her the news.

"Has your head been itching?" I asked when she answered.

"Something awful," she said, her tone suspicious. "Why?"

"We got lice from that hat at the thrift store."

She shrieked.

"Look, it's no big deal," I said. "You just have to wash with a medicated shampoo and throw out your hairbrushes."

"Oh my God! I told you we'd catch something from those secondhand clothes!"

"You thought we'd get an STD. Lice is nothing compared to syphilis."

She shrieked again.

My phone bleeped, Eddie calling. My partner had perfect timing. "Gotta go," I told Alicia. I hung up on her and answered Eddie's call. "Hey, partner."

"Bad news, Tara." Eddie's voice was tight, clipped. "Someone beat the shit out of the Pokornys and trashed the bakery."

Holy crap. The earth seemed to drop away under me. "What happened?"

"The details are sketchy at this point. Darina and Jakub are in surgery as we speak. Head injuries, broken bones. God knows what else."

I closed my eyes, saying a quick prayer in my head for the couple. "How'd you find out?"

"A nurse from the hospital called. Darina gave my business card to a medic on the ambulance and he passed it on to the ER staff."

"You think this has something to do with the loan?" This could just be a crazy coincidence, right?

"What do you think, Tara?" Eddie's tone told me exactly what he thought. Of course this wasn't a coincidence. Why else would Darina have given Eddie's card to the EMT?

"What hospital are they in?"

"Parkland."

"I'm on my way." Looked like the lice would get a brief reprieve.

I laid rubber to the hospital and eased into a tight space between a rusty pickup and an oversized SUV, risking door dings to my precious Beamer. But there were bigger things to worry about at the moment. I rushed into the waiting room of the Parkland Hospital ER, the same waiting room where I'd sat mere weeks before, waiting to find out if my partner would survive the bullet wound to his head. Luckily, Eddie had pulled through. I hoped the Pokornys would do the same.

Eddie sat with the Pokornys' children, who actually looked like children now despite the fact that both were in their early twenties. The son worriedly chewed the inside of his cheek, while their daughter sobbed into her hands, her shoulders heaving.

Eddie stood and introduced me to the Pokornys' children.

"I'm so sorry," I told them as I took their hands. As upset as I was, I couldn't even imagine what they were going through.

Eddie gestured to the automatic glass doors and we made our way outside to talk.

"How are the Pokornys?"

"Darina has three cracked ribs and a broken arm. The thugs fractured Jakub's skull. He's in a coma. The doctors won't be sure of the extent of his brain injury until he comes out of it." He paused a moment before adding, "*If* he comes out of it."

My hands fisted reflexively and it suddenly seemed as if there wasn't enough air to breathe. I couldn't believe it. *I didn't want to believe it.* "Eddie, this is . . ." Too terrifying. Too close. Too real.

"Some seriously scary shit?"

"Yeah."

It wasn't until midnight that we were able to see Darina Pokorny. Darina's children had gone into the room twenty minutes earlier. Her son had since moved on to intensive care to be with his unconscious father, but her daughter remained in the room, slumped in a chair next to the bed, holding her mother's small, pale hand.

When I first saw Darina's face, my fingers flew to my mouth, stifling my gasp. The figure lying in the bed looked nothing like the woman we'd met at the bakery only two weeks earlier. Her curly hair was matted and in disarray. Both of her eyes were swollen nearly shut and bore purplish-black circles around them, as if she were wearing a dark sleep mask. A long, deep cut slashed across her cheek, a dozen stitches holding the wound closed, pulling her skin taut. And didn't her nose used to be in the middle of her face?

As if the facial injuries weren't enough, a plaster cast encased her right arm from wrist to shoulder, indicating multiple fractures. The white bandage visible through the gaping armholes of her gown told me the doctors had also wrapped her ribs. An IV bag hung from a metal stand next to her bed, the plastic tube feeding into a vein in her left arm.

The injuries I'd suffered on the job were nothing compared to what Darina had suffered. Now my job wasn't just taking over my life, it was taking an emotional toll on me. With all the dead ends we'd encountered, I was beginning to think it might be easier to simply shoot Mendoza than to try to nail him for tax fraud. Heck, with my keen eye and sharp finger, I could take Mendoza out with a clean head shot from a hundred yards. Given the many loopholes in gun registration laws, my dad had a whole cabinet full of unregistered hunting rifles. Nobody would ever know it was me.

Very tempting.

Also, a bit scary that I was seriously considering this option.

Darina slowly turned her head to look at me and Eddie. The doctors had given her pain medication, so we weren't sure how much information we'd be able to gather from her. Still, it was worth a try. Who knew how much she'd remember later? Or if she'd even be willing to talk to us once her mind cleared and she realized that cooperating with federal agents could pose further risks?

"Mrs. Pokorny?" I stepped closer and put a hand on the cold metal bedrail. "Are you up to talking to us?"

She emitted a groan that sounded affirmative.

Her daughter released her hand and stood, offering me the chair. "I'll go check on my dad."

I nodded, thanked her, and sat down next to Mrs. Pokorny.

My gaze met hers. As I took in the fear and pain reflected in her bruised, bloodshot eyes, I felt the tingle of tears forming in mine. What kind of sick bastard could hurt someone like this? "Do you know who did this to you, Darina?"

She closed her eyes, letting out a long, slow breath and, for a moment, I thought she was going to submit to the sedatives and fall asleep. But, finally, she opened her eyes again, as much as she could open them in their swollen state, and answered in a barely audible voice. "Three young men, around my son's age. Two white. One black."

"Did you recognize them?"

She gave a small, nearly imperceptible shake of her head.

I asked her what the men looked like.

She told me all of them were tall, big, and muscular.

"You think this had something to do with your loan? The one we talked to you about?"

She nodded, just barely.

"How do you know that?"

She struggled in the bed then, trying to sit up, grimacing despite the pain meds dripping into her arm. I found the controller among the blankets and pushed the button to raise the top half of the bed so she would be more upright.

"How's that?" I asked.

"Better."

I laid the controller down on top of the white blanket.

She spoke slowly, so softly I had to lean in to make sure I could hear her. "The grocery store we made kolaches for filed bankruptcy a few days after we met with you. They didn't pay our last invoice. Without their money we couldn't make our full loan payment this month. I sent a money order for half of the amount with a note explaining we would pay the rest as soon as we could." She paused a moment, as if trying to work past the painkiller-induced fog in her head. "A man called the bakery a few days ago and told us to have the rest of the money today. But we had nowhere to get money from. The banks will not loan to us and we do not have wealthy relatives or friends. When we were closing up this evening, the men showed up and demanded the money." Tears spilled over her bruised lids then, running down her cheek. "The black man stood watch at the front door. The others took all of the money in our cash register and my purse and Jakub's wallet."

And then, obviously, the men beat the holy crap out of the Pokornys. I couldn't imagine how terrifying that must have been. Well, maybe I could. I'd recently been trapped in a hole with gunfire raining down on me. Still, the fractured arm I'd suffered was nothing compared to what the Pokornys had been through.

"Did you see what kind of car they were driving?"

"No."

"Did any of them refer to the others by name?"

She slowly shook her head. "No, but the man who attacked Jakub wore one of those leather western belts with his name printed on the back."

"What was the name?"

"Bubba."

Eddie grunted. Translation: *With a name like Bubba, the guy had to be a dumbass, white trash motherfucker.*

It was unlikely that Bubba was his given name. Still, even a nickname gave us something to go on.

When I asked for a more detailed description, her swollen eyes narrowed even further. "I'll never forget them. All of them wore dark clothing. Both of the white men had shaved heads and dark goatees. The one who beat me had dark eyes. The one who beat Jakub had light blue eyes, like ice." A cold heart, too, apparently. "The black man was a little smaller than the others. He wore his hair in short braids."

"Did you or your husband mention that we'd been by to see you?" I hoped they hadn't blown our case, though under the circumstances I could hardly blame them if they had.

"No," she said. "I think that would have made them even more angry."

"Good call," Eddie said, speaking for the first time, his voice cracking. Apparently he wasn't dealing with this all too well, either.

"They wore gloves," Darina said. "The thin latex kind. But the one who took the money from the cash register had trouble picking up the bills with his gloves on and took one of them off. There might be fingerprints on the till."

"Was that Bubba or one of the others?"

"Bubba."

That would've been my guess. A guy named Bubba would've been dumb enough to forget why he was wearing gloves in the first place. Weren't many Bubbas giving vale-dictorian speeches at high school graduation ceremonies.

When we'd gathered all the information we could from Darina, we wished her a speedy recovery and told her we'd be in touch if we learned anything. We found her daughter just outside the door and asked her to call us if there were any developments, if her parents remembered anything else that might be helpful. A nod was all the poor girl could manage.

CHAPTER SEVENTEEN

$\mathcal{A}$ Crack in the Case

By the time we arrived at the Pokornys' bakery, it was two A.M. Eddie and I parked in the lot and made our way to the door. The night was unusually cool for early May and I hadn't brought a jacket. I wrapped my arms around myself in a vain attempt to keep warm. When Eddie noticed, he slipped his suit jacket off without a word and draped it over my shoulders. I gave him a grateful smile.

The front door and windows were intact. The thugs likely realized that breaking the glass would've drawn attention from people at nearby businesses. Three crime scene technicians were still on the scene. Yellow crime scene tape stretched across the front of the store.

We rapped gently on the window and displayed our badges. The tech in charge, a short brunette, came to the door and pulled it open.

We could see inside now.

"My God," Eddie said. "It looks like a bomb went off in here."

The newly purchased display cases were cracked, crushed pastries strewn about the floor, a smear of chocolate a foot long indicating where someone had slipped on the mess. The framed recipes and photos of the Prague landmarks were broken, some in shards on the tabletops and booths, others hanging at odd angles on the wall, the glass smashed to smithereens. The frame containing the first dollar the Pokornys had earned was shattered, too, the bill they'd been so proud of now gone. The cash register lay on its side on the floor, the cash drawer hanging open like the tongue lolling out of a dead animal. Other than loose change scattered about the floor, all of the money was gone.

Eddie and I identified ourselves to the tech.

The woman scrunched her nose. "IRS? Why is the IRS interested in this?"

Eddie and I exchanged glances. The fewer people who knew we were investigating Mendoza the better. We had no intention of telling anyone with the Dallas PD about our investigation.

"The bakery was under audit," I offered. It wasn't entirely a lie. The Pokornys had been audited. In fact, the audit was what had led us here in the first place.

She still looked confused but fortunately she didn't press us for more information.

"Any luck here?" Eddie asked the technician.

"We've lifted quite a few fingerprints," the woman said. "Most probably belong to the bakery's customers, though. We won't know anything until we run them. And even then, we'll only get a match if the thugs have a record and their prints are on file."

Such an optimist. Then again, she was probably right to keep her hopes in check. Surely Mendoza had covered his tracks. Chances were the guys who'd assaulted the Pokornys and created this mess were hired muscle.

I passed on the information Darina had given me about the robber who'd removed his glove to clear the till, the one wearing the Bubba belt.

The supervisor nodded. "Good to know. We'll pay special attention to the prints we lift from the register."

"Any camera footage?" Eddie asked.

"Nope. There's no security camera on site and none anywhere close by that we could locate."

I turned and glanced around at the neighboring buildings. Although a couple of the shops had security company stickers on their windows, none had a visible exterior camera. Too expensive for a small business owner to justify. They were likely more concerned about what went on inside their stores rather than what took place outside on the sidewalks.

Eddie and I took a couple of steps into the bakery and glanced around the place, noting nothing that would tie this crime to Mendoza. Not that we'd expected him to leave a calling card, but we'd felt compelled to stop by anyway. Chalk it up to our type A personalities.

A tech kneeling by one of the smashed refrigerator cases used tweezers to remove something from one of the sharp edges of broken glass remaining. "Hair," he said, holding up the tweezers and eyeing the matter he'd removed. "Part of a scalp, too. They must've used Mr. Pokorny's head as a battering ram to smash the case."

Oh God. My head felt light and my stomach roiled at the violent mental image. I had to swallow hard to keep from losing the drive-thru burrito I'd scarfed down earlier on my way to see Ajay.

Eddie handed his business card to the lead tech. "Can you let us know what you find out?"

She took the card and tucked it into the breast pocket of her shirt. "Will do."

I suppose we could've pulled rank, told the Dallas PD to hand the matter over to the FBI. But given how little progress the FBI had made with Andrew Sheffield's murder investigation, I knew that Eddie and I were the only ones with any real chance of linking these crimes to Mendoza. Might as well let Dallas PD take a crack at it.

Eddie and I walked to his minivan and took seats inside. We simply sat there for a moment, doing nothing, saying nothing, just staring through the windshield at the side of the bakery. Finally, Eddie exhaled, long and loud. I echoed both the sound and the sentiment. Without words, we'd communicated that we felt the same way.

Frustrated. Incompetent. Powerless.

And it sucked.

CHAPTER EIGHTEEN

All Bets Are Off

It was four in the morning by the time I returned home. After changing into my nightclothes, I went to the kitchen and retrieved the mayonnaise from the fridge. Hanging my head in the sink, I slathered the white glop over my hair, making sure every strand was fully coated. I wrapped my hair in Saran Wrap for good measure. I had no idea how long I'd need to leave the stuff on my hair, but figured I'd rather err on the side of caution.

I climbed into bed wearing my plastic wrap turban. Despite the late hour and my exhaustion, I could hardly sleep. I prayed that Darina and Jakub Porkorny would make a complete recovery, that the criminals who had so brutally attacked them would be found and brought to justice.

Annie curled up by my side, licking my hand with her rough, moist tongue and purring a loud, rapturous purr that caused her entire body to vibrate. The poor thing had clearly missed me. Even Henry seemed lonely. Normally, he ventured upstairs only to use the litter box, but tonight he lay at the foot of my bed, swishing his tail angrily back and forth, letting me know he was none too happy I'd been ignoring him lately. Of course the snobby cat ignored me all the time. But he didn't like the shoe being on the other foot. Or should I say the other paw?

I slept fitfully and woke early, stirred by the cats licking mayonnaise from my face. The stuff had oozed out of the plastic wrap during the night, soaking my pillow. Guess it didn't much matter since I'd planned to throw the thing out anyway.

I felt physically and emotionally drained. I was worried sick about the Pokornys, about the Mendoza case, about his next potential victim.

I climbed out of bed and headed to the bathroom. Fingers crossed, I stepped onto my digital scale. The six extra pounds I'd gained courtesy of the extra-whip heavy-drizzle caramel lattes hadn't budged. I flipped the bird at the scale and used my foot to shove it back under the cabinet.

I took a shower and shampooed, twice, afterward doing my best to style my still-gooey hair. As I dressed, I tried desperately to put on a fresh attitude, too. I couldn't let this case get to me. I had to be professional. Stay objective. Learn to compartmentalize.

If I couldn't, this case would eat me alive.

I ran through the coffeehouse drive-thru on the way to work and picked up a skinny no-whip latte. I took a sip. The drink was a poor substitute for the deliciously sweet, creamy concoctions I was used to. Still, I needed to get back in shape. In this line of work, you never knew when you might have to run after someone.

Or *from* someone.

A head shot with a hunting rifle was looking better all the time, though a quick death was more than Mendoza deserved. He should be tortured first, forced to review an inventory ledger or compute a hard asset depreciation schedule. Nothing was worse than a depreciation schedule.

I kept hoping Nick Pratt would call again. I wanted to confront him. Figure out what the hell was going on.

I glanced at the clock on my dashboard. Eight-fifteen. Mom would have just left for the Nacogdoches Historical Society's weekly meeting, just like she had every Friday morning for the last twenty years. Dad would be home alone. Perfect. I dialed my parents' phone number.

Dad answered, sounding a bit surprised to hear from me. "Your mother's at her club meeting."

"I know. I need to talk to you, Dad."

"Problem with your car? Plumbing?"

"No. Nothing like that. I was wondering about your hunting rifles. What do you have that's unregistered?"

"Long range or short?"

"Long." No sense getting any closer to Mendoza than I had to. He might be carrying a weapon himself. Besides, a long-range rifle would make getting away undetected that much easier for me.

"I've got a Remington 7400 and a .308 Winchester I traded for at the swap meet last year."

I'd always been more of a Winchester girl. "Does the Winchester have an adjustable scope?"

"Wouldn't settle for nothin' less." Dad hesitated a moment. "You in some trouble, hon?"

"I'm working a difficult case. Let's just say I'm keeping my options open."

"Need me to take care of someone for you?"

I found myself smiling. "Nice of you to offer, Dad. But I'm the federal agent. Not you."

"You may be a federal agent, Tara," he said, "but you're my little girl first."

Daddy's little girl. I probably should've felt insulted, but instead I felt warm and fuzzy inside. "Thanks, Dad."

"Should I bring the rifle to you?"

Fast, free delivery? Tempting. But no, not yet. Not until I'd exhausted all of my nonlethal options. "Just keep it clean for now, and make sure you've got plenty of ammunition."

"Will do."

"Don't tell Mom, okay? She'll just worry."

He gave a mirthless chuckle. "You got that right."

"I love you, Dad."

"Right back at ya. Stay safe, you hear?"

By the time I pulled into the parking lot at work, I'd finished most of the latte and the caffeine had kicked in, giving me the artificial energy I needed to face the day. *Life is good,* I told myself, as I walked to the building. *Look at all of these people who aren't beat up. Think about Brett, what a great guy he is.*

The thoughts of Brett backfired on me. Today was the day the two of us had planned to leave for Florida. Instead, he'd be traveling to a virtual paradise all alone and I'd be stuck here working myself to death. All thanks to that asshole Marcos Mendoza.

I rode the elevator up with a male agent who'd been with the IRS for several years and played on the IRS softball team. Had he played back when Nick served as team captain? Was he Nick's inside contact?

I ran into Eddie as I stepped off the elevator. He jerked his head toward my office, indicating he wanted to speak with me alone.

We reached my office and ducked inside. Eddie shut the door behind us. I dropped my purse into my desk drawer and plunked down in my wobbly rolling chair, while Eddie perched on the corner of my desk.

"What's up with your hair?" he asked.

Turns out it's really difficult to rinse out mayonnaise. My greasy hair was glued to my head. "Lice treatment."

His upper lip curled back in disgust.

"Don't give me any shit today," I ordered. "I'm not in the mood."

"All right. I've got good news and bad news," he said. "Which do you want first?"

"Give me the bad news first." Might as well get it out of the

way, right? I pulled Nick Pratt's stress ball from my drawer
and began working it.

"The agent from Laredo called this morning. A young
guy came in yesterday to pick up the mail at the post office
box. His car had Mexican plates. He took the mail and drove
right back over the border. The agent tried to follow him but
he lost the car at the border crossing."

A fresh surge of frustration flooded me. "Dammit!" We
couldn't catch a break.

"Lu allowed me to call one of our agents in Mexico, see
what he could dig up. So I put in a call to Hector Gutierrez."
Eddie went on to tell me that Gutierrez was stationed in
Nuevo Laredo, the city where Torres lived just south of the
border in Mexico, essentially a sister city to the American
city of Laredo.

Besides the contingent of agents in the U.S., the IRS maintained a permanent staff of agents in several foreign countries,
including Mexico, Colombia, Canada, Hong Kong, Germany,
and even at Interpol in France. Unfortunately, although agents
were stationed in these foreign countries, their investigative
powers were much more limited than in the U.S. The countries
had to balance the rights of its citizens against the interests
of a foreign government and, in many cases, their citizens
won out.

Still, evidence could sometimes be obtained through direct surveillance or by convincing the governments of these
countries that its interests would also be served by allowing
our agents to investigate. Often, if someone was cheating the
IRS out of tax dollars, they were cheating the other government out of its due as well. Problem was, most countries,
Mexico included, preferred to assign one of their own to lead
the investigations.

There was no way we could let the Mexican authorities
know we were investigating Mendoza. We couldn't trust there
wouldn't be a leak or that Mendoza wouldn't buy off another
agent. But at least our guy in Mexico could trace the Mexican
license plate, follow the driver to see where he went.

I chose to be hopeful. I wanted this investigation over. Now. I was sick of this case hanging over me. "How much did you have to tell Gutierrez?"

"Fortunately, very little," Eddie said. "He's been an agent a long time. He understands the details of this case are on a need-to-know basis only."

Looked like we were finished with the bad news, at least for now. "So what's the good news?"

"Got another lead for us."

"Fantastic." I clapped my hands. "What is it?"

"Taxpayer named Carson McNabb. He was audited recently. Reported forty grand in gambling winnings over the past few years. A small part of the winnings were from bets McNabb placed at a racetrack in Hot Springs, Arkansas, that's owned by AmeriMex. The rest of the winnings were from a company called Double Down that takes bets by telephone. Double Down didn't report McNabb's winnings."

Assuming Double Down was located in the U.S., failing to report the payout would be a violation of the Internal Revenue Code's filing requirements. Suspicious. And precisely why the audit department had referred the information to Criminal Investigations.

"You think there's a link between the racetrack and Double Down?"

Eddie raised his hands, palms up. "You never know until you ask."

CHAPTER NINETEEN

$\mathcal{L}$ife's a Gamble

I'd been summoned to give a deposition that morning in a relatively small case against a barely legal self-employed personal trainer who'd underreported her earnings by over twenty grand last year. The cash deposited into her bank account far exceeded the earnings she'd reported on her tax return. Although she'd claimed a large portion of the deposits were gifts from various friends and relatives, not a single one of them substantiated her story. What's more, the gym where she'd provided her training services supplied us with logs detailing the appointments she'd had with their members. The logs indicated she'd been a far busier girl than she'd led us to believe.

It was an open-and-shut case. If she'd hired an attorney better versed in accounting and tax law, he would've realized right off he had a losing case and not wasted our time. Instead, she'd hired a local defense attorney who advertised on television, called himself "the Jail Breaker," and primarily represented defendants in DWI and drug possession cases. He was way out of his league here. But anything for a buck, right?

Ross O'Donnell was already at the attorney's office when I arrived. I nodded to Ross and turned to shake the Jail Breaker's hand. "Nice to meet you." As if.

"Likewise." Yeah, right.

We made our way to his small conference room and got down to business. An hour into my deposition, after I'd detailed how I'd verified the woman's earnings through bank records and the health club's training logs, the attorney seemed to realize that not only was his client in deep doo-doo but that he also lacked the proper shovel to dig her out. "Any chance my client can avoid jail time if she agrees to pay all taxes, interest, and penalties assessed?"

Ross asked my opinion on the matter. The girl looked terrified, realizing she'd sorely underestimated the ability of the IRS to detect fraud and nip it in its firm little twenty-year-old butt. I decided to show a little mercy. Payment arrangements were made, the trainer was admonished to be a good little girl from now on, and the case was closed.

If only the Mendoza case could be wrapped up so easily.

I stopped the girl on her way out the door. She might be a tax cheat, but she had the firmest biceps and glutes I'd ever seen. "I've gained a little weight recently," I told her. "Any suggestions on how to get rid of it quick?"

She looked me up and down. "Ten sets of squats every day," she said. "Same with lunges."

My muscles hurt just thinking about it.

That afternoon, Eddie and I drove out to Carson McNabb's property, a hundred-acre spread outside the town of Bonham, an hour's drive northeast of Dallas. Eddie climbed out of the car to open the rusty gate. I cringed as I pulled into the gravel drive, the rocks plink-plinking against the undercarriage of my precious Beamer. I hoped none would chip my paint.

The McNabbs' house was set back a quarter mile from the road in a stand of scrubby cedars. The rest of the land had been cleared, horses of different sizes and colors dotting the pasture. Fortunately, the area immediately surrounding the house was fenced off, so at least we wouldn't have to worry about stepping in horse droppings. A lone donkey stood at the barbed-wire fence, watching us like a small, big-eared sentry. He pulled back his upper lip and treated us to a hearty hee-haw.

The McNabbs' home was a sprawling single-story ranch, white stone with a sloped tin roof and expansive front porch. I parked next to a late-model Ford pickup on the side of the house. A warm, dust-scented breeze greeted us as we climbed out of the car and up the stone steps to knock on the door.

A pleasant-looking older woman answered. She wore a loose-fitting pumpkin-colored blouse and long matching skirt along with a pair of expensive riding boots. "Hello there. I'm Mary Lynn McNabb." Her eyes flickered to my oily hair as she held out her hand. "You must be Agents Holloway and Bardin?"

Eddie gave a quick nod. "That's us."

We shook hands and she invited us in, seating us at a rough-hewn pine table in their formal dining room. A delicious smell wafted from the adjacent kitchen. My guess was chicken and dumplings.

Mary Lynn left to round up her husband, returning with two large glasses of iced tea and Carson, who was a tall drink of water himself. We stood and shook hands with Mr. McNabb.

Carson McNabb was a good ol' boy if ever there was one. Wrangler jeans, old-fashioned pointy-toed cowboy boots, western-cut shirt with pearl buttons, and a straw Stetson.

After Mrs. McNabb set a glass of tea in front of me and another in front of Eddie, she took a seat next to her husband.

Eddie held up a palm. "Before we get started here, we want to make it clear that we've got no plans to bring you in on gambling charges. We're more interested in finding out who's running the operation so we can collect any taxes they might owe."

Carson nodded, removing his hat and placing it upside down on the table. "Didn't realize it was against the law to place bets by phone," he said, his drawl one hundred percent pure Texan. He ran a weathered hand over his close-cropped white hair. "Surely didn't mean to break the law."

His confession would have made a defense attorney cringe but, lucky for us, he hadn't employed one. Good thing, too. Didn't need any more people involved than absolutely necessary, especially people who could impede our ability to collect information.

A jingling sound came from down the hall, and a sizable brown-and-white birddog wearing a leather collar and tags trotted into the room. He lifted his pink snout into the air, sniffing, and turned his brown eyes on me.

The mayonnaise. Uh-oh.

The dog lunged full force at me, knocking me backward in my chair. When I hit the floor, he pounced on me, straddling my face and gripping my head between his legs like those creepy creatures from the *Alien* movie. His boy parts stared me in the face as he ran his long tongue over my hair, snuffling and slurping the greasy substance from my head.

That was the last time I'd try one of my mother's home remedies.

I wriggled on the floor, trying to push the dog off me, but didn't have much luck. I couldn't get much leverage and this pooch was persistent.

"Toby!" Mary Lynn cried, grabbing his collar and yanking him away. "Bad boy!"

"Sorry 'bout that," Carson said.

I sat up on the floor and raised a palm. "No problem. An IRS agent gets used to that kind of reception."

My partner held out a hand to help me up, then righted my chair for me. Once we were seated again, we opened our briefcases and pulled out our legal pads and pens.

Eddie began the questioning. "What can you tell us about the gambling operation?"

McNabb shrugged. "What would you like to know?" The man wasn't being evasive, he simply didn't seem to know where to start. He looked back and forth between me and Eddie.

"When did you first become involved in the telephone betting?" Eddie asked.

McNabb looked up in thought. "Three, maybe four years ago. The wife and I took a weekend trip up to Arkansas for our fortieth anniversary. They got a racetrack up there in Hot Springs. We bet a little on the ponies. Won a little money. Had some fun. Remember that weekend, hon?" He shot a wink at his wife.

Mrs. McNabb clutched at the neck of her blouse and blushed. Must've been some weekend. I wondered if the McNabbs had ever tried LuvLub or if Mary Lynn had had her vagina rejuvenated, whatever the hell that meant.

"How much did you bet at the track?" Eddie asked McNabb.

"Couple thousand dollars, give or take. Won 'round six grand, if memory serves me right. The girl at the counter had us fill out one of them tax forms before they paid out."

I nodded. Eddie'd pulled the McNabbs' tax records for the last decade and saw a Form W-2G had been filed by AmeriMex for the year in question, reporting McNabb had won sixty-two hundred dollars at the track. All of the legitimate companies operated by AmeriMex were run carefully, all i's dotted and t's crossed, the record-keeping meticulous. Mendoza ran a tight ship. Unfortunately, he seemed to run an even tighter ship with his illegal operations.

Eddie continued his questioning. "How did you get hooked up with 'Double D'?"

"About a month after our trip to Arkansas," McNabb said, "I got a call from someone saying he could place telephone bets on football games and the like."

"What about horse races?" I asked.

Carson shook his head. "I asked about that, but the person on the phone said they only did sports betting."

Probably another way to make it appear as if the bets had nothing to do with the racetracks owned by AmeriMex.

Eddie jotted a note on his legal pad. "Did the representative say how he got your name and number?"

"No, and I didn't ask, neither. I assumed that since we'd recently been to the track in Hot Springs, he must've been associated with that outfit."

Made sense. "How did you place your bets?" I asked.

"He gave me a phone number to call."

I held my pen poised over my pad. "Got that number handy?"

"Sure do." McNabb pulled out his cell phone and scrolled through his list of contacts, holding up the phone so I could read from the screen. The number displayed was a toll-free 800 number. Now we were getting somewhere. I jotted the number down.

"How'd you place the bets?" Eddie asked.

"With my credit card."

Eddie nodded. "Do you have any statements that would show the charges?"

"Reckon I might."

Mary Lynn stood. "I'll get them, hon."

Mrs. McNabb walked into the den through which we'd entered and rummaged through the top drawer of an antique roll-top desk. She came back with a handful of credit card statements and handed them to Eddie.

I scooted my chair closer to my partner and looked over his shoulder. The bills were in reverse chronological order, with the most recent bills at the top and the older bills at the bottom. The first two entries on their April statement indicated the McNabbs had enjoyed dinner at a local steakhouse and made a significant purchase at a feed store. The third entry listed the merchant as "DD Entertainment." The charge was two hundred and fifty dollars.

After reviewing the rest of the statements and pulling out those showing charges by Double D, Eddie looked up at Carson. "May I take these statements with me?"

"Sure," the man said. "They've done been paid."

Eddie launched back into his questions now. "When you won, how did you get your winnings?"

"They mailed checks to me."

Checks? My heart flip-flopped in my chest.

Checks left a paper trail. Checks could be traced.

Was this our big break? My eyes met Eddie's. He, too, looked surprised and hopeful.

"Any chance you might have one of those checks around?" Eddie asked.

Carson pulled out his wallet and removed a check. "Received this one yesterday. Haven't yet had a chance to get by the bank to deposit it."

He laid the check on the table. It was a basic blue business-style check in the amount of three hundred dollars with the name "Double D" imprinted on the top. No address was listed on the check.

Eddie inquired about their winnings and learned Double D had paid out various amounts over the years, the smallest being a mere fifty bucks and the largest being nine grand he'd won on a Texas-Oklahoma football game.

I narrowed my eyes at him. "You didn't bet against the Longhorns, did you?"

Carson chuckled and held up his palms. "Gotta plead the fifth on that one."

Mrs. McNabb looked from me to Eddie. "Do we have to stop making the bets?"

I couldn't blame her for asking. The gambling had paid off much better than the stock market.

Eddie and I exchanged glances. Technically, this type of gambling was illegal in Texas. But most law enforcement agencies had shown little interest in pursuing violators. It seemed silly to punish people for placing bets on sports when they could easily go to one of the horse or dog tracks in the state and do essentially the same thing. Splitting hairs, wasn't it? And after controversy surrounding the arrest of small-time gamblers and business owners offering "eight-liners," a type of slot machine, neither local police nor state law enforcement agencies had made gambling violations a priority. It seemed to be a victimless crime and, besides, the police had bigger fish to fry. Still, the thought of any more money going into Mendoza's pockets, possibly funding hits on his unsuspecting associates, turned my stomach.

I gave them a regretful smile. "Any more betting with Double D could get you in trouble."

Carson frowned. "Dadgummit."

"Sorry, folks. But we'll send this check back to you to deposit once we're done with it." I didn't want any more money going into Mendoza's pockets, but I sure as hell didn't mind more money coming out of them.

Eddie and I thanked the McNabbs and left, our spirits renewed. The McNabbs' credit card service could tell us where Double D was located and the bank would be able to tell us where the check had come from. Plus, the toll-free phone number could easily be traced to its source.

Surely one of these sources would provide a link to Mendoza. Then we could bring the murderous bastard in and I could focus instead on the upcoming party to celebrate the Lobo reaching the hundred-million milestone.

CHAPTER TWENTY

*W*rong Numbers

As we drove back to Dallas, Eddie called his wife to let her know he'd be late getting home tonight.

"Again?" I heard Sandra lament through the phone.

"Again," Eddie said. He didn't sound none too happy about it, either. This case was taking over his life, too.

I glanced at my watch. The banquet in Fort Lauderdale would be starting soon—the banquet I'd be attending if it weren't for this damn investigation.

I pulled out my phone and sent Brett a quick text. *Thinking of u*. Fat lot of good that did, huh?

Fresh anger surged through me. I wasn't just mad at Mendoza now, I was starting to feel pissed at Nick Pratt, too. He'd gotten me all hot and bothered, wondering what the hell he was up to, whose side he was on now.

I'd kept my phone with me at all times since his last call, even taken the darn thing into the bathroom when I showered.

Why hadn't he called back?

When we arrived at the federal building, Eddie headed to his office to research the phone number for Double Down, while I returned to my office and set about tracking down the banking information. It was well after five o'clock on a Friday evening and, other than the cleaning staff, we were the only people on the floor. Still, I closed my door. Couldn't hurt to be cautious.

I examined the line of numbers across the bottom of Carson McNabb's check and typed the bank's routing number into the research system. After a few seconds, the screen popped up with some information. The checks paid to Carson McNabb had been issued by an offshore bank.

I banged a fist on my desk, causing a trio of paper clips to jump out of their shallow plastic bin. "Damn!"

There'd be no luck getting any information on who had set up the account. Those Caribbean islanders would happily share a spliff, but under no circumstances would they share banking information, *mon*. That wouldn't be *irie*.

I made my way to Eddie's office, plopping into a chair while he finished his phone call. He had the receiver in one hand and a death grip on his skull with the other. This didn't bode well.

"Uh-huh," he said. "Okay. Well, thanks for the information." He slammed his phone down and threw his hands in the air. "The phone number for Double Down is an international toll-free number."

A what? "Didn't know there was such a thing."

Eddie stared out his window, glaring at the world at large. "There are several American companies that provide call forwarding services. The calls go through the forwarding company's toll-free number in the U.S. and are then routed internationally."

Clever. "That way Double Down has no physical presence in the U.S. and can't be called on the carpet here for running an illegal gambling operation."

"Exactly." Eddie turned back to me, his lips pressed into a thin line.

"Hate to tell you this, but the checks were a dead end, too."

"Let me guess," Eddie spat. "Offshore bank?"

"Yep."

Just to make sure we'd left no stone unturned, I placed a call to McNabb's credit card company. The representative informed me that the charges by Double D originated in Juarez, Mexico, a large city just across the Rio Grande river from El Paso, Texas. Plagued with violence related to drug trafficking, Juarez had seen hundreds, if not thousands, of murders in recent years, many of the victims shot with guns funneled south from the U.S. given that the sale of guns was illegal in Mexico. Drugs were one export that did nothing to positively impact the Mexican economy. Though a few arrests had been made recently, law enforcement had little control over the city. Juarez was the perfect place to operate a business such as this.

And, again, it was outside of our jurisdiction.

Ugh.

Ugh. Ugh. Ugh!

"The problem with this case is that we can't get close to anyone involved," Eddie grumbled, an edge in his voice. "Mendoza's done a great job of making himself untouchable." Eddie punted his plastic garbage can across the room in frustration. Fortunately, the cleaning crew had already come by his office and the can was empty.

I stood and walked over to the corner where the can landed. Rather than pick it up, I gave it another kick. Had to admit, it felt good to let out some of my frustrations, even if it was on an innocent piece of plastic.

"What now?" I kicked the can back in the direction of Eddie's desk. It seemed as if we had dozens of puzzle pieces that we were trying to fit together, but the pieces that would link them together were still missing.

Eddie picked up the can and set it back in its place. "Let's call Gutierrez, see if he can be of any help." Eddie dialed Hector Gutierrez, our agent south of the border. Fortunately, he was still in his office. Eddie pushed the speakerphone button so we'd both be able to hear, but kept the volume turned low.

"Gambling was recently legalized here in Mexico," Gutierrez informed us in a voice tinged with a heavy Spanish accent. Apparently the Mexican federal government realized it was losing tax revenue due to the giant sucking sound pulling Mexican tourists north into Las Vegas, Reno, and smaller gambling destinations such as Shreveport. "There's only a handful of casinos in the country now, but plans for more are under way. I'll look into who owns Double Down Entertainment and let you know what I find out."

"Thanks," Eddie and I said in unison. Sometimes it seemed we shared one brain.

"By the way," Gutierrez said, "I tracked down that license plate you gave me."

Eddie's head whipped my way and vice versa.

"And?" we asked, again in unison.

"The car belongs to a young guy in his early twenties. He works at one of the *maquiladoras*. A shoe factory operated by a corporation called Zapatos Superiores."

Eyes still locked on mine, Eddie cocked his head. "Any idea who owns Zapatos Superiores?" he asked Gutierrez, his tone deceptively casual.

"There are a number of minority shareholders," Gutierrez said, "but the majority of the stock is held by a man named Vicente Torres."

"Aha!" A possible link. After all, Torres held an indirect interest in AmeriMex.

Eddie put a finger to his lips.

I covered my mouth, realizing my reaction might have clued Gutierrez in to the fact that Torres was on our radar. Then again, a little niggle at the back of my mind told me Gutierrez might have already figured that out on his own. After all, the IRS don't hire no flunkies.

"Want me to talk to anybody down here?" Gutierrez asked.

"Not yet," Eddie said. "But we'll let you know if we change our minds on that."

We thanked him for his time and bid him *adios*. He bid us *buena suerte*—good luck.

"What now?" I asked Eddie. "There's got to be something we can do with this information."

"I'm not so sure," Eddie said. "Short of placing a mole in the shoe factory and hoping he can prove the money orders were delivered to Torres, which is highly doubtful, I don't see how we can use this information. And even then all we'd prove is that Torres is involved in a loan shark operation. That wouldn't prove Mendoza played a role."

"Then where do we go from here?" Throwing in the towel was not an option. I debated suggesting the head shot with the hunting rifle, but I was afraid my partner might take me up on it. At this point, Eddie's okay would be all the encouragement I'd need to follow through on the plan.

Eddie ran a hand over his short hair, letting out a frustrated huff. "Hell, I don't know what to do now. Never had a case like this before. Most people aren't this good at covering their tracks."

True. Most people didn't even try very hard, failing to give the IRS credit we'd be able to track down the financial information needed to prove their returns hadn't been on the up-and-up.

I hated to ask the next question, but I wanted an honest answer. "What do you think the chances are we'll bring Mendoza in?"

Eddie's gaze locked on mine. "Honestly, Tara? Slim to none. We're not dealing with an amateur here."

I sighed. "I like amateurs. They're so cute when they think they can get away with stuff." I closed my eyes, racking a brain that had already been racked, reracked, and re-reracked. "You think there's any point in talking to the widow?"

"The widow?"

"Lauren Sheffield. The wife of the guy Mendoza . . ." Again, I couldn't say it. Heck, I could still hardly even think it.

"Dismembered?" Eddie supplied for me.

My sphincter tightened involuntarily. "Yeah."

"We've read through her statements. There was nothing in there that looked helpful. She didn't seem to know much."

"You got any other bright ideas?"

He shook his head. "Guess it can't hurt to talk to her again. What's a little more wasted time at this point?"

I hung around the office after Eddie left, telling him I wanted to catch up on my e-mails. But it was a ruse. What I really wanted to do was find out who'd been in touch with Nick.

But how?

I stepped out into the hallway. The cleaning crew stood around their cart at the end of the hall. One of the women pulled a vacuum cleaner off the cart and headed into an office, another grabbed a feather duster and a roll of trash bags and followed her in.

The sound of the vacuum switching on met my ears as I slid into the office next to mine. The space belonged to another female agent, one who'd been with the IRS for five years or so. I rummaged through her drawers and checked her trash can but found nothing of interest other than a secret stash of gummy worms she'd never offered to share. And to think I'd given her a half dozen of Mom's pralines.

I continued down the hall, quickly searching each office, paying particular attention to the digs of those who played on the softball team. The team members not only practiced and played together, but they often went out for pizza and beer after the games. Maybe one of them had bonded with Nick over slices of pepperoni.

My search turned up a small bottle of wart remover in one office, a can of deodorant foot spray another, and, in the last office, a copy of Dr. Phil's *Relationship Rescue Workbook*. More than I really wanted to know about my coworkers. Too much information. And, unfortunately, not the right information.

My last stop was the Lobo's office. I eased past Viola's desk and slipped through Lu's half-open door. I found nothing incriminating in her workspace other than an empty can of Slim-Fast and a king-sized Snickers wrapper.

Would I ever find the answers I was looking for?

CHAPTER TWENTY-ONE

$\mathscr{P}$asta to Die For

The following Monday, Hector Gutierrez called us back with some interesting information. Double Down was owned by a small, privately held Mexican corporation. It had taken some digging, but he'd been able to verify that the stock of the corporation was held by two Mexican partnerships. Vicente Torres was the managing partner of one of the partnerships.

Given that Torres was also one of the owners of Ameri-Mex, Double Down could thus be linked to Mendoza. The link was tenuous at best, but it was nonetheless a link. Still, as expected, it didn't directly implicate Mendoza in any illegal activity.

We needed more.

The supervisor from Dallas PD's crime scene team called shortly thereafter.

"Any luck?" I asked.

"We matched several prints on the cash register till to Darina and Jakub Pokorny," she said. "No surprise there. But we also lifted one print from the till that didn't match either of them."

Bubba's, no doubt. Dumbass.

"Unfortunately," she continued, "the print didn't match anyone in the system. Whoever it belongs to doesn't have a record. Yet."

"What do you mean 'yet'?"

"The fingerprint matched an unidentified print lifted from a burglary last year. If the thug did something like this twice already, he's likely to do it again. In time, he might be arrested for another crime."

Problem was, time was in very short supply.

I gritted my teeth in frustration. It seemed as though Eddie and I were running through a maze that had no way out. The loan payments couldn't be directly linked to Mendoza. And even though Gutierrez found out that Torres owned Double Down, what could we do with that information? Not a damn thing. Not with Torres and Double Down sitting on the wrong side of the border and no definitive evidence that Mendoza had received any payments from the gambling operation. The fingerprints from the Pokornys' bakery had given us nothing to go on, either. Nick Pratt hadn't called back, either. Damn him.

At this point, unless and until something else developed, the only hope we had for a break in the case rested with Lauren Sheffield, the widow of Mendoza's most recent victim. I hoped against hope Lauren would give us something, *anything,* that might help in our investigation. Eddie and I were out of ideas.

After her husband's murder, Lauren had immediately put their house on the market and moved herself and her young son back home to Tulsa, Oklahoma, where she'd grown up. When I'd spoken with her by phone on the previous Friday, she'd agreed to meet with us this Wednesday, when she'd be in town to close the sale on the house.

In preparation for our meeting, I reread the files from the earlier investigations. The Texas Rangers and FBI had thoroughly investigated Andrew Sheffield's murder already and had come up with nothing. No evidence. No witnesses. No viable suspects. Mendoza had an ironclad alibi. At the time of the murder, he'd been out of the country attending a week-long financial conference in Frankfurt, Germany, seeking out venture capitalists who might want to invest in businesses owned by AmeriMex.

Obviously, just as he'd hired others to attack the Pokornys, he'd hired someone to kill Andrew Sheffield. The creep didn't have the *cojones* to do his own dirty work. Ironically, the fact that he didn't commit his own murders made me lose even more respect for him.

We'd arranged to meet Lauren at one-thirty on Wednesday, when the lunch crowd would be thinning and we could have more privacy. She'd chosen the spot, a small Italian restaurant in Garland, the suburban town she and Andrew had once called home.

I hoped she'd give us a new lead. I wasn't sure how much longer I could take the stress. I'd had to stop by a grocery store to buy chewable antacid tablets this morning. I'd washed them down with a tasteless skinny no-whip latte. On a brighter note, I'd lost a pound. The squats and lunges the tax-cheating personal trainer had recommended were doing the trick. The girl might not pay her taxes, but when it came to fitness, she knew her stuff.

Eddie and I entered the restaurant, pausing inside the door as our eyes adjusted from the bright sunlight to the dimly lit interior. The bar sat to the right, through a wide archway. Eddie and I made our way into the room, glancing around for Lauren.

Though neither of us knew what she looked like, we identified her immediately. The woman sitting on a stool at the bar bore the gaunt physique reserved for marathon runners, supermodels, and the grief stricken. She wore a pair of wrinkled black linen pants and a long-sleeved gray silk blouse she hadn't bothered to tuck in. Though both garments were clearly expensive designer pieces that had once fit her, the clothing now hung off her skeletal frame.

I stepped up to her. "Lauren?"

She turned to me and nodded. Her hazel eyes were sunken and underscored with dark crescents accumulated through dozens of sleepless nights. She wore no makeup, making no attempt to conceal the evidence of her despair. Her dark, dull hair fell haphazardly around her shoulders, brushed, barely, but not styled. She was so thin, so pale, so lifeless, it was as if some part of her had died along with her husband.

"I'm Tara Holloway." I stuck out my hand and she took it in hers, her grip light, hopeless.

Eddie also introduced himself. None of us bothered to say "nice to meet you." There was nothing nice at all about this meeting. If Andrew Sheffield hadn't been brutally slain, Lauren would have remained blissfully ignorant of our existence and vice versa.

"Shall we get a table?" Eddie asked.

Again, Lauren merely nodded. Words seemed too much of an effort.

She climbed off her stool to follow us. Eddie checked in with the hostess, requesting a private table. The woman grabbed three menus from a stack on her podium and led us to a table in the back corner.

Eddie and I took seats opposite Lauren.

Once the hostess had gone, she finally spoke. "This was Andrew's favorite restaurant. He always ordered the linguine formaggio. Said he could eat it every day until he died."

Oh God. What do you say in response to something like that? I glanced at Eddie, but his stricken expression told me he was as shell-shocked as I was.

"I'm so sorry, Lauren." Couldn't go wrong with that, right?

The woman reached into her purse, removed a photo, and set it on the table in front of me. I picked it up. A couple dressed in colorful aloha shirts smiled big, gaping smiles at the camera, a cruise ship visible behind them. On the woman's hip rested an adorable dark-haired toddler, a white sailor cap tucked squarely on his head.

Though the woman in the photo was Lauren Sheffield,

she bore little resemblance to the person sitting across the table. The Lauren in the photo looked lively, happy, in love. The man standing beside her had an average build, short brown hair, and a friendly smile, the grown-up version of the boy next door. His head angled toward his wife, his arm draped protectively and lovingly over Lauren's shoulders.

"That photo was taken on our vacation two summers ago," she said. "We took the trip to celebrate the launch of Andrew's consulting business. Andrew and Tyler had so much fun." Her voice caught and she struggled to maintain her composure. "Tyler is so young. He'll never be able to remember his dad. What am I going to tell him when he grows up and asks what happened to his father?"

I glanced at my partner. Eddie looked uncomfortable, fidgeting with his silverware. I wasn't sure whether Lauren's question was intended to be rhetorical but, regardless, there was no good answer.

"Can I keep this photo?"

She nodded. "It's digital. I can print another."

I slid the photo into my purse and pulled out a small note pad and pen. "I hate to put you through this again, Lauren, but the IRS may be the last hope for nailing the person responsible for your husband's death."

She looked me square in the eye. "You mean Marcos Mendoza." She spat out his name as if spitting out poison.

I met her gaze for a few seconds before responding. Even if Mendoza hadn't done the actual killing, he'd ordered the hit. He was as culpable as the man, or men, who'd slain Andrew. "Yes. Marcos Mendoza."

She sat up straighter in her seat. "I want to help in any way I can."

I looked down at my blank notepad, willing it to tell me what magic question I could ask that might elicit something new, some clue that had been overlooked. Unfortunately, the pad was silent. I glanced over at Eddie, then back at Lauren. "I'm going to be honest with you, Lauren. I have no idea where to start. My only hope is that we might elicit something new or different than the earlier investigations, that maybe a small tidbit of information that seemed insignificant to the other agencies might mean something to us."

Eddie chimed in now, giving us a place to start. "The earlier reports indicated that Andrew started working for Mendoza about ten years ago, at North Dallas Credit Union. Is that right?"

"Yes," Lauren said. "He started working there just after we graduated from Oklahoma State. Andrew was the first person in his family to go to college. He was very ambitious, worked hard. He started as a loan officer, then transferred into the accounting department. Eventually he was promoted to chief financial officer. It was a good job. Regular hours. The pay was good, too. But he'd gone as far as he could at the credit union. Andrew wanted more. For himself. For us."

Ambition was normally a good thing. But Andrew's ambition got him killed. If only he'd been a slacker he'd still be alive today.

The waiter arrived then to take our order. We all ordered the linguine formaggio, a culinary tribute to Andrew Sheffield. It seemed the least we could do.

When the waiter left, Lauren continued. "Andrew met Marcos Mendoza several times when Mendoza came to the credit union to check on things. Mendoza wore the right clothes, drove the right car, knew how to get what he wanted. Andrew was impressed. He seemed like the kind of man Andrew aspired to be." Lauren emitted a sharp, derisive breath before continuing. "Andrew figured getting a job with the credit union's parent company would open more doors for him. So he approached Mendoza about opportunities at AmeriMex. Mendoza told Andrew that no in-house positions were available, but that if Andrew opened his own business he'd hire Andrew as an outside consultant on special projects. Andrew was thrilled. He thought it would be a chance for him to prove himself, to be his own boss. Mendoza told Andrew how to set up a corporation and Andrew formed ARS Financial."

No doubt Mendoza had advised Andrew to set up a corporation because tax law did not require payments to a corporation to be reported to the IRS. Funds could change hands off the agency's radar.

She went on, telling us that Andrew had rented a one-room executive suite not far from their house. "Andrew dealt directly with Mendoza rather than one of his underlings. Mendoza even gave Andrew his private e-mail address and cell phone number. Andrew felt important, like his right-hand man."

Feeding the victim's ego. Typical MO for con artists.

"For the first few months things seemed normal. Financial information was provided to Andrew for various business ventures operated by AmeriMex, and Andrew prepared financial statements, did some projections and forecasting. AmeriMex paid Andrew ungodly amounts of money for the consulting work." Her voice grew softer, sadder. "We thought our ship had come in."

It had.

And it was the *Titanic*.

Our salads arrived then, along with a basket of warm garlic bread. While Eddie and I picked at our salads, Lauren continued.

"After a few months, things started getting weird. Andrew didn't tell me all the details. He probably didn't want me to worry. But I know Mendoza asked Andrew to funnel a large cash payment though the ARS corporate bank account. Mendoza claimed that he suspected an employee with access to the AmeriMex accounts had embezzled funds and that he didn't want to put the money where the employee might be able to abscond with it. Andrew agreed to transfer the funds that one time."

She turned away then, a guilty look on her face. My guess was the couple knew the exorbitant income Andrew received would come with some not-so-ethical strings attached. They just hadn't realized the strings would become the rope with which Andrew would later be hung.

Lauren took a shaky breath and turned back to us. "After that, the transactions became more frequent and in larger amounts. Mendoza had cash and money orders couriered to Andrew and instructed Andrew to deposit the funds in ARS Financial's accounts. He'd give Andrew instructions later on where to send the money. Proper accounting controls weren't being followed. The source of the income was questionable and when Andrew asked about it, Mendoza was evasive. Andrew became uncomfortable serving as a straw man with such large sums involved."

Rightfully so. Clearly, Andrew's consulting business had become a front for a money-laundering scheme.

Lauren took a small sip of her water. "Mendoza wouldn't allow Andrew to contact anyone at AmeriMex directly. He insisted that all communication go through him, via e-mail or his cell phone. Andrew felt like he wasn't getting the full story. He didn't like being kept in the dark and he was worried he could end up in trouble."

He'd ended up in more than trouble. He'd ended up in a Dumpster. Actually, four Dumpsters to be exact.

Tears pooled in her eyes now. "Andrew sent Mendoza a resignation letter politely thanking him for the opportunities he had provided, but stating that he no longer wanted to perform consulting services for AmeriMex. Mendoza offered Andrew even more money to continue on. Of course, Andrew declined. Two days later, Andrew was . . . gone."

She picked up her fork, gripping it so hard her knuckles turned white. "When the police investigated, the officers found drug paraphernalia and hard-core porn magazines in one of Andrew's desk drawers. I think Mendoza's henchmen planted them to make Andrew look bad and to throw off suspicion. Andrew would never have done drugs or looked at porn."

Eddie gave me a little kick under the table. This kick said *Never say never*. Lauren Sheffield may not have wanted to believe her husband would involve himself in drugs or sexual perversion, but Eddie and I had learned that looks could be deceiving and that nobody knew others as well as they thought they did. We'd recently sent a softball coach away for eighteen months for tax evasion, much to the surprise of his wife. She'd known nothing about the stash of unreported cash he'd earned in his roofing business and mingled with the team's accounts in an attempt to hide it.

Regardless of the extent to which Andrew had been a partner or pawn in Mendoza's game, the fact remained that Mendoza was a dangerous man, a man who'd gotten away with murder, more than once.

A man who would kill again.

I couldn't let that happen. "Any chance Andrew ever gave you the private phone number or e-mail address Mendoza had instructed him to use?"

Lauren shook her head. "The cell phone disappeared. The police kept the computer as evidence. But there wasn't anything on it. The hard drive had been wiped clean."

Just like Nick Pratt's hard drive had been wiped clean.

"All the money in the ARS bank accounts was gone, too," Lauren said. "Every penny had been withdrawn."

The FBI report had indicated that the funds had been taken out in cash rather than a check or wire transfer that could be traced. Unfortunately, it had been Andrew Sheffield himself who'd cleaned out the account, probably at Mendoza's request since most, if not all, of the funds belonged to Mendoza. Andrew probably thought he was doing the right thing returning the money, that it would get him out from under Mendoza's thumb.

"It wasn't until after Andrew disappeared that I learned that a former employee of AmeriMex had been found dead after a carjacking that was never solved. Another died in a suspicious fire. The FBI agent who interviewed me told me about those deaths."

And with Andrew Sheffield's death, the trail of bodies grew even longer.

After Andrew's murder, the FBI had interviewed Mendoza but he'd offered only vague, carefully crafted answers to a small number of introductory questions, politely declining to answer the more meaty inquiries on the advice of his attorney.

He'd even apologized that his counsel "would not allow him to respond." I'd read the transcript of the interview. It made me want to puke.

Eddie and I were the only hope for justice now, for putting Mendoza behind bars, for saving the lives of others who might be lured in by the promise of prestige and financial security. Chances were some other naïve soul was unknowingly being groomed to take Andrew's place. We had to solve this case before that person suffered the same fate as Andrew. But how could we find out who that person was?

Lauren stared at me now and, for the first time, her eyes showed signs of life. They narrowed now and sparked with vengeance. "Promise me you'll get Mendoza. Promise me you'll make sure that bastard gets what he deserves."

Eddie and I exchanged glances again. Hell, I didn't know if we could get this guy. Lauren had given us nothing new to pursue. But I had to give this woman some hope that justice would prevail. Hell, I had to give *myself* some hope. I'd never been the type to go down easily. And I wasn't about to start now.

"I promise."

Eddie promptly gave me another sideways kick under the table, a kick that said *You've done it again, stupid. Made another promise you may not be able to deliver on.*

I responded by putting the toe of my shoe on top of his and pressing down. My gesture said *Shut your piehole. I'll bust this bastard if it's the last thing I do.*

Andrew Sheffield had been wrong to involve himself with Mendoza. But he'd been right about one thing. The linguine formaggio was indeed delicious.

Absolutely to die for.

Too bad I could only choke down a few bites.

CHAPTER TWENTY-TWO

We'd followed every rabbit trail and found no rabbit. Eddie and I were like the Knights of the Round Table in the Monty Python version of *The Holy Grail.* They'd pursued the grail with never-foundering focus only to encounter obstacle after obstacle, ranging from the Black Knight to livestock launched at them from a castle. When the movie ended, they still hadn't located the Holy Grail, their goal having eluded them. At this point, it seemed that we, likewise, would never succeed in our quest to nail Mendoza.

There was only one option left at this point and it was a long shot.

The morning after we met with Lauren Sheffield, Eddie and I rounded up Ross O'Donnell and headed to the federal courthouse to seek an order from Magistrate Judge Alice Trumbull to allow a wiretap on Mendoza's personal phone lines and those at AmeriMex. To be honest, we weren't sure a wiretap would do any good. From the information Lauren Sheffield had provided us, it appeared Mendoza used untraceable cell phones to do his dirty business. We'd have no way of discovering what those phone numbers might be. And with all the free e-mail services on the Web, pinning down Mendoza's secret e-mail address would be like finding a needle in a worldwide haystack. Still, a wiretap seemed to be our only option.

I handed Ross the affidavits and evidence we'd collected, including the family photo of the Sheffields. The stack looked paltry. "Think it'll be enough?"

He glanced down at the papers, his face skeptical. "Hard to say with Judge Trumbull. But I'll do my best."

Judge Trumbull was one of the few liberal judges in Texas. She'd been a flower child back in the sixties and once had the crap beaten out of her by police during a peaceful sit-in at a congressman's office to protest the Vietnam War. She'd applied to law school shortly afterward and made it her life's mission to prevent further abuses of authority. Unfortunately, what she mostly accomplished was preventing us government employees from effectively doing our jobs.

Despite all of that, I had an odd sort of respect for the Bulldog, as she was known in local legal circles. She had her principles and she stuck to them. Kinda like the hot sun was making my jacket stick to my sweaty back as we walked from our office to the federal courthouse in the late May heat.

We waited in a short line at security, most of those ahead of us attorneys in business suits. When it was our turn, we placed our briefcases on the conveyer belt to be X-rayed and walked through the metal detectors. After showing our credentials to the deputies manning the security checkpoint, we were allowed to retain our weapons.

We rode the elevator up to Judge Trumbull's courtroom in silence. A lot rested on the decision Judge Trumbull would make today. Maybe the whole investigation.

When the bailiff called our case, identifying it only as "*Commissioner* versus *John Doe*," Ross approached the bench. "We have a highly sensitive matter, Your Honor. May we discuss this in your chambers, off the record?"

"What the hell." Judge Trumbull's jowls jiggled as she spoke. "Time for a potty break anyway." She banged her gavel, announced a short recess, and stepped down from the bench.

We followed her through a door and into a small hallway that led to her private office and bathroom. She waved for us to go into her chambers to the left, while she ducked into the restroom to the right.

Judge Trumbull's office was surprisingly feminine. Her desk chair and the set of wing chairs were a soft mauve. Her cherrywood antique desk sported a white marble top shot through with streaks of amber. A pink-and-white orchid sat on one corner of her desk, a small brass lamp with a Tiffany-style shade on the other corner. Her oversized floor-to-ceiling bookshelves supported an assortment of legal texts, knick-knacks, and photos of the judge with various bigwigs, including one of her in much younger days with then-President Jimmy Carter. Billowy curtains graced the plate-glass windows behind her desk, framing the view of the old-fashioned Dallas County courthouse and clock tower sitting catty-corner across the street from the relatively modern federal courthouse.

Ross gestured for Eddie and me to take the wing chairs, while he opted to stand near the bookshelves and peruse the judge's collection of law primers.

A few minutes later, Judge Trumbull sailed into the room, her unzipped robe flowing behind her like a superhero's cape. Underneath her robe, she wore Birkenstocks, faded blue jeans, and a T-shirt commemorating a chili cook-off held in 1997. "Have to practically get undressed to pee," she said, removing her robe and hanging it on a brass coat tree just inside the door to her office.

She flopped into her desk chair and folded her hands across her ample belly. "So? What do y'all have that's so gosh-darn secret?"

Ross deferred to Eddie, and my partner explained who we were after and why. He explained about Nick Pratt and how Mendoza had bought off Pratt in the previous investigation.

He explained that Carson McNabb was approached by Double Down after betting on the horses at a track owned by Ameri-Mex and that the Pokornys were approached by the loan shark after applying for a loan at North Dallas Credit Union which, again, was owned by AmeriMex. He noted that all three of the credit card fraud victims held accounts at NDCU. He informed her about the robbery and beatings at the Pokornys' bakery, about the earlier suspicious home fire and the deadly, unsolved carjacking that claimed two of Mendoza's former employees. He wrapped things up by telling her about our interview with Andrew Sheffield's wife, the information Andrew had shared before he was murdered, the questionable cash transactions run through the ARS Financial account.

Her expression was less than impressed. "All you've got is a bunch of people flapping their gums about this Mendoza character? No hard evidence? Nothing to tie all of this together?"

Ross opened his briefcase and handed her copies of the affidavits and other documentation we'd collected from McNabb and the identify theft victims.

Trumbull thumbed through the documents, reading over the parts I'd highlighted, ending with the pharmacy receipt. "What's LovLub?"

I felt a warm blush rush to my face, but my cheeks burning was far preferable to the burning LovLub had caused in my nether regions. "It's . . . um . . . a sexual enhancement product."

She harrumphed. "For $27.99 it better produce some pretty fantastic results."

I had some personal knowledge in that regard but wasn't particularly inclined to share, on or off the record.

The judge looked at me and Eddie, stuck out her hand, and waggled her fingers. "Show me what else you got."

Eddie and I looked at each other. We'd given her all we had.

Eddie cleared his throat. "Mendoza's left a trail of at least three bodies," Eddie said, merely putting a new spin on the information he'd already provided. "Maybe more."

"You mean you *suspect* he's left the bodies," Judge Trumbull corrected him. "He's never been convicted of any of these crimes, right?"

Not only had he not been convicted, Mendoza had never even been arrested.

This wasn't going well.

Ross interjected now, stepping closer to her desk. "Marcos Mendoza hasn't been convicted, Your Honor, but as we all know the lack of a criminal record doesn't mean someone is innocent."

"That may be true," Judge Trumbull said, looking up at him. "But the lack of a record means I don't have hard facts to back up my decision. A wiretap is a major invasion of someone's privacy. If I start granting wiretaps willy-nilly the ACLU will be crawling up my butt."

Now there's a visual.

"If I'm going to allow a wiretap," she continued. "It's gotta be clear it's the right thing to do. All you've got is secondhand, hearsay testimony from the widow, which has already been investigated by a number of law enforcement agencies who couldn't put a case together. You haven't been able to prove any direct link between this Mendoza and the murders or show me any hard proof that Mendoza is involved in any illegal activity. Everything you've shown me is circumstantial at best."

"That's exactly the problem, Your Honor." Eddie leaned forward in his chair, his jaw flexing with barely contained frustration, his speech slow and controlled. "Without a wiretap, we may never be able to get anything but circumstantial evidence and Mendoza will go on to kill someone else. If we're going to nab this guy, we need a wiretap to do it."

Judge Trumbull spun her chair around to look out the window behind her. After a moment, she stood and waved us over. Once we were standing next to her, she pointed down to a small area of grass outside the Dallas County courthouse.

"See that spot down there?" she said. "That's the very place where, back in 1972, me and three dozen other women burned our bras as an act of support for the Equal Rights Amendment." She looked down at her sizable bustline, which had now all but merged with her waistline. "In retrospect, burning my bra might not have been the smartest decision." She turned to face us now. "Civil rights is what this country is all about. It's why the pilgrims came over on the *Niña,* the *Pinta,* and the *Santa Maria.*"

Actually, the pilgrims came over on the *Mayflower.* Christopher Columbus was the one with the three ships. But none of us was stupid enough to correct her on that. No matter how erroneous the reference, she'd made her point.

"You don't have probable cause," she said. "Fact is, from a legal standpoint, you don't have diddly squat. Sorry, gang. Can't do it."

Before I could stop myself, the words flew out of my mouth. "But I promised my boss and Lauren Sheffield we'd get Mendoza."

Judge Trumbull gave me the evil eye. "You should know better than to make those kinds of promises, young lady."

"Told you," Eddie said.

I turned *my* evil eye on him then.

Ross forced out a thank-you, and Eddie and I insincerely agreed.

"You get something new," Judge Trumbull called after us as we walked out of her chambers. "You're welcome to come back and try again."

We parted ways with Ross on the courthouse steps.

"Sorry, you two," he said.

"You did your best," I replied.

"Yeah," Eddie spat. "It's not your fault Trumbull's a bra-burning, bleeding-heart liberal—"

"I need a drink," I said, interrupting Eddie's rant.

"Not a bad idea. You want to join us, Ross?"

Ross begged off. "Got a brief to prepare. Maybe next time."

Eddie and I headed into one of the downtown bars. He ordered a Heineken and I ordered a frozen margarita plus a platter of nachos to share.

When the waiter brought our order, I took a deep drag on my margarita, steeling myself against the inevitable brain freeze. I powered through it and licked my finger, running it around the rim of the frosted mug to collect some of the large-grained salt.

"What the fuck do we do now?" Eddie said. "Short of catching Mendoza in the act, we'll never nail him."

"And we'll never catch him in the act," I said, licking the salt from my finger, "because he never does his own dirty work."

Eddie swallowed a large swig of beer. "He's got to slip up sometime, doesn't he?"

We sat in silence for a few minutes. Well, relative silence. There's no quiet way to eat a platter of crispy nachos.

Alcohol supposedly kills brain cells, but the tequila in my margarita seemed to open my mind instead. "I've got an idea."

"It better be a good one," Eddie said.

"The problem so far has been that we can't get close to Mendoza, right?"

"Right. And?"

"Suppose we get close to him."

"You mean infiltrate his operations? Like Nick Pratt did?"

I shook my head. "Not that close. Too risky. But maybe we'd learn something if we played spy on our own. Kept an eye on him ourselves. Monitored his comings and goings."

Eddie tossed back the remains of his beer. "What the hell. I'm in."

CHAPTER TWENTY-THREE

$\mathscr{S}$ecurity and Insecurity

Judge Trumbull had told us to come back if we obtained more evidence against Mendoza and that's exactly what Eddie and I hoped to do. Of course the only chance we had for collecting hard evidence against Mendoza at this point was to spy on the guy, hope he'd lead us to something incriminating. Not that we really expected to learn anything from watching Mendoza. He was far too smart to make any stupid moves. But it was the only thing left to try before throwing in the towel.

Eddie and I scarfed down the rest of our nachos, paid our bill, and hopped into his minivan. Given that it was after five, it was too late to snag a car from the Treasury's fleet or impound lot. We could've picked up a rental, but the extra time and expense involved didn't seem necessary given that we'd only be taking a preliminary look-see at potential stakeout spots.

"Let's hit Crescent Tower first," I said, noting the first of our two destinations.

Eddie turned out of downtown and in just minutes we arrived at the Crescent Tower complex. The property was a nineteen-story European-style mixed-use property situated just north of the downtown financial district and on the southern edge of the Turtle Creek neighborhood, adjacent to the Ritz-Carlton Hotel. Since the fiasco of Nick Pratt's earlier investigation, Marcos Mendoza had relocated both his residence and the headquarters of AmeriMex to the prestigious Crescent Tower. Mendoza now lived in one of the building's exclusive penthouses. AmeriMex maintained a small office on the building's ninth floor. Must be nice to have only a twenty-second vertical commute each morning. No worries about traffic or gridlock. The worst thing he might experience is a stubbed toe.

The enormous structure boasted the largest order of limestone since the construction of the Empire State Building. The light-gray stone exterior featured filigree trim and a dark slate roof. Intricate painted grillwork graced the balconies. The place was beautiful, one of Dallas's signature buildings.

A gorgeous façade hiding a cold, murderous criminal.

I'd been to Crescent Tower once before, enjoying a fancy dinner at the private Crescent Club dining room on one of the higher floors of the office building. A client of Martin and McGee had invited me and the firm's managing partner to the club. We had provided the financial analysis to defend his company against an antitrust lawsuit and the meal was his way of saying thanks. He'd treated us to appetizers, dinner, wine, and dessert. The feast must have cost a fortune. But I'd worked overtime three months straight for the client. I'd earned it. Besides, the guy would get a tax deduction for the meal.

Eddie pulled into the underground parking garage. We circled past an assortment of late-model Mercedeses, Lexuses, and Infinitis, all in silver, white, or black, until finding an empty spot three levels down. Eddie's maroon minivan with the Mickey Mouse antenna ball stuck out like a sore thumb among the tastefully drab luxury automobiles.

We rode the elevator up to the lobby. Due to the late hour,

the lights in the open foyer had been dimmed. Eddie and I stepped out onto the pink-and-black granite floor, glancing around the space to familiarize ourselves with the layout. The building's lower floors housed a variety of upscale restaurants and high-end retail shops, all of which were closed and locked up now, though they were sure to be bustling during business hours tomorrow.

Eddie jerked his head toward the elevators. "Check out the team of rent-a-cops."

To the right of the elevator bank sat a wide console housing state-of-the-art security equipment monitored by no less than five security guards. The tenants and residents of the building would expect no less. A quick glance around the lobby confirmed eight visible security cameras, with probably more hidden in less obvious locations. The tight security likely explained Mendoza's decision to relocate here.

With eyes everywhere, there was no way we could check out AmeriMex's office space tonight. Not that we'd planned to. We were here simply to get a feel for the place, seek out spots from which we might be able to keep a clandestine eye on Mendoza's comings and goings. Still, at some point, I wanted to take a peek at his digs.

To keep the security guards from becoming suspicious, we headed across the lobby to the twenty-four-hour copy center, the one still-bright spot in the lobby. The large machines whirred, giving off heat and the acrid smell of hot ink. Two young men were hard at work, copying and collating.

I pulled a legal pad out of my briefcase and jotted down a quick memo for the staff of a fictitious business I created on the spot. I handed the memo to the young female clerk, asking her to make five copies of the Tardie Incorporated dress code policy. Nose-hair trimming was mandatory, but underwear was now optional.

"Tardie?" Eddie asked after the clerk stepped away.

"That's what our name would be if we were a celebrity couple."

Eddie shook his head. "You watch too much *Access Hollywood*."

While the clerk made the copies, Eddie and I glanced around the lobby. Several restaurants had atrium seating from which a stakeout could be run. What's more, it would be fairly easy to keep an eye on the elevator bank from the windows of various shops around the lobby. The random clusters of cushy chairs and coffee tables situated around the lobby could be used, too.

Memos in hand, we made our way back across the lobby, giving a friendly wave to the security guards when a couple of them glanced our way. *Yep, we belong here. Not casing the joint. Nope. Not us.*

Back in his van, Eddie loosened his tie and pulled it from the neck of his white dress shirt. Always the helpful side-kick, I took it from him, folded it neatly, and set it on the backseat on top of his briefcase.

"Where to now?" he asked.

I used my phone to access the Internet, found the address for NDCU, then plugged the address into the GPS feature. Per the map, NDCU was located in the Lake Highlands neighborhood northeast of downtown. "Take Central north."

Eddie took a right out of the parking lot and headed onto the nearly deserted street. In minutes, we were heading north on Interstate 75, the same general route we'd taken to the Pokornys' bakery. The late-spring drizzle kicked in again, halos forming around the streetlights, Eddie's tires kicking up a steady stream of rain, the white noise nearly lulling me to sleep.

We made a quick stop for coffee and I opted for another skinny no-whip latte. My thigh muscles still ached from my recent workout. I wasn't sure the whipped cream and cara-mel drizzle were worth an extra half hour on the treadmill. Then I took a sip of the plain latte and decided maybe they were.

A half hour later, we pulled into the parking lot of a florist across the street from the credit union. Eddie stopped his van and we looked across the road at NDCU. The building was a single-story structure composed of rust-orange brick. A stand of silver maples lined the left side of the building. On the right were two drive-up lanes, one marked for commercial customers, the other for personal banking. A piece of modern art that resembled a twisted strand of DNA stood to the left of the glass double doors on the front of the building. To the right was an ATM machine built into the brick wall. The building's front windows were dark, the lot empty, the floodlights reflecting off the wet asphalt. The security cameras mounted on each corner of the building made slow sweeps side to side across the building's parking lot, but I wasn't concerned. We were parked well out of camera range.

Eddie cocked his head as he stared at the building. "Looks like any other small bank."

"Mm-hm."

But clearly there was more to NDCU than met the eye. Someone there had accessed NDCU's client records and obtained personal information about Ernestine Griggs and the other fraud victims, information later used to produce counterfeit credit cards. Did Mendoza have one of the employees under his thumb, doing his dirty work? Or had he accessed the files himself and passed the information on to an outsider?

Given what Lauren Sheffield had shared with us, it seemed that Mendoza tried to keep his hands out of the cookie jar, instead recruiting others to handle the questionable activities. But it also seemed that Mendoza had taken to outsourcing the dirty work, keeping it away from the companies he managed, increasing the distance between himself and his minions. Probably a smart idea. Given that two AmeriMex employees had already died under suspicious circumstances, any more questionable deaths at such a small company would raise eyebrows.

I downed the last of my latte, cringing as the now-cold grounds from the bottom of the cup hit my tongue. I glanced over at the bank again.

What the hell?

One of the security cameras was raised high on its mount and appeared to be aimed in our direction. I watched it for a few seconds, waiting for it to continue its slow sweep over the premises, but it didn't seem to be moving. I put a hand on Eddie's arm. "Is that camera pointed at us?"

Eddie turned to me, then followed my gaze, squinting through the drizzle-dappled windshield and dim light. The camera moved then, swinging slowly to the right. "Nah. It's moving. See?"

I hesitated a moment. Had the camera been aimed at us? Or had the rain-dotted windshield and darkness played tricks on my mind? "Must've been my imagination."

But was it?

CHAPTER TWENTY-FOUR

 Spy

Darina Pokorny called to let us know she'd been released from the hospital. After several days in a coma Jakub had come to, though the doctors were keeping him heavily sedated to help him deal with the pain of seventeen—*my God! Seventeen!*—broken bones. But his prognosis was surprisingly good.

My prayers had been answered. Well, one of them at least. I was still waiting for the thugs to be apprehended. Of course, that might be up to me to accomplish.

Darina informed us that she and Jakub planned to move back to Czechoslovakia as soon as he was able to travel. Who could blame them? The American dream had turned into a nightmare for them. I wished her well and told her to stay in touch. I'd let her know when we nailed the people responsible for hiring the goons who'd beaten them.

Because we would nail Mendoza and his minions.

We simply had to. For Darina, for Jakub, and for their children. For Mendoza's other victims and their families.

And for every other unsuspecting person out there who might get sucked into Mendoza's vortex of violence.

So here I was on Friday morning, in a women's clothing store in the lobby of Crescent Tower, pretending to be window-shopping when, in fact, I was watching out the window, casing the lobby, hoping to catch a glimpse of Marcos Mendoza. I slowly made my way toward the jewelry display near the cash register. A pink beaded bracelet caught my eye. The piece had Lu written all over it. She'd insisted no one buy presents for the upcoming party to celebrate her hundred-million-dollar mile-stone, but the fact that she'd insisted no less than a dozen times negated her words.

"I'll take this one." I held the bracelet out to the sales clerk.

"Great choice," she chirped. "Would you like this gift wrapped?"

Eddie sat in a rented dark blue Ford Taurus on a nearby street, watching the exit of the underground garage, waiting to see if Mendoza left the tower. Given that Mendoza both lived and worked in this building, it could be days before he ventured out. The place was a virtual world unto itself, a microcosm housing a barber, a dry cleaner, even a full service spa. Groceries and meals could be delivered. About the only thing Mendoza couldn't do in this building was get a prostate exam.

I wasn't a patient person under the best of circumstances, and these undercover stakeouts had stretched my patience very thin, especially after the debacle at the post office. Time for more aggressive action.

I strode purposefully across the lobby, punched the up-arrow button, and rode the elevator up with two men, both in business suits, both carrying briefcases, both talking on their cell phones. One of the men got off on the fourth floor, the other got off on the seventh. Alone now. Just me and my telltale heart, pulsing so rapidly in my chest I feared it might explode.

The bell dinged as the elevator reached the ninth floor and the doors slid open. I stepped out onto the floor, eyeing the sign indicating suites 901 to 905 were to the left with suites

906 to 910 to the right. AmeriMex was in 901. I turned left and made my way down the hall, past a law office, a commercial property management company, and a collection agency. The doors and front walls to each of these offices were glass, giving the offices an open, welcoming feel and allowing a view into their reception areas.

AmeriMex was located at the end of the hallway, next to the door leading to the stairwell. Judging from the proximity of the stairs and the adjacent business, AmeriMex's headquarters were small, probably no more than twelve hundred square feet. But that was all I could tell. Unfortunately, there was nothing to see other than a solid wood door with AMERIMEX printed on it in three-inch gold lettering. The front walls were solid. No glass.

Damn.

Eddie and I had searched the IRS payroll filings on AmeriMex employees. Once we'd composed a list, we searched the Net to obtain information about the personnel, as well as photos of each of them. In addition to Mendoza, AmeriMex employed five staff, including three accountants, an administrative assistant, and one part-time human resources administrator. Typical for a holding company that simply owned other businesses and provided no products or services itself.

Was one or more of them in on Mendoza's schemes?

None of the information we'd collected about the workers was remarkable. Their reported salaries were fair but not unusually generous. The cars, houses, and other assets they owned were typical for workers in their salary ranges. No inexplicable Maseratis or vacation homes in Maui. Other than one of the accountants who'd served a short probation years ago for driving under the influence, none of the staff had a criminal record. If I had to hazard a guess, I'd say they were all legit. Still, I had hoped to get a glimpse into the office, maybe try to visually identify some of the employees, see if they looked as innocent in person as they seemed from our background check.

I'd reached the end of the hall and my only options were to enter the stairwell or turn around. I chose the latter. I slowly made my way down the hall in the other direction, pretending to be searching for an office.

A woman in a bright green T-shirt and white cotton shorts stepped off the elevator ahead of me, rolling a plastic tank behind her. She made her way up the hallway, stopping to water several potted plants placed here and there along the way, sticking the nozzle into the base of the plants to avoid spattering the liquid. She pulled a feather duster from a loop on the dolly and dusted the plant, then used a spray bottle to spritz the leaves.

I wondered if working as a professional plant mainte-nance person was as monotonous as watching a bank of el-evators all day. I'd been bored out of my skull.

I walked to the far end of the hallway, noting a security camera at this end of the hall. The camera was mounted over the door leading to another stairwell and aimed down the hallway where it could take in all of the space. No sense hanging around in the corridor where I might garner suspi-cion from the security guards monitoring the camera feeds I made my way back to the elevator and rode it down to the lobby.

Back to window-shopping.

I stepped into a different store this time, an upscale wom-en's clothing boutique. I slid several blouses aside on a rack, pretending to be looking through them.

A blond-bobbed saleswoman wearing one of the store's offerings, a silvery trapeze dress, wandered over. "Can I help you find something?"

I offered a cordial smile. "Just looking." *Out the window.* I didn't have two hundred bucks to spend on a blouse and, even if I did, I wouldn't. I liked the thrill of a bargain hunt.

She looked me up and down appraisingly, a smile tug-ging at her lips. She must have recognized my suit as Donna Karan. What she didn't know was that I'd bought it at Nei-man's Last Call. Underneath the paisley scarf tied around my neck was a hideous black slash, an accident with a permanent marker. But, heck, for seventy percent off its original price I was happy to take the damaged goods off their hands.

"Take your time," she said, virtually salivating at the commission she thought I might generate.

Darn. I was on her radar now. Time to find another spot from which to keep an eye on the lobby elevators.

I sorted through a few more racks, then slipped out the door when another customer came in and sidetracked the clerk. A few minutes later, I was seated at one of the restaurants on a mock patio surrounded by a wrought-iron railing that extended into the lobby. I sipped an iced tea and slowly picked at a spinach and walnut salad while pretending to read the *Dallas Morning News*.

An elevator dinged across the way and the doors slid open.

Oh my God.

There he was. The murderer himself. Complete with his expensive suit and dark widow's peak.

Mendoza stepped out of the elevator and strode across the lobby, heading toward the shops on the far side. My heart pumped fast in my chest, sending my blood rushing through my veins. I held the newspaper higher, watching him over the top of the business pages.

Mendoza stepped up to the glass counter of a small jewelry store. He spoke briefly to the salesman standing behind the case, then removed his watch from his wrist and handed it to the clerk.

Replacing his battery. Such an everyday activity for such an evil man. The incongruity made him seem more real, more vulnerable than the legend in my mind. He might be a cold-blooded killer, but he was still mere flesh and bone, right? He could be taken down.

He *would* be taken down.

He paid the clerk and made his way back across the lobby, raising a hand in greeting to the security guards at their desk. An elevator opened directly in front of him as if on command and he stepped in without breaking pace. Okay, maybe that seemed like the stuff of legend.

The doors slid closed and the man was gone.

I drove over to Brett's for dinner. He showed me the plaque he'd received in Florida, as well as photographs from the banquet. Judging from the pictures, he was the only award recipient without a significant other in attendance.

Guilt weighed on me. I'd let him down. Ugh.

Brett fired up the propane-powered barbecue grill on his patio and grilled thick salmon steaks with a lemon butter sauce, which he served with rice pilaf and a sweet moscato wine. I'd brought dessert. Double Stuff Oreos. Only the best for my man.

We ate on the couch, bypassing *Keeping Up with the Kardashians* on E! in favor of *Keeping Up Appearances* on the BBC America channel. What exactly was a Kardashian anyway? And why would anyone want to keep up with one?

After Hyacinth Bucket had wrapped up her silly antics on the TV screen, Brett retrieved the remote and changed the channel to the local ten o'clock news. I stood to go. It was a work night after all. But Brett took my arm and pulled me back to the couch. "You have to stay and watch," he said. "One of the reporters is doing a piece on Habitat for Humanity. She came to the house today when I was planting some bushes and interviewed me."

"Brett, that's fantastic!" I focused on the screen, eager to see my man on TV.

The intro provided sound bites of the news to come, including a nine-second shot of a cheesecake reporter named Trish LeGrande who was known for both her catch phrase— *"Tune in for Trish at Ten!"*—and her oversized breasts. Trish wore a tight, low-cut pink T-shirt that barely contained her cleavage, along with skimpy khaki shorts and a leather tool belt slung low across her curvaceous hips. Her long butterscotch-colored hair was pulled up into a sassy ponytail.

She held her microphone in front of full, pink-frosted lips. "I'm Trish LeGrande," she said in a soft and airy voice, as if she was having trouble catching her breath. Perhaps her enormous breasts were crushing her lungs. "I'm here at a house being built by volunteers for Habitat for Humanity. Stay tuned to learn more about the charity and this great group of volunteers." The camera panned farther out, showing Brett standing beside Trish with a shovel in his hand. Trish turned to him. "I see you've got some big equipment, Mr. Ellington. I hope you'll show me what you can do with it."

Big equipment? If that didn't call for a jeer I didn't know what did. "You've got to be kidding me."

Brett cut a disapproving look my way. "Don't be so critical."

I rolled my eyes. "Come on, Brett. I'm all for the happy-feel-good crap, but did the station have to hire someone like that for the job?"

"Someone like what?"

So he was gonna play dumb, huh? I leaned into Brett, rubbing my hand in circles on his shoulder, mimicking Trish's girlie voice. "Someone with such *big equipment.*"

Brett cocked his head. "She's not the bimbo she comes off to be. She earned a master's degree in journalism from Texas Christian University."

The same school that gave the news world Bob Schieffer. Not bad. *Wait a minute.* "How do you know where she went to school?"

Brett shrugged. "We talked while the camera crew was setting up. She asked about my business. Said she'd plug it in the piece. It was only polite to show an interest in her job in return."

Hmm. Not sure I liked that. The idea of another woman engaging in chitchat and tit-for-tat with my man put a burr in my britches. Especially when she had so much tit to exchange for his tat.

The full piece came on halfway through the news broadcast and ran only thirty seconds, but it was long enough for Brett to mention he worked as a landscape architect for Wakefield Designs. Not only was he helping a great cause, but the exposure for his business couldn't hurt, either. Dallas was a huge television market. More than two and a half million people lived in the area.

When the piece ended, Brett retrieved the remote, clicked off the TV, and led me to his bedroom.

Move aside, burr, there was someone else who wanted to get in my britches now. And I'd let him. Maybe it would make up for me missing the awards banquet. Then again, maybe I was afraid that if I didn't maintain my claim to Brett's equipment, someone else might try to get her hands on it.

Perhaps a butterscotch-blond bimbo.

Saturday afternoon I sat in a mid-sized rental car on a side street, keeping an eye on the Crescent Tower parking garage while Eddie attended his daughters' soccer games. Thanks to Eddie's mad coaching skills, their team had made the playoffs. Good news for Eddie, bad news for me. Their championship status meant I'd be stuck babysitting Mendoza all day.

In the early afternoon, Christina swung by with a homemade batch of virgin peach Bellinis in an oversized thermos. The perfect thing to keep us cool as we sat in the rental car, watching the garage exit.

Christina glanced around the sedan. "This is a step up from the toy car you were using to spy on the post office."

"Yeah, but the upgrade's coming out of my pocket." The government would pay three grand for a hammer, but provide a comfortable car for an undercover agent when a tiny compact would do? Forget it.

The day was warm, and a layer of sweat formed on our skin even with the windows down and a small, battery-operated fan blowing on us.

I updated Christina on the Mendoza case. It only took two words. "No progress."

She played with her straw, stirring her rapidly melting drink. "He sure is one slippery sucker."

"You can say that again. Got any suggestions?"

"Wish I did." She was quiet for a moment before turning

in the passenger seat to face me. "We can't eliminate all of the bad guys, you know. Occasionally there's one that gets away. Sucks, but that's just the way it is."

I knew what she said was true. Still, I couldn't accept that Mendoza might get away with his crimes. "This guy hasn't just ripped off the government, he's killed people. And he'll likely kill again." I chewed the inside of my cheek. Hell, I'd just about chewed through it.

Christina reached across the console and put her hand over mine in a rare showing of seriousness. "If that happens, Tara, you won't be to blame. You can't take on that kind of responsibility or guilt. What Mendoza chooses to do is his fault and his alone."

Somehow, that didn't make me feel any better.

CHAPTER TWENTY-FIVE

A Sighting

Eddie and I continued our surveillance. We did our best to vary our looks, dressing professionally some days, wearing more casual clothes on others. I styled my hair differently each day, going from bun, to loose and curly, to flat-ironed.

On Monday, I wore the maternity set again, this time stuffing a beach ball from the dollar store into the front pouch of the pants. Might as well make the most of my disguise, huh?

I waddled into the lobby of Crescent Tower, making my way to the coffee bar, my round belly eliciting friendly smiles from several of those who passed. But when I ordered a skinny no-whip latte, the woman behind me in line wasn't so friendly.

"Caffeine isn't good for the baby," she said, "and you really should be drinking whole milk when you're pregnant."

"The drink's for a coworker," I lied. I didn't want to debate prenatal care with this woman, especially when my baby-to-be was merely an inflated piece of plastic.

I waited until she left, then slid into a booth to watch the elevators. Unfortunately, the beach ball sprung a leak as I sat. Even more unfortunately, the leak was on the side of the ball pressed up against my skin.

A sound like a whoopee cushion came from my belly. *Blaaat.*

A man at the table next to me glanced up. "My wife had the same problem when she was pregnant."

A hot blush rushed to my cheeks. *Blaaat.* I stood up, spotted the closest ladies' room, and bolted toward the door.

Two short *blaaats* blasted as I slammed the door on the stall. I reached into my pants and removed the quickly deflating ball. Sheez. A buck doesn't go very far these days.

I wadded up bath tissue and used that to fill up the pants pouch, tossing the ball into the trash bin as I left. My new baby was slightly lumpy and lopsided, but at least this one wasn't flatulent.

The only glimpse I caught of Mendoza on Monday was when he came down late in the day to pick up his dry cleaning. Needless to say, I gained no helpful information from watching him pay for the shirts he'd had laundered and pressed. Maybe I should speak to the dry cleaner's staff, find out if they'd ever had to wash bloodstains out of his clothing or found a weapon in his pocket, maybe a handwritten confession drafted in a moment of weakness.

That was too much to hope for, wasn't it?

On Tuesday, I borrowed a portable watering tank from Brett, wore a bright green T-shirt and white shorts, and pretended to be from the plant service. I paid particular attention to the plants on the ninth floor, but there was no action at AmeriMex other than a guy from the sandwich shop downstairs delivering lunch to the office. The club sandwich looked particularly appetizing but the chicken salad appeared a bit soggy.

On Wednesday, I was doing duty outside when Mendoza made his first venture out of the building. Eddie texted me from inside Crescent Tower at two-thirty in the afternoon. *The rat is out of the cage.*

I started the engine on my rental sedan, suffering a momentary panic when it seemed to have trouble catching. All that sitting in the car and listening to my newest Carrie Underwood CD had run down the battery. Fortunately, the motor eventually kicked in.

I slid my sunglasses on, a pair of tortoiseshell Brighton knockoffs, and looked off to my left as Mendoza drove by on my right in his silver Mercedes E550. The car cost around sixty grand. Luxurious, sure, but still well within range for his purported salary. Not surprising. His lifestyle in the U.S. was controlled, measured, while the home he owned in Mexico was a fully staffed mansion. There had to be a lot of unreported, untaxed money being sent to his wife and daughter in Monterrey.

Once Mendoza had a block lead on me, I eased myself into traffic to follow him. He turned west on McKinney, then south on Olive Street, heading toward downtown. Where was he going? A meeting, maybe?

He took another turn onto St. Paul, then drove a short distance on Young Street before putting on his right blinker to turn into a parking lot. I continued past, watching in my rearview mirror to ensure he actually made the turn he'd signaled.

I made the block and drove back around, stopping to look up at the building. The Dallas Central Library. What was Mendoza doing here? Checking out *The Seven Habits of Highly Successful Tax Evaders*?

I called Eddie from my car and told him where I was.

"The library?" He sounded puzzled.

"Yep."

"What do you think he's doing there?"

"Not a clue."

Just in case Mendoza had noticed my car following him earlier, Eddie drove over in the rented Taurus to take my place. I headed back to Crescent Tower, parking three blocks behind the building, waiting for further instructions from my partner.

Fifteen minutes later, Eddie rang me back. "He's come out of the library, but he doesn't have any books or anything."

"Strange."

We weren't sure what to make of that. What had he been doing in the library if not checking out a book or video?

"Could he have returned an item he'd checked out earlier?" Eddie asked.

"It's possible." I hadn't seen Mendoza walk into the building so I couldn't be sure whether he'd carried something inside.

"Maybe he was doing research," Eddie suggested.

"I don't think so. He wasn't inside the library long enough to get much done." Besides, it's not like the guy had a term paper due on *Great Expectations.* "Think he was meeting up with someone?"

"Maybe."

But who?

And why?

Despite my protests, my mother insisted on making the three-hour drive from Nacogdoches to Dallas on Thursday. She claimed she simply needed a change of scenery, but I knew better. We hadn't seen each other in weeks and she'd grown suspicious when I'd repeatedly put off her visit. She was worried about my safety and had traveled all this way to check on me, assure herself I was alive and well.

Who could blame her? It had only been a few weeks since Michael Gryder had put a bullet in Eddie's skull and then tried to obliterate me. If not for Brett's bravery, neither I nor my partner would be alive today. Never again would I let myself run out of bullets. I'd since bought five extra clips for my Glock. Overkill, probably, but overkill was better than ending up six feet under.

I had no choice but to take my mother along on my stakeout. To be honest, I was glad for the company. I'd spent way too much time alone lately.

Mom and I spent some time browsing in the shops in the Crescent Tower lobby, then had lunch at a French bakery. I opted for a hummus and olive sandwich on sun-dried tomato bread. Mom ordered a traditional Reuben. We claimed a table near the front of the restaurant where we'd have an open view of the lobby.

Mom smiled at me across the table. "Playing spy is fun."

I smiled back. "We'll have to make bring-your-mother-to-work day an annual event." Especially if she'd bring me another full tin of her homemade pecan pralines.

Window-shopping with my mother was indeed fun, but this investigation had become anything but. My stomach felt tight and I could only nibble at my sandwich. I wondered if Eddie and I would ever get Mendoza. The longer this case dragged on, the less likely it seemed. After all the time we'd put in, we still had nothing to show for our efforts. We'd caught only brief glimpses of the man. How could we snag someone so covert, so elusive?

I kept a close eye on the elevators as I ate. My mother kept a close eye on me.

She set her half-eaten sandwich down on her plate and reached across the table to take my hand. "You've hardly touched your food, honey. I hate to see you so stressed out."

I wasn't merely stressed out. I was stressed in, up, down, backward, and sideways. "We can't seem to catch this guy doing anything wrong. It's incredibly frustrating. Sometimes I think we'll never get him."

She gave my hand a squeeze. "Well, Tara, the biggest part of getting something is wanting it bad enough." Mom was full of wisdom.

I, on the other hand, was full of piss and vinegar. "You've got a saying for every occasion. As if all it takes is the right adage to solve any problem." I rolled my eyes, a flashback to my petulant teen days.

"I'll have none of your backtalk, young lady." Mom pointed a finger at me, just as she'd done so many times when I was younger. Only this time the gesture was in jest. I was too old to be affected by a scolding from my mother and she darn well knew it. But I'd never be too old to appreciate the comfort she brought by coming to see me.

"You may scoff at my sayings, but they're tried and true."

Mom took a sip of her iced tea. "So, tell me. How much do you want this guy?"

"Bad."

"Just bad?"

"So bad I can taste it." I wanted to say *fucking bad*, but the mere thought of cussing in front of my mother brought another taste to my mouth, the taste of Ivory soap. Mom had washed my mouth out with the stuff each time I'd let a curse slip as a child.

"You want him bad enough," she said, "I have no doubt you'll get him." She picked up her sandwich again. "By the way, your dad sent his Winchester hunting rifle with me. Said you wanted to borrow it for target practice."

"Great. Thanks."

She eyed me one last time. "You realize I'm not buying that 'target practice' bullshit."

Now it was my turn to point at her. "Don't make me get the Ivory soap."

CHAPTER TWENTY-SIX

Checking Things Out

Friday morning, I wore a baseball cap and ponytail, figuring the look went hand in hand with the sporty tracksuit I had on. I carried a cardboard box with me, hoping to look like a courier.

I was on my way across the lobby, heading toward the pastry shop, when Mendoza turned around from the shop himself, a small white bakery bag in one hand, his keys in the other.

He wore an understated, perfectly tailored brown suit, a crisp white shirt peeking out from under the jacket, and a slate-blue silk tie. He looked awfully classy for such an awful guy. He'd already slipped on his sunglasses, so I couldn't see his eyes, but his widow's peak seemed extra dark and pointed today.

I hoped he didn't notice the brief hesitation in my step when I spotted him. My heart pounded in my chest, throbbing in my ears. There he was. The tax cheat. The murderer. *El Diablo* himself.

I continued across the lobby and he crossed a mere ten feet in front of me. I swear I smelled death on the man but perhaps it was only his cologne. *Eau de Muerte.* I glanced back to see him stop at the elevators and jab the down button, summoning a car to take him to the parking garage.

I made my way into the ladies' room. Since there were two other women in there with me who could eavesdrop on a phone conversation, I texted Eddie instead. *Passed M in lobby. He's heading out.*

Eddie called me shortly thereafter and informed me that Mendoza was heading north on Central Expressway, apparently making his way to the credit union. I left Crescent Tower then. No point in risking any AmeriMex employees seeing me loitering unnecessarily.

I wasn't sure what to do, so I decided to head over to the central library where Mendoza had gone earlier in the week. Eddie had stuck around for half an hour after Mendoza had left, watching the other patrons leaving the library, trying to see if any looked like someone Mendoza might have met with. Most had been college kids or mothers with school-age children, though there'd been a couple of men in the bunch. Given that none of them carried a sign reading I JUST MET WITH MARCOS MENDOZA, it was impossible to know whether the men were associated with our target.

I parked in the library's lot, walked inside, and looked around. If Mendoza hadn't been meeting someone on Wednesday, what else could he have been doing here?

Maybe the library had a pay phone he'd come to use. I passed the long bank of computers situated near the reference librarian's desk and walked the floors, searching. The only pay phone was in the basement by the restrooms. I made my way down the hall and looked at the phone, picking up the receiver and putting it to my ear. No dial tone. Of course not. You didn't get a dial tone until you put money in.

Had Mendoza made a call from this phone? If Mendoza used pay phones to make the private calls we'd hoped to intercept, a wiretap on his personal and business lines would prove pointless even if we somehow convinced Judge Trumbull to grant us a wiretap. It was highly unlikely Trumbull would include public pay phones in a wiretap order. She'd never allow us to listen in on the phone calls of random, unsuspecting people. Never mind the fact that, to make the call, they would have to be standing in a public building in an open hallway where any passerby could hear the conversation, or at least one side of it, anyway.

Damn. Mendoza really was an expert at making himself untouchable.

I made my way back upstairs and looked around. I loved to read, but I hadn't been to a library in years. I liked to read in the bathtub and librarians tend to get miffed when you return books with steam-wrinkled pages.

The library had a huge nonfiction area. Story time was going on in the children's area, a dozen slack-jawed tykes staring up at the children's librarian as she read an oversized picture book, something about a young giraffe being teased by the others in the herd for his extra-long neck. When a drought ensued and all the lower foliage had been eaten, the giraffe with the extra-long neck was the only one able to reach the higher-up leaves, which he shared with the others, who now saw the value in his aberrant neck length. The story was barely veiled plagiarism, Rudolph the red-nosed reindeer on the African savannah rather than the North Pole. How about some creativity here?

I wound my way through the fiction section, ending up in the audio books. Since I'd be on this stakeout for the foreseeable future, I checked out a couple of mystery novels on CD, as well as one historical romance featuring a tightly corseted young duchess and a hot stablehand taking a roll in the hay and breaking the class barrier. Good for them.

The librarian handed me an application for a library card. I filled it out and handed it back to her. She input my personal data into her computer, then aimed a handheld scanner at the bar code on the back of my newly issued card and on the plastic case for each of the audio books.

Bleep. Bleep-bleep-bleep.

She slid the books across the table to me. "Here you go. They're due back three weeks from today."

I wondered if we'd have Mendoza busted by then.

I feared we wouldn't.

Not unless something unexpected happened.

Since I hadn't heard back from Eddie, I went home to change into a business suit and headed back to the office to work on some of my other cases. Though my other investigations were far more routine and certainly less risky, they were also far less interesting. Run-of-the-mill tax fraud cases, including a bar owner who'd siphoned off thousands of untaxed dollars from his corporation and a woman running an eBay sales business who didn't bother to report over eighty grand in sales.

The woman's attorney had been trying to convince me to settle the case for pennies on the dollar. No way, Jose. Not only did we have solid evidence against her, but the cheating twit had plenty of assets to pay her tax bill. She'd just rather spend the money on herself.

I called the attorney, reminded him that interest and penalties continued to accrue, and threatened that if his client didn't pay up in the next week I'd arrest her. No more Miss Nice Girl. I was tired of tax cheats, sick of people who thought they were above the law.

Eddie called me that evening at six-fifteen. "Mendoza's leaving the credit union now, heading south."

That meant he might be coming back home. "I'll get into position."

I parked down a side street, waiting to see if Mendoza returned to Crescent Tower. A few minutes later, he drove down the street ahead of me and into the underground garage. There was probably no point in going into the lobby. By this time, he was likely going home for the night. Still, something told me to give it a few minutes. Instinct kicking in again.

Sure enough, after about forty-five minutes, Mendoza reemerged from the parking garage. I followed him as he took Maple to McKinney. He turned again on Pearl, then made his way to I-45 south. I followed him when he took the I-30 exit, keeping a safe distance and staying two lanes over, where he was less likely to notice me. After a short drive, he exited and entered the older but upscale Lakewood neighborhood. He slowed and I had to take a brief detour through a gas station parking lot to prevent myself from inadvertently gaining on him.

Finally, he pulled into the branch library on Worth Street. Was he was making a call from a pay phone here? This branch was small and there was no way to follow him into the building without being spotted. Instead, I parked behind a taco stand across the street, breathing in the smells of simmering beans, garlic, and onions.

When Mendoza emerged from his car, I noticed he'd changed into a pair of jeans and a knit polo shirt, looking more like a typical middle-aged father than a killer.

But I knew better.

While I waited, I listened to the steamy, romantic audio book. The duke was a prig, ignoring his wife and instead gallivanting around town, gambling and boozing with friends. The lonely duchess was riding the stablehand like a bronc when Mendoza emerged from the library.

I checked the clock on the dashboard. Mendoza had spent an hour inside. Couldn't the guy take another minute so I could find out if the stablehand satisfied the duchess better than the indifferent duke?

I phoned Eddie. "Elvis has left the building."

"Do I hear moaning?"

I jabbed the button to eject the audio book. "I have no idea what you're talking about."

Given that it was now the middle of the evening, we assumed Mendoza was heading back to Crescent Tower. Eddie said he'd drive over there to check. Meanwhile, I went into the library and looked around for a pay phone, but found none.

When I asked an older, bearded man at the front desk where the pay phone was, an amused smile played at his lips.

"We don't have a pay phone anymore," he teased good-naturedly, giving me a wink. "These days most people have a magical, newfangled device called a cell phone."

Except for criminals who don't want their calls traced.

I thanked the man and stepped away from the desk. No pay phone here. That meant Mendoza had come to the library for another reason. But what?

This library was a single story with the requisite children, teen, and adult areas, though all were much smaller than those at the central library. At the front was a series of long, narrow tables on which eight computers were placed side by side. All but one were in use. Off to the right were glassed-in study rooms, a group of high school kids in one of them laughing and eating Skittles they'd smuggled into the library against its strict no-drinks, no-food policy. Didn't look like they'd be getting much studying done tonight. Then again, it was Friday evening, a night intended for fun.

Not for me, though. Thanks to that bastard Mendoza, I was still at work.

When I arrived home, I gave my neglected cats some much-needed attention. Annie purred softly and rubbed her head against my chin as I cuddled her to my chest. Henry normally acted as if I didn't exist, but tonight he stretched a paw toward me when I reached up to his place on top of the armoire.

I scratched behind his ears. "Hey, boy."

He replied with a yawn and rolled over onto his back.

Brett was having dinner with some of the other Habitat for Humanity volunteers tonight and, as much as I'd have loved to see him, the thought of a quiet evening to myself, soaking in the tub, sounded wonderful. I'd hardly been home lately and I missed it. Besides, Eddie and I planned to double-team Mendoza tomorrow. We figured the weekend might mean a change in his routine given that AmeriMex would be closed. Maybe, just maybe, he'd finally do something to move this case along. I hoped so. I'd far exceeded my shopping budget at the shops in Crescent Tower.

After I bathed, I gave myself a manicure with shiny red polish. Not as fancy as a professional job, but I hadn't had time to stop for a manicure. The red polish would match the dress I planned to wear to Lu's party tomorrow night. I was glad to have something fun to look forward to, something to take my mind off Marcos Mendoza and the trail of body parts he'd left across the state of Texas, even if only for an evening.

CHAPTER TWENTY-SEVEN

$\mathscr{D}$iscovered

The following morning, I headed to Crescent Tower around nine, stopping on the way for a skinny no-whip latte. I'd lost another pound. Just a few more to go and I'd be back to my precaramel-latte weight. Still, I'd have to hold my breath in order to zip the dress I planned to wear to Lu's party tonight.

I pulled into the garage, circling slowly down the dimly lit levels, passing a security guard on a golf cart and giving him a friendly smile and wave. Mendoza's car was in his reserved spot. The guy was probably still in bed. Eddie's rented Taurus was parked on one of the lower levels. No doubt his girls had wakened him early, as usual. The car was empty.

I parked a few spots away and sent Eddie a text message from my phone. *Where R U?*

Twenty seconds later the reply came. *Restaurant in lobby. Gr8 waffles.*

Mmm. It had been a long time since I'd had a waffle. I rode the elevator up and stepped into the foyer. Compared to the hustle and bustle of the workweek, the place appeared nearly deserted today. Other than the print shop, the only business open was a small café. Eddie sat at one of the restaurant's tables in the atrium, where he'd have a clear view of the elevators. A stack of waffles covered in syrup, strawberries, and whipped cream graced the plate in front of him.

Dang, they looked good. But I'd fought hard to get rid of the caramel latte weight. No sense undoing all that work, right?

I planned to check in with Eddie so we could formulate a game plan for the day, but my plans quickly changed when Marcos Mendoza stepped off the elevator to my right. My heart lurched in my chest and my vision blurred as if I were looking through a kaleidoscope.

Get it together, I told myself. I paused and looked down, pretending to be searching for something in my purse. I watched from under my bangs to see if Mendoza would glance my way. He didn't, thank goodness. But, oddly and alarmingly, he seemed to be aiming straight for Eddie.

Holy shit.

Was he on to us? Probably it was nothing more than coincidence. Most likely, Mendoza was simply going for breakfast at the same restaurant where Eddie was seated. Maybe he wanted one of those great waffles, too.

Still, the guy was a cold-blooded killer. Best to stay close.

Eddie held the weekend edition of the *Wall Street Journal* in front of him, not looking up as Mendoza approached. He did a good job of pretending to be unaware of Mendoza's presence. Mendoza walked up to the railing and stopped next to Eddie's table.

There was no doubt now.

Mendoza had not come down for the waffles.

The man said nothing, his posture menacing as he towered over Eddie. Eddie eventually looked up. It was the only natural thing someone could do.

I was too far away to hear what Mendoza said to Eddie, but the exact words didn't really matter. The mere fact that he'd addressed Eddie directly said it all.

Eddie's cover was blown.

The case was blown.

All these weeks of work, all the sacrifices, all for naught. Shit. Shit! SHIT!

I ducked into the copy center and engaged the young male clerk in a pointless conversation about paper colors, all the while keeping a surreptitious eye on Eddie and Mendoza twenty yards away. Whatever Mendoza said, he kept it short. He turned abruptly, not glancing back as he made his way to the elevator bank.

Eddie wore a panicked expression, his posture more tense than I'd ever seen it. Everything in me wanted to run to him, to ask what Mendoza had said, but I had to remain cool. Just because Eddie's cover was blown didn't necessarily mean mine was, did it?

Eddie pulled out his wallet, placed some bills on the table, and rushed across the lobby to the elevator. I had no idea what to do, but figured it was best to keep up pretenses, at least until I knew for certain I'd been outed. "Do y'all do wedding invitations?"

The clerk nodded and handed me a heavy, oversized sample book to thumb through. I pulled the book aside so that he could help another customer, and flipped slowly through the papers, not really seeing anything.

When I believed enough time had passed that I could leave the building without necessarily being associated with Eddie, I took the stairs down to the garage, hopped into my rental car, and got the hell out of there.

Once I was a couple of blocks away, I pulled over and called Eddie. "What the hell?"

"Fuck!" he screamed, so loud I had to hold my phone away from my ear.

"What did Mendoza say?"

"He thanked me for keeping an eye on things at the credit union and Crescent Tower. Then he—" Eddie choked up.

"What, Eddie?" I cried. "What did he say?"

"He said to give his best to Sandra and the twins."

I felt light-headed, as if the world had dropped away under me. "Oh God! Oh Eddie! Oh . . . God!"

Mendoza's words were a threat. Veiled, sure, but clearly intended to let Eddie know he wouldn't be messed with. Mendoza had never met Eddie's wife or girls. The only way he'd know about them was if he'd done some checking up himself.

Or if Nick Pratt had told him.

Had Nick ratted us out to Mendoza? Or had I been right about that security camera at the credit union? Had it picked up Eddie's license plate? We'd been stupid—Stupid! Stupid! Stupid!—to drive over there in a personal vehicle.

I had no idea what to think. "What now, Eddie?"

"I'm getting home as fast as I can. Call Lu for me."

"Damn it all!" Lu shrieked through the phone after I told her what happened. "How in the Sam hell did this happen?"

How did this happen? Either Nick had served Eddie and me up to Mendoza on a silver platter or Eddie and I had fucked up, that's how. We never should have driven one of our personal vehicles on the investigation.

I didn't want to lie to my boss, but I didn't want to get Eddie in trouble, either. If I told the Lobo he'd driven his minivan to the credit union, she'd have a shit fit. Taking his car had been a major lapse in judgment, one brought on by exhaustion and the pressure to move this case along as quickly as possible.

I also didn't want to tell her about the communications I'd received from Nick. How could I tell her now, when I'd kept the information to myself for weeks? She might question my actions. Besides, what did it matter at this point? The case was blown.

"I . . . I don't know how this happened, Lu."

"Well, this a fine mess," she spat.

A fine mess thanks to Marcos Mendoza, the fucker. Pardon my language, but the guy had me more angry than ever. He'd threatened my partner.

He'd made this personal.

He shouldn't have done that.

Especially when I was now in possession of an unregistered hunting rifle.

CHAPTER TWENTY-EIGHT

Party Pooper

That afternoon, I stopped by the salon to have my hairdresser style my hair into a sleek updo. I normally enjoyed chitchatting with her, sharing secrets and gossip, but today I was in no mood for small talk. I was too upset, too devastated. To be more precise, I felt ashamed. George Burton and the Lobo had trusted me and Eddie to bring down Marcos Mendoza, and we hadn't been able to deliver.

My stylist brushed out my locks, pulling one section up in a plastic clip. She put her hands on my shoulders and tilted her head, eyeing me in the mirror. "You okay, Tara?"

I shook my head. "Not really."

"Anything you want to talk about?"

Yes! But I couldn't. "Wish I could."

"Confidential government stuff, huh?"

"Yeah."

She held up a sharp pair of shears, running a finger up and down the razor-sharp five-inch blade. "You need to take someone out," she said. "I'd be glad to help."

"Thanks. I'll keep that in mind." I forced a smile. "I'm sure everything will eventually work out fine."

As if. Nothing was fine. And nothing would be fine until Mendoza was behind bars.

Or dead.

Once again, I found myself seriously considering the head shot with a hunting rifle.

After what happened that morning, I was hardly in the mood for merriment. But since the other special agents had no idea what had taken place, I couldn't very well skip Lu's party. Heck, the celebration had been my idea. I had no choice but to play along as if nothing unusual had occurred, as if Eddie and I hadn't suffered a major career setback, an enormous defeat.

Back at home, I dressed for Lu's party, slipping my red chenille dress over my head, reaching around the back to zip it up. I took a deep breath and stood on tiptoe, hoping to stretch myself as thin as possible. I managed to zip up the dress, but breathing would be difficult.

The dress was the one I'd bought to wear to Florida. I'd felt beautiful in it when I'd tried it on at the store, but when I looked in the mirror today all I saw were seams stretched to their limits and worry lines creasing my forehead.

Brett arrived promptly at six. When I opened the door, he stepped inside, looking me up and down. "You look gorgeous." He took both of my hands in his, placed a soft kiss on the back of each, then another on my lips.

He looked handsome in his dark gray suit. The black shirt he'd worn under it was a nice, unusual touch. He'd added a white tie, the effect both trendy and slightly retro.

I returned his kiss, forcing a perky demeanor. "You're not so bad yourself."

I grabbed my tiny black evening purse and the gift-wrapped bracelet I'd bought for Lu, and we headed out to Brett's car. On the drive to the country club, Brett was too busy chattering on about the great deal he'd negotiated on azalea bushes for the Habitat houses to notice how quiet and pensive I was.

Twenty minutes later, we pulled up to the main clubhouse. The valet helped me out of the car, Brett handed him the keys, and we made our way inside.

Viola was already there, henpecking the club's catering staff, counting the appetizers on the trays to make sure they hadn't shorted us a single stuffed mushroom.

She glanced over at me as I walked in. Her wrinkled face seemed pinched, her smile strained, her usually perky curls droopy. Did she know about Eddie, that Mendoza had threatened him?

Even though Lu had sworn me and Eddie to secrecy about our investigation, it wouldn't have surprised me if Lu had shared the information with Viola. Even if the Lobo hadn't volunteered the information, Viola could probably have figured things out on her own. Not much got past her.

The double doors that led from the kitchen into the clubhouse swung slowly open and one of the kitchen employees backed into the room rolling a cart bearing an enormous mermaid ice sculpture.

"Wow." Brett tilted his head as he took in the frozen display. "That's . . ."

I looked up at him. "Is 'incredibly tacky' the term you're looking for?"

Brett pointed a finger at me. "That's it."

The sculpture had been a point of contention among the members of the party planning committee. Some called it art, others called it ridiculous. I'd been among the ridiculous faction. We'd lost out.

But the mermaid was the least of my concerns at the moment. I couldn't imagine what Eddie was going through, fearing not only for his own life, but even more so for the lives of his wife and young children. Surely he was suffering the same sense of failure I felt, kicking himself for driving his minivan to the credit union.

We should've gotten a rental. No matter how tired and

stressed we were, we should've followed procedure. I felt an urge to flog myself. Where's a whip when you need one?

Then again, it could have been Nick who'd sold us out. I wished the guy would call again so I could talk to him, figure out what the hell was going on.

I placed my gift bag on the side table near the door and surveyed the room. Colorful helium balloons with "100" printed on them floated above each table. They'd probably been intended for a centenarian's birthday party, but they worked just as well for celebrating Lu reaching the hundred-million-dollar mark. I'd ordered them from an online party supply outfit, along with napkins printed to resemble dollar bills and chocolate coins wrapped in gold foil.

Among the first to arrive at the party was Josh. He was dressed in his standard work clothes, khaki pants and a blue button-down, sleeves rolled up to just below the elbow. Sheez. Way to make the party feel special. Then again, the guy was known for his technical skills, not his social graces. He was alone. No date.

Josh eyed the buffet table, noting the covers had not yet been removed from the chafing dishes. "What? No food yet? I'm starving."

I directed him to a side table where crudités and a creamy spinach dip had been arranged on a shiny silver platter.

Several other couples wandered in, including Christina and Ajay. Since Christina and I had worked together to bust the drug-dealing, tax-cheating ice cream man, it earned her an invitation to the party, plus one of course. Although the case hadn't brought in oodles of money, it had nonetheless brought the Lobo closer to her hundred-million-dollar goal.

Christina looked beautiful, as always, in a high-necked lavender sleeveless top and matching palazzo pants. Ajay sported a bright blue blazer with matching bow tie over a white dress shirt and black pants, looking like a game show host. Only he could pull that look off.

Brett and Ajay did that half-hug shoulder-pat maneuver that men do. "Hey, Ajay."

"Dude," Ajay said, eyeing me over Brett's shoulder with a

cocky grin. This was the first time Ajay had seen me and Brett together since the LovLub fiasco.

I narrowed my eyes at the doc, giving him a look that said *If you know what's good for you, you'll keep your mouth shut.*

Brett gave Christina a hug next.

"Haven't seen Eddie and his wife," Brett noted, his gaze traveling around the room, searching for my partner.

Uh-oh. "Um . . . something came up. A . . . family emergency."

"Oh." Brett looked taken aback. "Is it serious?"

Eddie and his family running for their lives? Yeah, I'd call that serious.

Before I could respond, Ajay interrupted. "What the . . . ?" He stared at the entrance behind me, his mouth gaping.

I turned to see the Lobo standing in the doorway wrapped in a half-dozen yards of gold lamé that formed a long flowing dress and cape. Her gold platform shoes sported ribbons that laced in a crisscross pattern up her meaty calves. She wore her usual false eyelashes with even more blue eye shadow and orange lipstick than usual. Her strawberry-blond hair had been teased and coiffed into a series of distinct spikes atop her head. She looked like a cross between Cleopatra and the Heat Miser.

"That's my boss," I informed Ajay.

Lu made her way over to us. A discreet, knowing look passed between the two of us before she forced a cheerful, orange-lipstick-rimmed smile on the group. She nodded at Brett. "Good to see you again."

"Congratulations," Brett said. "A hundred million dollars is a lot of money to collect."

"Thank you," Lu said. "I couldn't have done it without my talented group of agents."

Lu's remark was like a knife in my gut. I was talented, sure. But apparently not talented enough to take down Marcos Mendoza.

The Lobo had met Christina several weeks ago at my internal affairs hearing on my first firearm discharge.

Fortunately, the hearings officers had deemed my use of my gun justified and I'd been allowed to keep my job.

Lu greeted Christina. "Nice to see you again, too." She turned to Ajay next. "Who do we have here?"

After I'd introduced Lu to Ajay and we'd engaged in several minutes of small talk, she excused herself to mingle with the rest of the crowd. Brett, Christina, Ajay, and I took places in line for the buffet, loading our plates with food as we made our way down the table. When we reached the mermaid ice sculpture, Ajay cut his eyes to her frozen breasts. A drop of water dripped from one of her nipples onto the bed of cocktail shrimp below. "If I lick her, do you think my tongue would stick?"

Christina gave Ajay a playful shove. "Behave, you perpetually horny man."

"It's not my fault," Ajay said. "I blame it on all the curry my mother forced me to eat as a child."

When we reached the end of the line, I looked around the room for a table with four available chairs. There was only one. Josh's. In fact, he was the only person seated there. Not surprising, yet a part of me felt sorry for him. Surely he had to get lonely on occasion.

I led the way over to the table, introducing everyone as we took seats. The others dug into the delicious food, but I had no appetite. Without Eddie here, the party felt incomplete. He'd been with the IRS for years, worked his ass off, brought in hundreds of thousands of dollars for Uncle Sam. He deserved to be here enjoying this celebration, dammit. But thanks to Mendoza, Eddie was missing all the fun.

As soon as I could, I snuck away from Brett's side and found Lu chatting with some of the administrative staff near the dessert table. She held a small plate bearing a slice of raspberry cheesecake, but she'd only picked at it. Not like Lu at all. I chatted briefly with the group.

"I'm going out for a smoke." Lu set her plate aside, her eyes seeking mine and issuing a silent invitation to join her on the patio.

I followed, trailing her out the door and onto the terrace.

A few couples had wandered outside to enjoy their drinks and dessert in the mild evening weather. As soon as we were out of earshot, Lu turned to me, flicking her lighter and holding the flame to the end of a cigarette. She took a long, deep puff then shot the acrid smoke out through her nose. "Eddie and his family have been moved to a safe house with round-the-clock protection."

Taking no chances. Good. But if I knew Eddie, and I did, he'd go nuts being cooped up. So would his active girls. Sandra, no doubt, would be worried to death.

"About the investigation, Lu—"

She pointed her cigarette at me. "There is no investigation, Tara. Not anymore." She took another deep drag. When she spoke again, her voice was resigned, disappointed, but firm. "This case is over. Now. Stop whatever you're doing. I've already lost two of my best agents to that bastard. I'm not about to lose another."

Stop the investigation? We'd spent weeks on this case with nothing to show for it and now Eddie'd be out of commission indefinitely. Still, I didn't want to admit defeat. Failure was not an option, at least not an option I wanted to accept.

I couldn't stomach the thought that Lu had trusted me with such an important case and I'd let her down. And not only Lu, but the Pokornys and Lauren Sheffield, as well. Wait, had Lu just implied that I was one of her best agents?

"But Lu—"

"No buts, Tara. If you and Eddie couldn't get this guy, no one can. Besides, if something happened to one of you, George Burton would have my ass. He gave me strict orders to stop the case."

"What if he hadn't, Lu? What if it were up to you?"

She took another pull on her cigarette and narrowed her eyes at me, assessing me through the fringe of her false lashes. "There's no point in discussing what-ifs. I'm in charge of the Dallas office but Burton is in charge of the national operation. What he says goes. This case is officially closed."

"But I don't think I've been compromised." Mendoza hadn't acknowledged me when I'd passed him in the lobby this morning and there'd been no flicker of recognition. "There's no need to call it off. I could continue on my own."

She flicked the ashes from the end of her cigarette. "If you and Eddie couldn't bring the guy down together, what makes you think you can do it by yourself?"

Tenacity?

Insanity?

Self-delusion?

I decided to go with, "Determination."

Lu snorted and threw her cigarette to the ground. She stomped the butt with her gold platform, crushing it with brute force as if it had personally offended her. She shot me a pointed look. "What part of 'this investigation is officially closed' do you not understand, Holloway?"

Now I was the one stomping my foot, like a petulant child who wouldn't take no for an answer.

Before I could open my mouth again, Lu sliced the air with a bladed hand, letting me know the discussion was over. "There's no more to say. Now get your skinny little butt inside and give me a toast, tell everyone how I'm the best goddamn boss you've ever had and it's a rare and special privilege to work for me."

I emitted a final huff of frustration and forced my words out through gritted teeth. "Yes, ma'am."

Inside, the waiters passed flutes of champagne. I returned to my table and stood to make the first toast, tapping a dessert spoon on my glass to gather the crowd's attention. I raised my glass high into the air. "A toast to Lu 'the Lobo' Lobozinski." I forced down the lump of discouragement that had formed in my throat. "A boss with smarts, gumption, and a unique sense of fashion."

A chorus of chuckles and "here-here" sounded around us, followed by the clink of stem glasses. Several other toasts followed, growing gradually more slurred and absurd as the champagne kicked in. One special agent toasted Lu's ability to apply lipstick while barking orders, while another toasted her for single-handedly keeping the beehive hairdo from fading into extinction.

The final toast was from Lu herself. She glanced around the room, raising her glass and nodding as her eyes met those of her staff. "To my team of special agents. The smartest, toughest, and best looking in federal law enforcement." She downed the last of her champagne and set her glass on the table. "Come on, you smart-asses. Let's dance!"

The overhead lights dimmed, the mirrored ball hanging from the ceiling began to spin, and the deejay cranked up the first song, a danceable disco number. Brett grabbed my hand and led me onto the dance floor. Ajay and Christina followed. Out of the corner of my eye, I saw the Lobo grab Josh by the collar and pull him out of his seat. His lips flapped in protest, but Lu wouldn't have it. She needed a dance partner and Josh needed to lighten up.

Lu was surprisingly agile for an older, large-bottomed woman. I'd given the deejay a playlist including a number of hits from the sixties and seventies, Lu's heyday. The woman could still hustle as well as she had forty years ago and her bump nearly sent Josh airborne.

As we danced, a heat began to build inside me, not solely due to the physical exertion. An image of Mendoza played in my mind, with his dark silver-streaked hair, his sharp widow's peak, his insincere yet sincerely evil smile. A fury as hot as molten lava flowed in my veins.

"How about some drinks?" I suggested to Brett when a song ended. If I drank enough, maybe I'd forget Mendoza had threatened the lives of my partner and his wife and children.

Once Brett and Ajay set off for the bar, I pulled Christina close and told her about Eddie.

Christina's brown eyes grew wide. "What now?"

What now? Now Mendoza could go about his business unhampered, living in luxury in his penthouse and Monterrey mansion while Eddie and his family would be forced to hide out God knows where for God knows how long. At the thought, the fury in me grew hotter than lava. Hell, hotter than the burn of the LovLub. "Lu says the case is officially closed."

Christina watched me for a moment, taking in my clenched jaw, the rabid resolve in my eyes. Her lips slowly curled into a sly smile. "And unofficially?"

I put one defiant hand on my hip and waved a red-tipped finger in the air. "It's on, bitch."

CHAPTER TWENTY-NINE

Going Rogue

Brett glanced my way several times on the drive home but said nothing. He pulled his Navigator into my driveway, shut off the engine, and issued a one-word command. "Spill."

I'd already defied direct orders by planning to continue the investigation, so what did it really matter at this point if I told Brett about the case?

So I told him.

Everything.

From the body parts in the Dumpsters, to the attack on the Pokornys, to the threats Mendoza had made to Eddie.

Brett's mouth hung open. When he finally spoke, his voice was enraged. "My God, Tara! I knew you were working on something big, but I had no idea it went this far."

"Look, Brett. If we don't get this guy now we never will. Maybe if I keep the pressure on, he'll screw up."

My heart pounded in my chest and I felt warm. Too warm. This was too much. Too much responsibility, too much stress.

I was just a rookie agent. How the hell was I supposed to bring this guy in alone?

But I couldn't let Mendoza get away with cheating the government, killing people, threatening my partner. If I didn't bring the criminal down, Eddie would spend the rest of his life looking over his shoulder, worrying about his wife and girls.

Angry, frustrated tears welled up in my eyes. "I have to bring Mendoza down if it's the last thing I do."

Brett emitted a mirthless chuckle. "Well, let's hope it's not the last thing you do." He gazed out into the dark of the night for a long moment before turning back to me. His voice was softer now. "This scares the hell out of me, Tara."

"It scares the hell out of me, too." I looked into his eyes. "But I really need your support right now, Brett."

He stared at me for a few moments, a mix of emotions playing across his face as he tried to come to terms with the situation, to figure out what to say. Finally, he pulled me to him, clenching me in a warm, strong embrace, and whispered in my ear. "Go get the bastard."

I knew encouraging me to do something so idiotic, so dangerous, was the last thing Brett truly wanted to do. But he'd set his feelings aside and given me exactly what he knew I needed.

I rewarded him in the bedroom that night and awoke surprisingly refreshed and with a newfound sense of purpose. That and a stiffy poking me in the back.

Brett nuzzled my neck. "How about a quickie before you head out?"

"I really should save my energy for the investigation," I teased. "And don't you have some more azaleas to plant today?"

Brett emitted a sad, resigned sigh.

He'd given me his support. But for the first time I wondered if I gave him what he needed from a relationship. I knew he was intrigued by my butt-kicking skills and respected my work with the Treasury Department, but I also realized I caused him a lot of worry and, with my crazy work schedule, wasn't able to be the consistent companion he wanted.

Was I being fair to him? Would he be better off dating someone with a less demanding, less risky job? Someone who could give him what he wanted, what he needed?

Oh hell no. I was not going there. At least not right now. I had enough on my plate at the moment without worrying about my relationship with Brett. Things were fine, right? Or at least fine enough. Once this case was over things would be different, better.

I turned to face him, taking in his rumpled T-shirt and mussed hair. The guy was freakin' adorable. Without further ado, I gave him the quickie he so deserved.

An hour later, Brett headed off for his charity work. I took a shower, threw on a pair of shorts and a tank top, and sat down at my kitchen table with a pen and notepad to formulate a plan for bringing Mendoza down single-handedly.

Now that I planned to go rogue, my options were wide open. I made a list of the alternatives, comparing the pros and cons.

Option #1: Head shot with hunting rifle. Pros—quick, easy, untraceable. Cons—jail time if caught.

Option #2: Place explosives in Mendoza's car. Pros— bastard gets his due. Cons—no clue how to rig explosives, potential for collateral damage, jail time if caught.

Option #3: Poison. Pros—slow, agonizing death. Cons—possibly traceable, difficult to administer, jail time if caught.

My eyes ran over the list. Had things really come to this? Was my only remaining option to kill the asshole?

I sighed. As much as Mendoza deserved to die, I simply couldn't bring myself to kill him. I couldn't risk spending the rest of my life in jail. And what would it say about my crime-solving skills if I had to resort to violence to resolve this case? I was a smart, resourceful girl. Somehow I'd find a way to take the evil bastard down without having to give in to my baser instincts.

But until I figured out what that way would be, I might as well continue the surveillance, see if I could learn anything new. I called Enterprise and had them bring me another rental car. I opted for a silver Mustang this time. If I were going to perform spy duty solo, at least I'd do it in style.

Off I went, now a rogue federal agent.

The house where Brett was working with the Habitat for Humanity crew was more or less on my way to Crescent Tower. Only a short time ago I'd vowed not to worry about my relationship with Brett, but apparently I wasn't too good at keeping my vows. He'd supported me and I should return the favor, right?

I stopped by a 7-Eleven and picked up an ice-cold sports drink for Brett, planning to run by the worksite and surprise him, show him how much I cared. I turned the Mustang onto the street and slowed, looking for the house. Brett's Navigator was parked in a driveway up ahead, the back hatch open, a flatbed trailer attached to the hitch. Large plastic bags of garden soil, compost, and cedar mulch were stacked on the trailer. A handful of people milled about, pulling bags from the stacks and carrying their loads to the flower beds.

Although a few of the workers were women, none of them had butterscotch hair or oversized breasts. Maybe Trish wasn't volunteering today. It wouldn't break my heart if she'd moved on to some other worthy cause. Maybe Trish had gone to save the baby seals up in Canada or the endangered dung beetle in South Africa. A girl can dream, can't she?

The newly completed house was modest but cheerful with fresh yellow paint and green shutters. Though the yard was bare dirt now, no doubt Brett and the rest of the volunteer crew would transform the plot into a virtual Eden by the end of the day.

I pulled to the curb behind an SUV parked across from the construction site. Just as I was about to hop out of the car, my cell phone bleeped. I checked the readout. Alicia. I hadn't talked to my best friend for days. Brett and my cats weren't the only ones I'd been neglecting. I hadn't been much of a BFF to Alicia lately, either.

I flipped my phone open. "Hey, Leesh."

"So you haven't fallen off the edge of the earth. I was beginning to wonder."

"Sorry I haven't returned your e-mails or texts. I've been slammed at work."

She launched into her usual updates, recounting the latest happenings at Martin and McGee, sharing the office gossip. As she chattered on, I kept an eye on the activity across the street.

Brett emerged from behind his SUV pushing a wheelbarrow full of smooth gray river rocks. He rolled the rocks over to the flower bed next to the front porch and upended the wheelbarrow, dumping the rocks into a pile next to the bed. He returned to his car, disappearing behind the open door.

When he emerged a second time, he once again had a full wheelbarrow. But this time it was filled with a bosomy butterscotch blonde.

Trish threw her head back and laughed, hanging on for dear life as Brett wheeled her into the yard, tilting the wheelbarrow from side to side, feigning as if he were going to dump Trish in the dirt.

My head felt light and my stomach hollow, as if I were on a roller coaster launching into a deep plunge. I didn't want to see this. I wish I hadn't seen this. Brett was flirting with another woman. Mere hours after doing the naked tango with me.

"Tara?" Alicia asked through the phone. "You still there?"

I closed my phone, ending the call. Alicia would think it had been dropped. I'd blame my carrier. Not the nicest thing to do, but I didn't trust myself to speak right then. I might burst into tears.

I started the car, shoved the stick into first gear, and floored it, leaving a cloud of dust and a trail of rubber in my wake.

I'd been wrong.

Brett didn't need me.

CHAPTER THIRTY

*W*hen a Stranger Calls

I pulled into the Crescent Tower garage, driving down to the reserved level to see if Mendoza's car was parked there.

Yep. There it was.

I circled back up, paying the attendant the minimum charge. I parked on a street a couple of blocks away. I rolled down the car's windows, letting in the already warm late-morning air. By the afternoon, the temp would be in the nineties and it would be miserable to be running a stakeout from a vehicle. But such is the price to be paid. At least I wasn't Eddie, having to hide out indefinitely. Poor guy.

I sat, watching Crescent Tower and thinking, trying to process what I'd seen earlier. So Brett had flirted with Trish. No big deal, right? They were just having some harmless fun. And he didn't appear to be the one who'd started it. He'd been innocently moving rocks when she'd jumped into his wheelbarrow. My reaction had been an overreaction. I should've taken him the drink. Or maybe I should have gone all *Glee* on Trish and tossed the drink in her face, told the bitch to back off from my man.

Shoulda, coulda, woulda. None of that mattered right now. Right now I had to focus on my work. After all, once I busted Mendoza, I could get things back on track with Brett.

The sooner the better.

I tried to put myself in Mendoza's place. My earlier assumption was that he'd be more discreet and careful now that he knew the IRS was after him again, which was probably correct. On the other hand, he might assume we'd back off temporarily to regroup. He might be forced to scramble, to make new arrangements for the operation of his illegal enterprises. If that were the case, I needed to keep the heat on.

As I sat there, waiting and watching, my cell phone bleeped again. I pulled it from the front pocket of my shorts and checked the screen. The call came from a phone number in the 713 area code, which covered a large part of Houston. I didn't know anyone in Houston. Could this be Nick Pratt again?

I pushed the accept button. "Hello?"

"Tara?" It was that same deep male voice with music in the background again.

"You're Nick Pratt, aren't you?"

"Don't hang up." His demand held undertones of desperation.

Instinctively, I sat up straighter in the seat. "Why shouldn't I hang up on the special agent who double-crossed his country and sold out to Marcos Mendoza?"

"Whoa, now," Nick said. "Don't believe everything you hear."

"It came from a reliable source."

"That doesn't make it true." The background noise grew louder, a bunch of young men whooping it up. "Look, Tara. I've got to make this quick. I'm in the men's room at Señor Frogs. I borrowed this phone from a college kid down here celebrating the end of the semester."

That explained the 713 area code.

"Then you better get to the point."

"All right. Here's the point. I can help you bring down Mendoza."

I snorted. "You're full of shit."

"Fuck, woman! Listen to me. I know what happened. That Mendoza threatened Eddie."

"You had something to do with that, didn't you? It wasn't enough for you to sell out, you sold out your former partner, too."

"I'd never do that!"

"Then how did Mendoza find out Eddie was after him?"

"Hell, I don't know," Nick said. "The guy's suspicious of everyone. He keeps a careful watch on what's going on around him."

Nick sounded sincere. But how could I be sure?

"Look," he said. "Come down here and talk to me, okay? If you meet me in person you'll realize I'm a good guy."

"Good guys don't sell out."

"I didn't sell out, Tara. I didn't have a choice. Mendoza was going to kill me if I didn't play along." Quickly, he told me how he'd landed a job with AmeriMex and used the position to spy on Mendoza. He'd begun to build a solid case when Mendoza asked him to work late one night. After hours, when the two were alone, Mendoza walked into Pratt's office. "From the look in his eye I knew he'd figured out who I was. But my weapon was in my briefcase and I couldn't get to it. Before he could say anything, I made him a proposition. I admitted I was an undercover agent but told him I was for sale. It was the only thing I could think of to save my life."

The story sounded plausible. Eddie had said Nick didn't seem like the kind of guy who'd sell out. And Nick had reported the bribe, paid taxes on it, even. That's not something a bad guy would do, right? Still, how could I be certain? "I'm not sure I'm buying this."

Nick emitted an angry growl. "Shit, Tara. You're even more stubborn than I was told. I want to bring Mendoza down as bad as you do. More, even. How do you think it feels for me being stuck down here, knowing everyone back there thinks I'm an asshole? Get yourself down here and let's talk. Noon tomorrow. Playa Las Perlas. "

I didn't know what to think. He sounded anxious, angry. If he were trying to lure me into a trap, he would've tried sweet-talking me instead, wouldn't he?

He must've taken my momentary silence as agreement, because he said, "Good. I'll be the guy in the tiger-striped bathing suit. When you see me approach, hold out a tube of sunscreen and ask me to put it on your back. That'll give us a minute to talk. I never know when I'm being watched, so we'll have to be careful. Tell no one you're coming down here."

Was I really going to do this? When I heard myself say, "Okay," I realized I was.

I don't know why I agreed. But there was something in his voice, something genuine, something sad, something that said I could trust him, that things weren't what they seemed.

My instincts again.

They'd never been wrong before.

Of course there could always be a first time.

"See you tomorrow at noon," he said.

"Wait. How did you find out about Eddie? And who told you I was stubborn?"

Before I could get my answer, *click,* he was gone.

CHAPTER THIRTY-ONE

A Quick Trip

Mendoza's car emerged from the garage an hour later as I sat contemplating the insanity of my plans to travel to Cancún later that evening. I'd phoned the airlines and made a reservation. The last-minute fare ran me eight hundred and seventy-nine bucks. ¡*Ay caramba!* This investigation would put me in bankruptcy.

Surely Mendoza would be extra attentive now, check his rearview mirror for a tail. Frankly, though, I figured the situation was a win-win for me. If he didn't realize I was following him, maybe I'd luck onto some useful information. If he did realize I was following him, maybe I'd foil his plans. Either way, neener-neener.

I started the car and eased away from the curb, willing an out-of-control eighteen-wheeler to slam into Mendoza's Mercedes, turning it into a fireball that would consume the devil within. *Case closed.*

No such luck.

I followed, making several lane changes, falling back and

keeping an eye on him from as far back as I could without losing him. Fortunately for me, Dallas has some of the worst drivers on the planet. Cars constantly crossed in front of me, creating enough obstacles that Mendoza might not notice me when he checked his mirrors.

Mendoza didn't drive far today, only a few blocks into downtown. He parked on a side street near the Magnolia Hotel, a famous landmark with a red neon Pegasus atop the building. He climbed out of his car, looking around him. He glanced my way, but didn't seem to give the Mustang a second thought. The sports car certainly wasn't the typical undercover vehicle. Apparently it had been a good choice.

Why would he be going to the hotel? The most likely scenario was that he was meeting someone there. If I'd been dressed better, I might have followed him in. But I'd stick out like a sore thumb if I went inside the posh hotel dressed like a slob.

I climbed out of the car, figuring I'd look less like a stalker if I weren't hiding out in a vehicle. Instead, I walked a block down and took a seat on a covered bench at a stop for the downtown trolley. An older woman in a hotel maid's uniform sat on the other end of the bench, singing softly to herself. I recognized the song, Patsy Cline's classic "Walkin' After Midnight." My granny had loved Patsy Cline, played her records on an old console record player in her living room when I was young.

I joined her in singing and the woman turned to me and smiled. When we finished the song, she asked, "You know 'She's Got You'?"

"Sure do."

We launched into song once again.

Mendoza spent only twenty minutes inside the hotel, looking around again when he walked out onto the sidewalk. He returned to his car and drove off.

I bade my duet partner adieu and sprinted back to the rental car. I hopped in and set off after Mendoza again. He made his way back to Crescent Tower and pulled into the garage.

Seemed doubtful he'd head out again anytime soon. I glanced at my watch. Might as well head on back home and pack for my trip to Mexico.

At eleven-thirty Monday morning, I tipped the cabana boy five bucks to set up a beach umbrella and chaise lounge for me. I spread my red-and-white-striped beach towel on the chair and plopped into it. A gentle breeze blew inward off the clear water, the waves gently lapping at the shore.

My God, Playa Las Perlas was beautiful. Shame this wasn't a pleasure trip, like one of those Corona beer commercials.

Despite the relaxing surroundings, my stomach twisted itself into a hard little ball. I'd called in sick that morning, claiming to have a stomach bug, an ailment about which even the nosy Viola wouldn't ask for details. Now I wasn't just defying orders, I was flat-out lying to my boss.

I didn't want to think of the penalties I'd face if I were caught. I'd lose my job, of course, but I could also face charges for abuse of authority, misuse of government property, obstruction of justice. For all I knew, working with Nick Pratt could constitute racketeering. I could serve prison time.

So what the hell was I doing here?

I slid my sunglasses on and pulled a paperback from my beach bag, opening it to a random page, using it as a prop so it wouldn't be obvious I was looking up and down the beach. I would've felt much more comfortable if I'd had a gun with me, but there hadn't been time to get the necessary clearances to bring it into Mexico and it was questionable whether the Mexican authorities would have approved it anyway.

Sitting on the beach, I felt exposed and vulnerable. Someone was on their way. But who? Was it really Nick Pratt? And, if so, was he truly on our side? Had I simply made myself a sitting duck for Mendoza's cohorts in Mexico? If the latter was the case, I hoped my parents wouldn't have a hard time getting my body back for burial.

Ugh. Nobody should have to have such ugly thoughts on such a pretty day in such a gorgeous place.

Over the top of page 73, I watched a young couple walk

by, hand in hand, their skin the warm, natural brown of locals. Farther down the beach, a young tourist boy tossed pieces of bread up to a flock of seagulls poised on the breeze. The birds dived down to catch the morsels, much to the delight of the squealing child.

"Drink?"

I nearly jumped out of both my seat and my skin when a waiter from the hotel stepped up to offer me refreshment.

"Margarita. Frozen, with salt." Might as well, huh? If I had been lured into a trap, maybe the alcohol would numb the pain when Mendoza's minions chopped me into little bits.

I checked my watch. Straight up noon, the scheduled time. I looked around while I waited for my drink. A tall man in long red swim trunks walked by, his sunburned skin nearly as bright as his suit. Another man in a baggy green suit moseyed by. A few more men puttered around the beach, but none wore tiger stripes.

I had no idea what Nick Pratt looked like. I'd checked online the day before but found no photos, no Facebook page. Not surprising since federal agents tended to lie low, but it would've been helpful if I had at least a clue. Was he tall? Short? Dark haired? Blond? Bigger than a breadbox?

The waiter returned with my margarita.

"*Gracias,*" I said. It was one of the few Spanish words I knew.

"You're welcome."

I gave the waiter a tip and took a sip of my drink. Looking out at the water, I kept my head straight but darted my eyes side to side, trying to see as much as possible out of my peripheral vision.

The kid down the beach had run out of bread and was now waving the empty plastic bag at the birds, who scolded him with screeching calls. The young couple had begun a game of Frisbee, laughing as the warm ocean breeze carried the disc inland much faster than either of them could run. An older barefooted woman in a wide-brimmed beach hat and rolled-up pants meandered along the water's edge, while two young women dressed in workout gear and carrying hand weights power-walked quickly by, their ponytails swinging behind them.

Still no man in a tiger-striped suit.

I'd been sitting there half an hour and had nearly finished my margarita when I spotted someone out in the waves, swimming toward shore. When the guy could reach the bottom, he stopped swimming and stood. From this distance, I couldn't tell much about him other than the fact that he had brown hair, slicked back with seawater.

I continued to look around the beach, occasionally glancing back at the man in the waves. His shoulders emerged as he made his way in and, *mmm,* what nice shoulders they were. Broad, tanned, muscular. Sure, I was in a serious relationship, but that didn't mean I couldn't enjoy the scenery, did it? Especially given Brett's recent flirting infraction. What's good for the gander . . .

The man continued toward the shore and a set of well-developed pecs broke the surface. *Nice.* Then two abs, four abs, yep, a whole six-pack. I put the straw to my lips and noisily slurped the dregs of my drink. When the man's muscular thighs emerged, framing a tiger-striped Speedo, I choked.

Holy.

Freakin'.

Guacamole.

The guy looked like Kurt Russell in his younger days, or Val Kilmer, who, coincidentally, had encountered his own problems with the IRS and had had to put his ranch on the market to pay delinquent taxes.

Lu had said Nick was a workhorse. But she hadn't mentioned he was a stallion. I'd like to think it was the flush of alcohol, but I knew the warm blush that rushed to my cheeks was a feminine reaction to Nick's raw masculinity.

He emerged from the water twenty feet away and turned to head up the beach. His tiger-striped suit left nothing to a girl's imagination. It looked like he'd packed an oversized potato in there. An extra-large, genuine grade-A russet that would win the blue ribbon, hands down, at the Idaho state fair.

I dug in my beach bag and felt around for my tube of sunscreen, readying myself to ask his assistance when he walked by. Nick approached, his eyes on the beach ahead of him. I held out my tube and called, "Excuse me? Would you mind putting some sunscreen on my back?"

He turned and looked my way. His eyes were a golden brown, the color of Southern Comfort, and caused the same warm burn inside me as the liquor. "Sure." He shook his head, drops of water glistening as they sailed through the air. Dryer now, his hair hung in a natural, shaggy fringe about his face, the ends tinged with blond, a sexy result of sun damage. He stepped over and took the tube from my outstretched hand.

I lowered my glasses and locked my gaze on his. Keeping my voice low, I asked, "Was the Speedo really necessary?"

"Didn't want you to worry that I might be packing a weapon."

My focus left his face, traveled to his crotch, then back up again. "I'm not so sure you aren't."

He gave me a crooked smile, revealing a slightly chipped bicuspid. A thick, short scar lined the top of his cheekbone below his left eye. He'd taken a right hook from someone. I wondered when and why. Somehow these flaws only made him seem more manly, enhanced his primal sex appeal.

He stepped behind me and I sat up on my chair. He knelt down in the sand, squeezed out a dollop of cream, and ran a warm, wet thumb across the top of my spine, sending a tingle down my backbone. His hands moved to the base of my neck and for a moment I wondered if this was it, if my instincts had been wrong, if he'd wrap his hands around my throat and try to choke me. I'd learned some evasive maneuvers in my special agent training but I'd never had to test them in the field. Still, if need be, I was ready.

"Here's how Mendoza operates," Nick said, his voice low, his warm breath feathering across the back of my neck. "He hires someone on the outside to keep his books for him off-site, usually someone running a solo accounting practice or working independently at a small firm. Some of them are willing pawns in his game, others are suckers who figure it out too late. All of the dirty money is run through that outside person, through their bank accounts."

Everything Nick said so far made perfect sense. The MO he'd described matched what Lauren Sheffield had told me about Mendoza's arrangement with her husband. My instincts had been right. I could trust this guy.

"Finding the puppet is the key. But it's not going to be easy. Mendoza's careful not to leave a trail. He uses untraceable cell phones, free e-mail services, public computers."

Public computers? A light bulb flashed on in my head. That's what Mendoza had been doing at the libraries. Using their public computers. Maybe at the hotel, too. Many hotels had courtesy computers in their lobbies for guests to print boarding passes, check their flight status or e-mail. "How can I track down the stooge?"

Nick had worked his way down to my lower back now, applying the cream in slow, sensual circles. If the guy hadn't become a federal agent, he'd have made one hell of a masseur.

"You're not going to like my suggestion, but it's the only thing I can think of."

"Lay it on me."

He lifted the strap of my bikini so he could spread the cream under it. His warm hand swept over my bare shoulder. "You need to get Josh involved."

Despite my attempt to remain professional, I felt my nipples tighten in response to Nick's touch. "Josh?" I glanced down at my traitorous nipples, willing them to remember they were involved in an exclusive relationship with Brett. "You're right. I don't like it."

"The days of paper trails are gone, Tara. Everything's electronic now. Josh has the best hi-tech skills in the office. He'll figure out a way to track down the information you need."

"But how can I ask him to help? The case is officially closed."

"Which is exactly why he'll agree. Josh was the last to be picked for every team in his life. He's an outcast, an outsider. But that's not who he wants to be. I invited him to join me for a beer once after work and he just about wet himself. He's like an insecure little puppy. He'll be thrilled you've asked him to be part of something secret."

Nick was probably right. On a recent case, Eddie and I had asked Josh to help us crack a computer password and he'd readily agreed to help, beaming with pride when we'd complimented him on his skills.

Nick motioned with his hand, directing me to lie flat on the chaise so he could slather sunscreen on the back of my legs. "Mendoza has an associate here in Mexico. Vicente Torres. You've probably heard of him. The two send buttloads of cash back and forth across the border. They're cheating both the IRS and the Mexican tax department. The Mexican government wants to put Torres out of business as bad as the U.S. government wants Mendoza. I've told the Mexican tax authorities everything I learned about Mendoza's operations. Some of the information could help them nail Torres, so in return the judge agreed to refuse the Department of Justice's extradition request. He knew I'd have no chance of defending myself back home. I would've ended up in jail."

For the past several weeks I'd thought Nick was a greedy chump. But, as I was learning, the guy was smart and savvy, a quick thinker, and, above all, a good guy.

A good guy who'd been forced into an untenable situation.

A good guy who needed my help.

A good guy whose warm hands were on my thighs making me have bad girl thoughts.

He'd worked his way down to my ankles and would have to leave soon lest anyone spying become suspicious of the amount of time he'd spent with me. "Get me back home, Tara. I miss my old life. I miss my family. I miss my dog." His voice cracked and he made a vain attempt to laugh off his emotional breakdown. "But most of all, I miss chili cheese fries and the electric slide."

I sat up in the chair and held out my hand for the sunscreen. "You had me at 'cheese.'"

He smiled softly and handed the tube back to me. "Never seen this brand of sunscreen before."

I looked down at the tube in my hand.

Shit.

The guy had just slathered me in LovLub.

CHAPTER THIRTY-TWO

Recruiting

Bright and early the next morning, I was back in Dallas, sitting at a coffee shop with the newspaper classifieds and a skinny no-whip latte in front of me. I was going to smuggle Nick back into the U.S. If you're going to go rogue, you might as well go all the way, right?

Problem was, I couldn't smuggle Nick out of Mexico in my BMW. The space behind the backseat that housed the retractable roof left a trunk far too small to conceal a grown man, especially one Nick's size. Thanks to George Burton's order to cease the Mendoza investigation, I couldn't borrow a car from the Treasury's impound lot. Because so many rental cars had disappeared south of the border, rental agreements prohibited driving the cars into Mexico. I couldn't risk driving a friend's or family member's car into Mexico for the same reason. I had no choice but to buy a car from a private party on my own dime.

I circled several of the ads. An eight-year-old Honda Accord for three grand. A ten-year-old Dodge Intrepid for two and a half. And a decade-old Chevy Silverado with "minor hail damage" for fifteen hundred. I decided to call on the Silverado first. I had a soft spot for Chevy pickups. Heck, I'd lost my virginity in the back of one. Besides, the way I was feeling, I might decide to make things easy on myself and simply run Mendoza over. I wasn't sure a Honda was up to the task, but I had no doubt a Silverado could splatter the prick from here to kingdom come. As the commercials say, "like a rock."

I spoke to the owner and made arrangements to take a look.

"Cash only," he said.

"Yeah, yeah," I replied.

The owner met me in the parking lot of a twenty-four-hour Wal-Mart. He was a scruffy, bowlegged cowboy, wearing scuffed boots and jeans with a telltale circle of Skoal chewing tobacco in the back pocket.

The owner looked me over, taking in my ratty tennis shoes, frayed denim shorts, and freebie T-shirt I'd received for donating blood at the annual Martin and McGee office blood drive last year. I'd purposely parked my BMW well out of sight, too. Didn't want this guy thinking I had a lot of money to spend. All part of my negotiation strategy.

While he checked me out, I walked around the dark green pickup, looking it over with just as much scrutiny. "You call this *minor hail damage*?" The hood looked as if Savion Glover had tap-danced his way across it. What's more, the windshield was cracked, the dashboard was split in several places, and the back bumper hung cockeyed, held on only by baling wire. But the tires were relatively new and the engine purred like a happy kitten. Plus, a large metal toolbox spanned the bed just behind the back window, the perfect place to secrete Dad's hunting rifle should I decide to take Mendoza out with a clean head shot.

"I'll go down to fourteen hundred," the man said, "but that's my final offer."

"I'll pay thirteen five." I crossed my arms over my chest. "And that's *my* final offer."

He stuck out his hand. "You got yourself a deal."

I gave him the cash, he gave me the title, and the deal was done.

After the man left, I went into the store and bought a wrench to remove the license plates. Didn't want to risk Mendoza tracing the truck if he realized I was watching him. Without plates, I ran the risk of being pulled over by local police or the DPS, but they'd let me go once I flashed my federal credentials.

I returned to the office early Tuesday afternoon. I lifted my chin by way of greeting and pretended to be speaking on my cell phone as I passed Viola's desk. Didn't want her quizzing me about my alleged sick day. I may have gone rogue, but I was still trying to keep my lies to a minimum. Hopefully Vi would think my pink skin was evidence of a lingering fever and not a sunburn. LovLub makes a poor sunscreen.

"I need to see all of the invoices," I said into my phone, ignoring Viola's persistent stare. "Send me the accounts receivable information, too." I turned the corner, out of her line of sight. All clear.

I stepped into my office, closing my door behind me. I dropped my phone into my purse, dropped my purse into the bottom drawer of my desk, and plunked myself into my wobbly chair. The vent rattled over my head as the air conditioner kicked on. I looked around my office then, almost as if seeing it for the first time.

My framed CPA license hung on the wall behind my desk next to the paper target from the firearms test I'd been given at the end of my special agent training. All six shots square in the center. A cheap bookcase standing on the side wall contained the five-volume set of the Internal Revenue Code, along with binders containing audit and investigation manuals. A stack of files sat on my desk next to an adding machine and a stapler that routinely jammed. A plastic cup full of number 2 pencils perched in the corner beside a framed photo of me and my family taken last Christmas, every one of us wearing Santa hats Mom had sewn herself.

This office wasn't much. But it was mine. And I could

lose it all in an instant if the Lobo realized I'd defied her orders and continued the Mendoza investigation.

What would I do if that happened? Assuming I could plead out and avoid jail time, would I return to Martin and McGee? Would the firm even be willing to take me back under those circumstances?

Years ago, I hadn't even known there was such a thing as a special agent for the Treasury Department. It wasn't until one of the agents came to Martin and McGee to seize the files I'd been working on that I realized the IRS had a criminal law enforcement division. I'd noticed the data in the client's records hadn't seemed kosher, had planned to discuss the matter with the partner in charge, but the IRS had beat us to the punch.

When I'd seen the gun holstered at the agent's waist, I'd driven the guy crazy, asking about his job. The job sounded exciting, each case different, posing a unique set of challenges. The agent traveled around the city rather than being trapped in his office day after day. How cool! I knew then it was what I wanted to do.

Being a special agent was more than just a job for me. Much more. I played a role in keeping things fair and just, making sure we collected as much as we could from those who owed it so that others didn't have to pay more than their fair share. I had a unique skill set. There weren't many people who had a mind for both accounting and weaponry. The job seemed tailor-made for me. I couldn't imagine doing anything else.

If I lost this job, I would lose a part of myself.

Nick Pratt must have felt the same way.

My resolve thus renewed, I picked up my cell and called Christina, giving her a quick rundown.

"You're going to be a *coyote*?" she asked, using the slang term for those who trafficked people into the country undocumented. "Have you gone loco?"

"Probably."

"You know how much trouble you could get into, right?"

"Yeah."

"And you're still going to do it?"

"Yeah." Crazy or not, it was the right thing to do. The end justified the means, right? Still, I didn't want to go alone. "Come with me. It's a long drive from Dallas to Mexico. I'll get bored without someone to talk to."

"Not to mention you're scared to death to do this alone."

Busted. "Well, yeah. There's that, too."

She hesitated, but only for a second. "Okay. I'm in. I know a great little jewelry place just across the border. They sell silver for next to nothing."

One down, one to go.

I made my way down the hall to Josh's office. He sat at his desk, sipping chocolate milk from a small carton. Chocolate milk? Seriously? This was the guy who would help me bring down a murderer? I rapped on the door frame. "Got a minute?"

He looked up. With his baby blue eyes, blond curls, and chocolate-milk mustache, he looked like a second grader. Hard to believe he was such a hotshot cyber sleuth. "I guess."

His baby blues narrowed in suspicion as I stepped inside and closed the door behind me.

I flopped down in one of his chairs. "I need your help, Josh."

The suspicion was replaced by an expression of smug self-satisfaction. "Oh my. Don't tell me the Annie Oakley of the IRS can't handle her job."

I ignored his sarcasm. "Not without you I can't."

"Let me guess. Your case needs computer skills rather than weapons skills."

"At least for now." Yep, still keeping that head shot in reserve.

"Who are you after?"

Could I trust this guy? I wasn't sure. The only thing I knew for certain was that I'd get no further without him. So I took a chance and laid it all on him, including Mendoza's threats to Eddie and his family, the details about Nick leaving the IRS, my recent contacts with the former agent. I crossed my fingers that Josh wouldn't refuse to help and rat me out.

But Nick was right. Josh virtually squealed with delight when I asked him to join in on my unauthorized operation. "I'll do it!"

That had been easy. Almost *too* easy. Had he been the one Nick had stayed in contact with? "You understand we'll be in deep shit if anyone finds out we continued this investigation against orders? We'd lose our jobs and possibly serve prison time."

"I know," Josh said. "But if we bring Mendoza down we'll be heroes."

Aha! Josh, the little squirt, wanted to be a big man, a hero. Probably to overcome some childhood playground trauma. But whatever his reasons, he was willing to help me out and accept the risks that went with it. I'd owe him. Big-time.

His blue eyes glittered eagerly. "When can we start?"

"No time like the present." I waved him after me. "Let's go."

CHAPTER THIRTY-THREE

Vamos a la Biblioteca

Two hours later, Josh and I rode in my hail-dented truck, following Marcos Mendoza. Josh had put on a pair of dark sunglasses, pulled up his collar, and slunk down low in his seat, a poor man's Magnum, P.I.

After a few turns on the surface streets, Mendoza pulled onto Harry Hines, one of the larger thoroughfares. Was he heading to the Dallas Love Field airport? I thought so until he passed the airport's entrance on Mockingbird and continued on. After ten minutes of driving, he turned right onto Gilford, once again pulling into a branch library.

"The library," I said. "Just as expected."

Josh bounced in his seat like a kid going to a carnival.

I climbed out of the car and followed Mendoza inside. When we'd swung by my house to pick up the truck, I'd changed into clothes that looked the least like an IRS agent as possible. A pair of dollar store flip-flops. Ripped jeans. A red tank top with my bra strap showing. I'd pulled my hair back into two short pigtails on either side of my head. I looked like a college kid. Okay, maybe a college kid who'd spent a few semesters partying and was a little behind the ball.

While Josh waited in the truck, I followed Mendoza into the building. He seemed to be familiar with the layout, taking a left through a set of low bookshelves. I headed straight into the magazine section and picked up a copy of *Southern Living,* turning to an article featuring a bed-and-breakfast in Fredericksburg, Texas, a popular weekend antiquing spot.

I watched Mendoza through a gap in the metal shelves. He stopped near a bank of computers and looked around the room, scanning for potential spies.

Here I am, asshole.

Seemingly satisfied that nobody was watching him, he sat down at a computer, leaning close to the screen to shield it from the view of passersby. He tapped a few keys then sat for a moment, staring intently at the screen. After another moment he punched a few more keys.

Mendoza spent half an hour at the machine before he stood to go. He glanced around the room again, his eyes stopping on a trim, thirtyish man in khaki pants and a plaid cotton shirt. The man stood at a kiosk, reviewing the announcements posted there. Eyes narrowed, Mendoza glared plainly at the man now as if waiting to see how he would respond.

Maybe I should've been insulted that Mendoza had overlooked me as a potential spy. After all, his failure to notice me implied that I was, well, overlookable. Okay, I admit that without makeup and decent clothes, I wasn't anything to write home about. And given my stature, I appeared deceptively harmless. Still, just once I'd like to make a man quake in fear without having to pull my gun. Heck, I'd settle for a quiver. A blink even.

A woman carrying a toddler walked up to the man in the khakis, put her hand on his arm, and smiled up at him. "Ready to go, honey?"

Mendoza's narrowed eyes returned to normal. He followed the couple into the library's lobby. The couple continued on, exiting through the front doors. Mendoza, however, ducked into the men's room. I slunk between the shelves, moving closer to the lobby. Not ten seconds later, Mendoza emerged from the men's room and headed out the front door.

Hardly enough time to do his business.

I watched from one of the windows as Mendoza returned to his car and left the lot. Scurrying into the lobby, I rapped once on the men's room door and pushed it open a couple of inches, my eyes averted. "Cleaning crew," I called. "Anyone in here?"

When no response came, I stepped inside. Typical men's room. Two stalls, two urinals, crumpled white paper towels in a shiny metal bin located under the towel dispenser.

Hmm.

I bent down and looked under the sink to see if Mendoza might have stashed something there. Nope. Nothing there but some rusty pipes. I glanced around again. Toilet tanks? Nope. Nothing there, either. The only other place to stash something was the waste bin.

Urk.

Sticking my hand in a bin of used, soggy towels was about the last thing I wanted to do. Nailing Mendoza, on the other hand, was at the top of my list. Cringing, I stuck my hand into the metal bin, feeling around the bottom.

Bingo.

At the bottom of the bin was a cell phone, one of those cheap basic models made to be used with a prepaid card. I turned it over and slid open the compartment for the sim card.

Empty.

Damn. Mendoza had probably flushed it. Even if his fingerprints appeared on this phone, it would do us no good. Without the sim card to tell us the phone number he'd been using, the device itself was useless.

Just to make sure I'd covered all my bases, I peeked into both urinals and toilets, checking to see if by some miracle the card hadn't been sucked into the sewer system. No such luck. But the fact that Mendoza had ditched the phone told me he was running scared now, being extra careful. We'd made things harder on him. That fact gave me some satisfaction.

I slipped the phone into my purse and stepped back into the lobby. What now? I glanced back into the library, at the bank of computers. Couldn't hurt to check the machine, right?

I headed to the PCs. A boy of about eighteen was sitting down at the computer Mendoza had been using. An MP3 player was strapped to his upper arm, tiny earplugs in his ears. He had three days' worth of stubble on his cheeks, two metal hoops through his nose, and one serious case of BO.

I stepped up next to him. "Hi." I gave him my friendliest smile. "I hate to inconvenience you, but I need to use that particular computer. Would you mind moving to another?"

He glanced up at me and turned back to the screen. "Yeah. I would."

Not the response I'd hoped for. "Please? There's five others available right here." I gestured to the empty seats around us.

"Exactly," he said. "Use one of those." He began to type on the keyboard.

"Look. I asked you nicely. Now I'm going to have to insist."

He shot me a go-to-hell look and continued typing.

I crouched down next to him. "If you don't voluntarily get up from this computer, I'm going to have to make you."

He looked me over and snorted. "I'd like to see you try."

"Oh yeah?" A quarter second later, I held him in a painful wristlock, his right arm sticking straight up behind him. "You like this, punk?" Okay, so I'd gone a little *Dirty Harry* on him. Sue me.

"Shit, lady! You're fucking crazy!"

"Yes," I hissed in his ear. "I am."

I let go of him and he leaped up from the chair, grabbing his grungy messenger bag and taking off. I knew he wouldn't report me. It would be too embarrassing for him to admit a five-foot-two-inch woman physically bested him. Wuss.

I slid into the chair, still warm from Mendoza's and grunge-boy's body heat.

During my six months of special agent training, we'd had several classes on computer searches, so I knew a little about cybersleuthing. Not as much as Josh, of course, but enough to get by. I pulled up the computer's history and reviewed the list of Web sites accessed. The most recent was a site selling secondhand term papers. That would be grunge-boy, no doubt. Before that, the most recent sites accessed were one for Chase Bank, another for Cayman Islands Bank & Trust, and Google mail.

Mendoza had a Gmail account? Interesting. I'd just discovered how he was communicating with his stooge. Too bad I didn't know how to hack into his account.

I texted Josh from my cell and he came inside, slipping into the chair as soon as I vacated it. I wasn't sure he'd be able to get anything more than I had, but it couldn't hurt to have him take a look, too.

I dropped into the seat next to him. "Well?"

Josh shook his head. "This history doesn't tell us much. I could get more information if I put key logger software on the system."

"What's that?"

Josh explained that a key logger program would track all keystrokes made on the keyboard, thus allowing us to extract account numbers, passwords, and, most important, e-mail addresses and communications. All the information we needed. Without permission from Judge Trumbull, though, any such computer search would be illegal and any resulting evidence would be inadmissible in court.

Dang.

Judge Trumbull had turned down our earlier request for a wiretap, but she'd invited us to come back if we obtained new evidence. So that's exactly what we'd do.

"Print out the search history for our records," I told Josh. "We'll need to follow Mendoza for the next few days and do the same if he uses a public computer again."

He hit the key to print out the history and held out his hand, waggling his fingers. "The library charges a quarter a page."

I rolled my eyes, dug in my purse, and handed him a dollar bill.

CHAPTER THIRTY-FOUR

$\mathcal{M}$y Backup Team

I arranged a double date for that evening. Brett and I met Alicia and Daniel at a Thai restaurant. The hostess seated us at a round table near the front windows.

Over a scrumptious plate of pad thai, I told the others that, as much as I enjoyed their company, I had ulterior motives for inviting them all out together. The three eyed me expectantly. I leaned toward them and spoke in a low voice so as not to be overheard. "I'm planning to do something really crazy and really risky this weekend." My eyes scanned their faces. "Why don't any of you look surprised?"

Alicia shrugged. "Crazy and risky is what you do."

"It's who you are," Brett added.

I looked at Daniel.

He raised both hands. "I plead the fifth."

"Typical lawyer." Sheez. I was tempted to argue the point, but since I might need their help, I figured it would be best to keep my mouth shut. "If things go wrong, I'll need bail money, legal representation, and someone to take care of my cats."

Brett lifted his index finger. "I'll post bail."

"I'll take legal representation." Daniel slid one of his business cards across the table to me. I slipped it into my wallet.

"Guess that leaves me with the cats." Alicia fingered her silver wristwatch. "Should we synchronize our watches?"

I paid for dinner. It was the least I could do for my backup team. Still, going rogue was costing me a small fortune. I wondered if I could get away with deducting the costs on my tax return.

Josh and I tag-teamed Mendoza the rest of the week. One good thing about Josh being a loner is that he didn't mind playing spy on his own. As long as he had his laptop to keep him company, he was fine. We did our best to cover our trail at work, claiming to be working on our other cases when, in reality, the files languished in our desk drawers.

Thursday evening, Brett and I took places on either side of his kitchen table and dug into the steaks he'd grilled. I unwrapped the foil from my large baked potato, trying not to think of Nick Pratt, of the supersized spud in his skimpy bathing suit, the feel of his hot breath on my neck, the touch of his fingers on my skin. The hot potato burned my finger, the pain bringing me instantly back to reality. Why was I thinking of Nick when I had a sweet, sexy, practically-perfect-except-for-watching-golf-on-TV guy right across the table?

Maybe I should give up potatoes. Then again, Brett had flirted with Trish. My lusting over Nick was merely payback. How's that for justification?

Despite the fact that each of us had downed a couple glasses of red wine, the mood was tense. Tomorrow I'd drive down to South Texas to smuggle Nick Pratt out of Mexico and back into the U.S. If things went wrong, which was a strong possibility, tonight might be the last time Brett and I would be together for a long time. Daniel was a good lawyer, sure, but even a good lawyer could only do so much for a client caught red-handed breaking multiple federal laws. The fact that I was a federal agent who should know better would only make matters worse for me.

Brett glanced across the table at me. "How many conjugal visits are prisoners allowed?"

"I have no idea." It didn't really matter. No way could I have sex with a warden standing guard outside the door, keeping time on a stopwatch. It would be tacky.

I looked back at Brett. His green eyes were dark with dread, worry lines radiating from the outer corners. My heart imploded in my chest. It wasn't right to put him through this, was it? I knew Brett respected my work, admired me for doing a job that mattered. Yet, at the same time, the demands of my job forced him to make sacrifices and the risks of my job caused him significant stress.

The two of us got along well, enjoyed each other's company, had begun to care about each other. But that didn't necessarily mean we were right for each other, did it?

CHAPTER THIRTY-FIVE

Wiretap Request, Take Two

I fidgeted throughout the Friday morning staff meeting, earning myself the evil eye from Viola and an ass-chewing from Lu. "Quit drinking those damn lattes," she snapped. "You've been squirming like a rattlesnake in a pillowcase all morning."

If she only knew. The squirming had little to do with the extra-large skinny no-whip latte I'd nursed during the meeting. Given my plans to travel to the border later in the day, my nerves were on edge.

After lunch, Josh and I armed ourselves with our printouts and followed Ross O'Donnell into Judge Trumbull's courtroom, prepared to plead, grovel, and beg for an order allowing us to install key logger software on the computers Mendoza had used. It was our final hope for nailing the man. Our final *legal* hope, that is. There was always the head shot option. Dad's Winchester stood at the ready in my coat closet at home.

The printouts would show that on Wednesday evening

Mendoza had used a computer at a Holiday Inn to access his Gmail account and another offshore bank Web site. On Thursday afternoon, he'd returned to the central library in Dallas, where he'd accessed not only the bank and Gmail sites, but also several airline Web sites, no doubt planning a trip. Whether it was to Monterrey to visit his family or a business trip was anyone's guess at this point. Without the key logger software in place, we couldn't verify his plans. Whatever he'd been doing, it was clear things were heating up in some way. He'd been especially active the last few days.

I felt guilty not telling Ross the case had been officially closed. But what he didn't know, he couldn't object to, right? He'd refuse to help us if he knew Lu had called the investigation off. Still, Josh and I were doing our best to follow the rules as much as we could. Hence here we were in court, seeking the judge's permission to cyberspy on Mendoza.

When our matter was called, the three of us approached the bench. "We'd like to speak in chambers, Your Honor."

The judge eyed me, one gray brow raised. "Back for another go?"

I nodded.

Her gaze moved to Josh then back to me. "Where's your usual sidekick?"

"That's part of what we want to talk to you about."

"Okeydoke. Let's get this party started." Trumbull stepped down from the bench, her black robe swishing behind her as she opened the door in the back wall that led to her private chambers. We followed her through. Once in her office, Josh and I took seats, while Ross stood behind me, his hands resting on the seatback.

Judge Trumbull flopped back in her chair and propped her feet, today clad in fuzzy purple slippers, on her desk. She put her hands behind her head, ready for our performance.

Wiretap request, take two.

Ross began. "Miss Holloway will explain the developments in the case since we last sought a wiretap. Her new partner, Josh Schmidt, will explain the technology they would like to use to gather evidence."

I leaned forward in my seat and launched into my spiel, telling Judge Trumbull how Eddie and I had attempted, unsuccessfully, to gather information with traditional surveillance. "We followed this guy for days," I told her, "but he's a pro at covering his tracks."

As my coup de grâce, I pulled out the framed photo of Eddie and his family that I'd swiped from his desk before we'd headed over. Weeks ago, when Lauren Sheffield had showed me the photo of Andrew and their son in front of the cruise ship, the sight of that once-happy family had pulled at my heartstrings. I hoped Eddie's family photo would pull at Judge Trumbull's.

She took the framed photo from me and looked down at it. "His girls are adorable." She handed it back to me.

"Mendoza threatened Eddie and his family."

She narrowed her eyes. "Threatened? In what way?"

I told her how Eddie was sitting in the coffee shop in the lobby of Crescent Tower, innocently eating his waffles, when Mendoza had approached.

"And what, exactly, did Mr. Mendoza say?"

I spoke slowly and deliberately, hoping to effect a convincing delivery. "He thanked Eddie for keeping an eye on the credit union and Crescent Tower. Then he told Eddie to 'give his best to his wife and daughters.'"

She pulled her feet off her desk and sat up in her chair now. "His best, huh? Had Mendoza met Eddie somewhere before? Met the wife and kids?"

"Never."

She frowned, realizing that despite the seemingly innocent language Mendoza had chosen, the fact he'd addressed Eddie at all said much more than his words. She turned her focus on Josh. "Tell me what you want to do."

Josh launched into a technical tirade about the key logger software, giving details about installation, configuration, and task management.

After a few seconds, Judge Trumbull formed a gun with her index finger and thumb and put it to her head, pulling the imaginary trigger. "Don't give me all that *Star Trek* mumbo jumbo, son. Just tell me what the software does in words an old woman can understand."

Josh offered a watered-down, simplified version this time. "The software will allow us to track the keys that are hit and from that data we can extract Web site addresses, e-mail addresses and messages, account numbers, passwords, that kind of thing."

"Gotcha." She picked up her ballpoint pen and held it poised over the written order Ross had typed up. As her eyes scanned the document, she chewed the tip of the pen. When she finished reading, she clicked the pen and marked through part of the verbiage. "I'll let you put the software on the Dallas library's computer system, but I'm not going to allow it on the hotels.'"

Though it wasn't exactly the full approval we'd aimed for, the limitation she'd imposed was understandable. The library was a public building, a government institution where complete privacy couldn't necessarily be expected. A person using a computer at a privately owned hotel would expect more security, however. Also, while the city attorney wasn't likely to give us any flack about the installation of the key logger software on the library computer system, the owners of the hotels might hire lawyers and put up a fuss about the invasion of their guests' privacy. If Trumbull's order were overturned, it would make her look bad. She didn't want to take that risk. We'd have to go with what we got.

Josh and I stood and shook the judge's hand, thanking her.

"Go get 'em, tigers."

CHAPTER THIRTY-SIX

Road Trip

Speaking of tigers or, more precisely, a hottie in a tiger-striped Speedo, Christina and I were now in the truck on our way to Mexico to pick up Nick Pratt. We'd left Friday afternoon, shortly after Judge Trumbull had granted the order allowing Josh to install key logger software on the Dallas library's network. Josh planned to continue tailing Mendoza over the weekend. We'd need to know which libraries Mendoza had visited and when in order to narrow down our later review of the key logger data.

After our seventh hour on the road, our butts had fallen asleep, our legs had begun to cramp, and the pleasure of each other's company was no longer such a pleasure.

Christina groaned. "Aren't we there yet?"

I sipped my third skinny no-whip latte of the trip. "Two hours to go."

"I'm sooo bored."

"Let's play I Spy."

"What are we? Five?"

I didn't point out that her whining was as childish as the game I'd proposed. "Come on. It'll be fun."

She rolled her eyes but gave a grunt of acquiescence.

I looked around. Not much to see at ten o'clock at night on a nearly deserted interstate. In the distance, I spotted a billboard advertising a barbecue joint. The sign featured a smiling cartoon cow. "I spy with my little eye something brown and white."

Christina pointed through the windshield. "The cow on that billboard."

"Wow. You're good."

"It wasn't exactly a challenge. That sign is the only thing around for miles." She fluffed up her pillow, placed it on the seat between us, and curled up to take a nap.

A hundred and twenty miles later, I pulled into a roadside motel in Brownsville, just a mile from the border crossing into Mexico. The parking lot was more potholes than asphalt and the fluorescent light in the lobby flickered eerily, but at least we wouldn't be here long.

When I killed the engine, Christina stirred, lifting her head. "What is this place? The Bates motel?"

"We're armed," I said. "We'll be fine."

"A Glock is no match for a bloodthirsty bedbug."

I woke the next morning, jittery with nervous energy. No need for a latte today. Christina and I planned to cross the border into Matamoros as mere citizens, worried that traveling as federal agents might put us on the border patrol's radar, subject us to increased questioning and scrutiny.

Federal agents or not, if the American border guards caught us smuggling an undocumented person into the United States, we'd be in deep doo-doo. What's more, Mexico had strict firearms laws. If the Mexican border agents discovered my guns, we'd be up to our chins in *caca*. But we were even more leery of traveling unarmed. Who knew if Nick Pratt had been followed to Matamoros? Even if he hadn't, there was always the chance, however remote, that my instincts had been wrong and that he was in cahoots with

Mendoza and Torres. In case I'd been duped, we needed to be ready to take Nick out or at least defend ourselves.

Step one was getting into Mexico. We pulled up to the border crossing and an attractive Mexican agent stepped up to the window. We showed him our paperwork and he took a cursory glance into the truck.

"Purpose of your visit?" he asked in a voice tinged with a heavy Spanish accent I'd have found sexy if I hadn't been so scared.

"Shopping and margaritas," Christina replied.

"Sure." I shrugged. "What else?" *Perhaps smuggling a wanted fugitive?*

"Have a good time, ladies. Be careful with the margaritas. Tequila makes nice girls like you do crazy things."

Little did he know we'd do crazy things without tequila.

He winked at us, backed up, and waved us through.

Things were off to an easy start. I took that as a good omen.

We drove over the bridge that spanned the muddy Rio Grande River and made our way into the city of Matamoros. Matamoros was a tourist town, with an array of shops, restaurants, and nightclubs within easy walking distance, or a drunken stagger, of the border crossing.

Christina directed me down Avenida Obregon to the jewelry mart she'd mentioned and we parked at the curb outside the shop. While the salesgirl helped Christina with the necklaces, I looked over the display of silver earrings, selecting a pretty teardrop-style pair. If we made it safely back to Dallas, they'd make a nice souvenir of this mission. If we didn't, they'd look good in my mug shot.

An hour later, we pulled up in front of Tekila's Canta Bar, a karaoke bar popular with American college kids in search of cheap beer and a good time.

Before the truck had come to a complete stop, Nick Pratt appeared at my window. He was dressed in a fitted black T-shirt stretched tight over his pecs, old-fashioned pointy-toed cowboy boots, and blue jeans that hugged his body in all the right places. "You're late."

I glanced at the clock on the dashboard. "Give me a break. It's only three minutes."

The beads of sweat on Nick's forehead told me the extra three minutes had been an eternity to him. Before he could respond, I said, "Sorry. I'll make it up to you. The chili cheese fries are on me."

After brief introductions between Nick and Christina, Nick told me to pull the truck down the alleyway. He stepped away from the truck to follow it on foot.

Christina glanced over her shoulder at Nick. "That guy's a walking orgasm."

"I know, right?"

I stopped at the end of the alley and Nick reappeared at my window. He gestured behind me to the bed of the pickup. "Open the toolbox. I'll hide in there."

I unlocked the box and Nick climbed up. We fished several empty Skoal cans out of the box, tossing them into the alley. I hated to be a litterbug, but a little bit of trash was the least of our worries right now.

As we cleaned out the box, I noticed the skin on Nick's fingers was red and raw.

He caught me eyeing his hands. "I had an allergic reaction to your sunscreen. My hands burned for three days. What the hell was in that stuff?"

I played innocent. "I have no idea." Thank goodness I'd run back to my hotel afterward and taken a long, thorough shower to remove all the LovLub, scrubbing my skin nearly down to the bone.

Nick stepped into the toolbox, first sitting then lying back, doing his best to fit inside. After much repositioning and two firm shoves from me and Christina, he finally managed to scrunch himself inside, though his knees were sure to end up bruised.

I closed the lid and locked the box.

"Hurry up and get across the border," Nick's muffled voice came from inside the metal box. "I ain't Houdini."

CHAPTER THIRTY-SEVEN

No Country for Young Women

Christina and I hopped into the pickup and made our way back to the border crossing. Unfortunately, the line into the U.S. was much longer than the line had been coming into Mexico. We inched slowly forward, the hot sun beating down on the truck. Neither Christina nor I spoke, too nervous for idle chatter. I silently prayed that Nick wouldn't suffocate or die of heatstroke in the toolbox.

As planned, we removed our blouses as we drew closer to the border patrol agents manning the gate, hoping two sets of breasts barely covered by bikinis might prove to be a distraction, even if one of the sets, mine, was only a pair of 32As.

Just as we reached the arm that blocked the entrance to the United States, the middle-aged guard stepped out of his glass booth and held up a hand. "It'll be just a moment, ladies. Shift change."

Shit.

We sat there for a couple of minutes in silence. Well, relative silence. I could virtually hear the adrenaline rocketing through my veins, my nerves buzzing.

The new agent stepped into place. The agent was tall, husky, and above all, female.

Christina emitted a soft and elongated *"Fuuuck."*

The female agent wasn't likely to find our breasts to be a distraction. In fact, she might want to give the two of us a hard time, Christina for receiving more than her fair share of beauty and curves, and me for befriending someone like Christina.

The agent stepped toward the truck, her expression as tight as the French braids keeping her hair out of her face. "Got your papers?"

We nodded and handed her our passports and identification.

She stood at the window and glanced around the inside of the cab, then stepped back and looked into the bed behind us. "You two buy anything in Mexico?"

I put a hand to my ear. "These earrings." My throat was tight with fear and my voice came out high and squeaky. Thank goodness the agent didn't know what my normal voice sounded like. For all she knew I always sounded like Kristin Chenoweth.

The agent cocked her head and took a look at my earrings. "Nice." Her focus shifted to Christina then. "How about you? Buy anything in Mexico?"

Christina put a hand to the silver pendant on her chest. "This necklace."

The guard eyed the necklace, her gaze slipping to the cleavage on either side. Hmm. Maybe the boobie trap would work after all.

The woman reached behind me and drummed her fingers on the toolbox. "Anything in here?"

My stomach tightened as I shook my head. "Nope." *Nothing but a man wanted for a laundry list of federal criminal charges.*

Relief flooded through me when she handed our paperwork back to us. But just as the officer was about to raise the arm to let us back into the U.S., movement in my side mirror caught my eye.

A German shepherd on a harness was coming up the line of cars behind us, his handler following behind, holding his leash. The dog sniffed along the side of each car, checking the doors, nosing around in the wheel wells.

No doubt the dog was trained to scent drugs, but he'd likely been trained to scent hidden bodies, too. Nick had already broken a sweat when we rendezvoused with him in the alley and hid him in the toolbox. Given the hot sun bearing down on the metal case, he'd smell completely ripe by now.

Come on, come on, I thought, willing the woman to raise the arm and let us through before the dog reached us.

No such luck.

The canine handler walked up beside my truck. Wagging his tail, the dog stopped. He sniffed at the wheel wells of my back tire. *Sniff-sniff.* Satisfied, he moved forward a few feet. The officer gave the dog a hand signal and the beast jumped up, putting his two front paws on the rim of the bed just behind the toolbox.

Oh dear God.

The dog snuffled the box briefly, then turned his head toward my open window, his nose twitching in the air. *Sniff-sniff.* The dog slid back to the ground and smelled around my door for a moment before plunking his hindquarters down on the cement and looking expectantly up at his handler.

The man ruffled the dog's ears. "Good boy."

I nearly lost bladder control.

This was it. I wasn't sure if the dog had smelled our guns or Nick hiding in the toolbox, but either way we were totally, absolutely, without a doubt, *fuuucked.*

The agent grabbed hold of the handle and pulled my door open. "Step out of the vehicle."

The jig was up.

My career was over.

My life as I knew it was at an end.

I'd spend the next decade in jail, frittering away my best reproductive years. By the time I was released, the alarm would have sounded on my biological clock. Brett would have married Trish, fathered a gaggle of busty, butterscotch-haired girls, and be living happily ever after.

I stepped out of the truck on legs that had turned to noodles. Christina climbed out on her side and I saw her surreptitiously glance at the arm blocking my truck, no doubt wondering if she could duck under the thing and make a run for it.

The dog hopped into the truck's cab, sniffing loudly along the driver's door—*sniff-sniff*—then the floor mat—*sniff-sniff*—then under the seat where we'd stashed the guns.

Sniff-sniff.

Sniff-sniff.

Sniff.

When he stuck his head under the seat, I knew it was all over. Instinctively I closed my eyes, unable to watch my world come to an end.

Crinkle-crinkle.

What the hell? I opened my eyes to see the dog pulling his head out from under the seat, a plastic bag of beef jerky in his mouth. The cowboy who'd sold me the truck must have left it there.

The dog's handler and the female agent laughed.

"Sorry, ladies," the handler said. "This darn dog can never get enough to eat."

I forced a laugh, Christina a high-pitched giggle. We climbed back into the pickup, the border patrol agent raised the arm, and we drove through, the truck lurching as my shaking foot slipped off the gas pedal.

As we continued on into America—*land of the free! Home of the brave!*—my laugh devolved into a crazed cackle while Christina's giggle became hysterical.

Banging came from the toolbox behind us. "Get me out of here!" Nick hollered.

I pulled into the parking lot of a convenience store, circling around back and parking behind the Dumpster where we wouldn't be seen. I jumped out of the truck and climbed into the bed, fumbling with my keys. Finally, I managed to unlock the toolbox.

Nick shoved the lid upward and sat up. The poor guy was drenched in sweat and gasping for breath. I stood in the bed and held a hand out to him. He took it and I helped pull him from the tight space.

On his feet now, Nick threw his head back and his hands in the air. "Oh, the sweet smell of freedom!" He took a deep breath of air and grimaced. "What the . . . ?" He noticed the Dumpster, realized that freedom smelled less sweet and more like festering garbage, and leaped over the side of the bed onto the pavement. I took the easy way down, climbing over the tailgate.

Nick knelt on the ground, kissing the asphalt. Then he jumped up and grabbed my face in both hands, planting a big, warm kiss on my lips. Despite the fact that the kiss was gritty and tasted like dirt, I enjoyed it far more than I should have given that I shouldn't have enjoyed it one bit. After all, I was in a committed, monogamous relationship with that great guy back in Dallas. Good old . . . what's-his-name.

Christina watched the interaction between me and Nick with a raised brow.

"Chili cheese fries?" I suggested, more to distract everyone than out of hunger.

Nick dropped his hands from my face. "You bet."

The three of us went into the convenience store, where I treated the others to frozen fruity drinks and large baskets of gooey fries.

CHAPTER THIRTY-EIGHT

$\mathscr{G}$oldilocks He Ain't

An hour up the road, the thrill of having rescued Nick from his forced exile had worn off and the stench of his sweat had stunk up the truck. I pulled into a truck stop with a banner that read HOT SHOWERS—$5.

I handed Nick a twenty-dollar bill, climbed out of the truck, and pointed at the door of the truck stop. "Shower. Now."

He glanced down at the bill in his hand. "There's enough here for you two to join me." He flashed that crooked, chipped-tooth smile.

Christina gave him playful shove. "Get out of here."

He slid out of the truck and went inside.

Christina watched Nick as he walked in, her eyes locked on his ass. "I don't know about you, but if he'd limited that offer to just me I'd have taken him up on it."

Hell, I didn't know about me, either. I adored Brett. But I had to admit, something about Nick appealed to me, too. We seemed to be kindred spirits.

Christina turned to me. "Think you'll get to partner up with him once everything's all cleared up?"

"A girl can dream, can't she?" Then again, working with Nick would probably be a bad idea. I wasn't not sure I'd be able to keep my mind on my work. Or on good old what's-his-name.

Nick emerged from the store twenty minutes later. He'd put his boots and jeans back on, but he'd used the extra fifteen bucks to buy a fresh T-shirt with the slogan SAVE A HORSE, RIDE A COWBOY. Also a bottle of Lone Star beer. He tossed his old, sweat-soaked tee into the trash can outside the door and headed to the truck, twisting the cap off the bottle as he made his way.

On the ride back to Dallas, Nick told us how he'd covered his tracks back in Mexico. He'd left his car in the parking garage at his condo, sneaking out in the dead of night and grabbing a bus to Matamoros. He knew his place was bugged, so he'd put his television on a timer to sound as if he were home. He'd also taped the water running, the microwave bell dinging, and the toilet flushing, the normal sounds of a bachelor pad. He'd left his computer playing the sounds on a loop.

"They'll figure it out eventually, so we'll have to work fast. But it should buy us a few days." Nick took a long, final swig of his beer and slid the empty bottle into a cup holder.

"What's the plan once you get to Dallas?" Christina asked.

"About that." Nick glanced my way. "I'll have to shack up with you until we bust Mendoza."

I could've sworn I heard my vagina scream, *Yikes!* But my mouth said, "Sure. No problem."

Big problem.

I hadn't been happy about Brett doing volunteer work alongside Trish. Brett would be even less happy about Nick living in my town house, watching the ten o'clock news with me, sharing my Fruity Pebbles in the morning. Again, I'd be forced to ask Brett to put his feelings aside, to make sacrifices for me, for my job.

Nick shifted in his seat, his warm thigh pressed to mine. Or maybe I could just forget to mention it.

By the time we'd dropped Christina at her apartment and driven to my town house, it was two in the morning. Both Nick and I were exhausted. We headed straight upstairs. Anne and Henry followed us. Poor cats. They were starved for attention.

I tossed a pillow and blanket onto the futon in my spare bedroom and gestured to the door of my guest bath. "Towels are under the sink. There's an extra toothbrush there, too."

Nick grabbed my arm as I was leaving the room, pulling me to a stop. He stepped in front of me, putting a strong hand on each of my shoulders and looking me in the eye. He opened his mouth to speak, but then closed it again as if unsure what to say. Though his mouth couldn't form words, his eyes spoke for him.

"Is 'thanks' the word you're looking for?" I supplied.

Nick laughed softly. "It's a start." He dropped his hands from my shoulders. "What you've done took guts."

"Eh." I waved a hand dismissively. "I don't scare easily."

He flashed that chipped-tooth smile, but then his face became serious. He stared at me a moment, something dark and dangerous flickering in his eyes. "You're one hell of a woman, Tara Holloway."

I turned to go, glancing back at him over my shoulder. "Don't you ever forget it."

I woke Sunday morning with a warm body pressed against my back and a heavy arm draped over me. My mind still foggy from sleep, I did what I always did. I snuggled back into the heat. And, as always, the response was a stiffy poking me in the hip.

But there was something a little different about this stiffy . . .

"Hey!" I leaped from the bed, upsetting Anne, who'd been asleep on my pillow. I turned to see the cat dart under the bed and Nick lying on his side in the middle of it.

He wore no shirt, exposing those *mmm* shoulders and a broad expanse of muscular chest covered in dark hair. The sheets were bunched around his waist, so I couldn't verify whether he was wearing underwear or had gone commando.

He chuckled, his eyes twinkling with mischief. "Don't take it personal. I always wake up with morning wood."

I emitted a huff of indignation. Still, a small part of me was disappointed by his statement. That small part wanted to think the stiffy had been personal, had been meant for, or at least *because of,* me.

"What are you doing in my bed?"

"Your brown cat kept staring at me. It was creepy." Henry did have a well-perfected death glare. "Besides, you ever slept on that futon? It's got more lumps than my mother's mashed potatoes."

"Enough with the potatoes already!"

His thick brows drew together. "What do you have against potatoes?"

If he only knew.

"You're not Goldilocks," I spat. "You can't just go climbing into beds that aren't yours. This is . . ." *Making me hot and bothered.* "Sexual harassment."

Nick shook his head. "You're wrong about that, darlin'. It's only sexual harassment if we work together. I don't currently work for the IRS. Besides, for my advances to constitute harassment, they have to be unwelcome." He shot me that chipped-tooth smile.

Cocky son of a bitch. "I was half asleep," I argued in my defense. "I thought you were my boyfriend."

"He's a lucky guy." Nick's self-assured grin softened into a sad smile and he dropped his eyes. "Sorry, Tara. It was wrong of me to take advantage of the situation. It's just that for years now I haven't been able to get close to anyone. I never knew who I could trust. I just needed some human contact."

Damn. One minute the guy had me ready to lynch him, the next he had me feeling sorry for him. I waved my hand. "Forget about it."

The mischievous twinkle returned to his eyes and the cocky grin returned to his lips. "You fell for that 'human contact' bullshit? Really? Maybe you aren't as smart as I thought you were."

"Jerk!" I grabbed a pillow from the bed and whopped him upside the head. Still, I realized that despite Nick's attempt to recant his statements there was likely some truth behind them. Surely he'd felt isolated living alone in Mexico with no family or friends.

Before Nick could respond, a knock came from my front door downstairs. It had to be Brett. Alicia never got up before noon on weekends and my parents always gave me advance notice of their visits.

"That's my boyfriend downstairs!" I hissed, pointing at the door. "Get out of my bedroom."

Nick chuckled. "Guess this could be a little hard to explain, huh?"

Why I had a naked Val Kilmer lookalike in my bed? "Yeah."

He climbed out of my bed. Turned out he was wearing underwear after all. Blue boxers. They covered more than the Speedo had. I tried really hard not to be disappointed by that fact. He quietly slunk out the door and into my guest bathroom.

I grabbed my bathrobe, slipped it on, and hurried downstairs to let Brett inside.

He was dressed for landscaping work in hiking boots, cargo shorts, and a T-shirt. "Sorry if I woke you. I had to see for myself that you got back okay."

I'd texted him from the convenience store yesterday, letting him know we'd cleared the border. His response? *Thank God. Now I can breathe again.*

He held up a large paper cup. "Brought you a latte."

"Skinny? No whip?"

He shook his head. "I figured you deserved the real thing today."

What the hell. I'd earned it.

I took the warm cup, gave Brett a kiss on the cheek, and jerked my head toward the kitchen. "I'll fix you breakfast."

We'd just sat down to two bowls of Fruity Pebbles when we heard the sound of the shower turning on upstairs.

Brett looked up at the ceiling. "Is someone here?"

I mentally squirmed. Still, it made sense for Nick to stay at my place, didn't it? No one else could know he was back, not even his family. It could jeopardize the case. "Yeah. It's Nick. He'll have to stay with me until we complete Mendoza's arrest. He slept in my guest room last night." Part of the night, anyway.

"Makes sense."

My gosh, Brett was so trusting. Maybe too trusting. Nothing had happened between me and Nick, but I felt a little guilty nonetheless. Also a little insulted. Shouldn't Brett be just a wee bit jealous? "Working at the Habitat House today?"

He nodded.

"Is Trish working with you?"

"I think I saw her name on the schedule."

Grr. "What are you doing out there?"

"Laying sod."

As long as he didn't lay Trish I guess I had no right to complain. Still, couldn't she find another charity to support? Maybe she could go help some orphans, preferably overseas.

A few minutes later, footsteps sounded on the stairs. Nick stepped into the kitchen. He wore the same clothes he'd had on yesterday, the only ones he had. We'd have to do some shopping today, buy him some new clothing, maybe a razor for that manly stubble on his cheeks.

I stood and introduced the two men.

They shook hands amiably, but it was clear they were subconsciously sizing each other up. Brett stood as tall as possible, and Nick's chest stuck out so much he looked like a rooster.

Men.

Sheez.

Still, it was flattering. I knew they wouldn't be acting like this if I wasn't around.

I offered to make Nick some coffee, but he declined, opening the fridge and grabbing the carton of orange juice instead. I retrieved a glass from the cabinet, our fingers touching as I handed it to him. I felt a warm blush on my cheeks and hoped neither of them would notice.

Lucky for me, my cell phone bleeped, giving me an excuse to turn away and dig through my purse on the counter. The readout indicated it was Josh calling. "Hey, Josh."

"The software is loaded," Josh said. "I finished that up yesterday afternoon. I programmed it to send the data directly to me. I've been keeping an eye on Crescent Tower, but Mendoza hasn't made a move today."

"We'll be over in a couple hours to relieve you."

"Roger that."

Brett stood then, rinsing his bowl and spoon in the sink and putting them in the dishwasher. "I'll let you two get to work."

Nick lifted his chin once in acknowledgment. "Later, man."

I walked Brett to the door. "Thanks for the latte."

"It's the least I could for my woman," he said, a bit louder than necessary. He pulled me to him, giving me a warm, possessive kiss. When he released me, his eyes cut to the kitchen, to Nick. "Be careful," he whispered.

"You, too," I whispered back. *Keep Trish away from your equipment.*

CHAPTER THIRTY-NINE

$\mathcal{M}$y New Partner

While I took a quick shower, Nick removed the license plates from my BMW. I'd followed Mendoza in the truck quite a bit recently and figured it would be a good idea to use a different vehicle.

"I'm ready." I hefted my purse onto my shoulder as I stepped into the garage.

"I'm not," Nick said. "I need a weapon."

"I'd figured as much." I pulled my Glock from my purse and handed it to him along with a clip. "Here you go."

He slid the gun into his waistband, the clip into his front pocket. "You got something for yourself?"

I pulled my purse open so he could see my thirty-eight tucked inside.

"Nice piece," he said. "One of these days you and I need to have a go at the firing range. I hear you're a pretty good shot."

"Who'd you hear that from?"

He slid a sly grin my way. "Wouldn't you like to know."

Before heading to Crescent Tower, Nick and I drove to a western-wear store. All of Nick's bank and credit card accounts had been frozen by the government when he'd fled to Mexico, so I had to play sugar mama, paying for his jeans, pearl-buttoned shirts, boxers, and socks.

"I'll pay you back once we clear things up," Nick promised.

"Okay," I agreed, steering him to the section with the cowboy hats. "But the white hat is on me."

We also stopped by a cell phone store. I added Nick to my plan and he selected a top-of-the-line smartphone complete with GPS, a data package, and dozens of preloaded apps.

"Did you have to pick the most expensive phone?" I asked as we climbed back into my car.

He plugged the charger into my cigarette lighter and inserted the other end into his shiny new phone. "Don't fret. You can have it when we wrap up this case. I think it has a vibrator feature."

"I'll choose to ignore that comment."

Nick chuckled.

"Why can't you buy your own phone? Don't you have access to Mendoza's bribe money?"

Nick's eyes darkened with anger. "I'm not touching one more dime of that dirty money than I absolutely have to."

Understandable.

A half hour later, we pulled up across the street from Josh's black rental car. He'd parked on one of the side streets with a view of the Crescent Tower parking garage.

Nick called Josh from his new cell phone, activating the speaker so I could hear the conversation.

Josh waved through his window. "Welcome back, Nick."

Nick raised a hand back at Josh. "Thanks, man."

Josh continued to look at Nick through the glass. "For what it's worth, I never would have believed you'd turn on us."

"That's worth a lot, Josh." Nick made a fist and bumped it twice against his chest, guy shorthand for *You've touched me emotionally, but I'm a man so I can't say such girlie things and have to beat my chest like a gorilla instead.* "We'll be in touch."

"Over and out." With that, Josh drove off.

Hmm. So Josh wasn't the one Nick had stayed in touch with. It was clear Nick had been well liked when he'd worked at the IRS. It wouldn't surprise me if his contact had been one of the other female agents. His manly charms were damn hard to resist.

Nick repositioned his white hat to better hide his face and slid on the pair of cheap sunglasses he'd snagged from the display at the store's register. He focused on the exit of the parking garage. "Come on, Mendoza. Show your ugly face, you cock-sucking motherfucker."

Not exactly polite language to use around a lady, but who could blame him? Mendoza had taken three years of Nick's life, forced Nick to leave behind his family, his dog, the electric slide. If a person who'd do that wasn't a cock-sucking motherfucker, I didn't know who was.

Unlike Eddie, who abhorred country music, and Brett, who merely tolerated it for my sake, Nick liked country. Although Nick looked like Val Kilmer, his voice was one hundred percent classic Waylon Jennings. We sang along with the songs on the radio as we waited to see if Mendoza would make an appearance.

Eddie was right. Nick and I had a lot in common.

More in common than me and Brett.

An hour into our watch, when I'd dozed off in the warm afternoon sun, Nick slapped his hand down on the dashboard, the noise jerking me from my slumber. "There he is."

I sat up, stretching and shaking my limbs to wake myself up. Nick leaned forward in the seat beside me, all raw nerves and barely contained energy. I now understood why Eddie had called Nick "intense." From Nick's behavior, I could tell he'd love nothing more than to hurl himself at Mendoza's Mercedes, rip off the door, and tear the evil man inside limb from limb.

I started up my car, eased away from the curb, and followed

Mendoza from a safe distance. Today he hit the library in Oak Lawn, one of the larger branches. He probably thought that using computers at different libraries would make his use more difficult to trace. Since all of the libraries were linked by a single network and central server, however, his game of musical chairs wouldn't slow us down.

While he pulled into the library parking lot, I drove on past, turning into a fast-food place a block away. Now that the key logger software was in place, there was no sense in taking unnecessary chances. I pulled out my cell and called Josh. His voice sounded tired. Must've woken him from a nap.

"Mendoza's in the Oak Lawn library as we speak."

"Logging on." I heard some clicking noises as Josh tapped the keys of his laptop. "Let's see." *Click. Clickety-click.* "That branch has thirty-two public computers. I'm capturing the data."

Gotta love technology, huh?

Mendoza spent only a short time in the library today, emerging thirty minutes later.

I called Josh from my cell. "Mendoza's left the library."

"Roger," Josh said. "I'll send you the data for the last half hour. Let's meet up to look it over."

Nick and I met up with Josh at a coffeehouse. Fortunately, now that it was mid-afternoon, the place had few patrons.

Two young women at a table near the front bore the telltale signs of a fun-as-hell Saturday night and a not-so-fun Sunday morning hangover. Bloodshot eyes, black raccoon-like rings of mascara around their eyes, slouching postures. They wore clothes they'd clearly slept in, one of them wearing a ribbon pronouncing her the BRIDE-TO-BE. Must've been one heck of a bachelorette party. Despite their exhaustion, the two glanced up appreciatively as Nick passed.

While Nick and Josh set up shop at a small round table in the corner, I ordered a skinny no-whip latte for myself, two regular coffees for the guys, and three club sandwiches. I carefully maneuvered through the tables with the loaded tray.

After unloading our lunch, I took a seat between the two

men. Nick scooted his chair closer to me so he could see my laptop screen. I ignored the fact that Nick's knee brushed against mine, ignored the frisson of heat that raced up my thigh, ignored the heat coming from his arm draped over the seat behind me. A kick-butt special agent wouldn't let herself be distracted by such things, right? Business before pleasure. Not that there would be pleasure later, but you know what I mean.

Josh began maneuvering his wireless mouse on the table. "You and Nick look over the activity on computers one through sixteen. I'll review the others."

I booted up my laptop, logged on, and, between bites of my sandwich and sips of my latte, began reading over the key logger data Josh had sent via e-mail. The keystrokes were somewhat difficult to decipher out of context. Without seeing the screen to which the input responded it was like hearing only one side of a conversation. But after a minute or two, when I'd become accustomed to the format, things became more clear.

Nick polished off his sandwich in six bites, drained his coffee, and leaned in to read my computer screen.

"Ew," I said. "Here's an e-mail where someone asks how penis enlargement works. Think that's Mendoza?"

"Nah," Nick said. "The guy's already a big dick."

Josh snickered. "Good one." He leaned over, trying to read my screen. "How does it work, exactly?"

Nick's lip curled back. "Dude."

Josh turned pink and turned back to his own screen.

Nick's eyes skimmed the screen while his finger ran down it. "Got someone researching John Steinbeck's *Of Mice and Men*. Somebody watching squirrels having sex on YouTube. That's some stupid shit, huh? Somebody looking to hook up on the dating sites."

The key punches from the next computer seemed odd, like words but . . . not exactly. "I can't make heads or tails of this data."

"Yo puedo." Nick slanted a grin my way. "For gringos like you, that means 'I can.'"

"You speak Spanish?"

"I lived in Mexico the last three years, remember?" His expression said *duh*.

"Oh. Right." Guess I'd deserved the *duh*.

Nick's eyes skimmed over the information, his hands fisting and unfisting with nervous energy. "This is him. This has to be Mendoza."

Josh pulled his chair and laptop closer. Josh's knee bumped mine, but his bump caused no frisson of heat to rush up my leg.

The data indicated Mendoza had accessed Web sites for a bank in Mexico and several others spread across Latin America. Bolivia. Guatamala. Peru. I pulled a pen and notepad from my purse and jotted down the URLs for the Web sites, along with the user IDs and passwords Mendoza had used to access them. Mendoza had also logged on to sites for three large American banks. I set the pad next to Josh so he could read my notes.

While Nick continued to review the key logger data, Josh pulled the bank sites up on his computer, re-creating the steps Mendoza had gone through. His brows drew together. "The accounts in the Latin American banks are all business accounts with nominal balances, just a few dollars in each."

I leaned over to look at the account information on Josh's computer screen. All of the names of the businesses were in Spanish. Servicios Financieros Peruanos. Turismo Internacional Exclusivo. Anuncios Publicitarios Creativos. None sounded familiar.

"Any of these names ring a bell to you?" I asked Nick. I rattled off the names on the accounts, doing my best to pronounce them properly.

He shook his head. "The names are for a travel agency, an advertising firm, and a financial services company."

All service-oriented businesses that would require only a minimal physical presence in the countries, no factories or large staff needed.

"Think Mendoza owns them?" I asked.

Nick shrugged. "Who knows?"

I turned back to the computer screen, using Josh's mouse to page back and forth between the accounts. "Looks like there was a large withdrawal from each of the accounts last Monday." Monday had been the first banking day following Mendoza's exchange with Eddie at Crescent Tower. Was it mere coincidence? Or was there a connection between the two events?

Josh pulled up the sites for the American banks next. He let out a whistle. "There's over two million in one of these accounts, one point eight in another, and six hundred G's in the last one."

Nick stopped typing on his computer and leaned forward, looking past me to Josh. "What name is on the accounts?"

Josh turned back to his screen. "Claudia's Accounting Service."

"Address?"

Josh frowned. "It's a post office box."

"What's the Zip Code?" I asked.

Josh rattled it off and I plugged it into my computer, locating the post office. "The Zip is located in southeast Dallas."

Nick jerked his head at Josh's screen. "Can you get Claudia's full name from any of the banking sites? She's Mendoza's new puppet. We need to find her. ASAP."

"I'll see what I can dig up." Josh squinted at his screen, looking over the bank's site for a menu that might lead him to the information he sought.

Meanwhile, Nick and I continued to review Mendoza's key logger data. The next entries indicated he'd accessed his e-mail. The communication had been sent from a Gmail address listed as *chief_financial_exec* to a Hotmail account for *claudiasaccounting*. The e-mail began with *Mi cariño Claudia*. I understood a few words of the communication, such as *banco, dolares,* and *mañana,* but beyond that the Spanish was Greek to me. In several places there were dollar amounts listed, in one place a series of ten numbers beginning with 214.

Nick read from the screen, pointing at the ten-digit number. "He's sent this Claudia a new contact phone number."

I'd shown Nick the cell phone Mendoza had discarded in the library's men's room a few days earlier. It made sense he'd have a new phone and new number. Too bad there wasn't a decapitation code we could dial to make his phone explode when he answered. Why isn't there an app for that?

Nick's finger moved to one of the dollar figures. "He's instructed Claudia to go to the banks first thing in the morning and move the entire account balances to something called CIB&T."

"That's got to be Cayman Islands Bank & Trust," I said.

The e-mail was signed only "CFO." Not surprising. Mendoza wasn't dumb enough to sign the thing "with all my love, Marcos Mendoza, Professional Money Launderer and Murderer."

"Seems odd that he's moving all of the money at once," I said. "That'll leave a paper trail." Small transactions required no reports to the government and could be accomplished online, but transactions of the size Mendoza had proposed would require his puppet to provide identification and fill out all kinds of forms at the bank.

"I'll check the account history." Josh maneuvered his mouse to pull up the account activity.

I looked at Josh. "Where should Nick and I go from here?"

"Log in to his e-mail account. Check his inbox and the file for sent e-mails. Maybe there's something there we can use."

While I watched over Nick's shoulder, fighting a strong urge to bite into it, he logged in to Mendoza's Gmail account. "They're empty. Dammit! He deleted everything. Even the e-mail he just sent to Claudia."

Smart move. Mendoza had left a trail of bread crumbs for us to follow, but he'd left as few crumbs as possible.

"I've got the history for each account pulled up now," Josh said. "There's a series of deposits here. Two or three each week in each account. All cash and all in the seven-thousand-dollar range. No withdrawals or transfers."

Nick looked thoughtful. "Sounds like Mendoza's been saving up. That's not his typical MO. He doesn't normally trust his puppets enough to leave the money in their hands for long. Something's up."

Nick and I continued to review the keystroke data. Farther down, the information indicated Mendoza had accessed both the American Airlines and Aeromexico Web sites. We extracted his user IDs and passwords and Nick accessed the airlines' online systems, retrieving his account information.

I could hardly believe my eyes. Mendoza had purchased a one-way ticket for himself from Dallas to Monterrey. His flight was scheduled to leave at noon on Tuesday. The Aeromexico records indicated he'd bought three one-way tickets from Monterrey to Nassau, Bahamas, one in his name, the others in the names of his wife and daughter. The flight from Monterrey to the Caribbean was scheduled to leave only two hours after Mendoza's arrival in Monterrey Tuesday afternoon. His wife and daughter must have been planning to meet him at the airport.

"Fuck!" Nick boomed.

The bachelorettes and the coffeehouse staff glanced our way, their expressions wary.

Nick noticed and raised a contrite palm. "'Scuse my French." He flashed that winning smile of his and all was forgiven. The guy had charisma dripping from his pores. He lowered his voice. "Mendoza's set to flee. We've got less than forty-eight hours to get him. We have to find this Claudia person. Now. It's the only way we can nail him."

"Problem," Josh replied. "I've been all over the banks' Web sites but there's nothing here showing who the authorized signatories are. I can't find Claudia's last name."

"You're the tech expert, Josh. Find something, for shit's sake!" Nick spat his words with far more venom than necessary and Josh shrank in his seat.

I felt a twinge of sympathy for Josh. He was doing his best. Then again, this case wasn't a normal investigation for

Nick. This was personal. Nick's outburst was understandable under the circumstances.

"At least we can narrow it down," I said. "Her e-mail address is 'Claudia's accounting,' so she's probably a CPA, right? How many CPAs can there be in Dallas named Claudia?"

CHAPTER FORTY

$\mathcal{M}$ad Scramble

As it turned out, there were thirteen CPAs in Dallas with the first name Claudia. I jotted down a quick list from the Texas State Board of Public Accountancy's Web site.

Nick snatched the pen from my hand and crossed through five names on the list. "We can rule out the ones who work for major firms. Mendoza wouldn't use one of them. Too much oversight and too many internal controls."

That still left us eight Claudias.

Unfortunately, given that it was a Sunday, we couldn't simply make the rounds of their offices. We'd have to try them at home. We didn't want to risk contacting them by phone and having Mendoza's puppet tip him off. We figured we'd have better luck convincing Claudia to cooperate with us if we spoke to her in person.

Nick divvied up the list, suggesting we approach them in order of their proximity to the post office where the bank statements had been mailed, starting with the closest ones.

He assigned half of the names to Josh. "Tara, you go with Josh. Okay?"

"We could cover more ground quicker if we divided the list in three," Josh pointed out.

Nick put a firm hand on Josh's shoulder. "Look, Josh. No offense, buddy, but you're not the most intimidating guy in the world and your people skills need work. I'm not sure you could convince Claudia to work with you."

Josh's eyes narrowed and his lips pressed into a thin line.

Nick gave Josh's shoulder a squeeze. "Don't sweat it, man. Nobody has it all. If it weren't for your computer skills, Tara and I would be sitting here with our heads up our asses."

His words may have appeased Josh, but now it was my eyes that narrowed, my lips that pressed into a thin line. Head up my ass. Who did Nick think he was?

I glared at him. As soon as Josh turned his attention back to his computer, Nick shot me a wink, the gesture communicating what he couldn't say. All of that BS about me and Nick having our heads up our butts was solely to keep Josh from getting his tightie whities in a bunch.

We headed out to the parking lot and I handed Nick my keys, admonishing him not to put a single scratch on my baby. I'd worked hard for my BMW.

I climbed into the passenger side of Josh's rental and off we went in search of Claudia.

The first Claudia we visited was Claudia Smith, a stay-at-home mom with a moody two-year-old daughter. The current mood was psycho-on-a-bad-acid-trip. Claudia Smith stood in her doorway, her red-faced toddler clinging to her right leg and projecting a bloodcurdling scream at a million decibels. "I don't do accounting work anymore," Claudia shouted over the din. "But I'll tell you, there are days when I miss going to a quiet office."

According to the board's records, the next Claudia, Claudia Morecki, worked as the controller for a utility company. She shook her head when we asked if she did any work on the side, particularly for a man named Mendoza. "No. My position pays well. There's no reason for me to take on extra work."

There was also no reason for me and Josh to doubt her story. There'd been no uneasiness on her part, no flicker of apprehension in her eyes when I'd said Mendoza's name.

The third Claudia was Claudia Andrews. She wasn't home, or at least she wasn't at the home address listed in the licensing records. Her estranged husband answered the door in a mismatched pair of socks, a wrinkled pair of Bermuda shorts, and a foul mood. "I have no idea where that bitch went. But if you find her, tell her I want my big-screen TV back and that she was right, I did love that thing more than her."

As we walked back to Josh's car, he asked, "Think his Claudia is the one we're looking for?"

"Probably not. The post office box on the bank accounts is way on the other side of the city. But we can always go by her office tomorrow if we have to."

The final Claudia on our list was Claudia Fryberg, an older woman in her late fifties. "No," she said when we asked if she had a client named Mendoza. "I used to do taxes for quite a few people, but I'm easing myself into retirement now. I haven't taken on a new client in years."

Josh and I had struck out. We could only hope Nick's search would turn up the Claudia we sought.

We drove back to my town house to wait for Nick to complete his rounds.

The minute we walked in my door, Josh began sneezing. "You have cats?"

"Yep. Two. You allergic?"

He nodded once before launching into another sneeze.

"Let's wait for Nick on the patio then."

We were sitting in plastic lawn chairs on my back patio a half hour later, eating the last of Mom's pecan pralines, when Nick showed. He slid the glass door open and stepped outside. I could tell from his pissed-off expression he hadn't had any luck, either.

Nick threw his hands in the air. "I'm at a loss."

"Maybe she's not a CPA." I turned to Josh. It wasn't so hard for someone to hide in the real world, but given the scope of the Internet, it was much harder to hide online. "Can we run another Internet search? Maybe see if this Claudia person has a Web site or something?"

Josh booted up his computer and ran several Internet searches, trying to find a Claudia's Accounting Service in Dallas. No luck. "She doesn't seem to have a Web site and she's not listed on any of the business referral sites."

"Either she's really small or she's not legit." Nick put his hands behind his head, angled his face upward, and closed his eyes, thinking. A few seconds later, he opened his eyes again. "What about the county clerk's assumed names office?"

"Good idea," I said. Anyone who operated a sole proprietorship doing business under another name had to register their business with the clerk.

Josh logged on to the county's searchable database. A few seconds later, his face brightened. "That did it. I've got a physical address for Claudia's Accounting Service. The name was registered six years ago by a Claudia R. Dominguez."

"Woo-hoo!" I jumped onto my laptop and ran a search of the driver's license records. Though a license had existed in that name years ago with a Dallas address, there was no current license issued to a Claudia R. Dominguez anywhere in the Dallas vicinity. "What does this mean?"

Josh raised his palms. "Who knows? I checked the address on her expired license. She and a Ricardo Dominguez used to own the house at that address, but they sold it a few years ago."

"There's just one thing we can do." Nick grabbed my keys from the table. "Let's roll."

The three of us loaded into my car, Nick at the wheel. He plugged the address for Claudia's Accounting Service into his phone's GPS and drove like a bat out of hell all the way there.

Claudia's office was located in a small strip mall that had seen better days but hadn't yet given up on itself. The stucco building bore a fresh coat of green paint and the park benches placed on the sidewalk were relatively new. Although the light fixtures were outdated, hi-tech security cameras perched on the corners of the roof, aimed to take in the parking lot and sidewalks.

Claudia's Accounting Service sat in the middle of the mall, in a narrow space only twelve feet wide. A karate studio flanked the office on the left, a pawn shop to the right. Claudia's window bore white stick-on lettering with the name of her business, as well as BOOKKEEPING, TAX, AND NOTARY SERVICES, along with SE HABLA ESPAÑOL and the word NOTARIO. Dark window tinting lined the inside of the windows, making it difficult to see inside the office from this distance.

We climbed out of the car, stepped to the window, and peered inside. Up close, visibility was better. The space was small and crowded, yet nevertheless clean and tidy.

A series of metal file cabinets lined the side and back walls. A large L-shaped wooden desk faced the front door, a banker's lamp with a green glass shade placed to one side. A clear plastic water cooler topped with a stack of cone-shaped paper cups stood in a corner next to a brass coat tree. Four wooden chairs sat in a row next to the front door, the small coffee table in front of them bearing copies of *Money* magazine and *Fortune*.

The space wasn't anything to be ashamed of, but it wasn't exactly the digs of a highly successful financial whiz, either.

Josh cupped his hands around his eyes to better see into the dark space. "She's got a stack of business cards on her desk but I can't read them from here."

I darted back to my BMW and retrieved Dad's field glasses from the glove box. "Try these." I handed them to Josh.

He held them to the window. "Pulido," he said. "Claudia's using the last name Pulido now."

Nick grabbed Josh by the shoulders, just as he'd done with me in the bed of the pickup after I'd sprung him from Mexico. I wondered for a second if he was going to embrace Josh, too.

Nick smiled. "If you were a woman, Josh, I'd kiss you."

Josh smiled back. "If I were a woman," he began, "I . . . um . . ." His face contorted as he realized he'd backed himself into a very awkward corner.

Nick released Josh's shoulders, letting him off the hook. "Let's find Miss Pulido."

We returned to my car and both Josh and I logged on to our laptops, running searches for a Claudia Pulido who lived in the vicinity.

"There's nothing in the property tax records," I told Josh after I'd run a search.

"I'll try the motor vehicle registrations," he said. Several clicks later, Josh looked up. "Found her."

Nick raised a palm for a high five. "Way to go, Josh!"

Grinning from ear to ear, Josh slapped Nick's hand.

While Josh read the address aloud, Nick plugged it into his new phone. He consulted the readout on the GPS when the map popped up. "She lives just a few blocks from here."

Less than a minute later, we pulled up in front of a modest one-story brick home. One of the shutters was missing a slat, a balsa-wood airplane lay on the roof, and the lawn, though mowed, lacked the crisp edge that comes from regular trimming. Apparently there wasn't a man in the picture or, if there was, he was a lazy man. An older model blue minivan was parked in the driveway, the back hatch open, several bags of groceries visible in the cargo bay.

We parked at the curb and climbed out of the car. I brought my briefcase with me, all of the documentation on the Mendoza case inside.

As we made our way up the driveway, a Hispanic woman in her mid-thirties emerged from the front door of the house. She was pretty, with smooth brown skin and dark hair that hung in loose curls down to her shoulders. She was petite, about my size, though her figure was much curvier than mine, even with my latte-enhanced cleavage. She wore a red short-sleeved dress in a soft fabric with low-heeled black sandals.

Three boys ranging in age from five to ten trailed behind her, all three dressed in crisp gray pants and white short-sleeved dress shirts. No doubt they'd attended a late-afternoon Mass and stopped at the grocery store on their way home.

Claudia stopped when she saw the three of us approaching, putting out a protective hand to stop her boys from walking past her. Her brow furrowed in concern. "Can I help you?"

CHAPTER FORTY-ONE

There's a New Puppetmaster in Town

Nick held up both hands, one of which was holding his badge. Guess he'd gotten away with it when he fled to Mexico. "No need to worry, ma'am," he said. "We just need to speak with you for a moment. We're from the IRS."

All color drained from the woman's face. She simply stared at us for a moment as if overcome, unable to think. Tears formed in her eyes. She quickly brushed away one that had escaped down her cheek. "Please come inside," she said, gesturing for us to follow her. "Boys, finish bringing in the groceries."

The boys looked from their mother to the three of us but said nothing, doing as their mother said and heading to the van to grab the remaining bags.

I eyed Claudia's left hand. No ring. I'd been right. No man in the picture.

Claudia led us inside. The décor was typical single mom, inexpensive furniture with an excess of female touches. She made her way to the kitchen and motioned to the rectangular table, which was covered with a cheap floral-print vinyl tablecloth. The four of us took seats.

Nick, Josh, and I introduced ourselves. The hand she extended across the table was trembling. I shook her hand and gave her what I hoped was a reassuring smile. Sure, she'd been Mendoza's puppet, helped him cheat the government. But, if she knew what was good for her, she'd also help us nail the bastard.

Nick sat rigid in his chair, his entire body tensed. Only one person stood between us and Mendoza now, and that one person sat at the table with us. We were close now, so close I could taste it. Once Claudia positively identified Mendoza as the man she'd been dealing with, we'd have probable cause to arrest the guy.

He'd never get a chance to use that one-way ticket to Monterrey.

Neener-neener.

Nick glanced my way before turning to Claudia. "Miss Pulido, I get the feeling you know why we're here."

She nodded.

"If you cooperate with us," Nick said, "we'll go easy on you. But if you don't, you may end up in jail and not see your boys again until they're grown and have no use for their mother anymore. Understand?"

Wow. That seemed a little harsh.

I glanced at Josh. He shrugged. Nick's words may have been harsh, but they were effective. Claudia nodded, terrified, tears openly running down her cheeks now. I grabbed a napkin from the plastic holder in front of me and handed it to her. She nodded gratefully and wiped her eyes.

Nick's focus locked on Claudia. "Tell us everything you know about Marcos Mendoza."

A mix of confusion and surprise sprang to her face. "I—I don't know a Marcos Mendoza."

Nick, Josh, and I exchanged glances. She had to be lying, yet her surprise seemed sincere.

Nick cocked his head, his eyes narrowed. "Tell us the truth, Miss Pulido."

She leaned forward. "I am telling you the truth." Her voice was frantic now. "I don't know anyone named Marcos Mendoza." Her brown eyes were wide, scared, as they traveled from Nick's face, to Josh's, to mine.

When our gazes met, I asked, "If you don't know Mendoza, then what did you think we came here for?"

"I thought this was about Robert Ruiz."

Who the heck was Robert Ruiz?

Nick began to say something but stopped himself as Claudia's boys came in with a load of groceries. When the three had left the room again, he turned back to Claudia. "Describe Ruiz."

"I don't know what he looks like," she said. "I've never seen him in person."

"Fuck!" Nick slammed his fists down on her table, causing everything on it to jump. The clear plastic salt shaker tipped over, spilling white granules across the flowery tablecloth.

This was not good. Spilling salt was a bad omen. I quickly grabbed a pinch and threw it over my left shoulder to counteract the bad juju Nick had generated.

"Hey!" Josh cried, his hand over one eye.

Looked like my aim had been a little off. "Oops," I said. "Sorry."

Now it wasn't just Claudia's hands that were shaking. Her entire body quaked in fear.

I shot Nick a look, hoping my eyes conveyed the message *Calm down or you'll freak this woman out.* Still, I could understand Nick's frustration. Without Claudia's ID, we wouldn't have probable cause to arrest Mendoza. We needed a link and we needed it quick.

As much as I didn't want to think about it, there was always the chance that Mendoza would skip the country and leave the funds behind. Although the amounts in Claudia's accounts totaled over four million dollars, it was chump change to Mendoza. With his extensive illegal enterprises, he could easily replace the funds in a few months' time. Still, we had to give this a shot. Claudia was the only chance we had of following the money trail, of tying the loose ends together, of finally getting enough evidence to constitute probable cause.

I put a hand on Claudia's arm, hoping the gesture would be comforting. "The man you've been dealing with may have told you his name was Ruiz, but his real name is Marcos Mendoza. The IRS has been after him for years."

She chewed her lip.

I removed my hand. "You got his e-mail today instructing you to wire all of the funds in your accounts to an offshore bank?"

Her eyes widened. "You know about that?"

"We know a lot of things," Nick said. "Now, tell me. When and how were you first contacted by the man you know as Ruiz?"

"A few months ago," Claudia said. "He telephoned my office and said he was looking for someone to do bookkeeping for him."

"Let me guess," Nick said. "He made you an offer you couldn't refuse?"

Claudia nodded. "He offered me five times what I normally charge. He didn't even ask about my usual rates." She turned to me then, apparently expecting a fellow female to be more sympathetic. Or maybe she was just afraid to make eye contact with Nick. His intensity could be intimidating. "I'm a single mom. I got divorced a few years ago. My ex-husband has been out of work and can't pay his child support. I've been having a hard time making ends meet."

The divorce explained the name change.

"Did his offer seem suspicious to you?" Nick asked.

Claudia averted her eyes, guilt emanating from her. "If I hadn't been so desperate . . ."

She left her sentence unfinished, letting us fill in the blanks. If she hadn't been so desperate, she wouldn't have been sucked into Mendoza's schemes. But if she hadn't been so desperate, Mendoza wouldn't have targeted her to be his puppet, either. The guy knew how to choose his minions.

We heard the slam of the van's door from out front and

Claudia's boys came in with another load of bags. "That's all of them, Mommy," said the middle one.

She forced a smile at her boys. "Thanks. You boys change out of your good clothes and go out back to play, okay?"

The younger two darted off, but the oldest one stayed behind, eyeing his mother, worry on his face. "Are you crying?"

Claudia made a choking sound. "Yes, honey. But everything's going to be all right. Don't worry."

The boy gave us a suspicious look but obeyed his mother and went to change his clothes.

"Go on," Nick urged Claudia, eager to hear all the details.

Claudia twisted the napkin in her hands. "At first he only asked me to do some bookkeeping for his business—"

"What business?" Nick asked.

"His furniture manufacturing company," Claudia said. "He owns a factory in Arizona."

As if. The alleged furniture company was nothing more than a ruse.

"And then what happened?" Nick prodded.

"After a few weeks, he called and asked if I would open an account that he could put some cash in. He said he suspected his inside accountant had been stealing from him."

Aha! That excuse was the same one Mendoza had used to convince Andrew Sheffield to start laundering funds for him.

"I didn't want to do it," Claudia continued, "but he said the money would be in the account for only a few days at most. He'd been so generous to me I felt like I owed him a favor."

Claudia described how things had escalated. Mendoza began having cash couriered to her office, instructing her to deposit it in her newly established business account. He then directed her to open two additional accounts at different banks. By spreading the funds around and keeping the balances lower, the transactions would be more likely to go unnoticed.

"He insisted I give him access to the online account information so that he could make sure I'd deposited the funds he sent me." She broke into out-and-out sobs now, gasping for breath between words. "I was so scared. He never threatened me outright, but he made it clear that I had no choice but to do what he said or bad things could happen to me and my boys."

From my file, I pulled the newspaper clippings on the suspicious deaths of Mendoza's former employees, placing Andrew Sheffield's at the bottom. "Bad things do happen to the people who work for Mendoza." I handed the clippings to her.

Claudia's eyes scanned the reports. When she began reading the report on Andrew's murder, she put a hand to her chest. "Oh God." The hand moved to her mouth as she read on. She jumped up from the table, ran to the kitchen sink, and retched, tossing up her communion wafer and wine. I'm guessing she'd reached the part about Sheffield being dismembered. Hard to read that without becoming queasy, especially when you might be next on the list.

Nick stood and walked over to the sink, snatching a kitchen towel from the oven-mounted rack and handing it to her. "We can keep you and your children safe," he said, "but you've got to cooperate with us and help us catch this guy."

Claudia held the towel to her mouth, using it now to stifle her sobs, and nodded.

CHAPTER FORTY-TWO

What Goes Around Comes Around

We'd taken Claudia and her boys to a safe hotel suite Sunday night. I slept on the foldout couch in the suite's living room while Nick slept on a rollaway situated in front of the door. He wasn't about to take a chance that Claudia might have a change of heart and try to escape. Nick had even confiscated her cell phone and laptop, and removed all of the telephones from the bedrooms. He wasn't taking a chance she'd contact Mendoza and warn him off, either.

First thing Monday morning, Nick and I took turns showering in one of the suite's bathrooms. I dressed in loose tan slacks, a navy blazer over my shoulder holster, and an ivory silk tank, along with my steel-toed loafers, a look I referred to as business casual butt-kicker. Nick wore jeans, a dark brown western-cut shirt that hugged his shoulders and biceps, and his pointy-toed cowboy boots, looking like a regular old shit-kicker.

We left the boys at the hotel under the supervision of Claudia's sister. Claudia was too scared to allow the boys to attend school that day. The boys, on the other hand, were thrilled. Skipping school, swimming in the hotel pool, ordering pizza in? Heck, this bust was a vacation for them.

While Josh kept an eye on Crescent Tower, I escorted Claudia to the banks. Claudia emptied each of the three business accounts containing Mendoza's ill-gotten revenue, but she didn't wire the funds to Mendoza's offshore bank as he'd instructed in his e-mail. Instead, at my direction, she withdrew thirty grand in cash and transferred the remaining amounts to her personal checking account.

An account to which Mendoza had no access.

Once we'd completed the transfers, we drove to her office in her minivan. Nick tailed us as a security measure. He situated himself nearby, keeping an eye on the strip mall from the truck.

Nick, Josh, and I had held a strategy session at the hotel last night. We'd made plans, backup plans, and alternate backup plans. Although Mendoza had instructed Claudia to delete their e-mail communications, she had kept copies in a separate file. Some part of her must have realized she could end up in trouble one day and that the e-mails could prove she'd been a mere pawn in his dirty, dangerous game. We'd read through all of Claudia's e-mails with Mendoza, giving ourselves a better sense of their interactions and relationship. Basically, Mendoza had told her to jump and she'd asked how high. We couldn't be certain how Mendoza would react to his funds being stolen, but his typical response had been to send thugs after anyone who dared to cross him. The only question now was when these thugs would show up.

Would they come to Claudia's office today? Or would they wait and go to her house tonight?

Either way, we'd be ready for them.

I forced back the thought that Mendoza might simply make a break for it and forfeit the money Claudia had taken. He had already made plans to leave the country tomorrow. Whether it was because he knew the IRS was after him again or for some other reason, I couldn't be sure. But there was no doubt the guy was about to make a move.

A move that could put him forever beyond our reach.

The minutes crept by, delineated by the painfully slow ticking of the wall clock in Claudia's office. *Tick . . . Tock . . . Tick . . . Tock.* My nerves were on edge and the clock wasn't helping. It was all I could do not to rip the damn thing off the wall and stomp on it. Claudia attempted to work on some projects for her other clients, but quickly gave up, unable to concentrate.

Two hours later, an e-mail from Mendoza popped up in Claudia's inbox. As usual, the communication was in Spanish.

¿Dónde está mi dinero?

Claudia translated for me. "He's asking where his money is. What should I say?"

Josh had furnished me and Nick with walkie-talkies so we could be in instant contact. I pushed the TALK button on my unit and told Nick about the e-mail. "How should Claudia respond?"

After a brief discussion, we reached an agreement.

"In your own words," I instructed her, "tell him it seems that he's cutting you off without warning and that you want to know what's going on since you need his business."

In Spanish she typed: *I'm very sorry, Mr. Ruiz, but I have come to rely on your business. It seems you are ending our arrangement without notice. Please explain.*

We waited for several long minutes before his response came back. *Cariño Claudia. Please understand that I am not terminating your services. I need the funds to purchase a manufacturing facility overseas. The deal is scheduled to close tomorrow. The funds must be transferred immediately or the deal will fall through. The expansion of the business will provide new opportunities for both of us.*

A clever response on his part. Nonthreatening but urgent, placating Claudia's concerns about the loss of his business and the revenue it provided her, hinting that the deal could bring her even more revenue.

I rousted Nick again on the walkie-talkie.

"Have her tell him she wants to meet with him in person," Nick suggested. "Maybe she can lure him out here."

Claudia sent a response to Mendoza. *Something this important should be discussed in person. Can we meet up today?*

Again, it was several minutes before Mendoza got back to her. *I'm not in Dallas,* he responded. An outright lie. Josh confirmed Mendoza's car was parked in the Crescent Tower garage. The fact that Mendoza was sending e-mails from his office or penthouse, presumably from one of his own computers, indicated he'd become desperate. He seemed more interested now in making tracks than covering them.

Again I consulted with Nick via the two-way radio.

"Don't respond," Nick said. "Force his hand."

Over the next few hours Mendoza sent a series of e-mails that grew progressively more insistent.

Don't steal from me, Claudia. You are a Christian woman and you know stealing is wrong.

Mendoza was going to bring religion into this? Seriously? What a hypocrite. Apparently he'd forgotten the whole "Thou shalt not kill" commandment.

Claudia, why aren't you responding? If you do not return my money, I will be forced to report this theft to the authorities.

Nick and I got a good laugh out of that one.

You are making a huge mistake, Claudia. If you do not transfer the funds immediately, you will regret this decision for the rest of your life.

A life Mendoza would no doubt attempt to cut short.

His final e-mail raised some possibilities. *I will send my associates to discuss this matter with you. They will come to your office at nine this evening.*

"Associates" was no doubt another term for "thugs." The fact that these alleged associates would arrive after dark when the other businesses in the strip center would be closed and no witnesses would be around was a clear tip-off.

I pushed the talk button and read the e-mail to Nick. "What do you think?"

Nick exhaled a long breath. "I'd rather Mendoza come himself, but he'd never agree to that. He's too smart, too wary."

I mulled things over for a moment. "You think his thugs could provide the link we need, give us the probable cause to arrest Mendoza?"

"There's no guarantee of that," Nick replied. "But, hell, I don't see anything we can do or say at this point that won't make him suspicious."

"Me, neither."

"We'll have to be extremely careful how we handle things tonight," Nick said. "It'll be dangerous."

Claudia's already round eyes grew rounder.

"Piece of cake," I said with much more bravado than I felt.

"All right," Nick said. "Let's do it."

At my direction, Claudia sent Mendoza a final e-mail that said simply *Sí*.

Claudia wasn't stupid. She knew exactly what Mendoza had in mind. She fell to pieces then. But better to fall to pieces than to be chopped to pieces.

I put a reassuring hand on her shoulder. "Don't worry, Claudia. Everything's going to be fine."

I wasn't only trying to convince her. I was also trying to convince myself.

I was scared absolutely shitless.

But I wasn't going to let a little thing like sheer terror stop me. Special Agent Tara Holloway had a job to do and, by God, she would get the job done.

Or die trying.

CHAPTER FORTY-THREE

These Guys Put the Ass in Associates

At eight o'clock that evening, we readied ourselves for the arrival of Mendoza's goon squad. We left Claudia's minivan in the parking lot and positioned Claudia in a rental car a block away, armed with a walkie-talkie. We taped the TALK button down on our unit and positioned it on a shelf to provide a constant transmission from her office. She'd been instructed to call 911 for backup if we said the code word "latte." Also if she heard gunshots or screaming. Guess that kind of goes without saying, though, huh?

After her breakdown earlier in the day, the woman had rallied, resolving to do all she could to help us nail Mendoza. She seemed to consider it a penance of sorts. She wanted to make things right, ease her conscience, even her score with the Big Guy Upstairs. Or maybe she realized cooperating with us was the best chance she had for keeping her butt out of jail. Either way, she was on our side.

Josh continued to keep an eye on Mendoza at Crescent Tower. Nick and I weren't sure how many thugs Mendoza would send to Claudia's office, but since there'd been three at the Pokornys' we wanted at least one more agent on our side to even the odds. Given that this was an unauthorized operation, we couldn't recruit anyone else from the Treasury's Criminal Investigations. Lucky for me, Christina was more than willing to help me out again. All she asked for in return was a margarita—served by Nick wearing nothing but the skimpy tiger-striped swimsuit she'd heard about. I readily agreed on his behalf.

The three of us donned our ballistic vests under our clothes. Although my build better matched Claudia's, my fair skin and chestnut hair would be a dead giveaway to Mendoza's hit men that I wasn't the woman they were after. Christina thus landed the lead role in our charade. In her attempt to impersonate a bookkeeper, Christina had worn a black blazer over a white shirt and donned a pair of cheap reading glasses. She'd also pulled her long hair back into a bun.

"Do I look like a financial nerd?" she asked, turning to and fro to model her outfit.

"You look *professional*," I snapped back.

We moved Claudia's desk back a few feet and rearranged her file cabinets to form a bunker we could hide behind should a gunfight break out. Better safe than sorry, right?

Preparations now complete, Christina lowered Claudia's chair so she'd appear shorter. She sat at Claudia's desk while we waited for Mendoza's "associates" to arrive for the scheduled meeting. Nick and I hid behind file cabinets on either side of the desk, guns at the ready.

Christina pretended to be typing in data from a file on her desk, while in reality she played Farmville on Facebook. The second hand on the wall clock continued making its jerking rounds, the ticks and tocks loud and insistent, as if counting off the remaining seconds of our lives.

A few minutes after nine, there was movement outside the front window of Claudia's office. My entire body went on high alert. My gaze met Nick's across the room. He gave me a thumbs-up. I returned the gesture and tried really hard not to wet myself.

I peeked out of the narrow slit between the cabinets as the door opened. There were one, two, three men. Two white, one black. All in their early to mid-twenties. All big and muscular. The white guys had shaved heads and dark goatees, the black guy sported cornrows. These guys matched the description Darina Pokorny had given me of their attackers. They wore jeans and T-shirts, making no attempt to look like businessmen.

The door swung shut behind them as Christina looked up from her desk. Though the thugs couldn't see her right hand, I could. She held her loaded Glock firmly gripped in it. "Are you Mr. Ruiz's associates?"

The biggest guy chuckled, turning slightly to address the others. When he shifted, the lettering on the back of his leather belt became visible. *Bubba*. There was no doubt whatsoever now. These were the ass-wipes who'd put the Pokornys in the hospital.

"What do you say, guys? Are we *Mr. Ruiz's associates*?"

The other white guy snickered. The black guy merely fidgeted with nervous energy, glancing back at the front window as if to assure himself they couldn't be seen from the outside.

Bubba stepped up to the desk, putting out a hand to cup Christina's chin. He looked at her with cold, ice-blue eyes. "I bet it would be a lot of fun to *associate* with you."

She jerked her head out of his hand. "What do you want?"

Bubba grabbed her by the hair this time, twisting the bun in his fist and pulling her face to his as he leaned in over the desk. Christina pulled her right hand up to her hip, readying herself to shoot if needed. I felt guilty putting her through this, though I knew the situation was nothing new to her. Still, it was creepy, scary.

I glanced at Nick. He'd shifted closer to the edge of the cabinets, preparing himself to pounce.

"You need to transfer the money like you were told. Every last cent of it."

Nick gestured at the other white guy, who'd moved closer in now and stood beside the desk. "He's mine," Nick mouthed, pointing to his chest. He motioned with his gun toward the black guy, who was standing lookout now near the front windows. "You get him."

I nodded.

That left Christina to deal with Bubba. Big as he was, I hoped she was up to the task.

"What money are you talking about?" Christina asked Bubba.

"Gonna play dumb, bitch?" He released her hair and raised his arm to backhand her across the face. Fortunately, she jerked her head back just in time to avoid the blow and Bubba managed only to knock Claudia's banker's lamp off the desk. The green glass shattered as the lamp hit the floor.

Bubba's eyes narrowed. He grabbed Christina across the desk by the front of her jacket and put his face only inches from hers. "You tryin' to make a fool of me?"

I had a feeling he could do a good job of that all by himself.

Nick held up one finger, counting.

Christina shook her head and looked at Bubba. "No. I j-just didn't w-want to get h-hit." The frightened stutter was a nice touch. Christina played her part well.

Bubba released her jacket and took a step back. With her left hand, she grabbed the telephone receiver on her desk.

The other white guy ripped it out of her grip. "Nice try."

Nick held up two fingers now.

Bubba grabbed the water cooler and dragged it to the door, turning it over on its side to form a barrier, blocking any escape. The cone-shaped cups rolled across the tile and water ran out of the overturned cooler, forming a puddle on the floor.

Bubba cracked his knuckles. "Let's get down to business."

Just as Bubba cocked his fist, Nick held up three fingers. He leaped from his hiding place. "Federal agents! On your knees! Now!"

Before Bubba could say, *What the fuck?* Christina had pulled her gun and aimed it point-blank at his ugly face.

I dashed forward, hurling myself toward the black guy. He turned and tried to flee out the front door, but the water cooler was in his way. His feet slipped in the water and he ended up on his hands and knees in the puddle. "On your stomach!" I shouted from where I stood over him, my gun aimed at his back. "Put your hands behind you!"

"Okay! Okay!" He flopped onto his belly in the pooled water, curling his hands up behind his lower back.

I pulled my cuffs from my pocket, and in two clicks he was restrained. I turned to find Christina engaged in a standing wrestling match with Bubba. Idiot. He could now add resisting arrest to his list of charges.

The guy Nick dealt with wasn't giving up easy, either. Nick had knocked the chunky man off his feet, but the guy kept trying to get back up. Nick brought the handle of his gun down on the guy's head. It didn't knock him out, but it stunned him enough for Nick to kick and shove him into position for cuffing.

Bubba's meaty fingers wrapped around Christina's wrist, squeezing, trying to force her to drop her gun. I wasn't sure how best to help Christina, but no way could we let Bubba get a hold of the gun in her hand.

I jumped onto his back, crooking my elbow around his neck. Fortunately, my maneuver threw him off kilter and he released his grip on Christina. Unfortunately, he fell over backward. Onto me. On the hard, wet floor.

Whoomp.

All of the air left my lungs as we hit the tile. I was surprised my spine didn't snap in two. With Bubba's weight crushing me, I couldn't breathe. White sparks danced around the edges of my vision and I felt myself losing consciousness.

No.

No way was I going to die being crushed to death by someone named Bubba. It would be too embarrassing.

Remembering the moves we'd been taught in training, I jerked to one side and dislodged Bubba enough to take a breath. Nick and Christina pounced on him then, pulling him off me, rolling him over, and slapping cuffs on him.

Click-click.

There's nothing as satisfying to a federal agent as the sure sound of handcuffs snapping shut.

I lay in the puddle of water flapping around and gasping for air like a fish stranded in a tide pool. After a few seconds, I caught my breath and was able to sit up.

Nick lined the men up in the middle of the floor, forcing them to sit in the puddle. The two white guys glared up at Nick, pissed. The black guy was the only one smart enough to look worried.

Nick sat on Claudia's desk, looking down at the oversized brutes. "We know why you're here and who sent you. You might as well save yourself some trouble and spill your guts now."

"Miranda's," I reminded Nick. Until we read them their rights, any confessions or statements would be inadmissible in court.

Nick glanced my way and rolled his eyes before turning back to address the goons. "All right, you sorry-ass bum fuckers. Listen up. She's going to read your rights. Not that you deserve any."

I pulled my cheat sheet out of the wallet that held my badge and rattled them off. Right to remain silent, right to a lawyer, blah-blah-blah.

"I want a lawyer," Bubba said.

Not to be left out, the other white guy said, "Me, too."

Sheez, you'd think we were handing out free beer.

Nick rolled his eyes again. He jerked his chin at the young black man. "Let me guess. You want a lawyer, too?"

He shook his head. "I want to talk about immunity."

Nick's upper lip crooked into a grin. "At least one of you has some sense."

Nick and I moved the upended water cooler back into place. While Christina stayed inside to stand guard over the other two, Nick grabbed the black guy by the upper arm, helped him up from the floor, and led him out front to the curb. I followed. The front of the guy's shirt and the back of his pants were soaked, water dripping from him as he walked.

I wasn't in much better shape. My blazer was drenched and the back of my head was wet, too.

Outside, the guy spilled his guts. He'd obviously watched a bunch of crime shows on television and thought that by being the first to talk he'd walk scot-free. Not exactly how it works, though. We hadn't struck any deals with him yet, hadn't promised he'd be off the hook. TV shows left out the boring yet crucial details. Unlike Frizzy Lizzie, who'd been through the routine before and had insisted on a signed immunity deal before she'd talked, this guy didn't ask for a written agreement. But we weren't about to advise the creep he'd be digging his own grave here.

"What's your name?" Nick asked him.

"Jared Jackson."

Nick hiked his thumb toward Claudia's office. "How'd you get hooked up with those shits-for-brains?"

"I know Bubba and Mack from high school," the guy said. "We played football together back then. They work as bouncers at Cowtown Cabaret."

I'd heard of the place. Cowtown Cabaret was a popular strip club in nearby Fort Worth. The place sold itself as a "distinguished gentleman's entertainment venue." As if there was anything distinguished or gentlemanly about horny middle-aged men getting lap dances from barely legal half-naked girls. Urk.

"Bubba got a phone call from a guy offering big bucks for some muscle to rough up a bookkeeper who'd stolen from him."

Nick and I exchanged glances. "What was the guy's name?"

Jared shook his head. "Don't know. I don't think he told Bubba, neither. But he sent some cash and instructions and said he'd pay another five thousand after Bubba got Claudia to return the money she'd stolen."

Clever strategy on Mendoza's part. "Did any of you ever see the guy who hired you?" I asked. "Meet face-to-face?"

Jared shook his head again. "No. It was all very secret. Like James Bond."

Not exactly an appropriate analogy, but he'd made his point.

I eyed Jared. "You were at the bakery, when your friends beat up the owner and his wife."

Jared's eyes flashed surprise. "You know about that?"

I nodded.

Jared tried to raise his palms, but couldn't manage well with the cuffs on. He settled for lifting his shoulders. "I didn't have any part of that. I was only the lookout."

I fought the urge to kick the guy in the kneecaps. Without a lookout, Bubba and Mack couldn't have carried out their plan. Jared may not have committed the violent physical acts himself, but he was as much to blame for the Pokornys' injuries as his friends.

I jerked my head to indicate the two men inside. "They killed Andrew Sheffield, too, huh?"

Jared's eyes flew open and his voice rose three octaves. "Kill somebody? What?" He looked from me to Nick, panic in his eyes. "I don't know nothin' about them killing anyone. Honest."

Nick's gaze met mine. "I think he's telling the truth."

I thought so, too. Still, I had to wonder if Bubba and the other thug had been responsible for Andrew's disappearance. Something told me they didn't do it, though. Andrew's murder didn't quite fit their MO.

"What was the plan after you three came here?" Nick asked.

Jared looked from me to Nick. "The guy who hired us is going to call Bubba's cell phone at ten, to make sure things worked out."

I glanced at my watch. Nine-forty. Mendoza would call in twenty minutes. That gave us only a short time to come up with a plan.

CHAPTER FORTY-FOUR

$\mathscr{B}$aiting the Trap

Nick stepped to the door of Claudia's office and pushed it open, sticking his head inside and looking down at the men on the floor. "Either of you want to talk?"

Bubba glared up at him. "Fuck you."

"Yeah!" Mack said. "Fuck you!"

Nick chuckled. "Tough guys, huh?" He turned to me. "I'll get the phone." He stepped inside and searched the pockets of both men, giving Bubba a swift, hard kick in the thigh with his pointed cowboy boot when Bubba attempted to resist the frisking. He found the cell phone in Bubba's back pocket. Phone in hand, Nick stepped back outside and motioned for me to follow him. We walked down the sidewalk, out of earshot of Jared.

"Any ideas?" I asked.

"Only one," Nick said.

"And?"

"And hopefully it will lure Mendoza out here."

"What if it doesn't?"

Nick closed his eyes for a moment. When he opened them, they were sad, resigned. So was his voice. "If it doesn't, he gets away."

"That's unacceptable!" I'd worked too hard to let Mendoza get away. So had Eddie and Josh. Nick, too.

"We've got nothing but circumstantial evidence, Tara," Nick said. "We don't have enough to arrest him or to force him to stay in the country. This is it. Either he shows up tonight or it's all over."

"But what would that mean for you? For Eddie? For me and Josh?"

Nick looked past me as if trying to look into the future but unable to see beyond this moment. "I go into hiding. Eddie and his family stay in protective custody indefinitely. You and Josh keep mum and hope nobody finds out what you've been doing."

Bright headlights illuminated the parking lot as a car turned into it. I raised my hand to shield my eyes.

The car pulled up to the curb. Josh's rental. Claudia unrolled the window. "I've been listening on the walkie-talkie. You got them, right?"

We nodded.

Nick stepped to the car and put his hands on the open window ledge. "We need you to do us a favor, Claudia."

I had no idea what favor he was referring to, but figured it had something to do with his plan to lure Mendoza out of hiding.

Nick and I escorted Jared back into Claudia's office and she followed us in.

Her eyes widened in fright when she took in the three men, their size and bulk. "Oh my God." She put a hand to her chest, swaying slightly as she realized what could have been.

"Here's what we're going to do," Nick said. He ran through the plan. "Everybody got it?"

We nodded.

Nick removed Jared's cuffs, admonishing him not to make any dumb moves.

"No way, man," Jared said. "I'm in this with you guys now."

What did this dipshit think, that he was our new BFF? But I wasn't about to set him straight. We needed his cooperation.

Christina pulled a roll of duct tape from her purse and we taped Bubba's and Mack's mouths shut. Didn't want to risk them shouting a warning to Mendoza when he called. She slid the roll back into her bag. "Amazing how often this stuff comes in handy."

Then we waited. Ten o'clock came, but Bubba's cell didn't ring. We continued to wait. Christina and I sat in the wooden chairs while Nick paced back and forth through the puddle on the floor.

Soon it was five after ten.

Then ten after.

A layer of nervous sweat glued Nick's shirt to his back. He glanced at me, our eyes meeting. This phone call meant everything to Nick. The rest of his life depended on it. "Come on," he willed Mendoza under his breath. "Call."

At ten-fifteen, we nearly jumped out of our skin when Bubba's phone blared the George Thorogood classic "Bad to the Bone." The perfect choice of ring tone for the bully.

I glanced over at the brute. "Your mother must be so proud."

Nick checked the caller ID, nodding at me to indicate the number on the readout matched the new cell phone number Mendoza had sent to Claudia via e-mail.

Jared answered the phone, holding it so Nick could lean in and hear Mendoza's side of the conversation. "Go."

Nick quickly wrote something on the notepad in his hand. Jared read it off. "Bubba's busy with the bookkeeper. He messed her up pretty good."

There was a short pause as Mendoza responded. Nick scribbled furiously on the paper.

Jared squinted at the notepad, speaking slowly as he followed Nick's chicken scratch. "We got a problem. You offered Bubba five grand to take care of this, but she's offering us twice as much to back off. She's got money here in her safe. Mack went with her to her house to get the key."

Mendoza shouted so loud into his phone all of us could hear him at this end. "That's my money! Don't you fuck with me!"

He didn't sound at all like the calm, cool, and collected man who'd issued the polite threat to Eddie. He sounded like a man who was losing it.

Nick scribbled on the pad again, and Jared repeated the words aloud. "We gotta do what's best for us. You understand. But you want to make a better offer, we're listening."

There was another pause as Mendoza spoke and Nick scribbled. "How do we know you'll follow through? She's got cash right here. You want to negotiate, you come here with some green."

At that, Nick grabbed the phone from Jared's hand and snapped it closed.

CHAPTER FORTY-FIVE

Mano a Mano

The role of Claudia was now being played by Claudia herself. I dressed her in my spare ballistic vest. Christina applied some dark blush to Claudia's cheekbones to make them look bruised and the two of us messed up her hair. She'd been crying so she already had mascara running down her face, adding authenticity to the scene we were setting. Eat your heart out, Steven Spielberg.

Claudia sat at her desk. Bubba and Mack sat in two chairs off to the side, facing the front windows, their cuffed hands hidden behind them. Jared stood at the front window, pretending to be on watch duty. Before taking our places behind the filing cabinets, Christina and I removed the duct tape from Bubba's and Mack's mouths, warning the men one last time not to try any funny business. Then again, I almost hoped they would do something stupid, give me a reason to shoot their sorry asses, give them a taste of what they'd done to Darina and Jakub Pokorny.

Nick hunkered down in Claudia's minivan out front. If things went as planned, Nick would snag Mendoza on the sidewalk before he could enter the office. If things didn't go as planned . . . well, I decided not to think about that. Nobody likes a negative Nellie.

I phoned Josh, who was keeping watch on Crescent Tower, and told him about the phone call from Mendoza.

"He's making a move," Josh said. "His car is leaving the garage as we speak."

"Follow him," I said. It couldn't hurt to have another agent here in case we needed backup.

Josh phoned a few minutes later. "He's on Interstate Thirty, eastbound."

Heading our way.

Nick's plan just might work.

I texted Nick to let him know Mendoza was on his way.

Twenty long minutes later, Josh rang me again. I'd put my phone on vibrate. I answered the phone in a whisper. "Yeah?"

"He's parked his car down a side street a block away." Mendoza must've known Claudia's building had security cameras. "He's out of the car now, heading your way on foot."

I texted this information to Nick.

Three minutes later, a shadowy figure appeared at Claudia's door. He wore a dark hooded sweatshirt pulled out around his face, obscuring it from view. He rapped on the locked door, then stuck his hands back into the pockets of the hoodie. "It's Ruiz," he called. "Let me in."

As Jared stepped to the door, pretending to unlock it, Nick slid the door of Claudia's minivan open. With a primal war cry, he rushed at Mendoza.

Mendoza spun on his heels and pulled a gun from his pocket. He got off one shot that shattered the windshield of Claudia's minivan before Nick tackled him to the ground.

Christina and I darted from our hiding places. She remained inside to make sure the muscle men couldn't take advantage of the situation. I unlocked the door and tried to step outside to help Nick.

The two men squirmed and fought on the sidewalk right in front of the door. I couldn't get it open more than a few inches.

Nick landed a solid punch to Mendoza's face. The man's head snapped back and hit the door, the glass giving off a sickening crack. Mendoza's gun lay on the sidewalk, but so did Nick's. The two were going at it hand to hand now.

Nick grabbed Mendoza's jacket and hauled the man away from the door, tossing him over the curb. But Mendoza had a firm grip on Nick's shirt and pulled Nick to the ground with him. The two rolled around together like tomcats in a tussle, then came apart.

As I stepped outside, Mendoza put a hand on Claudia's van. He managed to get to his feet and pulled a second gun from his waistband. Seeing me in the doorway, he let loose a round that whizzed past my shoulder and shattered the glass behind me.

Screams came from inside Claudia's office. I glanced back to see Claudia's mouth open, her hands clawing at her face. No one had been hit, though Mendoza's shot had taken out the wall clock. It had ticked its last tock.

I pulled my gun and aimed it at Mendoza. "Drop it!"

But he didn't drop it.

Nick was on his feet now and lunged at Mendoza before he could fire again. The two went at each other again, wildly throwing punches and kicks. Mendoza lost this gun, too, the weapon clattering as it was knocked from his hand and slid across the parking lot.

Josh ran up then, stopping beside me, panting with exertion. "What do we do?"

By that point, Nick had Mendoza backed up against Claudia's van, his body covering Mendoza's, his hands at Mendoza's throat. Josh and I ran over to the van.

"We've got your back, Nick," I said. "You can let go of him now."

But Nick didn't let go. Mendoza's face turned dark purple, the light in his eyes dimming.

"Stop, Nick!" I tried to pry his fingers from Mendoza's neck.

He'd kill the man if he didn't stop. Sure, Mendoza deserved to die. But what would killing Mendoza mean for Nick? Even if Nick convinced Internal Affairs he hadn't willingly turned his back on the agency three years ago, there was no way he'd ever get his job back if he killed a man who clearly could have been taken into custody alive.

I pulled on Nick's arm but couldn't budge it. "Let go!"

Nick still didn't release Mendoza.

I looked at Nick's face, into his eyes. I saw pure hate, uncontrolled rage, a raw and crazed aggression. His teeth were gritted, his lips curled back in a vicious snarl, an inhuman growl coming from his throat.

Something had come over Nick. He'd snapped. He couldn't have stopped himself even if he'd wanted to.

I'd have to do it for him.

Josh stood to the side, hopping around and flapping his arms, totally ineffective. He was a great cybersleuth, but clearly he wasn't cut out for hand-to-hand combat.

I stepped back and pulled my gun. It was the only thing I could think of. I tried to find a nonvital part of Mendoza to put a bullet in, but the only part of him that was exposed was his crotch. I had only one choice.

I aimed.

I squeezed my trigger.

And I took out Mendoza's nads.

At the sound of the shot, Nick dropped his hands from Mendoza's neck, letting the man slide to the ground. Mendoza had no breath yet to scream, but jerked in pain on the asphalt, his hands at his groin.

Nick whirled on me, the crazed look in his eyes flashing one last time before quickly retreating. He glanced down at Mendoza for a moment, then back at me. The look in Nick's eyes spoke for him. *Thank you for keeping me from killing the bastard.*

Mendoza launched into a high-pitched shriek while I

grabbed my cell phone from my pocket and dialed 911, summoning both an ambulance and local police.

"Does that woman need help, too?" the dispatcher asked. She must've heard Mendoza's cries.

"Nah," I said. "She'll be fine."

CHAPTER FORTY-SIX

$\mathcal{P}$atching Things Up

Christina, Nick, and I arrived at the medical clinic an hour later. Ajay was working the late shift tonight. His white lab coat hung open over a T-shirt that read DOCTORS DO IT WITH PATIENCE. He ushered us back to an examination room immediately.

Christina received the doctor's attention first. "I'm fine," she said, holding up a palm. "The only thing I've got is Bubba cooties."

"Me, too," I said, though I could feel a long bruise forming along my backbone from my fall in Claudia's office.

Ajay turned to Nick, who took a seat on the examination table. Ajay shined his little light in Nick's eyes. "Looks like someone used your face for a punching bag."

Nick chuckled and cut his eyes my way. "You should see the other guy."

I shot him a stern look. Already he'd replaced my former

title as the Annie Oakley of the IRS with a new moniker—
the Sperminator.

Nick had a black eye, several scrapes, and a cut on his jaw-
line. Ajay sewed up Nick's chin and gave him a cold pack for
the eye, while a nurse applied antibiotic ointment to the scrapes.

The worst part was the glass in Nick's arm. He and Mendoza had rolled around in the shards from Claudia's shattered
windshield and sharp bits had lodged in Nick's skin. Using a
pair of tweezers, Ajay pulled them out one by one, dropping
them into a metal bowl. "You can take these to class for
show-and-tell."

When Ajay finished extracting the broken glass, he cleaned
the area and applied a series of small bandages to Nick's
arm. The doc jotted a note in Nick's new file and slid it into
the plastic bin on the door. "You'll live to fight another day."
He reached into the pocket of his lab coat and pulled out a
green lollipop. "Here's a little something for being such a
brave boy."

It was well after two A.M. once things settled down, but Nick
didn't want to wait a second longer. He gave me directions to
his mother's house, calling her from his new cell phone as
we pulled into the driveway.

"Hi, Mom," he said. "Everything's okay. In fact, it's more
than okay." He slid a smile my way. "Come to your front
door. There's a surprise waiting there."

He ended the call and handed the phone to me. "It's yours
now."

"Gee. Thanks."

He let out a breath and looked at me. "Tara, I—"

I cut him off with a raised palm. "No need."

He simply stared at me for a moment, then leaned over to
give me a soft kiss on the cheek. He climbed out of the car
just as the front door opened. His mother stood in the doorway, putting a hand to her eyes to shield them from the harsh
porch light. A big and fluffy golden-haired dog stood next
to her.

As Nick made his way up the sidewalk, the dog sniffed the air, perked up as he recognized his master's scent, and bounded forward, leaping onto Nick, barking and wagging his tail. Nick's mother rushed after the dog, grabbing her son in a huge bear hug, wailing joyfully. Her shoulders heaved as she sobbed.

Nick's did, too.

I put my hand to the spot on my cheek where Nick had kissed me.

Then I put my car in gear and drove straight to Brett's house.

I let myself in with his hidden key. It probably wasn't right to wake Brett so late, but I needed him. I needed to feel his strong arms around me, needed him to hold me, to comfort me. Sure, we'd kicked ass back at Claudia's office, and some rather big asses at that, but now that the showdown was over and the adrenaline was wearing off, I was shaking like an addict who'd gone too long without a hit.

I needed a Brett fix.

I stood in the doorway to his dark bedroom. Reggie lay on his back on my side of the bed, shedding on my pillow and snoring. Napoleon lifted his head from his spot next to Brett and gave a half growl, half bark, chewing me out for interrupting his slumber.

Brett shifted in the bed and opened his eyes, looking toward the doorway. "Tara?"

"Yeah," I said. "It's me."

He sat up, running a hand over his tousled hair. His voice was raspy with sleep. "You okay?"

"It's done," I said. "We got him."

"Thank God!" Fully awake now, Brett jumped out of bed and dashed over to me, grabbing me tight, his arms wrapped around my back. Given the bruises down my spine, his embrace hurt a little, but I wasn't about to stop him. He breathed a warm sigh of relief into my hair. "You have no idea how glad I am this case is over."

He wasn't the only one. Now I could have my life back. So could Eddie. And Nick.

"Wait a minute." Brett stepped back, removing his arms. "You're wet."

I gave him a soft smile. "It's a long story."

CHAPTER FORTY-SEVEN

The Prodigal Son Returns

Around ten the next morning, I arrived at the office to find Viola and Lu in the conference room. Colorful streamers hung from the ceiling, helium balloons floated in the air, and the table held an enormous frosted sheet cake that read WEL-COME BACK, NICK! The corners of the cake boasted thick, gooey roses. Yum. Just the thing to go with the skinny no-whip latte in my hand. I'd ordered an extra-large one this morning, figured I'd need some caffeine-induced courage to face the Lobo.

I'd done a lot of wrong things. But I'd done them for the right reasons. I wasn't sure where that left me as far as my boss was concerned.

I stepped into the room and looked at the two women. "Guess you heard, huh?"

Lu turned and marched straight at me. She stopped just inches from me, putting one hand on her hip and pointing a meaty finger in my face. "You directly defied my orders. You broke a multitude of federal laws. You dragged Josh into this. For Christ's sake, you shot a man in the testicles! What do you have to say for yourself?"

There wasn't much I could say in my defense other than, "Actually, it was only one testicle." The marshal who'd landed guard duty at the hospital had filled me in earlier this morning. Mendoza's left nut had gone *adios*.

Her scowl softened into a smile and she dropped her finger. "Good work, Holloway."

I smiled back. "Thanks."

The scowl and finger returned. "But if you ever do anything like this again, you'll be tossed out of here faster than you can say 'boo.' Understand me?"

I nodded. "Yes, ma'am."

She threw her hands in the air. "I don't know how I'm going to explain this to George Burton."

"Got that covered," came Nick's voice from behind me.

"Nick!" Lu rushed past me to grab him in a bear hug. She held him, one hand on each arm as she stepped back to look up at him. "I can hardly believe my eyes."

Viola walked over to Nick and accepted a hug from him, too. She looked up into his face, putting a maternal hand on his cheek. A knowing look passed between the two.

Aha! So Viola was the one who'd been in contact with Nick. No matter how much I had pleaded and prodded last night, Nick had refused to reveal his source. But I had my answer now, plain as day.

Viola frowned at Nick's black eye. "That's one hell of a shiner."

Nick was tough. He'd survive. At the moment I was more concerned with placating George Burton and, hopefully, keeping my job. "What's this about George Burton?"

Nick grinned. "I got in touch with a contact in the Mexican tax department after we looked over Mendoza's key logger data. I gave him the access codes to the bank accounts in Latin America. They were able to link those accounts to shell businesses Vicente Torres had used to launder money."

According to Nick, the Mexican agent determined the accounts had been shared by Torres and Mendoza, and that

Torres had ripped off his partner in crime, moving the funds to an account only he could access after learning the IRS had renewed its pursuit of Mendoza.

"Our information gave them enough evidence to bust Torres," Nick said. "They caught him boarding a flight to Ecuador. They've been after Torres for years. Burton's counterpart in the Mexican tax bureau was thrilled, called me himself this morning. He said he'd put in a good word for us with Burton."

No way would Burton fire the agents who'd performed an international coup and brought down a dangerous crime syndicate, even if the agents' methods were less than exemplary.

Lu sent Viola to round up the staff. The other agents received Nick back into the fold with open arms, both literally and figuratively. When they learned everything Nick had gone through the last three years, that he'd been living in forced exile in Mexico, they were stunned.

As I licked the last bit of frosting from my plastic fork, Eddie entered the room. He seemed to have aged years since I'd last seen him, yet he looked relieved, too. While he and Nick greeted each other, I cut him a piece of cake and brought it to him along with a cup of fruit punch.

"How was your vacation?" I teased, knowing living under protective custody was anything but a holiday.

Eddie shook his head. "The twins were bouncing off the walls, Sandra was worried sick but trying her hardest not to show it, and I couldn't do jack shit about any of it. It was hell."

"So you're glad to be back at work then?"

"Damn straight."

Christina, Alicia, and I sat in plastic lawn chairs on my back patio, sipping frozen margaritas prepared and served by Nick, who wore nothing but a few small bandages, a chipped-tooth smile, and his tiger-striped Speedo. A deal's a deal, even if I was the one who'd negotiated it for him without his express consent.

God, it felt good to relax.

The Mendoza case was out of my hands now. Dallas PD's crime scene techs had matched Bubba's fingerprint to one found on the till at the Pokornys' bakery. His print had also been matched to a prior burglary. Having linked the thug to three crimes, the DA made sure Bubba wasn't going anywhere. While his cohort's bail had been set somewhat lower, nobody had shown up to post bond for either of them.

Jared had been released on his own recognizance. While he wouldn't enjoy full immunity, it was likely he'd work out a plea deal and only serve probation, avoiding jail time. Hopefully he'd learned his lesson and would keep his nose clean from here on out.

Bubba's fingerprints tied Mendoza to both the loan shark operation and the attack on the Pokornys. The key logger data Josh had obtained directly linked Mendoza to the e-mails sent to Claudia and to the foreign bank accounts. Given this new evidence, the FBI had reopened Andrew Sheffield's murder investigation. They'd sought phone records for the two cell numbers Mendoza had used to communicate with Claudia. From those records, they were able to trace Mendoza's calls and thus identify a number of his minions, including a new accounts officer at NDCU who'd stolen credit card information from the bank's clients. When the FBI dug a little deeper, they discovered that, lo and behold, one of Mendoza's henchmen had placed two calls to a suspected hit man, a former butcher at a slaughterhouse. Andrew Sheffield's killer, no doubt.

Heads would roll. Dozens of them. On both sides of the border. The Mexican authorities had made widespread arrests, too.

The vast financial empire Mendoza and Torres had built now lay in ruins. Mendoza would spend the rest of his life in jail.

How did I feel about all of this? I had just one thing to say. *Neener-neener.*

When I finished my first drink, I snapped my fingers and sent Nick back into my kitchen to make another round.

"My God," Alicia said, gazing appreciatively at Nick through the window. "Even with a black eye that man is so sexy it's ridiculous."

I watched Nick, too, as he revved up the blender to prepare our second round. His skimpy bathing suit left nothing to the imagination, but it sure had us girls imagining some very naughty things.

"His office is directly across from mine," I said. "I have no idea how I'll get any work done."

"You could always shut your door," Christina suggested.

"And you could always shut your mouth," I suggested right back.

CHAPTER FORTY-EIGHT

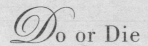

Do or Die

My life was mine again.

With the Mendoza case now over, I had more time to spend with Brett. We spent hours in the bedroom making up for lost time, toured the new exhibit at the Dallas Arboretum, went out for sushi and a movie with Alicia and Daniel. I even helped Brett plant some seedlings at one of the Habitat houses. Trish had been on the job site and I'd finally met her face-to-face. Despite my urge to take a shovel to her butterscotch-colored head, I managed to restrain myself.

I'd taken a couple of days off from work and driven to Nacogdoches to visit my parents. I returned Dad's unregistered hunting rifle, exchanging the weapon for a fresh tin of Mom's pecan pralines. Both Mom and Dad had been happy to see me, relieved my dangerous case was over.

I'd devoted an entire afternoon to quality time with my cats, playing with them, hand-feeding them treats, petting and stroking them until they'd forgiven my neglect.

I'd gone by the bakery to visit the Pokornys. With Mendoza

now in jail and the insurance payout in their pockets, they'd reconsidered their plans to move back to the Czech Republic and were in the process of rebuilding their bakery.

I'd even had lunch again with Lauren Sheffield, again enjoying the linguine formaggio. Mendoza's arrest gave her the closure she needed to begin moving on, to make plans for her and her son's future.

Life was good.

Two weeks later, I sat at my desk, multitasking.

Task number one was trying not to stare at Nick. His desk faced mine from his office across the hall. His snakeskin cowboy boots were propped on his desk as he leaned back in his chair and looked over some paperwork. Even in a white dress shirt and navy slacks he exuded a primal masculinity. His black eye had faded to a pale yellow and the stitches on his chin had been removed, leaving a wide pink scar that begged to be touched. His left hand worked the blue stress ball he'd reclaimed from me, the squeezing motion oddly sensual. I couldn't help but wonder how his hands would feel squeezing me.

Task number two was trying to forget how warm and hard and inviting his body had felt pressed against my back when he climbed into my bed half naked mere days ago.

Task number three was trying to dislodge a crimped staple that had jammed in my stapler. After fighting with the stupid device for ten minutes, I tossed it into my trash can. I'd stop by an office supply store on my way home and buy one of those expensive electric jobs.

"What do you think you're doing?" Lu's voice came from my doorway. "That's federal government property."

"That's a piece of junk," I replied.

She held a stack of files in her arms. She stepped forward and dropped them on my desk, sending dust and cobwebs into the air.

I eyed her for a moment. Something was different. She reeked of her usual industrial-strength hairspray but, for the first time since I'd met her, she didn't smell like cigarette smoke. "Did you quit smoking?"

She cocked one pinkish-orange brow. "My, aren't you the observant one." She flopped down in one of my chairs. "Yes, I quit smoking. Had to. The doctor found a spot on my lung."

A spot on . . . "Lu! Oh my God!" I instinctively stood once my mind processed the information.

When Nick eyed me across the hall, I sat back down and tried to compose myself.

The Lobo? Cancer? My world seemed to be spinning in the wrong direction. How could this be? Lu had always seemed, well, invincible. I could hardly believe cancer cells were brave enough to invade the body of such a tough old broad. "Lu, I'm so sorry."

She waved a hand dismissively. "It's only a small spot. I'm gonna beat this thing. I'm gonna beat the hell out of it."

I was glad to hear her confidence. She'd need hope and sheer will to get through the next few months. They wouldn't be easy.

"But just in case I don't beat it," she said, banging a fist on top of the files and releasing a fresh cloud of dust, "I want these jerkwads brought down. I've set these files aside for years because they weren't worth the hassle. I want to see these cases closed before I die. And seeing as how my death might be more imminent than I thought, I figure I better get someone working on them."

My reservations must have been written all over my face. She glanced back across the hall at Nick and lowered her voice. "You know why I assigned these to you instead of another agent?"

I shook my head.

"'Cause no matter what it takes, Tara, you get the job done."

Gee. No pressure, huh?

Read on for an excerpt from

Death, Taxes, and Extra-Hold Hairspray—

the next novel starring Tara Holloway, coming soon
from Diane Kelly and St. Martin's Paperbacks!

"Damn." I dropped the phone back into its cradle on my
desk. I needed help on a case, but it seemed no one was available
this afternoon. I'd called every special agent in the Dallas
IRS Criminal Investigations office.

Make that every special agent *but one*.

That one sat directly across the hall, his cowboy boots
propped on his desk, his right hand rhythmically squeezing
a blue stress ball as he eyed me. I sat at my desk, pretending
not to notice.

Why didn't I want Nick Pratt working on this case with
me? Because the guy had whiskey-colored eyes that drank a
girl in, an ass you could bounce a quarter off of, and more
sex appeal than George Clooney, Brad Pitt, and Johnny Depp
combined.

I realize these factors might all sounds like reasons *to
want* to work with him. Problem was, I was in a committed
relationship with a wonderful guy and, despite that fact,
wasn't entirely sure I could resist temptation.

Better not put myself to the test, right?

My usual partner, Eddie Bardin, had received an unexpected temporary promotion to Acting Director three weeks ago when doctors found a spot on the right lung of our boss, Lu Lobozinski. Lu had taken time off for her chemotherapy treatments and recovery, appointing Eddie to take her place until she was able to return.

Eddie's promotion left me to handle a buttload of cases on my own. And not just any old buttload, but cases that had been purposely put on the back burner for years because each case was guaranteed to be a major pain in the ass.

One of the biggest of these cases involved an eighty-three-year old chicken rancher who'd served seven consecutive terms as vice president of a radical secessionist group. Another involved a popular, charismatic preacher who financed a lavish lifestyle via his congregants' tax-deductible donations to his mega-church. It was almost enough to send me back to my boring old job at the CPA firm.

But not quite.

The phone on my desk rang. The caller readout displayed the name *N PRATT.*

Dang. No way could I ignore the guy now. It would be too obvious.

I looked across the hall as I picked up the phone. Nick looked back at me, one thick brown brow raised. How the guy could look so damn sexy in a plain white dress shirt and basic tan slacks was beyond me. Maybe it was the oversized gold horseshoe-shaped belt buckle that did it, drawing attention to his nether regions like a flashing neon sign that said WANNA GET LUCKY?

"Big Bob's Bait Bucket," I said in my best southern twang. "We got whatcha need if whatcha need is worms."

You got me. I'm a bit of a smart ass. But I had spent two summers in high school working for Big Bob. Minimum wage plus all the free nightcrawlers I wanted. Which was none.

Nick shot me a pointed look across the hall. "Why haven't you asked me up to help you?"

Because you make my girlie parts quiver in a very un-professional manner. But I couldn't very well tell him that now, could I? Better think quick, Tara.

"You looked . . . um . . ." *Gorgeous? Sexy as hell? Absolutely boinkable?* I went with "busy."

He grinned, flashing his chipped tooth, an imperfection that somehow only added to his primal appeal. "I fake it pretty good, don't I? That's how I got fast-tracked to senior special agent."

Nick's career as a special agent with the IRS had indeed been meteoric, at least until three years ago when he'd been forced to flee the country or die at the hands of Marcos Mendoza, a violent, money-laundering tax cheat.

Lucky for Nick, Lu had later assigned me and Eddie to renew the case against Mendoza. After the creep threatened Eddie and his family, I'd smuggled Nick back into the U.S. and the two of us had brought Mendoza to his knees. Literally. Hard for the man to stay standing after I'd shot off his left testicle. I'd considered taking the gonad to a taxidermist for mounting, but I doubted my mother would let me hang it over the fireplace back home next to Dad's sixteen-point trophy buck.

Nick sat up at his desk, his expression serious now. "You gave me my life back, Tara. I'll never be too busy for you."

Nick was directly offering to help me out. No girl in her right mind could say no to that, even if she had been avoiding him. There's only so much willpower to go around.

I hung up the phone. "Saddle up, cowboy," I called across the hall as I stood and grabbed my purse. "We've got a chicken farmer to check in on."

We snagged a car from the Treasury's fleet and drove for what seemed an eternity through flat, dry country. The radio was tuned to a country station to combat our boredom and the air conditioner turned on full blast to combat the outdoor temperature, which had topped out at one-hundred and three. That's August in North Texas. Brutal.

Nick had brought his stress ball with him and manipulated

it in his right hand, slowly turning it and squeezing. His movements were oddly sensual and had me wondering how his hands might feel squeezing certain parts of me.

Splat.

We drove past a farmer driving a green John Deere tractor though a field, kicking up dust and scattering insects, most of which veered on a suicidal path toward the windshield of the car. I was glad I wasn't driving my precious red convertible BMW out here.

Splat.

Splat-splat.

Splat.

A colorful assortment of bug guts now decorated the windshield like miniature Rorschach ink-blot tests. One of the spots looked vaguely like our boss, who'd sported a towering strawberry-blond beehive since the sixties. Her hairdo had to be at least eight-inches tall, held together by a thorough coating of extra-hold hairspray.

I pointed at the pinkish goo. "What's that look like to you?"

Nick squinted at the glass. "The Lobo."

"My thoughts exactly."

Nick glanced my way and my crotch clenched reflexively. He always looked hot, but he was especially attractive at the moment. He'd topped his stylishly shaggy brown hair with the white felt Stetson I'd bought him shortly after sneaking him back out of Mexico. Yep, I'd always had a soft spot for cowboys. Make that *two* soft spots—one spot was metaphorical, the other was between my thighs.

Nick flashed a mischievous grin. "You know what's the last thing to go through a bug's mind when he hits your windshield?"

I shrugged.

"His asshole."

I rolled my eyes and pulled to a stop behind another white government-issue sedan parked by a rusty gate. "Here we are. The middle of BFE."

A spray-painted plywood sign affixed to the barbed-wire

fence read PROPERTY OF THE REPUBLIC OF TEXAS. TRESPASS-
ERS WILL BE VIOLATED.

Nick groaned. "You didn't tell me we'd be dealing with
idiots."

"You didn't ask," I said. "And need I remind you that you you
volunteered for this assignment?"

"Next time I'll ask for more details before I commit," he
muttered.

The Republic of Texas was a separatist group, a bunch of
anti-government loonies who referred to themselves as
"Texians" and operated an unofficial sovereign state. For
such a small organization they'd proved to be a huge pain in
the ass. The group had issued numerous bogus court sum-
mons and filed frivolous lawsuits with both the Supreme
Court of Texas and the International Court of Justice at the
Hague, challenging the annexation of Texas in 1845 by
the United States.

That's what happens when rednecks have too much time
on their hands.

After shootouts between federal agents and armed ex-
tremists in Ruby Ridge, Idaho, and Waco, Texas, the government had received a lot of flack, virtually all of it from
whack jobs and nearly all of it undue. There's no clean way
to take down these types of people. They don't exactly think
and act reasonably.

Government agencies had learned to be extra careful in
handling interactions with members of such groups. In 1997,
state troopers had negotiated a surrender with Richard
McLaren, the former leader of the Republic of Texas, after
he'd been accused of fraud and kidnapping. Still, two of the
group's members had refused to cooperate and one of them
had been shot dead after they'd opened fire on a police heli-
copter.

Thus, despite the fact that August and Betty Buchmeyer
hadn't filed a tax return since Ronald and Nancy Reagan
were bumping uglies in the White House, Lu had made a
strategic decision not to arrest the couple. Rather, she'd
instructed me only to see what we could collect from the

elderly deadbeats, perhaps make an example of them to the dozen or steadfast Texians who stubbornly stuck to their beliefs.

Collections work was boring as hell, essentially standing guard while staff from the collections department seized any non-exempt assets. While most tax evaders cursed and glared, others moaned and sobbed, lamenting the loss of their RVs, their collection of mink coats, their limited-edition prints. But sheez, by the time it got to that point they'd been given ample opportunity to make payment arrangements and had stubbornly refused. It wouldn't be fair to honest, hardworking taxpayers to let scofflaws off the hook.

So here we were.

Nick and I climbed out of the car. The intense midsummer heat caused an instant sweat to break out on my skin. Nick shrugged into his bulletproof vest and a navy sport coat. I slipped my protective vest on over my white cotton blouse and secured my gun in my hip holster, covering them both with a lightweight yellow blazer. Standard precautions. After all, it wasn't likely a couple of octogenarians would put up a fight. Right?

A hundred feet inside the gate sat a weather-beaten blue single-wide trailer in a thick patch of weeds. The house stood slightly cockeyed from settling unevenly into the reddish soil. The metal skirting had pulled away in places and there was no telling what manner of vermin had made a home under the structure. An enormous, outdated satellite dish mounted on a sturdy five-foot pole stood between the trailer and a lone, misshapen mesquite tree that struggled for life in the bare, dry dirt. An ancient pickup with faded two-tone brown paint sat on the far side of the dirt driveway. Two rusted tractors, a dented horse trailer, and a broken-down trampoline, its springs long since sprung, littered the yard.

Fifty yards beyond the house stood a series of long metal barns. The hot breeze blew toward us, carrying with it the faint sounds of clucking and the stench of bird poop. Over it all flew the Burnet flag, an azure background with a single gold star in the middle, the last flag flown over Texas when it was still an independent country.

Nick gave a whistle. "Boy howdy. This is quite the presidential palace."

"Buchmeyer's only the VP," I corrected.

"Whatever. It's still a dump."

No correction needed there.

The collections agent stepped out of her car and met us on the asphalt. She was slender, fortyish, with curly black hair. She wore a floral-print dress with sensible flats, and introduced herself as Jane Jenkins.

"This shouldn't take long," Jenkins said. "I'm not expecting to find much. Other than the trailer, twenty acres of scrubland, and the pickup, there's no other property in their name."

"What about the chickens?" I asked. "They've got to be worth something." After all, a two-piece meal at KFC ran about four bucks. I should know. I'd had some extra crispy for lunch.

Jenkins shook her head. "We've got a strict policy in collections. We don't seize anything that eats and craps. Costs too much to care for animals."

Made sense. Better to wait for the owner to sell the birds, then seize the resulting profits. Problem was, the IRS had levied the Buchmeyers' bank account years ago, garnering over six grand in one fell swoop just after the couple received a large payment from one of their customers. Since then, they couple had taken to operating on a cash-only basis.

Where the cash was being held was anyone's guess. With any luck, we'd find some in their trailer today, maybe under a mattress or in their toilet tank. Eddie'd once collected ten grand from a delinquent taxpayer who'd hidden large bills in his bowling bag, including stacks of hundreds stashed in his bowling shoes under a pair of Odor Eaters. When Eddie couldn't find the cash he was sure the man had somewhere in his possession, he'd left the apartment and pulled the fire alarm at the complex. On hearing the alarm, the guy ran outside with the bowling bag. A dead giveaway.

Yep, sometimes being a special agent calls for creative tactics.

Nick, Jenkins, and I carefully stepped across the metal cattle guard and walked up to the gate. The opening was secured by two large, rusty padlocks joined with heavy gauge chain thick enough to anchor an aircraft carrier.

I stepped forward and tugged on the locks. They didn't budge.

Jenkins frowned. "I called ahead and told them to unlock the gate for us."

It wouldn't be the first time a taxpayer refused to cooperate. Wouldn't be the last, either. For some reason, people didn't like turning over their sports cars, big-screen televisions, and jewelry collections to the IRS. Not that we were likely to find anything like that here. The Buchmeyers' profits had been modest. If they'd paid on time, their tax bill would've been paltry. But once three decades of interest and penalties were tacked on, those tiny tax bills had grown to over a hundred grand.

The three of us spent a few minutes searching for any keys that might be hidden about, turning over rocks, checking in and under the mailbox and behind the fence posts. We came up empty-handed.

I glanced back at the trailer. The faded blue-and-white-striped bath towel serving as a curtain in the front window was pulled back, an older woman's face visible. She raised a gnarled hand and gave me the finger. Wouldn't be the first or last time that happened, either.

"Got their phone number handy?" I asked Jenkins.

She rattled it off, and I dialed the Buchmeyers on my cell.

After five rings, someone picked up the phone. "Hello?" an old man's voice rasped.

"Mr. Buchmeyer, this is IRS Special Agent Tara Holloway. We need you to come on out here and unlock your gate."

An elderly man's face appeared in the window now. "I ain't going to do that, young lady," he spat. "I don't recognize the authority of the United States government to tax me nor seize my property. This here place belongs to the Republic of Texas. Didn't you see the sign?"

"The sign doesn't mean anything, Mr. Buchmeyer."

"Like hell it don't! If you all dare to enter my property, I'll be obligated to defend it. Now you go about your business and let me go about mine." With that, he hung up the phone and yanked the curtain closed.